PRAISE
CHARLIE N. HOLMBERG

THE NUMINA SERIES

"[An] enthralling fantasy . . . The story is gripping from the start, with a surprising plot and a lush, beautifully realized setting. Holmberg knows just how to please fantasy fans."

—Publishers Weekly

"With scads of action, clear explanations of how supernatural elements function, and appealing characters with smart backstories, this first in a series will draw in fans of Cassandra Clare, Leigh Bardugo, or Brandon Sanderson."

—Library Journal

"Holmberg is a genius at world building; she provides just enough information to set the scene without overwhelming the reader. She also creates captivating characters worth rooting for, and puts them in que situations. Readers will be eager for the second installment in umina series."

—Booklist

HE PAPER MAGICIAN SERIES

vibrant writer with an excellent voice and great world roughly enjoyed *The Paper Magician*."

on Sanderson, author of *Mistborn* and *The Way of Kings*

"Harry Potter fans will likely enjoy this story for its glimpses of another structured magical world, and fans of Erin Morgenstern's *The Night Circus* will enjoy the whimsical romance element . . . So if you're looking for a story with some unique magic, romantic gestures, and the inherent darkness that accompanies power all steeped in a yet to be fully explored magical world, then this could be your next read."

—Amanda Lowery, *Thinking Out Loud*

THE WILL AND THE WILDS

"An immersive, dangerous fantasy world. Holmberg draws readers in with a fast-moving plot, rich details, and a surprisingly sweet human-monster romance. This is a lovely, memorable fairy tale."

—*Publishers Weekly*

"Holmberg ably builds her latest fantasy world, and her brisk narrative and the romance at its heart will please fans of her previous magical tales."

—*Bookli*

THE FIFTH DOLL

Winner of the 2017 Whitney Award for Speculative Fiction

Spellbreaker

ALSO BY CHARLIE N. HOLMBERG

The Numina Series

Smoke and Summons

Myths and Mortals

Siege and Sacrifice

The Paper Magician Series

The Paper Magician

The Glass Magician

The Master Magician

The Plastic Magician

Other Novels

The Fifth Doll

Magic Bitter, Magic Sweet

Followed by Frost

Veins of Gold

The Will and the Wilds

Spellbreaker

AUTHOR OF *THE PAPER MAGICIAN*
CHARLIE N. HOLMBERG

47NORTH

Text copyright © 2020 by Charlie N. Holmberg
All rights reserved.

No part of this book may be reproduced, or stored in a retrieval system, or transmitted in any form or by any means, electronic, mechanical, photocopying, recording, or otherwise, without express written permission of the publisher.

Published by 47North, Seattle

www.apub.com

Amazon, the Amazon logo, and 47North are trademarks of Amazon.com, Inc., or its affiliates.

ISBN-13: 9781542020091
ISBN-10: 1542020093

Cover design by Micaela Alcaino

Printed in the United States of America

To Emily Schwarzmann,
the mighty Em'terprise,
who stands fast in the storm,
dances through the currents,
protects her tribe,
and shouts LOVE from the rooftops.
Step back, world,
and hear her roar.

PROLOGUE

Abingdon-on-Thames, England, 1885

Elsie hadn't meant to burn down the workhouse.

She hadn't mentioned this to the constable when he'd come around to question her and the other children. She hadn't said anything at all.

It wasn't a matter of who had started the fire. Everyone knew it had been Old Wilson, whose knuckles ached when it rained and whose body trembled a little more every year. He'd dropped the lamp. Broken the glass. Spilled the kerosene. But that's not why the rug and walls had lit up. It wasn't why the big block of a building raged orange and yellow behind them, its smoke stinging Elsie's eyes.

She hadn't known the pretty rune on the wall was a fireguard. She hadn't known it was important. She'd pointed it out to both Betsey and James, but neither of them could see it. She'd wanted only to touch it, trace it. And when she did, it had vanished beneath her fingertips. She hadn't told a soul. Didn't want to get into trouble. Didn't want the workhouse to throw her away, too.

That had been a month ago. So when Old Wilson had dropped his lamp, there'd been no magic to stop the fire from eating up the whole place.

Elsie hated the workhouse. She didn't feel so terrible watching it crumble, but she did feel bad that everyone had been put out of their beds, that the constable was being so mean, and that Old Wilson would get in trouble.

Elsie didn't know where they would send her now. Another workhouse? With new people, or the same ones?

One of the boys beside her started to cry. Elsie didn't know what to say. She wanted to help, but telling the truth wouldn't help them—it would only hurt her. She didn't want to give them a reason not to love her.

She stepped away. The police had told everyone to stay put, but the fire was so hot. Elsie didn't go far, just a few steps, then a few more. Turning her face toward the tree-shadows behind her, she let it cool off in the damp air that smelled like storms.

She was picking out shapes in the shadows when a hand touched her shoulder. She flinched, sure it was the constable. Sure Betsey or James had tattled on her, saying she had seen a rune and broken it—

But it was a cloaked figure who stood beside her, face obscured by a cowl. "My dear," the voice within said, "what is your name?"

Elsie swallowed, her throat tight. She glanced back to the fire, to the shouting men trying to contain it.

"Don't mind them. You're safe. What is your name?"

Elsie peered into that cowl, but the darkness hid any discernible features. The voice was quiet and feminine. "E-Elsie. Elsie Camden."

"Such a pretty name. How old are you?"

The compliment took her by surprise. "E-Eleven."

"Wonderful. Come with me, Elsie."

Her feet were slow to move. "Are you taking me to another workhouse?"

The cowl shook from side to side, revealing a weak, fleshy chin. "Not if you do as I say. You're very important, Elsie. I need your help to make the world a better place. I need to use that special talent of yours."

Elsie dug her heels into the soft earth. She knew it. She knew she was one of them. A spellbreaker, born with one kind of magic instead of taught a hundred.

"If you register me, they'll know I did it," she whispered.

The hand on her shoulder squeezed. "Yes, they will. And you'll get into a lot of trouble. Noose around your neck, no doubt. But I would never ask you to do such a thing. You'll help me, and I'll help you. We'll keep you safe, and you'll never be the government's pet. We've a lot of good work ahead of us, sweet Elsie. Helping those who need it, not those in power. Come on, then. I know a good place to hide, and we'll get you a bite to eat. How does that sound?"

The heat of the fire prickled Elsie's scalp.

She was wanted? She was important? Her spirit felt too big for her body, blooming like a wild rose. Elsie smiled, and the cloaked woman led her away.

She never did see her face.

CHAPTER 1

London, England, 1895

Elsie could just barely hear the toll of Big Ben in the distance. Four o'clock. A decent enough time for breaking the law.

But when the law wasn't fit, was it really a bad thing to break it?

Slipping around a corner, Elsie pulled the letter from her pocket. Although London was only an hour's ride by omnibus or carriage from her home in Brookley, she was not familiar with this particular neighborhood. She usually burned the letters right away, but she'd feared she might get lost if she didn't bring this one along.

The note had found its way to her despite the fact that it hadn't been delivered by post. As always, the sender had not signed it, although the small seal of a bird foot stamped over a crescent moon was identification enough.

The Cowls.

That wasn't their real name, obviously. But Elsie didn't know what else to call them. She hadn't seen any of them since she was eleven, ten years ago. But they kept in contact. More often than usual, lately. Either the world was getting worse, or they were on the cusp of making real change, and including *her* in that change.

At first, they'd given her small tasks, local tasks. She'd dis-spelled an unbreakable wall, magically fortified centuries ago, which had sat in the middle of farmland. The local tenants had spent months writing to their lords, petitioning for the spell's removal for the sake of planting, but *she* was the one who'd helped them. Some of the early tasks she'd been given didn't even require her fledgling spellbreaking. Delivering bread baskets to an orphanage had been the first to take her away from her home, and she'd managed it, getting lost only once. As her gifts improved, so the tasks she was given became bigger, more important. *Elsie* became more important, and the occasional coin or candy left with her missives told her the Cowls were grateful, that she was of real value to them.

Mind returning to the present, Elsie rechecked the address. A young woman hawked roses from a basket on one corner, and across from her was a small shop with a bright-blue sign reading **WIZARD OF ALL TRADES**. Elsie rolled her eyes. Not at the boldness of the color, but at the idea of being a wizard-of-all-trades. Only someone needing a very small spell or someone with no comprehension of magic would visit such a place. For when a person learned magic in all four alignments, they would be very weak in each of them, no matter how much magical potential they possessed. There was a reason people specialized.

Not that it pertained to Elsie. Specializations were only for spell*makers*.

Pulling her eyes away, she crossed at the next intersection. This neighborhood was so large and so winding . . . she was sure she'd passed her turn. But she couldn't retrace her steps. Couldn't do anything to draw suspicion. So she shoved the letter back into her pocket and strolled, enjoying the sunshine, trying not to think too hard on the novel reader she'd finished just before getting this latest missive. Oh, but it was hard not to think on the mystery! The baron in disguise had just confided his secret to Mademoiselle Amboise, completely unaware that she was betrothed to his enemy! There were so many ways the plot could unwind, and the author had cruelly ended the piece right there, forcing Elsie and thousands of others to wait for the continuation. Were it Elsie's novel—that is, she was no writer, but if she *were*—she would have Mademoiselle Amboise get into some sort of trouble. Perhaps with a highwayman? The lady would be forced to relinquish the information before she could give it to the villainous Count Neville, only to later learn the highwayman was actually the baron's long-lost brother and rightful heir!

And to think she had to wait another two weeks to read what happened next.

Oh, wait, here she was. Swallow Street. She glanced up at the rows of large houses, thinking on how many families could fit into one of the behemoths, before walking down the road. The elaborate homes on one side of the street were guarded by wrought iron fences. The houses on the other side were closed in by a high brick wall. She found Mr. Turner's house easily enough on the brick side. It was three stories high and white with navy tiles, windowed on all sides. Black shutters, blue drapes, a large elm growing up along its east side. Bold white cornices, bay windows, everything a wealthy person could want.

These folk didn't want the poor traipsing around their doorstep, that was for sure.

Elsie hid her frown as she approached the end of the street, then turned onto the next road and looped back to approach the Turner home from behind. Despite the crowded nature of the city, these estates didn't have a second row of buildings at their backs. The wealthy demanded nice gardens to accompany their nice houses. Meanwhile, their tenants worked their land and paid their dues without so much as a *cheers!* sent their way.

Which was precisely why Elsie didn't feel bad about breaking the law.

It would be sneakier to do it at night. Surely a burglar or the like from one of the tales in her novel reader would have acted at night. But Elsie was already a single woman venturing about on her own; she needn't ruin herself by doing so after sundown. Times were changing, yes, but people's minds were slow to keep up.

A man passed by her, tipping his hat in greeting. Elsie smiled and nodded back. Once he'd left, Elsie touched the brick wall encircling the Turner home, letting its roughness pass beneath her fingertips. Searching for anything magicked.

A few feet ahead of her, a rune shimmered once and shied away, as though embarrassed by Elsie's scrutiny. A physical spell, if she could see it. Different spells manifested themselves to her in different ways. She could feel rational runes, hear spiritual ones, and smell the temporal. Physical spells, however, liked to be seen. They were the dandies of the magic world.

The thing all runes had in common was their knot-like quality. At least, Elsie liked to think of them as knots. And like knots, they could fray over time. The more masterful the spellmaker's hand, the more stubborn the knot was to untie. The ones she could *see*—physical spells—were made of light and glitter, bright and pretzel-like, loose if the man casting them had been lazy or simply wasn't talented.

Aspectors were usually men, anyway.

There were two kinds of wizards in the world—those who cast spells, and those who broke them. The spellmakers, known as aspectors, paid a king's ransom for the spells they took into their bodies, yet another means of benefitting the rich and rebuffing the poor. But God had a way of making things even. He'd been generous with the other side of the coin, for spellbreakers were *born* with the ability to dis-spell magic, and it didn't cost them a farthing.

Elsie couldn't handle any of the four alignments of magic herself, but she could *detect* spells and unravel them like knots. This spell was decently tied, but not terribly so. An intermediate or advanced physical spell of hiding. It concealed a door, Elsie was sure of it. And it just so happened that Mr. Turner had a habit of "losing" his tenants' rent and forcing them to pay double. The people who depended on him for their livelihoods could barely keep food on the table, while this man lounged with the peerage and had servants at his beck and call. This was the sort of injustice the Cowls often addressed—with Elsie's help. She would disenchant this door, and the Cowls would take back the money he had stolen. Very Robin Hood of them. And Elsie was their Little John.

Pushing her palms into the spell, she pulled on the ends of the knot. There were seven of them, and she would need to unravel them in the reverse order of their placement. Fortunately, Elsie had encountered this spell before. She'd know how to proceed, once she found the loose end.

In a matter of heartbeats, the spell faded, and the creases and hinges of a brick-heavy door became visible to her eye.

"Who goes there?"

Elsie's heart leapt into her throat. She pulled away from the wall as though it had stung her. It was not a constable, but a man in a fine waistcoat and trousers, a gold watch chain swinging from one of his pockets. Upon recognizing his face against the late-afternoon sun, however, Elsie almost wished it had been a constable.

Squire Douglas Hughes. The squire who presided over her hometown. Brookley was close enough to London that it wasn't particularly odd for her to see him here. But it *was* bad luck.

Not because she feared he'd recognize her—despite the fact that she'd worked in his house for a year, she doubted he would—but because Squire Hughes was the epitome of everything she hated. He was rude to the common folk and a sycophant to the aristocrats. He hoarded his money and passed off his squirely duties whenever he could, and when he could not, he bore them with the utmost disdain and didn't attempt to hide it. He held his nose when he passed farmers. And he'd once trodden upon Elsie's foot and not even stopped to see if she was all right, let alone apologize for it.

This was the beast the Cowls fought against, though thus far the secretive group had not deemed him important enough for action.

How she wished they would. If the Cowls were Robin Hood, this man was Prince John.

Forcing a relaxed demeanor, Elsie walked up to meet him instead of letting him come to her. She didn't want him to notice the seams of the door. Mr. Turner was a wealthy man, and therefore the squire might actually care that Elsie had been snooping about his property.

Biting the inside of her cheek, she curtsied. "I apologize if I'm disturbing anyone. I work for a stonemason; I was just admiring the brickwork." It was only half a lie.

The man raised a fine eyebrow. "The brickwork? Surely you jest." He eyed her, but not with any recognition. Rather, he seemed confused by her clothing—particularly her skirts, as if it confused him that a woman could work outside of service. Elsie certainly wasn't dressed as a maid.

Elsie couldn't make herself blush, but she glanced away as though embarrassed.

Squire Hughes said, "Don't loiter. Your employer would be angry to see you wasting time."

She was tempted to snap back, to insist her employer had given his blessing for her to be here, but that wouldn't strictly be true. While Ogden was undeniably generous with her time, he hadn't a clue what she spent it on. If she left now, she could get back to Brookley by dinner and he'd be none the wiser.

She curtsied again. "I beg your pardon."

The squire didn't so much as nod, so Elsie excused herself wordlessly, walking a little too fast to be casual. Once she turned the corner, she straightened her spine and squared her shoulders.

No, she didn't feel bad about breaking the law. Not one mite.

The sun was setting when Elsie made it back to Brookley; she'd paid a hansom cab to take her as far as Lambeth and had walked the rest of the way. She shredded the letter from the Cowls in her pocket. The oven would be hot about this time, and she could cast the bits into the coals without any trouble.

Sometimes she wished she had a confidant, but she counted herself lucky all the same. The Cowls had rescued her from the workhouse and lifted her from a destiny of poverty. The least she could do was protect their secrecy.

Brookley was just south and a little east of London, wedged almost equidistant between Croydon and Orpington. It was an old town well kept by those who lived there. The main road spiraled through the center like a river of cobblestone, a thoroughfare that led south to Clunwood and farmland before continuing on to Edenbridge. It was small and quaint, yet had everything a reasonable person could need—a bank, a post office, a dressmaker, a church. Granted, if one wanted a millinery, they'd have to head into either London or Kent, but seeing as Elsie was set on hatwear, that didn't bother her particularly much.

One of the best things about Brookley was that the stonemasonry shop sat on its northern side, down a small road curving off the main one, so it was a fairly private affair to walk to and from the direction of London.

Elsie kicked dirt from her shoes before letting herself in through the back door of the house attached to the studio. There were a few shirts hanging on a clothing line overhead. The smell of mutton wafted through the air. In the kitchen, Emmeline, the maid, stirred a pot on the stove. Elsie had been in that position for several years after escaping the squire's household, until Ogden had promoted her to his assistant and brought in a new employee.

After hanging up her hat and setting her chatelaine bag on a table, Elsie waved to Emmeline before venturing down the hallway, around the corner, and into the studio, which was by far the largest room in the house. The counter by the door served as a storefront, and the rest of the space was filled with tarps, uncarved and half-carved stone, easels, canvases, blankets, and an array of shelves holding a collection of tools and utensils in every shape a person could imagine, as well as a great deal of white paint; a man who could change the color of anything with a simple touch needn't spend money on pigments. Cuthbert Ogden hunched on a stool just shy of the center of the room, surrounded by two lamps and three candles, delicately placing snow on the tiles of a manor he'd painted on a canvas half as tall as he was. There was something comforting about seeing him working like that, something familiar, something safe. Elsie needed those kinds of *somethings* in her life.

"You'll need glasses if you keep squinting by candlelight." She picked up a nearly extinguished candle and set it closer to his work.

"I am young and hale yet." His low voice seemed to creep along the floorboards.

"Hale, yes," Elsie said, and her employer glanced over to her, his turquoise eyes sparkling in the light. His dark brows crooked in a mock disapproving manner.

"Fifty-four is not old," he quipped.

"Fifty-five is."

Ogden paused, nearly touching his paintbrush to his lips in thought. "I'm not fifty-five, am I?"

"You turned fifty-five in February."

"I turned fifty-four."

Elsie sighed and tried to hide the smile on her lips. "Mr. Ogden. You were born in 1840, the same day the queen married Prince Albert. You brag about it to everyone."

Ogden's lip quirked. "I'm sure they married in 1841."

"Now you're just being difficult." She stepped up behind him, avoiding a lamp, and surveyed the painting. Ogden had managed to make a gray winter sky look cheery. A heavy wreath with red ribbon on the front door denoted Christmas. Snow at the top of the house, the chimney, the bottom two corners. Ogden had a strange thing about adding details at the edges of the canvas first before moving in toward the center.

"Does it snow often in Manchester?"

Ogden shook his head. "No, but it was the client's request."

"Christmas is seven months away yet. Seven and a half."

"But I will need to put this away and look at it again in a few weeks." Ogden's eyes stayed on the painting, squinting and scrutinizing. "And then have you take it to the framer's. That will take up another month, and then if they request corrections . . . you know how it goes. How was your evening?"

Elsie shrugged. "Uneventful. A long walk and some window browsing."

Ogden stuck his pinky finger in the white paint on the palette in his off-hand. Elsie felt the spell as it sparked out of him, and the white brightened until it nearly glowed. He was a physical aspector, but not a very strong one. Strength in aspecting varied from person to person, although it seemed to be bestowed at random, not by genetics. The spells Ogden knew were all novice level. Spells that made only slight changes to the physical world around him—like changing the color of paint. Ogden didn't seem to mind, though. Enough for an artist to get by. He'd told her that himself on more than one occasion.

Elsie watched him dip his brush and touch its fine tip to the eaves of the manor and the leaves of a tree on the grounds. It looked like real snow. With artistic talent such as his, Ogden didn't need powerful magic.

He worked for a few more minutes before putting the brush down. "Would you help me clean up?"

Elsie picked up one of the candles, shielding its flame with her cupped hand.

"I'm expecting Nash," he added.

"Is he staying for dinner?" Elsie asked.

Ogden shook his head. "Have Emmeline set a plate aside for me, would you?"

Nodding, Elsie carried the candle to a nearby table, then gathered the lamps and stuck them on the counter. She blew out the remaining candles—no point in wasting them. Ogden rinsed his brush and carefully carried the easel holding his latest work to the corner; Elsie rolled up the stained tarp underfoot. Even as she did so, she knew it was pointless. First thing tomorrow Ogden would be in the same spot, doing the same work, but she strived to make herself useful. Had strived for it these last nine years, ever since she'd advanced from being a scullery maid for a pompous jackanapes.

Elsie brushed off her hands and took the still-lit candle down the hall with her. Movement on the stairs made her gasp and set her heart racing.

"Emmeline!" Her whisper was nearly a hiss. "Why are you skulking about in the shadows?"

The maid, four years younger than Elsie at seventeen, darted her dark eyes over the railing. "Is he here yet?"

"Who?"

She licked her lips. "Nash."

The name was barely audible.

Elsie rolled her eyes. "Not yet, and don't worry, he's not staying for dinner. Ogden said to leave his plate for him."

Emmeline nodded, but fear tightened her face. She was always uneasy around Ogden's messenger boy. Why, Elsie didn't know. He was a tall man, yes, but so slight a strong wind might snap his torso like a twig. That, and he was an abundantly pleasant fellow; he always had a grin on his face and a bounce to his step. He wasn't crude or

14

cruel—indeed, although he rarely spoke to Elsie and Emmeline, he was unfailingly kind when he did so.

Emmeline shifted, and the stair creaked underfoot. "Would you set the table with me?"

Elsie let out a long breath through her nose. "Really, Emmeline."

"Why does he always come at night?" she asked, defensive.

"Because he has other clients? Because that's when Ogden is ready for him? And he doesn't always."

"Often," the maid countered. "*Often* at night. There's a look to him, Els. I don't like it."

Oh, Elsie knew it well. Emmeline had always been wary of Abel Nash, from her first day in Ogden's household. It was an odd reaction to a man who was reasonably attractive and had a rather cheery disposition.

Elsie had teased her about it, once, asking if the true reason for her interest in the blond errand boy was a hidden affection, but Emmeline had responded so coldly that Elsie dared not mention it again. Ogden was more likely to court the man than Emmeline was.

Elsie's shoulders drooped. "Yes, I'll help you."

Emmeline looked so relieved she might have fainted. "Thank you. I'll serve you breakfast first tomorrow."

Elsie snorted. "We'll see how Ogden likes that." Climbing a few steps, she took the girl's arm in hers and walked her to the kitchen, noting how Emmeline gave the hall to the studio a nervous glance. The action made her feel like something of an older sister. The thought niggled something painful in her gut, however, and she pushed the notion away.

The two set the table and ate together. Emmeline listened intently as Elsie regurgitated the story of the baron from her novel reader, and together they speculated what his fate might be. Ogden still hadn't come in for his plate when they finished, but that wasn't unlike him. Like most artists, he could be a little absent at times.

Grabbing a candleholder, Elsie ventured toward the stairs, but voices in the studio caught her attention. Nash was quiet even in motion—she'd never heard the front door open.

She peeked in. Nash looked fragile next to Ogden, who had the broad, stout, muscular build of a stonemason—work he still did on occasion, when commissions from his paintings and sculptures grew sparse. Nash was taller, his hair dandelion yellow, his face young and narrow. He was in his midtwenties, dressed simply. Pale. Completely unthreatening.

Elsie couldn't overhear their discussion, not that it mattered. Nothing interesting ever passed her employer's lips, and she'd spied on them enough to know they were strictly business partners and nothing else. No, Elsie had to depend on Emmeline and the local merchants for good gossip. Not that she ever spread it herself. But the vicar didn't preach against *listening* to gossip.

And yet, as Elsie turned away to venture to bed, Abel Nash looked over Ogden's shoulder, his light eyes finding her for only a moment before refocusing on the man before him. In that brief moment, Elsie felt a chill course down her spine.

CHAPTER 2

After three weeks aboard a merchant ship, Bacchus's head ached for land almost as much as his legs did. He swore he could feel his sanity slipping. He'd made the trip more times than he could count in his twenty-seven years, and yet he never had accustomed himself to it. The Atlantic always felt so much broader than he remembered it. On a voyage that long, he craved solid ground. And oranges. These merchant ships abounded in good food, but all of it was for profit, not for crewmen or passengers.

As Bacchus looked up at accumulating rain clouds and listened to the English lilt of the sailors hurrying to dock, his home in Barbados felt very far away. He'd spent just as many years in England with his father as he had on the island, but he'd never truly felt he belonged anywhere but the Caribbean. He'd visited his mother's homeland, the Algarve, only twice. His poor grasp of Portuguese had always made him feel like he stood on the outside looking in. He had no desire to return.

He nodded to John and Rainer, servants from his household, who scrambled to collect his suitcases. He'd tried to pack light, but he didn't know how long his stay would be. He could be in England for a mere week, or he could be here for months. It all depended on how accommodating the Physical Atheneum would be.

He had a feeling accommodation wasn't the atheneum's strong suit.

Grabbing a bag himself and urging strength into his limbs, Bacchus marched for the gangplank leading to the dock. A few of the sailors stepped aside to let him pass. He was not yet a titled man, certainly not here in England, but he was a well-dressed landowner and an aspector ready to test for master status, which in this uptight society would shove him somewhere above a clergyman and below a baron. Unfortunately, the test was not the only hurdle he faced in English society. As soon as he stepped ashore, he felt eyes on his face, his hair, his hands. Even the finest clothes couldn't hide his foreign heritage. Despite having an English father, he didn't *look* English, and his skin was all the darker from a lifetime in the sun.

But Bacchus was accustomed to stares.

Fortunately, as a breeze reeking of fish blew through his thick hair, bound at the nape of his neck, he saw a familiar face among the onlookers, standing on the edge of the road across from low-lodging houses. It was a face as pale as the whites of Bacchus's eyes, framed by hair even lighter. A hooked nose, a regal bearing despite his years. A waistcoat embroidered with gold thread.

Isaiah Scott, Duke of Kent.

Bacchus grinned and charged forward. This time, when the Englishmen scattered from his path, it was because his stride demanded it, as did his height and breadth. He may have been a copper coin against a sea of silver, but he was a large coin—a fact he often used to his advantage. He clasped hands with the duke. Bacchus's father had become close with the family after attending university with the duke's youngest brother, Matthew. He'd maintained the connection from afar after moving to Barbados to claim his inheritance. The first time Bacchus's father had brought him to England, or at least the first time Bacchus remembered, had been to pay his respects to the Scotts after Matthew passed away in a hunting incident. Although Bacchus's father had since passed on, Bacchus had stayed close with them. They felt like family.

"I didn't think it possible, but you've grown." The Duke of Kent had a glint in his eye.

Although the man had turned seventy last month, his grip was strong as ever.

"Only because we're at sea level." Bacchus's tongue easily slipped into a British accent. "Once we ride up those green hills by your estate, we'll see eye to eye."

The duke chuckled. "You need a lesson in physics. Are you sure you picked the right alignment?"

Bacchus had studied physical aspecting—magic that affected the physical world—since he was an adolescent. His father, being a land-owner on a prosperous sugarcane plantation, had been able to fund his studies. It hadn't been hard for him to choose a specialization. The last thing he wanted was to give the English another reason to distrust him, so the rational arts were out. He didn't need anyone suspecting he'd bewitched their thoughts. Spiritual magic dealt fundamentally with blessings and curses, which seemed a poor investment for day-to-day life. And temporal magic had always come off as vain to him. A temporal aspector couldn't change time, only time's effects. And while aging plant sprouts and turning back the clock for livestock could prove beneficial back home, Bacchus knew he'd more often be hired to lighten wrinkles and strip the rust from antiques. He used to think poorly of those who spent their life's savings on temporal spells, assuming they were driven by vanity.

Until the day he'd needed one for himself.

His men, John and Rainer, stepped up beside him, bug-eyed as they looked around. John, the older of the two, had been to Europe once before, on Bacchus's last trip three years ago. Rainer was new and absorbed everything as though the cobbles and clouds were nails pounded into his bones.

He wouldn't like it here.

"Come." The duke placed a hand on Bacchus's shoulder and led him down the narrow road to a carriage awaiting them. "You must be tired from such a long journey. Your room is ready, and I brought a cushion in case you can't wait the hour it will take to arrive there."

"Truly, I'd like nothing more than to run until my legs give out." Which took less time than it once had. Hiding a grimace, Bacchus glanced down at his legs, then rubbed a spot on his chest. "That ship is a cage, and the ocean its bars."

"So poetic," the duke said. One of his servants opened the carriage door, and Bacchus stepped back to allow his friend—though he'd always been more of an uncle—to enter first. Bacchus followed after, feeling the carriage shift as he sat down.

"If it isn't much trouble," Bacchus said after the carriage door shut and his bags were loaded onto the back, "I'd like to contact the Physical Atheneum as soon as possible."

The duke clasped his hands over his knees. "Is there a reason for the rush?"

"Not a rush, merely a desire to utilize the time given me. I'd rather not waste it."

"Ah, so time with me is wasted?" The duke quirked his brow.

Bacchus chuckled. "I suppose that depends on what leisure you have planned for us. I did receive your letter about the estate; I'd be obliged to help you where I can."

The duke nodded. "I greatly appreciate it. As for the atheneum, I've been trying to throw my weight to get you an earlier meeting. I think it's working. With luck, I'll hear back in the morning."

Not wanting to seem ungrateful, Bacchus nodded his thanks before looking out the window as the carriage jerked forward. As an aspector registered with the London Physical Atheneum, he was entitled to a meeting. But as with everything, there were politics involved, and his appointment had been set for the end of summer. The four-month wait was preposterous, especially given that he'd petitioned for the meeting in February. While the duke was not a spellmaker of any sort, he was an influential aristocrat with money to his name, and thus could hopefully bend the politics in Bacchus's favor. Either way, he feared his meeting would not go smoothly.

He watched the docks pass by, rubbing the light beard encircling his mouth. While such a thing was fashionable here, his long hair certainly wasn't. But long hair ultimately required less upkeep than short. He supposed he'd *consider* cutting it if it would make a better impression on the Assembly of the London Physical Atheneum.

He knew the spell he wanted. He'd known it for years now, and aspired to claim it far more vigorously than he did any title. The ambulation spell would allow him to move an object—any object—without touching it. The trick was convincing the self-righteous hermits in the atheneum to let him have it. Although hundreds of spells existed for each alignment, the atheneums guarded the powerful ones as carefully as a miser did his money, selling them only to those deemed worthy and reliable. And even if a spell was made available to an aspector, there still remained the challenge of absorbing it—a costly procedure that did not always work.

Bacchus rubbed his eyes. Perhaps he was more tired than he cared to admit. It would do him well to get a full night's rest at the Duke of Kent's estate before tackling his mission in the morning. He needed to think clearly and tread carefully if he didn't want to mix himself up in these aspectors' games.

CHAPTER 3

After Elsie finished logging Ogden's receipts the next morning, she wrote and folded a letter, put on her nicest hat, and strode into town with a basket on her arm and Emmeline's shopping list in hand. She headed first toward the church, which was at the other end of Brookley's high street. The farmers from the nearby town of Clunwood often set up there to sell their goods, and Elsie was in the mood for a walk. The clouds had parted to reveal a brilliant morning sun, while a subtle breeze kept the air from getting too warm.

Elsie took on a pace neither brisk nor leisurely, and allowed herself to wander from one side of the road to the other, glancing into windows as she went, both shops and homes. Elizabeth Davies, she noticed, had her fine china out on the breakfast table. What was the occasion? The glazier was working on something rather large that did not look like a window. Was it an elaborate bowl, or some sort of chandelier? Elsie couldn't tell, and preferred to speculate over asking. It was better for everyone that she go unnoticed, besides.

A familiar gasp sounded just to Elsie's left as she turned away from the glass shop. A smile pinched her cheeks. None other than Rose and Alexandra Wright were passing by, their hats extravagant and their satin skirts brushing the ground. They were the banker's daughters and terrible gossips. Even now, they had their heads pushed together, mumbling to each other. They really should be ashamed of themselves.

Stepping around a wagon, Elsie trotted up behind them, straining to listen.

"He was a *baron*?" Rose asked, fingertips to her bottom lip.

"Not just any," chirped Alexandra, "but the very one who visited here not two summers ago."

Rose gasped. "The squire's guest?"

"And," Alexandra's voice lowered, "it happened right in his own bed."

Rose shook her head. "But it might not be murder. You can never be sure with their type."

Elsie nearly stumbled as she kicked her own heel. *Murder?* And a baron! It was as if her novel reader had come to life, although crime was much easier to stomach in fiction. Her mind quickly unraveled the rest of the sisters' words.

Never be sure with their type.

Had the man been an aspector? When an aspector of any type or talent died, he did not become a corpse to be buried like everyone else. Magic changed aspectors. When they perished, their bodies morphed into opuses. Spellbooks of all the enchantments they had learned in life. Granted, *spellbook* wasn't an adequate term. The form they took varied depending on who the aspector had been as a person. Though Ogden was a weak aspector with very few spells under his skin, he, too, would transmute into an opus when he passed. Elsie had always imagined he'd become an elaborate, if small, stone tablet.

The stonemason had no spouse and no children—for reasons Elsie suspected but never said aloud—so she wondered if he would bequeath his opus to her or Emmeline. Usually a spellmaker's opus became the property of his or her atheneum, a safety precaution lest dangerous spells fall into unscrupulous hands, but she couldn't imagine the London Physical Atheneum caring about a small, novice spellbook.

That was the special thing about opuses—*anyone* could cast a spell from an opus. Ogden had told her about it. The person could just rip out a page and say, "Excitant," and the spell would cast itself (if the opus was not composed of pages, they could run a hand over the spell instead). They could be used in such a manner only once, for the page or engraved spell would vanish afterward, but it made opuses priceless.

And yet, Elsie didn't think she could ever bring herself to cast Ogden's opus spells. She'd likely just treasure it and keep it close, reminding her of the good years they had spent together. By all means, Ogden was the closest thing to a father she had.

Focus! she chided herself, daring to step close enough that she almost trampled the women's skirt trains.

"Then he vanished splendidly." Alexandra's voice took on a mocking tone. "Murdered, I tell you. And his opus stolen. Even the newspaper speculates it. Perhaps he was kidnapped, but who could lug a grown man down so many floors without leaving a witness? The opus could have been carted off with no one the wiser."

A man hurried across the street, one hand on his hat to keep it from flying off. "Misses Wright! I have a question regarding your father—"

The two women paused, and Elsie quickly sidestepped to avoid running into them. She walked as far as the carpenter's home before glancing over her shoulder, but the conversing trio didn't pay her any mind.

She certainly hoped the baron would turn up someplace unexpected. To think of someone being killed in his own home, his own bed . . . Elsie shuddered at the thought. Even members of the upper class didn't deserve such a fate. And yet she knew she would check Ogden's newspaper the moment she got home, to glean any additional details.

Still mulling over the story, Elsie found a smattering of farmers, their wives, and their children selling produce on the side of the road. Checking Emmeline's list, she purchased two cabbages, a bundle of carrots, and an onion. She quite loathed onions, which was why she bought only one. Emmeline would have to make it stretch, which meant less onion in their meals. It was ultimately better for the household.

Stepping out of the way of two men on horseback, Elsie turned back, glancing once more into Elizabeth Davies's home. They were seated at the table now, but no strangers dined with them. It wasn't a visitor that had her pulling out the china, then. Curious.

The post office sat just past the row of terraced housing, its location indicated by the tidy storefront attached to Mr. Green's home, one of the larger buildings in town. He certainly did well for himself, delivering post and telegrams day in and day out.

Elsie stepped in just as a fellow stepped out. She nodded to him when he held the door. One of Mr. Green's employees, Martha Morgan, manned the front desk today, and she smiled as Elsie approached, and one of the post dogs—animals trained by spiritual aspectors to deliver letters and packages—wagged its tail behind the desk. The thumping almost hid the light buzz of the spells at work beneath its fur.

"Just a penny stamp." Elsie set her letter on the desk before her. She smoothed her lace-gloved fingers over the paper. It had been six months since she'd last sent a letter to Juniper Down, and five months since she'd received a response from Agatha Hall. She always wrote to Agatha rather than her husband. Agatha was more kindhearted and quicker to reply. Elsie's letter was brief, containing many of the same words as her previous missives.

Dear Mrs. Hall,

*I hope all is well with the children and your health. I am,
of course, inquiring again to learn if anyone has come
looking for me, or if anyone bearing the name Camden
has passed through? I do greatly appreciate your report.
You have my utmost thanks.*

  Sincerely,

  Elsie Camden

Elsie had lost count of the number of letters she had sent west to Juniper Down. She had written more frequently in her younger years, after Ogden hired her and taught her how to read and write. Another reason to be grateful to him. Had she remained in the squire's employ, she might never have learned to decipher the Cowls' missives. They'd started to send them a few months before her thirteenth birthday.

Martha handed her the penny stamp, and Elsie carefully placed it on her letter. Memories flooded into her as she looked at Agatha Hall's name spelled out in her own hand across the envelope. The Halls had offered Elsie's family shelter that cold winter night. Elsie couldn't remember where they'd been going, let alone where they'd started, and neither could the Halls. Come morning, her parents and siblings—the Halls confirmed she'd had three siblings, two brothers and a sister—had vanished without a trace. Much like the baron from the Wright sisters' story. The whole town had banded together to search for them, to no avail.

Of course, the Halls didn't know Elsie. And they had little money and five children of their own, so after all hope was lost, they'd sent six-year-old Elsie to the workhouse. And she'd stayed there until she was eleven, when it burned down.

That night, her rescuer had hastened her to a simple one-room cabin miles away, hooded the whole time, and left her there with food and blankets and the instruction to stay put and not feel guilty for her part in the fire, but Elsie had stewed about it, especially as the days passed with no word. Four days, to be precise. But she'd been bolstered by hope, good food, and the giddy feeling that someone actually *wanted* her. Finally, she'd woken up on the fifth day to find a map, a train ticket, and an address pinned to the inside of the front door. She'd followed the directions without complaint, and found herself on Squire Hughes's doorstep.

Although no one there was expecting her, it turned out they were in need of a new scullery maid, something the Cowls must have known. She'd hated the work almost as much as she hated the squire, so a year later, when Cuthbert Ogden announced he was hiring help, she'd run to him straightaway and begged him to take her on, even promising to work for only food and board.

Fortunately, Ogden had still given her a wage.

Elsie had never told any of them, even Ogden, about the cabin or the fire. She hadn't wanted to give them a reason to cast her aside.

"Miss?"

Elsie blinked, wrenched back to the moment, and smiled. "Yes, if you would post it."

She offered the letter, and Martha added it to a small stack. "Nothing for Mr. Ogden today," she added.

"Just as well. Thank you."

Perhaps Agatha Hall would finally have news of the family Elsie hadn't seen in fifteen years. Perhaps desire, guilt, or curiosity had finally driven one of her relations to ask, *Whatever happened to Elsie?*

Shifting her basket to her other arm, Elsie excused herself silently and stepped back into the sunshine, taking a moment to soak it in until another postal customer forced her to move so he could access the door.

When Elsie got home, Emmeline was scrubbing the floor near the back door, lost somewhere in her thoughts, for she didn't even look up and beg Elsie to remove her shoes. Elsie did it, anyway, precariously balancing her basket of produce while aiming for dry spots so as not to dampen her stockings.

"Is Ogden in?" she asked upon reaching the stairs.

Emmeline shook her head. "He went out right on your tail. Mr. Parker himself came by for him, wanted his eye on the new stonework for the wall, or something like that."

Mr. Parker, who worked for the abominable Squire Hughes. Elsie sniffed in disdain. But the squire paid well, which meant Ogden could afford to keep both her and Emmeline on staff.

Elsie would need to man the studio, then. It was usually a boring task, as unlike the post office, a stonemason's shop was not one people frequented. But her novel reader would keep her company. If she reread it with a scrutinizing eye, she might discover a clue she'd missed the first time.

Hurrying up the steps and down the hallway, Elsie ducked into her room and tossed her hat onto her bed. Her novel reader was tucked away on the small shelf in the corner. As she pulled it free, however, a gray note fell to the floor.

She recognized it instantly, even with the seal facedown.

Although she itched to open it, she crossed the room first to shut and lock the door. That done, she knelt to pick up the folded paper. Turned it over. The symbol of a bird's footprint overlaying a crescent moon looked back up at her in vivid orange wax.

So soon? she wondered. The notes had been more frequent lately, and more *intimate*. Left on her bed, under her covers, now on her bookshelf. What if she hadn't decided to reread the latest installment of *The Curse of the Ruby* today? Perhaps this mission wasn't urgent. Perhaps they were watching her more closely than she'd thought.

Elsie turned toward the window, which was two stories up. How absurd it would be for someone, especially a cloaked someone, to hover on the precipice, watching her and learning her habits. She could almost laugh at the notion.

And yet the letter had been waiting.

She used her fingernail to break the seal. A few shillings fell into her lap.

Power taints all. Someone at the Duke of Kent's estate has enchanted the servants' door, forbidding them outside after sundown. It is a spell of heat. Be prepared. Take a carriage, but be discreet. At the wine shop in Kent, ask for Mrs. Shaw's basket.

That was it. No name, no date. She'd have to find a wine shop near the duke's estate—the note didn't include an address. What would she do if there was more than one?

Her stomach squirmed. In truth, the wine shop was the least of her troubles. This was the riskiest task she'd ever been given. Hopefully this duke was not a spellmaker as well—they tended to ward their property with all sorts of nasty things, a precaution passed down from the revolts two centuries past. And she'd have to trespass onto his property, not merely brush her fingers across an exterior wall. Swallowing, she reassured herself that the Cowls would not ask her to do anything she wasn't capable of doing. Perhaps Mrs. Shaw's basket would lend some aid.

Elsie tried to imagine what it would feel like if Ogden bespelled the stonemasonry shop to keep her and Emmeline locked indoors. The note had said it was a fire spell . . . Did it burn the servants when they attempted to escape? What was it about wealth that made the upper class treat other human beings like they were livestock to keep penned?

She pressed her lips together. Kent wasn't far. If she took a carriage, she could be there and back before nightfall. The squire would be a fool not to hire Ogden, which meant her boss would likely be busy for the next few days.

It was settled, then. Elsie would rush through her work and ensure everything was in order before leaving. Emmeline could listen for the door and see to any late-day customers.

Replacing her novel reader on the shelf, Elsie tore the silvery note in half, then in half again. Despite the warm weather, she lit the fireplace in her room and tossed the pieces onto the flames, making sure they disintegrated to ash before she ventured downstairs.

∽

There was a wine shop a good walk's distance from Seven Oaks, the Duke of Kent's estate. It had a very fine storefront, so Elsie straightened her shoulders and her hat before going in. A rotund man greeted her, and as directed, she requested Mrs. Shaw's basket.

She hadn't a clue who Mrs. Shaw was, nor whether or not she existed.

The man stepped into a small back room and brought out a sturdy basket with two bottles of an expensive Madeira, as well as a few cheese wedges and a layout of grapes that smelled strongly of earth. The grapes were just fine, they'd simply been enchanted with a temporal spell to keep them fresh. The scent was off-putting, which was why Elsie didn't often eat temporally enchanted food. The Christmas turkeys Ogden brought home usually had a similar rune on them, but she'd always subtly removed it before enjoying the meal.

The food was already paid for, so Elsie thanked the man, hung the heavy basket on her arm, and departed.

Although no note had been tucked into the basket, Elsie understood the tactic. The spell in question was on a servant's door, so Elsie would need to approach it as a salesman—and given the finery in this basket, she probably had something the housekeeper would want. She wondered how much the food cost and what she should do with what she didn't sell. Would the Cowls want it returned somehow? They'd left no directions in her note, but it didn't feel right, keeping it, when someone else could enjoy it so much more than she could.

She paused by a few select merchants on her way, purchasing a used book with her own money and trading one wedge of cheese for a buckle clasp and shoeshine. Best to have an array of goods. If not to tempt the duke's servants, then to better disguise herself as a peddler.

She glanced over her dress. She tried to keep up with fashion, but being too fashionable might make her suspect. When she finally reached the enormous estate, her arm aching from her load, she forced herself to pluck the adornment off her hat—she'd pocket it and fix it later—and did her best to wrinkle her skirt. Clean and trustworthy, but not well-to-do. That should be enough.

She wasn't sure which side of the house the servants' entrance was on. The house—*do not ogle the house*—had to fit at least twenty bedrooms. But it would not do to dawdle. She wanted to look like a local, like someone who'd done this before. A businesswoman. The ruse would have been easier if she were a business*man*, but one had to work with what one had.

She spied a narrow path leading off to the left and took it around until she found a relatively plain-looking door near the back. A skinny wisp of a girl was dumping out a small washbasin nearby.

Elsie spied the slightest wisps of orange light emanating from the doorknob. She reached for it—

The door swung open, and a wide-faced woman of about forty startled, her hand flying to her chest. Pieces of sweaty curls stuck out from her cap.

"Goodness, girl, you scared my blood cold!" she exclaimed, looking Elsie up and down.

"Forgive me, I was about to knock. I've come hoping to sell." She gestured to her basket.

The woman—she looked like a cook—was about to wave her away, but her hand stilled when she saw the Madeira. "What are you selling those for?" She gestured to the bottles.

"Two and five for both," she answered, purposefully choosing a low number.

The cook's eyes bugged. "Two and five? Don't you know what—never mind. Wait right here."

She turned around, leaving the door ajar. Inside was a narrow room lined with hooks. A pair of dirty boots sat on the floor. Beyond that, Elsie could just see the opening of a pantry on one side and a kitchen on the other. She thought she felt a tingle cross her face as she leaned in—was there a rational spell nearby, or was that just nerves? Perhaps the duke had a large illusion on display in a nearby room, or someone could be using a mental spell to keep their memory sharp. In a place as rich as this one, spells were likely to abound.

Setting her basket down, Elsie glanced over her shoulder for the wash girl. She'd vanished. Footsteps sounded deeper within the house. Nearby, a horse nickered.

Taking half a step back, Elsie put both hands on the enchanted doorknob. It was a small physical spell, but not a simple one. A knot made of light instead of rope, pulled tightly together. It was a bright white at its center, twinkling like a shy star, and slightly blue around the edges. Her eyes unfocused a bit as she found the start. The spell resisted her—it was well made. An intermediate spell formed by a master's hands. She loosened the rune and picked it apart string by string until it ceased to exist, fizzling out like the last sparks of a firework.

The cook returned moments later with a cheery disposition. She handed over three gold coins. "I'll take both bottles and a wedge of that cheese." She pointed to the paler option.

Elsie handed the goods over and thanked the cook, who had no idea she'd been liberated. Soon enough, that cheery disposition would be genuine, not the fleeting excitement of having nabbed a good price on wine.

It would likely take a few days before Elsie's work was discovered. It wouldn't be reported in the newspapers or shouted from the rooftops, but prestige had never been the goal.

Feeling accomplished, Elsie swung her much lighter basket at her side and left the estate grounds.

She hoped the Cowls were watching.

CHAPTER 4

The London Physical Atheneum was one of the most eye-catching, prestigious, and ancient buildings in England. Built in medieval times, it looked something like a mix between a castle and a university. In a sense, it was both. It boasted the largest aspector library in the world. The immense windows were fitted with enchanted glass to protect the spells inside and prevent them from leaving without the proper permissions.

Bacchus had left John and Rainer in Kent and excused his driver. A few people milled about the meticulous grounds, complete with gardens that even the queen could envy. Only one seemed to notice him. Bacchus did not maintain eye contact. Impressing this man was not his agenda today.

The atheneum grew ever larger as Bacchus approached, and if he hadn't known any better, he would have accused the walkway of lengthening as he strode down it. He knew spells for enlarging objects, but none of them would work on such a path, not without ripping the stones from the ground. No, this was merely his nerves. Bacchus wasn't used to nerves. He berated them with a soft growl, but at least they lent him energy.

Two sentries stood guard at the heavy double doors at the entrance of the grand library. Bacchus nodded to them and gave his name. He half expected to be turned away, but fortunately the guards had been alerted to his visit. They opened the right door and allowed him inside.

It took a moment for his eyes to adjust from the bright morning to the darker interior. Rugs and tapestries masked swathes of stone walls and floors, but a soft chill permeated the air. Bacchus felt a bit like a time traveler; the modernizations in the place were minimal.

Beyond the short antechamber stretched a long table, adorned only by elaborate silver candlesticks the style of which matched the low-hanging chandeliers above them, their tips glowing with intermediate light spells. Short rows of books lined the far walls, broken up by woven art. That chamber ended in an archway, and the true library started beyond it. Immense shelves stuffed with tomes that gave way to shadow. He thought he caught faint whispering echoing between the stonework.

Bacchus took a step forward, only to have one of the sentries raise his hand, urging him to wait. Bacchus let his impatience drain down his arms and into his hands, where he crushed it with tight fists. After a few minutes, a new guard came around the corner—there must have been a hidden hallway in the chandelier room.

"Mr. Bacchus Kelsey?" the man asked, looking Bacchus up and down.

Bacchus nodded.

"Your court is ready. Please follow me."

Bacchus did so without word. *Court. Do they think themselves kings, or am I about to be sentenced?*

They took a corridor circumventing the library and passed through a small room lined with bookshelves, several acolytes buried in their work. Lamps hovered without cords, likely bespelled by teachers to keep the light where it was needed. But there wasn't time to notice anything else, for Bacchus and his guide were already cutting through another massive room with a high ceiling, poorly lit, approaching a wide and winding set of stairs. They were old but in excellent repair, which likely meant they'd been hardened and bullied to hold their shape with magic. Perhaps a temporal magician had been hired to remove centuries of wear, but Bacchus suspected the heads of the Physical Atheneum were too proud to ask for help from another alignment.

The guard led Bacchus past the second floor, which appeared to have classrooms and dormitories, to the third, where they traversed a long hallway in which the portraits of English royals hung across from those of famous aspectors. Bacchus's limbs began to grow weary despite the early hour, but he stood straighter, refusing to let the fatigue show. Sunlight filtered in through the large windows to his left, illuminating the portraits of the aspectors. All English save for one with a French name. All male. Women, the lower classes, and foreigners hadn't been allowed access to spellmaking until the early seventeen hundreds, after the riots. Even so, society was slow to catch up.

His guide took him up one more flight of stairs. *This place is a labyrinth.* One more stairwell and Bacchus would know something was magicked; the atheneum wasn't *that* large.

But the stairs ended, and Bacchus found himself in a narrow corridor facing doors even heavier than those at the entrance. Two more sentries stood at attention. As they approached, one of them retreated back down the stairs, perhaps to take up the position vacated by Bacchus's guide. The guide then knocked thrice, opened the door, and made his announcement.

"Mr. Bacchus Kelsey, advanced aspector of the physical alignment, Barbados, to meet with the assembly."

There was no reply. The guard stepped back into the hall and gestured for Bacchus to enter.

He did so with his shoulders squared and his head held high.

It was a cold room, though not so much in temperature as in aesthetics. A few draperies adorned the walls, but they were cast in shadow and seemed little more than caves of ink. There were no chandeliers, sconces, or candlesticks; all the light came from the windows in one wall. The only rug was a long red strip that led directly from the door to the raised row of seats protected by an overly tall stone partition. Bacchus stood six foot three, but the assembly sat ten feet above ground level.

Eleven aspectors in all, the youngest being perhaps in his forties and the eldest holding on to his health in his seventies. They very much matched the portraits in that long hallway, save for the single woman in their ranks, who sat in the second-to-last chair on the right.

Bacchus knew all their names, but not all their faces. He could, however, identify the man sitting in the center of the assembly, his seat jutting forward. His hair was a pale gray, his face deeply lined as though he'd spent his entire life scowling. Master Enoch Phillips, a titled earl, and head of this atheneum.

Bacchus bowed deeply. "My thanks that you have agreed to meet with me."

"You've traveled far," Master Phillips said, his tone both impressed and disgusted at the same time. "Welcome to London."

Bacchus nodded his thanks.

"Your portfolio is most impressive," said the woman. Her name was easy to place: Master Ruth Hill. She shuffled a few papers Bacchus could hear but not see. She was in her fifties and carried her age well. White wisps of hair streaked the blonde tresses pulled back at the nape of her neck. "You started at a good age and progressed well, despite your limited resources."

Spending half his life in Barbados, she meant. The island was small, and its magical community was even smaller.

"And all of your testing has been performed here," added the man to her left. "A wise choice."

"England is my second home." Bacchus laced his words with as much politeness as he could muster. He *needed* this, and not just for his mastership. "I have much respect for the country as well as this atheneum." Not to mention the tedium of getting his records sent back and forth across the seas.

"Yes," interjected Master Phillips, rubbing his pointed chin, "that is evident. And a pure spellmaking history. I do appreciate a man who knows what he wants. Purity is essential for longevity."

Master Phillips cast a pointed glance at the man beside him, who gave no reaction other than the tightening of his mouth. That was Master Victor Allen, then. Although he had become a master regardless, he'd spent his first two years of apprenticeship under a spiritual aspector before switching to the physical alignment. Such a thing was not uncommon, but the magical strength a man earned in one alignment could not be transferred to another, and it would hinder him for the rest of his life. Indeed, most men would not have the capacity to reach masterhood in a second discipline after expending some of their abilities in a first, which only went to show Master Allen was a very powerful man. Perhaps that was the real reason Master Phillips seemed to dislike him.

"I have known my desires since I was a boy, even before I showed promise," Bacchus explained. "I have not faltered from my chosen path."

He fought the desire to twitch under the scrutiny of eleven pairs of eyes.

"Indeed. Another admirable quality." Master Phillips nodded. He folded his hands against the edge of his pedestal wall. "Your résumé and references speak for themselves, Mr. Kelsey. The assembly has discussed your petition previously, and we have agreed to approve your promotion to mastership."

A bubble of pride swelled in Bacchus's chest. All he had to do now was learn a master spell—prove he could absorb it—under the eye of an assembly member, and the title would be his.

"However, your request for the master ambulation spell is denied."

The bubble popped, and it took every bit of Bacchus's will not to let his shoulders slump. Not to look as though he'd been punched in the gut. Not to show his anger.

His throat tightened as he said, "I thank you kindly for the approval." He bowed, if only to buy himself a few seconds to sort out his tangled thoughts. "Forgive my impertinence, but why have I been denied the requested spell? I do not ask for any others." Desperation drove him to ask. It would be virtually impossible for someone to *guess* the words to a spell, which were both lengthy and in Latin. Certain spells could be acquired directly from spellmakers or opus collectors, but master spells tended to be dangerous, and were thus much more closely regulated. There was, of course, the illegal route, but the punishment for misusing magic in any way was hard and swift, and any aspector caught doing it would immediately lose his license, assuming he didn't lose his head as well. "I will not drain any of the atheneum's resources. I will not share the knowledge with any, save on the bed of my death."

His mastership meant *nothing* if he did not have that ambulation spell.

His future would mean nothing, too.

"It is a powerful spell. Rare, valuable. As you know," Master Phillips replied. He appeared to be looking just over Bacchus's head rather than at his eyes.

"I am aware." Bacchus carefully measured out his words. He could not unball his fists, so he stowed them behind his back. "But I do not request it for the sake of its rarity. It would prove very useful at my estate." Not a lie. "I will compensate the atheneum generously and the drops, of course, will come from my own pocket."

One could not master even a novice spell without paying for it in aspector drops—the universe's wizarding currency—but Bacchus had been saving a long time. He was prepared for that.

"I do not doubt its usefulness, young man," Master Phillips replied, "but the master ambulation spell is a treasure of the atheneum. It must stay among its people."

His brow twitched. "Pardon?" He'd been a student of this atheneum since his childhood.

Master Phillips sighed very much like a parent tired of scolding his child. "Although none can dispute your talent, you are not truly of this atheneum, Mr. Kelsey. You are not one of *us*. Your request is denied. However, were you to make a substantial donation to the atheneum, we could work out another master-level spell for your repertoire and provide the necessary witness."

Bacchus's muscles tightened to steel. He understood every unspoken word. "My father was just as English as you, Master Phillips. And as stated by the assembly, my aspector lineage is pure." Though they likely knew he was a bastard, and he did not doubt they'd gossiped about it prior to his visit. "The London Physical Atheneum administered all my prior testing."

Master Phillips picked up a gavel and struck it against the edge of the wall. "Thank you, Mr. Kelsey. You are dismissed."

His steel muscles instantly turned to pudding. That was it? He could not defend himself? Yet every defense surfacing in his tumbling mind would not win the favor of this court. No, the words piling upon his tongue were laced with anger; if he spoke any of them, he'd likely lose the chance of promotion entirely. So he kept silent as the assembly members rose from their seats and began filing out through a back door. The only person to give him a second glance was Master Ruth Hill. The pity in her eyes left a sour taste in his mouth.

The door behind him opened, his guards expectant. They forced his retreat, but this battle wasn't over. One way or another, Bacchus *would* get his spell, the atheneum be damned.

He'd have to tell the duke he was extending his stay.

CHAPTER 5

Mr. Ogden had forgotten his trowels.

Emmeline discovered the error not thirty minutes after Ogden departed for another day of work at Squire Douglas Hughes's estate. He'd left the plaster-stained bag by the front door—and then exited out the back. Elsie wasn't sure he *was* plastering today, but if the man had taken the effort to stick the bag where he'd thought he wouldn't forget it, then he must need it for something. And though Elsie was loath to get any closer to the squire than was absolutely necessary, she would be more loath if Ogden lost the job and could no longer fund her own. So she took the bag, holding it away from her so as not to get bits of dried plaster on her dress, and crossed Brookley to the squire's home.

Squire Hughes's home was very much like himself. Distant from the riffraff, gaudy in appearance, and generally pointless. Elsie's sides were stitching by the time she arrived. Unwilling to wait in the line of servants at the back door, she decided a direct approach would be best. Striding up to the front door, she slammed the iron knocker against it.

It took a minute, but the butler answered the door, and Mr. Parker, the squire's steward, approached as it was being opened, dismissing the butler with a nod of his head. Mr. Parker was an older man, with white hair and a well-fed belly. He dressed primly, if a little out of fashion, and had a receding hairline that was quite symmetrical. He was one of the few tolerable people in the squire's employ, though during her time as a scullery maid here, Elsie hadn't interacted with him often.

He blinked in surprise. "Miss Camden! How may I help you?"

She was surprised he remembered her. She looked different now than she had as a dirty eleven-year-old scrubbing dishes, and she very rarely saw the steward in town. Hefting the bag, she said, "I'm afraid Mr. Ogden forgot his trowels."

She needn't explain further—the steward nodded sagely and invited her in. "He's just this way." Once they reached a well-polished set of stairs, he added, "Would you like me to carry this?"

She would indeed, but it struck her that she'd have little reason to stay if she handed over the bag. If she'd walked all the way here, she might as well get a good look at the squire's accommodations. See if he'd changed anything. Hidden anything. To sate her curiosity.

"I'm fond of the exercise, Mr. Parker." She smiled. He looked only a little perplexed as he offered her a gracious nod and led the way through the house.

It was a far larger house than a simple squire should have, in Elsie's opinion—more suitable to a baron. The sparse yet costly décor had not changed, nor did it seem to have aged, although her perspective was slightly different since she'd grown several inches in the interim. It struck her that perhaps the squire had kept things the same because he had not yet managed to convince a woman to marry him and refresh the place. All wood was polished, all windows were free of smudges. Every light fixture seemed dotted with crystal. Something with thyme in it was being baked in the kitchen, but Mr. Parker led her into the courtyard before she could determine what.

The courtyard was completely engulfed by the house, about twice the size of Ogden's studio. A stone path looped through gardens lush with greens and spindly trees. A bench sat in the shade on the far side. Brick lined the walls of the house where the garden met them, and atop it was a border of plaster. Or rather, the start of one. Elsie imagined that Ogden's artwork would be carved into that plaster, providing visitors with something to admire as they walked the stone loop. Elsie had tried to walk that loop once, but the housekeeper had caught and scolded her. She'd had her hand switched for "going where she didn't belong," which had made scrubbing pots the next day miserable.

Ogden crouched at the northeast corner, barely visible behind some well-trimmed dogwood.

"Mr. Ogden, you've a guest." Mr. Parker spoke with the slightest hint of cheer. How anyone could be cheery in Squire Hughes's employ, Elsie didn't know.

"Not so much a guest as a deliverer," Elsie said as Ogden turned around. His eyes immediately went to the trowel bag, and relief lit his face.

He crossed the path—"You're an angel"—and took the bag.

"More so Emmeline. She's the one who noticed it."

Ogden gave her a look that said, *I know you and your desire to ogle,* which she steadfastly ignored.

Brushing off her skirt and checking for remnants of plaster dust, Elsie said, "Well, that will be that. I'm afraid I'll get lost in this enormous house, Mr. Parker." It had been ten years, after all, and her station had been so low she'd rarely seen the main floor. "Would you see me to the door?"

The steward smiled. "It would be my pleasure. Good day, Mr. Ogden."

Ogden nodded and returned to his work.

Once inside, Elsie said, "Is it a lot of trouble, keeping on top of all the workings of such a large household?"

Mr. Parker shook his head. He moved at a leisurely pace, which allowed for good conversation. "Not at all. I keep all the books in order, and the squire isn't a frivolous man. Makes things simple."

Feeling daring, Elsie remarked, "I'm not sure anything would be simple, with the squire."

To her relief, Mr. Parker merely chuckled. "I understand your point, Miss Camden. He has been out of sorts lately, what with the passing of the viscount."

The viscount?

She'd hoped for some talk of the baron, who'd stayed with the squire two summers past if the Wright sisters were to be believed, but who was this viscount?

Elsie's stomach did a little flip at the promise of gossip. Yet Mr. Parker had said it with the assumption that she would know to whom he referred. He was not baiting her. Thinking quickly, Elsie asked, "Is he distraught?"

"Of course." They entered a long hallway. "There was only an empty bedroom between them. Right under his nose, yet no one heard a thing. He hasn't been himself since returning from London. They were not terribly close, but it is a reminder of our own mortality."

Her mind spun, craving the pieces of the puzzle she was missing.

As they neared the entry hall, the squire himself came around the corner, tall and brooding. Elsie was so involved in her own mind that he startled her, eliciting a small gasp from her lips, which she quickly shut. Decorum mandated she not speak to her *better* first, and she was grateful for the excuse to ignore him.

Unfortunately, Squire Hughes did not ignore her. He stopped abruptly, eyeing Elsie as if he were some bull and she a red flag. His fiery gaze flew to Mr. Parker. "What on earth are you doing with your time, Parker? Who is this woman, and why is she in my house?"

Anger burned up Elsie's neck. She bit down so many heated retorts her teeth hurt. At least he didn't seem to recognize her from their brief meeting in London.

"Just an aide to Mr. Ogden, who is doing fine work on your inner courtyard. I'm seeing her out now. I do believe Markson was looking for you regarding your luncheon."

Squire Hughes's lips curved in a most unpleasant fashion. Instead of answering, the despicable man merely pushed past the both of them and continued on his ornery way.

Well, I never. She didn't dare say it aloud, so she merely folded her arms.

"My apologies." Mr. Parker crossed the entryway and took hold of the door handle. "The squire is very . . . old fashioned." There was a glint in his eyes Elsie couldn't quite interpret. "Please do send my regards to young Emmeline, hmm?"

She paused a step from the door frame, taking in Mr. Parker's aging but wise features. "You know Emmeline?"

He smoothed his cravat. "It is my business to know all things Brookley, my dear." Did he wink, or was there perhaps something in his eye?

Did he know about her? About *them*?

Elsie nodded slowly. "Of course. Thank you."

She walked out, listening for the door to shut behind her. She never heard it click, but when she turned back, it was closed. She paused a moment, studying the front of the house.

Was it a steward's business to know? And what *did* he know? And why had he imparted the information about the viscount?

Elsie contemplated the questions the entire way home, never once deciding on a definitive answer for any of them.

∞

"It's been like this a long time . . . years," Thom Thomas, known locally as Two Thom, held up a small plaster Christus statue in aged hands that trembled ever so slightly. Part of the Christus's robe had chipped away, and its left hand had snapped clean off. The old farmhand offered a light chuckle. "Since my boy was still at home. He's the one knocked it off the mantel, you see. We haven't displayed it since."

Elsie nodded as she gingerly took the small statue and its severed hand and fit them together. She'd left the shop again that afternoon to pick up a few supplies, hoping to distract herself from overthinking her visit to the squire's estate. Two Thom had apparently been on his way to the studio when he spied her on the street.

"Should be an easy fix." She could probably even do the repair herself, but Ogden's hands were far more practiced than her own. "I don't think he'd charge more than a shilling or two, and only that because he'll have to shape the plaster for the robe."

Two Thom smiled, exposing two gaps in his bottom jaw. "That will do." He fished two tarnished shillings from his pocket and handed them to her. "She'll be so surprised. It's our anniversary next week. Forty-three years."

He had already mentioned the anniversary, but Elsie smiled. "It's a very thoughtful thing to do. I'll carry it like my own babe back to the shop. You can pick it up the day before your celebration, hmm? Or I can deliver it."

Two Thom shook his head. "I'll make the walk. I can get away."

He shook her hand. Elsie took off her gloves and wrapped the plaster pieces in them before nestling them in her basket.

Turning back for home, Elsie slid the shillings into her chatelaine bag, only to have her fingertips brush a folded piece of paper there. Her first thought was that she needed to stop by the post office and post her letter. The second was that she had not written a letter to be posted.

She let the coins slip from her fingers and pinched the paper's edge, pulling it free. It wasn't even a full sheet of paper, but a quarter sheet with a silvery hue, folded tightly and sealed with a crescent moon and bird's foot.

Heart leaping, Elsie whirled around so quickly she nearly swung the plaster Christus right out of her basket. Two Thom had already crossed the road back to Clunwood. But he'd never been near her chatelaine. No one had. And . . . well, he couldn't be a Cowl himself, unless he was a fantastic actor. Two Thom had lived in Clunwood all his life and was as simple as a man could be. Yet she was certain her chatelaine had been note-free that morning! Where had she gone, besides . . .

Mr. Parker passed through her thoughts, but he hadn't touched the bag, had he? Still, he'd *known* so much about her, more than he should, given their weak acquaintance. She tried to remember how closely they had stood . . . and the speculation only made her heart beat faster. Her fancies were getting away with her! She needed to focus, not dawdle on potentialities.

But if it *was* Mr. Parker . . . if she could finally *know* at least one of the people guiding her . . .

She couldn't read the note here. Not where someone could see. So Elsie tucked the note back into her little pouch and clutched it to her, forgoing the road and cutting through the wild grass behind the butcher shop. She popped out into a cul-de-sac of houses surrounding a well. Spied Alexandra Wright strolling toward Main Street with her arm knit through that of a ginger-haired man—

Her heart thudded once against her chest before dropping to her feet, the note in her pouch forgotten. That couldn't possibly be . . . not *here* . . .

But the man turned his head to Miss Wright as he chuckled at something, and in his profile Elsie saw a complete stranger.

The relief was instant, though her heart was slow to reclaim its place in her breast. He merely looked like Alfred. Her former beau hadn't graced Brookley with his presence for nearly two years. Why should he do so now? Still, she didn't like being assailed with memories of the man, even if it was hardly the fault of Miss Wright's companion.

Picking up her feet, Elsie carved out one more shortcut before passing behind the post office and the saddler on her way to the masonry shop. She went in through the side door and did not remove her shoes before venturing upstairs to her room.

Closing the door and leaning against it, Elsie tore open the note.

It is urgent that you break the spell in Kent.

That was it.

She blinked and stared at the paper. Break the spell in Kent? But she had! Not even two days ago. Surely they knew the wine basket had been picked up. Did they think her a failure?

Gooseflesh erupted under Elsie's fitted sleeves. She had *never* failed the Cowls. She was too afraid of what it might cost her. Not afraid of the Cowls themselves, but of being discarded. Of being deemed useless. Of losing her purpose. Of never learning the identity of those who secretly employed her. Surely every mission was a test, and once she proved herself . . .

There was no way to reply to the letter. No way to defend herself. No proof and no ability to provide it if she'd had any.

She tore up the letter and threw it into her fireplace, though her hands fumbled with the match. She had to return to Kent. She'd have to buy the Madeira herself—and it was certainly expensive! Would it look questionable were she to return to the servants' door so soon? Would they want more, regardless of the price?

She chewed on her lip and paced the floor as tiny flames ate up the letter. It would be too suspicious, she decided, to repeat the ruse of being a saleswoman. She raked her mind for a better excuse. Looking for a job? The cook would recognize her, but that wouldn't be so bad. A bigger stumbling block was the need for a letter of reference. She could forge one. But what happened if someone recognized it as a forgery? If there was one thing Elsie needed to avoid, it was the law. Unregistered aspectors, spellbreakers included, faced harsh and unsavory penalties. The most common was the noose.

Think, think. She could just walk right up, disenchant the thing, and walk away. She might not be noticed. But that was trespassing, wasn't it? Was it permissible only if she had a basket of goods on her arm?

She'd have to go at night. She'd done missions for the Cowls at night before, but rarely. Yes, she'd go at night, and if she was caught . . .

She thought of Miss Wright, arm in arm with the mystery man. Elsie could claim a romantic tryst with one of the footmen. She was there to see him. If they asked for his name, she could deny the request, insist on protecting him. Or realize she'd come to the wrong estate. Or that her beau had lied about his employment. She could feign heartbreak and cry. Surely she'd be sent away without penalty if she cried!

Then again, this was a household that imprisoned their own staff, so perhaps not. But Elsie didn't have any other ideas.

She'd sneak away just after dinner. Return before dawn. Maybe Ogden wouldn't notice her absence—

A knock on the door startled a squeak from her throat. Glancing to the fireplace and seeing her pathetic flames had already died, she marched to the door and opened it with more force than was necessary.

Emmeline blinked at her in surprise. "Mr. Ogden is requesting you."

Elsie whirled toward the window. The day was nearly over—had so much time passed already? Ogden must have just gotten home from the squire's.

"Thank you, Em." She snatched up the basket by the door and hurried downstairs, the maid calling "The studio!" behind her.

Ogden leaned against the countertop near the front entrance to the studio, hovering over a sketch pad. He still had his work trousers on, stained with plaster. "Ah, there you are," he said as she approached.

"Thom Thomas stopped me in town." She tried to relax her body so her nerves wouldn't creep into her speech. She set the Christus in front of him and dug out the two shillings. "Asked for it to be repaired by next week."

Ogden paused a moment before setting down his pencil and studying the statue. "Easily done." He eyed her. "Are you quite all right?"

Elsie felt herself blush. "Just fine. The walk exhilarated me, is all."

Ogden set the statue on a shelf below the counter. "Do you remember that little supply store in Westerham?"

Elsie rubbed her eyes, forcing her brain to switch from one channel to another. "Yes, the one with the cherry trees?"

Ogden grinned. "That's the one. I'm in need of that metallic paint they have. I was hoping you'd venture down there to fetch some. It's quicker than requesting delivery." He shook his head, and for the first time Elsie noticed how tired he looked. "The squire is a persistent man, but I need that paint for another client. Now, Elsie, hold your tongue."

He knew her so well. She swallowed the words *The squire is a ratbag* and nodded. Then straightened.

Westerham was south of Brookley, and Kent was southeast . . . Couldn't she swing by the duke's estate on her way back?

"I can go tonight, if you'd like." She stretched her mouth into a cheerful smile. "I have a friend in"—*think*—"Knockholt. Since it's a bit of a trip, perhaps I could dine with her tonight and come back in the morning?"

"You're welcome to hire a cab," he said. "But yes, that should be fine, so long as you're back in the morning to assist customers. I won't be here most of the day. Let Emmeline know. Did you get those chops?"

"I will and I did."

Ogden gave her a paternal smile. "You're a treasure, Elsie." He turned back to his sketchbook.

And you have impeccable timing, she thought, assembling her darkest outfit in her head for tonight's venture. She tagged it with a little prayer—she'd need all the extra help she could get.

⌒9

She'd stashed the paint behind the woodpile of a bakery.

A few stars gleamed overhead as Elsie approached the duke's estate. It seemed so much larger and more ominous in the dark. It had a heavy stone wall that faced the road, but the back of it opened up onto woodland. Land only the duke and his guests could hunt on, though that was a gripe for another evening.

Elsie did not much like ambling through the woods in the dark, yet her choices were limited. She could only pray no one mistook her for a poacher.

She stepped quietly, holding her skirts in her hands. Modern fashion did not take into account a woman's need to be stealthy amidst brambles. There was decent moonlight, but the trees and clouds played peekaboo with it, forcing Elsie to move very slowly or risk falling. Wouldn't that be something, stranded in the Duke of Kent's wood with a twisted ankle?

Would her tale of secret love wriggle her out of *that* predicament?

Fortunately, the excursion through the wood proved uneventful. The trees thinned, the ground evened, and a manicured lawn sprawled ahead. She stepped onto the hunting path leading from the back of the estate with a sigh of relief.

She made it only a few steps before her foot was sucked into the path. Not mud—it hadn't rained the last few days. No roots or holes, either. The glimmer of a rune revealed the truth, its feeble gleam highlighting the earth that popped up around her shoe, grabbing it in an iron-like grasp. It was not unlike the one she'd disenchanted on the doorknob, but it was more complex, with several tight, interlocking loops.

More spells to keep your servants in their place? she wondered, making a half-hearted attempt to tug her leg free. Crouching, watching her surroundings, Elsie touched the spell. She didn't recognize this one—a physical spell, but not one she'd disenchanted previously. She tugged at the knot one way, then another, before finding a loose end and unraveling the rune bit by bit. The spell flashed—she almost thought it pouted—before vanishing, and the earth holding her in place crumbled back to dust.

Elsie shook off her shoe and proceeded carefully. Runes weren't bold things; she couldn't merely glance down the path ahead of her to see where any copycats lay. They would reveal themselves only as she got closer. Sometimes close enough to touch, for more masterful spells. Stepping just off the path, Elsie tiptoed carefully, catching sight of another foot trap several yards ahead. She searched the shadows, waiting for movement. Listening for sound. She smelled the stables but didn't hear horses. Seemed all was well and proper. *Good.*

The servants' door loomed ahead. Elsie might have missed it had she not made the Madeira delivery two days ago; the shadows hid it well. Heart pounding in her ears, she snuck closer, closer, and pressed her back against the cool wall of the mansion. She wasn't terribly far from the woods. Perhaps she could run back to safety without being caught. She'd been quite a climber in her youth. If anything gave chase, she could ball her skirts between her knees and hide up a tree.

Her palms sweated, and her mouth grew dry. *Get it done and get out. The Cowls will know you did it this time.*

The door seemed so far away. Elsie sidestepped, cursing the moonlight when it peeked between its misty curtains. She reached for the doorknob, the spell of heat licking at her fingers. It was activated; Elsie snatched her hand away as the metal singed her fingertips. How many servants in this household had blister scars from this damnable thing?

She attacked it with her nails. The unwinding came easier this time. She knew the pattern, knew which thread to loop through. It took only seconds—

A hand seized her upper arm. Elsie barely had enough sense to bite down on a scream as someone yanked her away from the door.

"So *you're* the conrad breaking my spells!" a gruff baritone snapped, the speaker making no effort to be quiet.

Elsie turned into her assailant's grip, coming face-to-face with an exceptionally large man whose hold was tighter than that of the bespelled hunting path. She reeled and twisted, desperate to free herself. Her pulse drummed war beneath her skull.

"A woman," he growled. "Who are you? What's your name?"

Elsie didn't answer, only fought. Aimed a kick for his shins, clawed at his sleeve. Full panic was setting in now. She became directionless save for the desperate need to escape. *Don't answer, don't answer!* If she did, he would know her voice, and perhaps he could use it against her. She had the cover of darkness. She just had to *get away*—

The man jerked her forward, toward the rear of the house. "Fine. I'm sure the authorities will get answers out of you."

Caution snapped.

"No!" she cried, dropping all her weight. Her captor stumbled as her knees hit the ground. "No, please!" Desperation wrenched the words out of her, making her hoarse. "I'll do anything, but don't call the police!"

The man snorted. "You should have thought of the consequences before you trespassed." He pulled her up.

Elsie dropped again, earning a curse from the man's lips.

She saw a faint glimmer before her dress hardened to rock around her, hindering her movement. *Physical aspector.*

He turned to grab her other arm. When he did, Elsie leaned her stiff body into him and, with a wrist still mobile, untied the spell of hardening near her hip.

Her dress relaxed into cloth again, and she slammed her shoe hard onto his.

It didn't have the effect she wanted—it didn't hurt the blasted man, only surprised him. She made it all of two steps before his enormous hands grabbed her arms again. And Elsie could disenchant only physical spells, not physical strength.

"You talk of morals to me, yet you forbid your staff from leaving the house!" She pushed off the ground, trying to throw him off balance.

He took a half step back before hauling her upright. "That spell is a security measure. Against thieves like you." He dragged her toward the back entrance.

"I am *not* a thief!" She tried to turn one way, then the other. Attempted to gouge his eyes. But his strength easily surmounted hers. *Fight with magic and make this fair, you towering oaf!*

"Who sent you?" he barked.

"No one did! Please, have mercy!"

He merely grunted. The door was in sight. Surely someone would hear them any moment, and her chance of escaping would become that much slimmer. It would take only one more man to apprehend her, and then—

"I'm not registered!" she hissed.

He paused only a moment. Surely he knew the penalty for working any sort of magic without registration was grave. It made the thieving accusation sound like afternoon tea.

"Please," she pressed. "I'm not a criminal. I wanted to help the servants." Pieces of loose hair fell into her face.

Another growl sounded low in the man's throat. "Who hired you?"

Elsie pinched her lips shut.

His grip tightened. "Who. Hired. You."

"I couldn't tell you if I wanted to," she muttered. Would the Cowls free her if she went to jail? But if her spellbreaking abilities went public, they'd never use her again. "My only crime is freeing the common man!"

"It's a *security measure*," her captor responded, and Elsie caught an unfamiliar lilt in the statement. Something about the sound snapped her senses into place. Whoever had her wasn't the duke—Elsie knew him to be getting on in years, and he wasn't an aspector, besides. In the streak of moonlight falling over them, Elsie noticed the darkness of her assailant's hands. He was a foreigner.

"I won't trespass again if you just let me go," she pleaded, the fight leaving her. She couldn't outmaneuver him. If she couldn't barter her way out of this, she'd be staring at the inside of a jail cell for the rest of her life, which might be rather short.

Would they hang her?

But the spellmaker seemed to consider her words. Sourly. Sourness poured off him like the stink of brandy. "Common man," he scoffed. "I don't believe you. What does a secure door do to hurt the people inside? They are free to go as they choose. They contribute decently to society. Something you should learn." He moved toward the door.

"Excuse me!" Elsie huffed as the man dragged her to her doom. Being silent no longer mattered, nor did attempting to pacify the brute. "I contribute to society! Do I look like a ruffian to you?"

He paused again. Looked her up and down. In the daylight, it might have made her self-conscious.

"You'd better explain yourself." His voice was low, like a threat. But his grip loosened a fraction.

"Please. I'm an assistant to a stonemason. I was nearby to get paints. *Someone* told me the servants were being mistreated. I came to help. I'm begging you"—her voice choked; it wasn't an act, but real fear strangling her—"let me go. Let me pay you for the spell. Or work off the price. I'll sign a contract never to step on the grounds again!"

The man considered. "You're a spellbreaker."

Obviously. She nodded, hopeful.

He drew back his left hand, keeping hold of her with his right. Stroked the beard Elsie could just make out in the poor light.

"Tell me your name."

Elsie pursed her lips.

"Tell me honestly, or the constable will have it."

Lies pooled in her mind. *Betty. I'm a baker.* He was no spiritual aspector—he couldn't detect the lie. Could he? And what if he did?

She deflated. "Elsie Camden. You can look me up. I haven't lied."

"You *will* work off the debt," he said. "I have work that needs to be done, and spellbreakers are hard to find and expensive. Work for me. Or for your life. However you choose to see it."

Elsie gaped. He released her, but she didn't run. She'd been too honest to run.

"I already work full time," she countered. And that was not including her missions for the Cowls.

He shrugged. "Not my problem."

Elsie straightened. "I have to be home in the morning. But I can come back the day after." Hopefully the squire's work would hold out and Ogden wouldn't notice her absence. Three employers . . . How would she make this work?

But she had to.

"Dawn."

"I'm not local."

He motioned toward the back door. On the second floor, someone lit a candle.

Nerves crawled over Elsie's skin like beetles. "Fine. *Fine.* I'll do my best. And who do I ask for?"

"Come to the servants' door and ask for Kelsey." He turned for the back door now, but without her in tow. "If you choose not to show, I *will* find you and ensure you are prosecuted to the full extent of the law."

Elsie swallowed. Knit her fingers together. The man said nothing more, only disappeared into the house.

Another candle lit in a third-story window.

Heart jumping, Elsie ran, avoiding the hunting trail. The woods swallowed her.

She didn't want to anger the Cowls, but she very much believed Mr. Kelsey's threat.

If she didn't show, his punishment would be swifter than theirs.

CHAPTER 6

"Elsie, could you hand me that pitcher? Elsie?"

Elsie blinked, climbing out of the mental hole she'd fallen into. She leaned against the wall in the kitchen, staring blindly into nothing. She noticed Emmeline standing over the stove, watching her. Spied the pitcher of water near the sink.

"Sorry." Elsie retrieved the pitcher and handed it to Emmeline, who poured its contents into the pot she stirred. Calf's foot jelly, one of Ogden's favorites.

"You've been absent this morning," the maid said.

Elsie merely nodded. She was tired, yes. Last night, she'd spent an exorbitant amount of money on a midnight carriage to drop her off at the edge of Brookley, and although she'd snuck into her room for a few hours' sleep, she'd had to leave again before the household awakened so she could pretend to arrive at the appointed time. She'd started on Ogden's financial ledgers only to find the numbers swirling before her eyes. Her brain was tied up in Kent.

Could Mr. Kelsey *really* track her down? Her name wasn't listed in any directory, she was certain. Her workhouse records had burned to ash long ago. What would he do, stop at every post office in the country until her name popped up?

She should have lied after all, but he'd been so serious, so dour, she'd suspected he would somehow know. Would the Cowls be angry when they saw the heat spell intact? Was Mr. Kelsey lying about the security measure? Elsie felt like she was drowning in a pool and desperately trying to find purchase on slick porcelain walls.

It's just for a little while. She'd balance it somehow. The Cowls might not ask for another favor for months, for all she knew. Ogden was often busy and was lenient with her schedule—she'd earned it, after so many years of good service. Kent wasn't far. She could manage it for a week or two. Surely that would be enough work to repay her perceived debt, and Mr. Kelsey would let her go.

He couldn't be too terrible if he'd given her the option to flee.

A bell rang in the kitchen, startling both Elsie and Emmeline. Ogden didn't often use the bellpull, only when he was very busy or needed to make a good impression on a visitor in his sitting room. Elsie and Emmeline exchanged a glance before Elsie said, "I'll take it."

Emmeline nodded her thanks. Picking up her maroon skirt, Elsie hurried up the stairs to the sitting room. The door was cracked open, and they had no visitors, so she didn't bother knocking.

"Mr. Ogden?" she asked, but she needn't have. Ogden sat on a stool by the unlit fireplace, a fine-tipped brush in his hand. He'd worked Latin letters down his arm in blue ink.

He was learning a new spell.

"My drops, Elsie, if you would," he said over his shoulder.

Elsie hurried from the sitting room to Ogden's room. It was simply furnished and smelled very much like man—shaving cream, plaster, spice. It was just as well that Elsie had answered the bell. Emmeline didn't know where Ogden kept his drops. She'd been employed at the stonemasonry shop for almost two years, but information so valuable could be entrusted only to so many.

Crouching, Elsie felt under Ogden's side table for a small key hidden there, then took it to the squat cupboard near the locked window. It fit into a small door on the side, and Elsie withdrew a small leather bag from within, the drops clanking against one another. She worked the bag open as she returned to the sitting room.

Inside were seven drops, each worth more than its weight in gold. Although roughly the size of shillings, they were imperfectly round—a strange, beautiful amalgamation of quartz, rose water, and gold. They were translucent, rounded but not smooth, and glinted in the sunlight. Drops were the currency the universe—or perhaps God—required for spells. They didn't require magic to create, an aspector *could* make his own, but the measurements were so precise and the process so expensive it was simpler just to exchange coin for them at the nearest atheneum. A lot of coin. The more advanced the spell, the higher the price. Drops were one of many reasons an impoverished person could rarely raise his fortune through magic.

Of course, it cost no money to break a spell, only to learn one.

"I need seven," Ogden said when Elsie slipped into the room.

"Just enough." Elsie turned the drops into her hand and stood behind Ogden, waiting for him to finish his work. The words of the spell, always in Latin, needed to be written precisely down his arm, and Elsie didn't wish to disturb him. If the spell took—if Ogden's innate talent was enough—the words would absorb into his skin, making the spell a part of him. A page in his future opus. The drops would vanish as well. Some said they became part of the body, generating power for magic. Others claimed they reabsorbed into the universe, or plunked into God's own coffers. Wherever they went, they could not be used a second time. Drops were one of magic's most compelling mysteries, perhaps rivaled only by the spells themselves. Who had penned the first spell was as shrouded in enigma as who had penned the last. None of the authors were known, and spells across all four disciplines were set. Many had studied the language and style of spellmaking enchantments in an effort to expound upon them, or create one anew, and not one had ever been successful. The magic was as set in stone as the Commandments themselves.

Ogden's handwriting was in blue ink, for physical aspecting. Red was used for rational, yellow for spiritual, and green for temporal. Why, she didn't know. That was just the way God had made it.

She settled down on the nearby settee, the drops warming in her hands. Her eyes fell to a folded newspaper beside her—Ogden's morning read. She opened the thin paper, her eyes instantly falling to the main headline.

Viscount Aspector Struck by Lightning on Clear Day.

Its subheading read:

Opus Not Recovered.

Furrowing her brow, Elsie brought the paper closer to her face. Viscount Byron had been struck down in London after a meeting of Parliament, in the late hours of the evening. Though there was no storm, lightning had forked from the sky through his window and into his person. The witness, who had asked not to be identified, ran screaming from the house, but when the family—and later authorities—arrived on the scene, there was no sign of the viscount or his opus.

A chill coursed down Elsie's spine as Mr. Parker's words came rushing back to her: *He has been out of sorts lately, what with the passing of the viscount . . . Right under his nose, yet no one heard a thing.*

Her mouth went dry. Had the steward been referring to Viscount *Byron*? Could Squire Hughes be the unidentified witness?

Her thoughts ran rampant. According to the Wright sisters, the squire had also been connected to the baron who had passed. Quite a coincidence that he should know both of the men whose opuses had been taken. And why the sudden increase in opus-related crime? This wasn't the seventeenth century—

"Elsie?"

She set down the paper and forced her thoughts to the present, tucking away the information for later study. Crossing to Ogden, she placed the drops in his waiting hand. They seemed so bright at first, but it was only a trick of the sun, for when Ogden shifted his hand, they glowed only faintly.

This was another aspect of drops—they reacted to a person's magical fortitude. Glowed. The stronger the spellmaker, the brighter the drop. They did not, however, react to a spellbreaker's magic. If Elsie held them in her hand, they remained unlit and translucent. Ogden had some ability, but not much. The spells she'd encountered at the duke's estate would be far beyond his grasp. But he did try, and occasionally succeed.

"Which spell is this?"

"Temperature change." Ogden held his painted arm out straight in front of him. "Would make some of my work easier. Maybe help with pottery."

Elsie stepped back, and Ogden chanted Latin. Elsie understood only a few words of the old language, and none of the ones passing her employer's lips. She tried to follow the words on his arms, for that was what he read, but Ogden's body hair was thick, and he had turned the top of his forearm away from her. When he finished, his fist closed around the drops. They brightened slightly, then dulled.

Ogden sighed. The spell hadn't taken.

"Maybe try again," Elsie suggested. "I can check your handwriting; the brush could have slipped."

"It's an intermediate spell." Ogden lowered his arm, looking fatigued. "It was a long shot to begin with. Seems I must appease myself with novice learning only."

Elsie rested her hand on his shoulder. "You still know more magic than I do." It was both a truth and a lie.

He offered a weak smile and patted her hand. "It's fine. I am an artist, not an aspector. This is really just a hobby."

"At least you'll only ever have to buy white paint." Ogden's most-used spell was the color-changing one, although he couldn't mimic the metallic glints in the paint Elsie had retrieved for him last night. "I put the new paint in your studio."

"Thank you. Mind getting me a tea cloth so I can wash this off? Emmeline hates scrubbing ink from my shirts."

She nodded and turned, but paused. "Did you read the paper already?"

"I have."

"What do you think . . . of the murders? And the opuses?" The opuses that had been stolen were from master magicians, people who knew the most powerful of spells. The spellbooks' value went far beyond money, and in the wrong hands, they could be incredibly dangerous. In the riots of the late seventeenth century, opus spells had been used to make a general forget which side he fought for and attack his own king. Another had set an atheneum on fire.

Ogden frowned. "I hope they are merely stories sensationalized by journalists to sell more papers. Let's pray the viscount is the last we hear of."

Elsie nodded before hurrying downstairs to do as asked, her thoughts flitting between murders, opuses, and Kent.

∽

When the door to the studio opened, Elsie jumped and dropped the paintbrushes she'd been organizing. She half expected a large, shadowy man to be standing there. He would say, *I meant dawn today,* and then step aside, revealing the police force assembled behind him, ready to drag her to the nearest atheneum for punishment.

To her relief, it was merely a lad no older than fourteen. Small in stature, dressed in gray servants' clothing. Completely harmless.

She craned to check the road behind him just in case, but it seemed God did not mean for her to meet her reckoning today.

Letting out a long breath, Elsie scooped up the paintbrushes and headed over to the counter, where the boy waited. "Can I help you?"

"I'm looking for Elsie Camden?" He scratched the side of his freckled nose.

She set the brush down. "I'm she. What can I do for you?"

His eyes darted around the studio, though it seemed to be more from curiosity than nervousness. Remembering himself, he shot his gaze back to her. "Oh. Uh, Mr. Parker sent me. From Squire Hughes's estate. Said . . ." He paused, trying to remember. "Needs your assistance with an addition, and Mr. Ogden 'asn't got the paperwork."

Mr. Parker. Her pulse quickened at the name. Why send for her when he could simply wait until tomorrow and have Ogden bring the paperwork himself? Why was a man who had so pointedly *not* been in her life—almost as though he'd been trying to conceal himself—now suddenly popping up again and again?

Could she be right about his connection to the Cowls? And if so, did this mean they were finally preparing to bring her into the fold? She'd been waiting so long . . .

The boy was watching her, so she pushed out a confirmative "Ah." The metallic paint would not be needed yet after all. If the squire meant to add *more* work to Ogden's plate, he wouldn't have time for it. Not today. Leave it to a nobleman to assume he was the only one worth serving. "Wait for me one moment, will you?"

The boy nodded, and Elsie retrieved the ledger used to record Ogden's open orders, trying not to let excitement shake her hands.

The ledger chronicled names, dates, the type of work, estimates, and final prices. Squire Hughes had a page all to himself. Ogden, being a wise man, wanted the extra requests recorded now so they'd be charged properly when the time came. Elsie would even make Mr. Parker sign the page. She wouldn't put it past Squire Rat to shortchange them.

Maybe she could get Mr. Parker to print his name as well. See if it matched the handwriting in the letters she received. Although she always promptly destroyed them, they were all written in the same hand. She felt certain she'd recognize it.

After retrieving her hat, she tucked the ledger under her arm and gestured for the lad to lead the way. He did so without word, and walked too slow for Elsie's liking. She wanted to arrive straightaway. She needed to *know*.

It was a bit too cloudy today, but the sun peeked out just often enough to keep the air warm. The Wright sisters hunched together outside the saddler. They were gossiping, no doubt, which made Elsie both roll her eyes and wish to get closer to see what garnered their interest. Levi Morgan, her closest neighbor, passed by with a bundle under his arm, tipping his hat to her. Elsie nodded in turn.

They crossed the street and passed the dressmaker, the courthouse, and the constable's home. Continued down the road until it narrowed and grew dusty, past a stream, and through a smattering of woods, all the way to the squire's home. Elsie was quite out of breath when she arrived. Her guide was gracious enough to lead her to Mr. Parker's study before continuing on his way. The door was ajar, and Mr. Parker sat at his desk, a dainty pair of spectacles resting at the end of his nose, making him look quite old. He scrawled something on a piece of paper. Elsie let herself in. She wasn't quiet about it, and when the steward glanced up and saw her, he immediately slammed his left hand down, covering what he had written.

Elsie, of course, took immediate interest in the writing, but Mr. Parker's wide hand successfully covered all of it. Surely he'd smeared the ink! What was so private that he felt the need to hide it? And so obviously?

It was as she lifted her gaze from the steward's hand that she saw a stick of wax to one side of it. Her pulse quickened. It was a vivid orange wax.

Just like the wax the Cowls used to seal their letters.

Her lips parted, but no sound escaped them. Of course more than one person, or people, could have orange wax on hand. Elsie knew that. But the orange wax in addition to the covering of the letter . . . Was Mr. Parker *trying* to hide his handwriting?

She feared he'd hear her heart thundering in her chest. *If it's him, then he's not ready to reveal himself.* It took the bulk of her willpower not to launch herself at the desk and forcibly remove that note so she could read it, or simply blurt out, *Are you the one who's been directing me all this time?*

It made sense. His age, the wax, his interest in and knowledge of her, the ease with which she'd landed that initial job in the squire's home. It made sense, and yet Elsie could do nothing about it until he moved first.

All of these thoughts swept through her mind in a matter of seconds, leaving her fingers cold and head dumbfounded.

Mr. Parker snapped her to attention. "Miss Camden, thank you for coming on such short notice. Squire Hughes wished to add some stonework to an outer wall, and I understand Mr. Ogden has a process for that."

Elsie met the steward's blue-eyed gaze. Swallowed. "Um, yes, of course." She pulled out the ledger, trying to keep her hand from shaking. *Act normal. It's just speculation.* But the wax, the secrecy . . . and Mr. Parker had specifically mentioned Viscount Byron to her on her last visit. Because he knew something? Because he knew *her*?

It is my business to know, he'd said.

Clearing her throat, Elsie opened to the squire's page in the ledger. "If I might borrow a pen and ink."

"Oh yes, of course." Mr. Parker slid whatever he'd been working on under the desk and pushed the pen and ink vial toward her. He gestured to a chair.

Elsie pulled it over and sat. She was so flustered, so excited, so confused, that she couldn't stop the question from bubbling up her throat. "What was that you were working on? That is, I hope I didn't intrude. I wouldn't want you to have to rewrite it."

Was she talking too fast? *Slow down, Elsie. Or he'll know you suspect.*

Was it wrong for him to think she knew? But there must be a reason the Cowls kept their identities from her. Like they were waiting for something. Like she had to prove herself. They'd provided her with so much already; they'd saved her from the workhouse and from being discovered as an illegal spellbreaker, which she surely would have been severely punished for despite her age. They'd arranged for her to find a good job—what *should* have been a good job, at least. She'd always wondered if it had angered them when she left it for Ogden's employ, but she'd still been a child. Certainly they couldn't hold it against her!

They used to send follow-up letters, telling her of the good she'd done, the results of her clandestine activities, but they'd stopped the practice years ago. Likely because double the letters meant double the chance of getting caught, and besides, she'd grown from a child to a woman. Still, she yearned for their praise, and they gave it in the best way possible.

They kept her on. They gave her more complicated and more important work, more frequently. Something was about to bend. Elsie could *feel* it, and then she'd finally have the answers to the mystery she'd been living for half her life.

"Just a list." Mr. Parker sounded cheery, but the tone wasn't genuine. It piqued her interest all the more.

Focus.

She dipped the proffered pen. "If you could detail the addition Squire Hughes is requesting."

He did so, and Elsie wrote it down, her penmanship not what it should be. The pen quivered in her anxious hand. She hoped Mr. Parker didn't notice.

She calculated the costs and wrote them in the first column of numbers, then, at the bottom of the page, drew an *X* and a straight line after it. Beneath it, she wrote, *Mr. Gabriel Parker.* Turning the ledger toward him, she said, "If you might review and sign, Mr. Ogden can get started right away."

Adjusting his glasses, the steward did just that. Meticulous—a good quality for a steward. Elsie took a moment to study him, his white hair, the writing calluses on his hand. The smeared ink on his left palm. He *had* ruined the letter. No list would have inspired him to do such a thing. Could he really be one of them?

Could Mr. Parker be working for the squire to watch him? To bring down his household from within?

Then there was his talk of the viscount, and the Wright sisters' gossip about the baron who had once stayed in this house. Could the squire be responsible for the deaths of the aspectors?

He was no spellmaker, but one didn't have to be to use an opus spell. Even the pageboy could unleash a master spell if it came from a master's opus.

Elsie's thoughts spun so fast they were making her dizzy. She desperately needed to get away and think.

Mr. Parker signed. Elsie glanced at his signature as he returned the ledger, but of course the scrawl wouldn't match his natural penmanship.

She desperately wanted to see what the steward was hiding under the desk. But alas, she could not force him to show her, and if she were to evince more than a natural interest, she risked revealing herself.

Standing, Elsie thanked Mr. Parker. He did not stand to walk her to the door—but of course he was busy, and he had *that letter*—so she saw herself out. Her nerves were so raw that she walked back to the stonemasonry shop at an even faster pace than she'd set earlier. She was distracted the remainder of the day, trying to piece together what she knew of Mr. Parker with what she knew of the Cowls. Wishing she had kept the letters to compare them to how he spoke.

It wasn't until night settled and Elsie turned in for bed that she recalled a much more pressing situation.

Come dawn, she had to report to Seven Oaks, and the man who knew her most protected secret.

⌒⍉

Why was it that every time Elsie returned to the Duke of Kent's estate, it seemed to have grown larger in her absence? When she stood before it now, it appeared as foreboding as a castle.

It had not been difficult to get away; Ogden was busy again at the squire's estate—something that tempted Elsie's thoughts to return to the mysterious Mr. Parker—and Emmeline was so focused on her chores she often didn't notice when Elsie left the house. After completing her deliveries and taking stock of supplies in the masonry shop, Elsie had brought the financial ledgers with her and finished them in the carriage, albeit with shaky penmanship. She would do her work for Mr. Kelsey and return swiftly, staying up late to sharpen the sculptor tools Ogden would need for his work at the squire's house. She'd still get enough sleep to function, and none would be the wiser. Perhaps she'd be so useful Mr. Kelsey would excuse her after her first day.

That certainly sounded fictional, even to her.

If Mr. Parker knew of her predicament, would he swoop in and save her?

Of course, she didn't *know* he was a Cowl. She couldn't tell him anything. Not yet.

She entered the grounds as she had the first time—through the front gate. The duke was neither a king nor an aspector; he didn't post guards, though he did have a number of footmen about. She didn't see any people at all as she trudged around to the servants' door, which was for the better. Whatever Mr. Kelsey had planned for her, she couldn't let anyone else, even a scullery maid, know what she was.

She knocked, noticing with dismay that her hard work had already been undone. The enchantment had been returned to the doorknob, though it was currently inactive. A few seconds passed before a girl—the one with the washbasin from before?—peeked out, only to instantly close the door in Elsie's face. Gritting her teeth together, Elsie waited a full minute, then another, before lifting her hand to knock again.

The door swung open fast enough to create its own wind. A large man filled its frame. "You're late."

Elsie gawked a moment. It was one thing to have an altercation with a shadow. It was another to see the shadow in bright morning sunlight.

He was over six feet tall, broad and well dressed. His skin was deeply tanned, a light sepia, and a dark half beard encircled his mouth. His wavy walnut hair was worn *long* and pulled up at the back of his head in a folded tail. A few pieces of the dark mass were sun bleached, as though the overall color could not decide if it wanted to be dark or light.

His eyes were a rather remarkable shade of green.

Elsie caught herself quickly and squared her shoulders. "I am an educated woman, monsieur. I have certain morning grooming rituals that cannot be overlooked, especially if I'm to appear at the home of a duke." If she didn't stand her ground, the spellmaker would walk all over her.

She thought she caught Mr. Kelsey rolling his eyes, but he stepped out of the door frame, forcing Elsie to step back. He shut the door

69

behind him. Elsie glanced longingly at the glimmering spell she'd disenchanted twice already.

Surely the Cowls knew she'd tried.

Mr. Kelsey strode toward the back of the estate without word. Elsie followed him, nearly having to jog to keep up with his stride.

"There are some slapdash spells on the estate I'd like voided." Mr. Kelsey looked straight ahead. "Previous hires of the duchess. Some are old, some are a smattering of intermediate spells that would be better replaced by a single advanced one." He glanced toward her, studying her for the space of a breath. "I take it you are untrained."

"I am more than capable of breaking slapdashery, Mr. Kelsey. I trust that you have kept your end of the bargain?"

He nodded, and a trickle of relief cooled Elsie's vitals. "The family is away, and most of the staff has been given the day off. The rest know better than to snoop. And if any of them do, they'll assume I hired you from a reputable source."

Elsie frowned. At least he'd ensured her safety.

He led her to the east side of the estate, to the large stone wall that surrounded the main grounds. The wall was speckled with fortification spells—one every twenty feet!—and Elsie unraveled them one by one. She got rather quick at it, and Mr. Kelsey followed behind her, replacing the spells with spells of his own—knots larger and more intricate than those falling to pieces under Elsie's hands. Brighter, too. He didn't say any magical words—aspectors didn't need to, once they had absorbed a spell. The words became part of them, part of their opus. He simply put his hands on the wall and placed his runes. Runes only a spellbreaker would be able to see. And see them she did, each neat and shiny and symmetrical, though they vanished from sight the farther she moved from them. At most, she could spy three at a time, if she focused, and only because she knew where to look.

He'd said *advanced* spells, which suggested he was an advanced physical aspector, not yet a master. He looked a few years shy of thirty.

He must have been raised to the magic, but he wasn't a nobleman. Not a local one, anyway. Perhaps he'd gotten a sponsorship, but gauging by the way he dressed, his sponsor would have to be *very* generous. A foreign landowner, most likely. She doubted he was a merchant, what with his gloomy demeanor.

By the time she got to the front gate, her wrists began to itch fiercely. Scratching did little to abate the discomfort, and Elsie paused and pulled up her sleeves, expecting to see an ugly rash. But her skin was unblemished, minus the pinkness caused by her own fingernails.

"Have you done work like this before?" Mr. Kelsey asked, sounding disinterested.

"I've disenchanted walls, yes." She sounded offended.

But the man shook his head. "I mean the repetition."

Elsie eyed him.

He gestured to her wrists. "Overextending of magic takes a toll. Itching, soreness, fatigue . . . it varies from aspector to aspector."

Elsie tugged down her sleeve. "I'm aware."

She was not.

She worked for another half hour—trying hard not to scratch—before a servant appeared with a small basket of food. Mr. Kelsey accepted with a nod, and the man retreated back to the house.

He offered her a wrapped sandwich.

Elsie hesitated.

Mr. Kelsey sighed. "I'll not starve you. There's more than enough to go around in this place."

If only to give her fiery wrists a break, Elsie accepted the food. "Thank you."

Mr. Kelsey grunted an acknowledgment and unwrapped his own quick meal. They were on the green without any immediate shade, and the closest bench was a short walk away, so Elsie ate her food where she stood.

"You don't live here," she stated, "normally, I mean."

She'd addressed him informally, and the look he gave her said he'd noticed. "Given the nature of our relationship," she added, "I hardly think it necessary to address you 'properly.' And if you're only an advanced aspector, you do not have a title, and therefore you are not my better."

His lip actually quirked at that. "Perhaps, but I am legal, and you are not."

Elsie blanched.

He went on. "I'm staying with the duke's family while I earn my mastership. My father was a friend of the family."

"Oh." Then he certainly *would* be her better, not that she'd satisfy him by saying as much. "So he has you doing menial chores about the grounds?"

He cocked a dark eyebrow. "Regardless of what you've chosen to believe, Miss Camden, the duke is a good man. I work willingly, out of gratitude."

"As I work unwillingly to keep my head on my shoulders."

He glowered. Elsie shrugged and took a bite of food. The bread was exquisite. She chewed, swallowed, and let herself relax.

"Well," she continued, "fair is fair. But how long must I toil to earn your favor? Or rather, your silence?"

"Until the work is done."

Elsie frowned. "Leave it to a man to be unspecific."

Another lip quirk. At least the boor appreciated humor. "The estate and its holdings are extensive; I have yet to walk all of it."

"And its *holdings*?" Elsie repeated, leaning against the wall as her knees weakened. "Good sir, you will work me to death. I have another occupation." Two, considering how often the Cowls had been contacting her of late. "One I am putting at risk for this."

"I needn't remind you that you made the initial risk yourself."

Elsie sniffed and attacked her sandwich. She ate half of it in silence, and while the lack of conversation bothered her, Mr. Kelsey seemed utterly unfazed by it. *Ridiculous man.* When she could bear the quiet no longer, she blurted, "So where are you from? Turkey?"

His eyes narrowed. "That is your first assumption? *Turkey?*"

"I am no duchess, Mr. Kelsey. I am not well traveled, though I highly doubt you're French."

He popped the last of his meal into his mouth and brushed off his hands. Returned to the wall. Ran his palm over it. There was a crack there, and without a word he bespelled the stones on either side of it, growing them until their own girth filled it.

It was only a little impressive.

"I'm from Barbados, if you must know." He tilted his head toward what remained of her food. "Don't dawdle."

Elsie gave him a pointed look and took her time finishing her meal. Mr. Kelsey, in the meantime, caught up to her with his fortifying spells. Despite the meal, he looked a little fatigued. Tired around his eyes.

They continued their work with the second half of the wall, disenchanting and re-enchanting it until they reached the woods. The itching spread nearly to Elsie's shoulders, but she scratched only when she was sure Mr. Kelsey was not looking. Her knees and lower back ached when the work was finished, and she very much yearned for a bath.

"That's enough for today." Mr. Kelsey looked back over his work. His shoulders slumped, and he looked older. She wondered if overuse of magic was the cause, but Mr. Kelsey seemed to feel more tired than she did itchy. "Until tomorrow."

"Tomorrow is the Sabbath."

He looked down at her. His glare certainly hadn't lost any energy. "You don't strike me as a God-fearing woman."

Folding her arms, she retorted, "I fear him on Sundays."

Mr. Kelsey actually laughed. Softly, barely loud enough to hear, but it was a chuckle, nonetheless. Much to Elsie's dismay, she found it to be a very pleasant and masculine sound. "As most do."

Elsie loosened her arms. "Monday is as good a time as any. My employer is away working on some grand scheme of stonework for our squire. Best I use the time as I am able."

"His name?"

Elsie glared.

"I could find out for myself."

"Do that." Elsie offered him a mocking curtsy. "Good evening, Mr. Kelsey. It's been lovely."

"If you're willing to wait," he said, turning as she passed him, "I'll have the footmen bring around a carriage."

"Thank you, but no." She paused a little too close to him, then caught herself and stepped back. Her thoughts spun, flashing from the close fit of his shirt to something else . . . something curious . . . but she squashed them. "It would be best if I did not arrive in Brookley in a duke's carriage."

"Brookley," he repeated with an obnoxious smirk.

She pinched her lips together. Next time she'd merely refuse to speak and bear the silence just as she bore this infuriating itching. The lace on her cuffs aggravated it. "I'll escort myself, thank you."

She turned and did just that. And once she reached the road, she finally let her turning thoughts surface. She'd sensed something strange about Mr. Kelsey those last few minutes.

A spell. She *smelled* it. A less experienced spellbreaker might have thought it Mr. Kelsey's musk of choice, but Elsie knew better. Knew the scent of fresh-cut wood and citrus was a natural smell—and not unpleasant—but the earthy smell beneath it, not unlike mushrooms, indicated a spell. A temporal spell, planted somewhere on Mr. Kelsey's person.

But whatever could it be?

CHAPTER 7

Ogden announced they would be going to church in London. Specifically, Camberwell, to a church they'd attended once before. That was a strange thing about Ogden—he wasn't a very religious person, and yet he insisted on the household attending church every Sunday. Only the church they attended changed more often than the season.

The Brookley chapel was a pleasant walk from the masonry shop, but Elsie didn't mind the travel into London, even if the Wright sisters would surely gossip about the Ogden household's "path to hell" again. After all, Squire Hughes went to the Brookley chapel whenever *he* was not in London, and he had a very obvious and annoying way of twisting the vicar around his fat finger. If the squire had his way, he'd rewrite the whole Bible. Still, it was a pity she would not be able to observe Mr. Parker from afar.

It was a gray day. Thick, brooding clouds stretched pale across the sky, making the air cool enough for a shawl. The three of them shared a carriage together—Elsie, Ogden, and Emmeline. Elsie peered out the window, searching the bustling streets and tight-fitted homes. A horseless carriage, propelled by aspected wheels, passed by them, and a few minutes later they passed a mill, far from any water source, that used the same spell to turn its turbine. Such spells were common in the city, but seen only on occasion in Brookley. Rumor said people were starting to use energy from such things to power lights in glass bulbs that had nothing to do with magic, but Elsie would believe it when she saw it.

The church was an old but lovely building, kept in good repair. Ogden led them toward the front of the chapel. This church employed a spiritual aspector, as many did. Although they were schooled in theology, they were not part of the clergy. Rather, they were icons to the faithful. Many of the devout viewed them as a means for miracles. Some believed the spell for invoking inner peace actually summoned the Holy Spirit, although Elsie suspected it was nothing more than a feel-good spell for the soul. Spiritual aspectors could also invoke truth and make it impossible for a person to lie, which could be useful in religion. It was certainly useful in law enforcement.

Not every church employed a spiritual aspector, but it helped their numbers to guarantee some sort of blessing at the end of a sermon. Simple ones, like good fortune, peace, or discernment—ones that couldn't go sour or be misinterpreted. If someone wanted a blessing greater than that, well, he would have to pay for it just as he would for any other spell.

Elsie swallowed, and adjusted the collar of her dress, her corset feeling a little too tight. If Mr. Kelsey turned her in, would they send a spiritual aspector to force her to spill every secret she'd kept from infancy up?

"Oh, pretty," Emmeline said beside her, and Elsie followed her gaze to what, at first glance, appeared to be an angel. But a closer look revealed the translucent image was simply a man. A rather normal-looking one despite the fact that he was translucent. An astral projection spell—a master-level spiritual spell, if Elsie remembered right.

Leaning toward Ogden, she asked, "Who is that?"

"I believe . . . yes, I think that's Master Allen. He's of the Physical Atheneum. Another aspector must be doing the projection for him."

Master Allen's ghost nodded to the vicar and sat in an invisible chair as the vicar approached the podium.

"If he lives in London," Elsie went on, "then why does he need to be projected? And why here?" Though with how fuzzy his image was, he must be on the other side of the city. Close as she was, if Elsie were to project herself to the front of the room, it would be crisp enough for it to appear she had an identical twin.

Ogden shrugged. "I don't know. Curious."

Curious indeed. Elsie watched the master aspector for several moments after the sermon began, studying his faded features. A man present yet not. A man with nebulous motivations.

It made Elsie think of the Cowls.

They had not been in contact since the night she was caught. Part of her worried they would make no more use of her, either because she'd failed or perhaps because she'd identified Mr. Parker. And yet, spellbreakers were valuable. Maybe they needed her. She hoped they did.

Something else troubled her. Mr. Kelsey had been adamant the heat spell was merely a security measure. The cook Elsie had spoken to hadn't seemed unhappy, although perhaps she'd been excited for an opportunity to win the favor of an overbearing employer.

Had Robin Hood ever made a mistake?

Quietly clearing her throat, Elsie forced herself to stare at the vicar and absorb his words, though his low voice quickly lulled her to drowsiness. Emmeline began to sway after a half hour, but Ogden was alert, his attention shifting back and forth between the man of God and the spiritual aspector who stood beside the podium. When the preaching concluded, the spiritual aspector waved his arms over the congregation. The slight tinkle of bells reached Elsie's ears, and suddenly she felt very calm, as though an anvil had been lifted from her lap and a fur stole coiled around her shoulders. She might not have recognized the sensation as a spell had she not heard it first. A general blessing of peace was a novice-level spell, but to be able to cast it upon an entire congregation was actually a master-level spell. A spell that could be chained to pass from person to person, almost like a disease.

It tingled on the skin around her shoulders, and pretending she had an itch, Elsie swiftly removed it. She liked calmness, of course, but she'd rather feel it genuinely than have some wealthy stranger stick it to her like a briar.

She bowed her head with everyone else as a final prayer was offered. Elsie's lips moved with one of her own—that the squire would keep Ogden thoroughly busy for the next week.

Hopefully the old church would magnify her heaven-directed plea.

ᗑ

"The new earl is selling his father's collection to pay off debts, supposedly." Rainer rubbed his hands together as he spoke. "It includes a master opus from his great-grandfather."

Bacchus traced his beard with his thumb and forefinger. He stood in one of the balconied windows in the gallery, one that had a nice view of the duke's gardens. The sun was behind him, making the shadowed alcove too cold for his liking. "It's very unlikely the atheneum would allow the auction of such a valuable opus. You shouldn't heed rumors."

Rainer parted his hands as though offering an apology. "You're right—the London Physical Atheneum wants it, but the earl took them to court, and the High Court of Justice itself ruled in his favor. Somewhat. He's allowed to sell a *copy*, although whomever buys it will need to have their paperwork in order. They'll probably also be asked to sign an agreement not to share the spells. Lord Bennett was a physical aspector. From what I could gather, it's very likely he knew the spell you're looking for."

Bacchus straightened, hope spreading its wings. He'd asked both of his men to help him figure out a way around the assembly. Could it be this easy? He didn't need the opus itself—a copy would give him exactly what he required. "Excellent, Rainer." He grinned. "Get me a seat at that auction, and you can have the rest of the day to do whatever you please."

Rainer shrugged. "There is little that interests me here."

"How about a couple of pounds to spend at the tables?"

Rainer cocked an interested eyebrow.

A woman cleared her voice behind them.

Bacchus turned to see his other servant, John, standing beside Miss Elsie Camden. Despite John's larger stature, he seemed almost cowed by the woman. She stood upright with her chin held high like she was a duke's daughter, and though her clothing was not as fine as that, it was well fitted and hardly inexpensive. Her stonemason paid her well—that part of her story was true, at least. Rainer had already confirmed it.

Elsie looked at him as though amused. The expression was cocky and oddly attractive. For an Englishwoman, anyway.

"Thank you, John. You're dismissed." Bacchus nodded to Rainer, and the two of them departed. The walls were taupe, decorated with portraits of the duke's family and red velvet curtains.

Elsie watched the two men go before speaking, and when she opened her mouth, she also planted her hands on her hips. "Do *they* know about me?"

Bacchus shook his head and passed through the gallery, forcing Elsie to follow or miss his answer. "None do, as promised. As far as anyone knows, you're a consultant."

She considered that a moment. "I do have remarkable taste."

She was oddly confident, for the employee of a stonemason. Bacchus normally liked confidence in women, but in this case, it made him suspicious. She still hadn't told him precisely *why* she'd been on the grounds that night—he didn't believe the story about the servants. He'd stayed at Seven Oaks several times throughout his life, and the staff were always treated well. "We'll be working in the ballroom."

Her step slowed. "And where is the family?" The confidence fizzled as easily as it had come.

"The duke is in his study and has better things to do than follow us around." He noted Miss Camden nearly trotting to keep up with him and slowed his stride, slightly. "The duchess has taken her daughters into town."

"And her sons?" she pressed.

"There are none."

"Only daughters?" Her tone shifted to mocking. "How sad."

Bacchus did not reply.

After a moment, she said, "Why do you speak falsely? Your accent, I mean."

This caught him off guard, and he slowed even more. "Pardon?"

That amused look returned to her face. She reminded him of a sugar merchant's wife, the way her expression so easily slipped from earnest to conniving. "When you were speaking with your servant—you spoke differently than you are with me."

Had he? He hadn't noticed. He turned the corner, the doors to the ballroom in sight. "I grow tired of repeating myself. Many men seem incapable of understanding English if it is not spoken to them the way they've always heard it. That said, I am just as much English as I am Bajan or Algarve." He sounded slightly defensive.

"Algarve?" She paused. "Well, I thought it sounded quite intriguing."

He slowed again, studying her from the corner of his eye. Oddly, the comment sounded genuine. "Then you are a rarity, Miss Camden."

"I could understand you just fine."

He paused at the doors. She would not win him over with flattery. "And how long were you standing there before you announced yourself?"

She merely smiled. He ignored her bait and pushed open the doors to the extravagant ballroom. The floors were well polished and showed only minimal wear of dancers' feet. Two rows of white columns followed the long walls, and the short walls featured intricately carved panels, painted with floral patterns, separated by red drapery. Three unlit chandeliers hung from the ceiling, and a set of glass doors led out toward the gardens.

"The duchess requested that I change the scheme of this room to burgundy." He sighed inwardly at the request; party décor was not his forte. But an aspector of any alignment had to occasionally take work he or she wasn't fond of, so this was good practice. He pulled her instructions from his waistcoat pocket once more to review them. "I can overlay the existing spells"—it was quicker and tidier to use magic to paint the walls instead of actual paint—"but the job will have more integrity if the slate is clean, so to speak."

He turned. Miss Camden gawked at the splendor around her, taking it in slowly, craning her head back to see the angelic mural on the ceiling overhead. Bacchus understood her wonder—he'd felt very much the same when he'd first beheld the rich house as a boy. His holding in Barbados was nothing to scoff at, but the island was small, and the plantation house was not nearly as elaborate as the ancestral homes owned by England's elite.

He'd once hated all of it. Now he tolerated it fairly well.

"The spells?" he asked.

Miss Camden shook herself and strode toward the unlit fireplace on the far side of the room. She ran her hand over the mantel, then across a carved panel to a red drape. She paused. "Oh, yes. I see it." She undid the spell quickly, and the curtain changed to an unfortunate teal. "Hmm." She leaned closer, wiggling her fingers, and it changed again to blue.

Stepping back, she examined her work. "If one is to change fabric with spells, why not start with black or white? Something neutral?"

Bacchus rubbed his eyes. "I beg you not to discuss the décor choices with me, for it is a conversation I am loath to participate in." He lowered his hand and caught that amused smirk on her face once more. "Please continue, before the duchess returns."

Her expression blanched. She nodded curtly and moved on to the next drape, dismissing its overlaid spells until it, too, returned to blue. Bacchus, meanwhile, used novice spells to shift the color of the first curtain to burgundy. Color-changing spells were some of the first he'd learned as an adolescent. Hopefully it was the shade the duchess had in mind, for he might go mad from the tediousness of it if she asked him to do it again.

After the curtains came the columns and walls, until everything was burgundy and cream instead of red and white. A tight headache bloomed in the center of Bacchus's forehead, and his customary exhaustion began to suck at his limbs, despite the early hour. He could think of a few people, his late father included, who would have had a fine laugh hearing about how he'd spent his day.

Somewhere in the house, a door opened and closed, the sound of it echoing through the halls. Miss Camden froze, her alarm apparent enough that Bacchus felt pity for her, earlier trespassing aside.

He gestured toward the double doors leading outside. "Head out this way. There's work to be done with the tenants."

"The tenants?" she repeated, but she hurried through the doors and did not slow until her feet were on the stone path that led toward the gardens. "Mr. Kelsey, it must be two in the afternoon by now. I must be getting back to Brookley. I only have so many excuses for my absence, and some of those I need to save for future excursions."

Bacchus clasped his hands behind his back. "And what would those future excursions be?"

Miss Camden blushed; the extra color in her cheeks had a lovely effect, though her forehead wrinkled with annoyance. "Nothing that concerns you."

"Then you should not have concerned me in the first place."

She stomped her foot. Like a child. Bacchus was tempted to laugh.

"You are impossible, Mr. Kelsey." Lowering her voice, she added, "Were I a registered spellbreaker, I would have charged you a good sum for the work I've done. Certainly ample enough to cover any fine for trespassing."

"But not enough for bail, if I understand correctly."

She blanched again, but the effect wasn't as stark this time. Drawing herself up, she said, "It would be easier for me to return tomorrow than to stay much later today. I ask that you be considerate of my predicament. Please."

The crack in her stubbornness softened him, and he nodded. "Just a brief consultation, then."

"And how will I work with the tenants without them noticing what I am?"

"It is not their homes that concern me, but their fields." Few landowners paid to have physical or temporal aspectors bespell their tenants' homes. If they were built well enough, they didn't technically need it, although Bacchus had volunteered his time to place fortifications for most of the duke's tenants. "Perhaps you can pose as a steward."

She pressed her lips together, considering.

"Ah, Bacchus, there you are!"

Bacchus turned at the sound of the duke's voice; he came striding down the steps from the ballroom. If his appearance made Miss Camden uncomfortable, she didn't show it.

The duke's eyes slid to the spellbreaker for a brief moment before returning to Bacchus. "It looks marvelous, if I may give my uneducated opinion. I'm sure the duchess will approve; thank you for giving in to her whims."

Bacchus nodded. "It's the least I could do."

The duke smiled and turned to Miss Camden. "Surely you will introduce me to this young woman?" He had a glint in his eye that Bacchus didn't like.

Bacchus cleared his throat. "Of course. Miss Camden, this is Isaiah Scott, the Duke of Kent. Your Grace, this is Miss Elsie Camden."

Miss Camden executed a well-practiced curtsy.

"My pleasure, Miss Camden." The duke was grinning now. And of course he would be. Bacchus had made no calls in England save for his ill-fated visit to the Physical Atheneum, and now he had been caught *strolling* in the gardens with a well-dressed young woman. He could have kicked himself.

"My dear," the duke continued, "we are at a loss for dinner guests as of late—"

No.

"—and it would be lovely to see a new face at the table."

Bacchus narrowed his eyes at the duke, but it was clear the man would not be dissuaded. The duchess had threatened matchmaking in her last letters before Bacchus had boarded the ship for Europe, but he hadn't thought she was serious about it, let alone that she would recruit her husband to the cause. He'd always intended to marry someone from the island, when he found the right one.

"Perhaps tomorrow, if you do not have other plans?" the duke finished.

Miss Camden blushed again. "I-I . . . that is, th-thank you for the offer, but I'm no one of importance—"

"Nonsense. A friend of Bacchus's is a friend of mine."

Miss Camden looked arthritic. After a moment almost long enough to be awkward, she nodded with a stiff neck. "Thank you, Your Grace."

Bacchus remained silent.

The duke was jovial. "Excellent! But I will not interrupt you further." He nodded to both of them before returning to the house.

A sigh escaped Bacchus's lips. "I may be able to make your excuses."

Miss Camden nodded dumbly, but once she came to herself, she said, "Bacchus."

He eyed her.

She grinned. "The god of the harvest and eternal consumption. Hmm, yes, I think it's very fitting."

His expression darkened. "It is not an unusual name."

She pulled out her chatelaine bag and thumbed through it. She retrieved nothing; perhaps she merely needed something to occupy her hands. "I think it is rather too late for that consultation you requested, Mr. Kelsey. Do send word once you inform the duke of my utter unimportance. Otherwise, I will see you tomorrow morning to pay off my debts."

She gave him a sloppy curtsy and again saw herself out, not so much as allowing him a chance to demand another hour's work or to offer the use of a carriage. Not that he was feeling particularly charitable at the moment.

He turned back toward the house, working out how he would explain the situation to the duke without betraying Miss Camden's trust. He did not think her a particularly trustworthy individual, but he had made a promise, and he would keep it.

However, he had a sinking feeling that the duke would merely cajole him and that the man's mind, set, would be impossible to change.

CHAPTER 8

Elsie had just prepared herself for another day out and was reaching for the back-door handle when Ogden yanked it from the other side, causing her to shriek.

Hand on her chest, chatelaine bag in her hand, she said, "Mr. Ogden! Are you not at the squire's today?"

She'd been preparing to set out for the Duke of Kent's estate, *again*, while pondering how she could adjust the route to deliver two bids. She'd already prepared a couple of orders in the studio for Nash to pick up.

Ogden looked frustrated. "I am, but not yet. I tell you, Elsie, a stonemason's job in a town like this one is a leisurely pursuit three hundred and sixty-four days of the year!" He marched past her, a man on a mission, into the studio. Opened a drawer beneath the counter. "Where are my granite tools?"

Brow furrowed, Elsie hurried over to him and checked the drawer. Empty. She checked the one next to it, and the one next to that. "I put them right here."

"Emmeline!" Ogden bellowed. "I need my granite tools!"

"Is everything all right?" Elsie asked, following Ogden like the tail of a comet.

Ogden searched a cupboard. "Fine." His head struck the top of the cupboard, and something sharp seasoned his breath. Pulling free, he sighed. "It's fine, really. Just . . . people."

Elsie leaned her weight on one leg. "You've always been fond of people."

Ogden snorted. "I won't give in to rumor, Elsie, but the squire has his hands in all sorts of nefarious affairs, and they bleed all over that house. Emmeline!"

Nefarious affairs?

Her shoulders slackened. "Did the Wright sisters say something?" Perhaps they were saving her the trouble of solving the mystery of the squire, the baron, and the viscount.

Ogden didn't answer. Emmeline came racing around the corner, wiping her hands on her apron. "Yes, I think I know where they are—"

A knock sounded at the front door.

Setting down her chatelaine, Elsie hurried to the door and found herself face-to-face with the vicar.

"Mr. Harrison, how are you this morning?" Her pulse was beating too quickly for her short run.

The vicar removed his hat. "Quite well, quite well. Thank you. I've come to officially commission that tile work. Mr. Ogden and I discussed it some time ago—March, perhaps. For the church."

He emphasized *for the church* as though doing so would earn him a discount.

He continued, "Is Mr. Ogden available?"

But Ogden had already vacated the area. Somewhere down the hall, something—many somethings from the sound of it—clattered to the floor. Elsie's best guess was that Emmeline had knocked something over in the space beneath the stairs.

"He is, unfortunately, preoccupied." Elsie smiled, falling into the persona of the helpful secretary. She retrieved a ledger from beneath the narrow counter separating herself from the vicar and opened it to the first blank page, glancing once at the clock. Mr. Kelsey would no doubt comment on her tardiness, but he couldn't keep her under his thumb forever . . . Could he? "Why don't you tell me about your request, and anything specific you discussed with Mr. Ogden?" She thought she recalled Ogden mentioning a mosaic of sorts for the chapel but didn't remember any details.

The vicar fumbled through his pockets for a folded piece of paper, opened it, and handed it over. On it was a simple design sketched in pieces. Elsie could not really describe it other than to think it looked very "Ogden." Dark tiles made a design against white ones, giving an illusion of two almost-circles, one inside the other. There was something familiar about it that she could not put her finger on. It made her fingers itch to touch it.

The vicar proceeded to ramble about his discussions with Ogden. Elsie's pencil stayed poised to record the relevant information, and she scrawled down numbers in the far-right column, occasionally prying for more information.

"Blue and white," she repeated.

"Peacock blue. A muted peacock blue, that is. I don't wish to distract from worship."

Elsie wrote *muted* and underlined it. "We'll be in touch about the timing and cost."

"We did discuss a budget," the vicar continued.

"Mr. Ogden has an impeccable memory, I assure you." The door opened again, and a flash of blond hair caught Elsie's eye. She glanced up at Abel Nash, but he merely scoured the room once, offered a cheery nod, and departed again, ignoring the deliveries she'd prepared. That addlepate. Did he expect her to *hand* them to him?

Elsie sighed. "Thank you, Mr. Harrison."

The vicar left, and Elsie found both Emmeline and Ogden, the latter cursing up a storm, in the hallway, surrounded by an array of boxes and knickknacks pulled from the cupboard below the stairs.

"Are they not in the kitchen?" she asked, and was ignored. "The vicar came by about a mosaic at the chapel. And Nash was here."

Ogden cursed again. "Is he waiting?"

"The vicar or Nash?"

"Nash, damn it."

"Mr. Ogden." Emmeline looked uncomfortable, though Elsie didn't think it was due to the wording of his reprimand.

"No," Elsie answered. "He left."

"Of course he did."

Elsie looked over the mess. "Might your granite tools be misplaced in the studio?"

Ogden paused in his rifling, shoulders drooping. "Do check, Elsie."

She nodded and returned the way she had come, setting the ledger back on its shelf before rummaging for the tools. She'd searched three-quarters of the studio when Ogden shouted, "Eureka!" from the hallway. He stumbled into the studio a moment later, a heavy leather bag in hand. Elsie would bet a shilling the bag had been in the kitchen the whole time.

"I have details for those chapel tiles in the binder." He wiped his forehead. "I need you to go to the quarryman and request the stone."

Elsie swallowed but nodded. That would take her another two hours, most likely. Perhaps Mr. Kelsey wouldn't detain her long, and she could do it on the way back? But she'd received no telegram regarding the duke's invitation to dinner, which likely meant she was obligated to go. Maybe she could go to the quarryman's home after hours and make her apologies.

"Of course," she managed.

Ogden relaxed. "Thank you. I'll be back." He tromped through the studio and out the front door, leaving it ajar in his wake. Elsie shut it.

She'd never make it to Kent in decent time. Would Mr. Kelsey hold it against her? But she'd *told* him she had this job to worry about!

She pressed her forehead to the cool wood of the door. This was some sort of twisted nightmare. Blackmailed by an aspector and *invited to dinner by a duke*. The latter was unheard of. She was no gentlewoman! Even her finest dress wouldn't suit their table. Surely the man hadn't mistaken her for someone of rank, so what was he getting at?

The duke would ask questions. Barrage her with them. He'd judge her. His whole family would judge her—

"Elsie, whatever is the matter?"

Pulling her forehead from the door, Elsie turned to see a very concerned-looking Emmeline standing in the doorway of the studio. Elsie slumped.

"Oh, I wish I could tell you. But on top of it all, I have a dinner invitation." It would be unbelievably rude to ignore the invitation. The man didn't actually *know* her . . . but he was a *duke*, for heaven's sake!

Elsie drew a harsh breath through her nose. *Look on the bright side. It will provide an opportunity to determine just what spell Mr. Kelsey is hiding on his person.* Perhaps he was secretly older than the duke and merely used magic to make himself appear so rugged and masculine. *Stupid spellmaker and his stupid rich friends.*

Emmeline lit up like a child on Christmas morning. "Dinner invitation? With whom, the vicar?"

Elsie snorted. "You would never believe it."

Emmeline hurried across the room and grabbed Elsie's hands. "Do tell me."

"I have to visit the quarryman."

"Oh, Elsie, you've time to tell me quickly. Please."

She chewed on the inside of her cheek a moment. "Well, I met this aspector in . . . town . . . and he apparently works for the Duke of Kent—"

"The Duke of Kent!" Emmeline squealed. Elsie might have as well were their positions switched. But gossip involving oneself was nowhere near as interesting as digging into someone else's business.

"And I'm to come to dinner, and if I say no . . . Who says no to a duke?" Elsie might have cried.

"A duke!" Emmeline had stars in her eyes. "This is absolutely wild!" Emmeline spun about. "Was the man very handsome?"

Elsie flushed. "Handsome? He's quite old—"

Her friend rolled her eyes. "Not the duke, you ninny. The aspector! What's his alignment?"

"Uh . . ." Elsie glanced around the studio, if only to take her eyes from Emmeline. "Well, he's not a bad-looking fellow."

"This is so exciting. You must go, and you must tell me all about it. You'll head to the quarry right away, and I'll rush through my chores so I can do your hair."

Elsie touched her pinned locks. Emmeline hadn't done her hair for a long time. Not since Alfred—

Alfred can choke on a rotten tart, she told herself, but it didn't soothe the sourness in her belly.

She stiffened. "I am certainly *not* looking for affection, Em." And Mr. Kelsey would certainly have none for her if she showed up too late to do any of her prison work.

The maid released Elsie's hands. Of course, Emmeline knew all about Alfred and that nonsense. Elsie needn't have snapped at her. But her friend's natural good cheer pushed through. "But it's not a bad thing, having a reason to fancy up."

Elsie folded her arms. "I own nothing fancy enough for a duke's table."

"I think you're fancy." She beamed.

Elsie smiled. Considered. Sighed. "You're right, I might as well make the best of it." Maybe a few well-placed words would embarrass Mr. Kelsey right out of their spoken contract. "Would you . . . keep an eye out for any messengers or telegrams?" Though it was unlikely at this late hour, she still prayed for a cancellation.

"You're expecting something from Juniper Down?"

The name of the place where she'd last seen her family hit her chest like a blow. Time had softened that wound, but it still sat there, a faded memory that made Elsie feel small. She was in a strange state of mind this afternoon, like she had a bad head cold that made her sensitive to everything around her. "Something like that," she muttered.

Emmeline nodded. Elsie accepted her chatelaine bag, found a good hat to place on her head, and ventured out into the streets for the quarryman.

She thought up her excuses as she went.

No cancellation arrived from the duke's residence, so Elsie found herself in her best dress at Seven Oaks that evening.

Wasn't this everything she hated? Everything she stood against? The wealthy snacking on crumpets in the comfort of their mansions while the poor boiled down cabbage for their supper? In the workhouse, it had been easier to count the days she didn't have cabbage than the days she did.

God bless Cuthbert Ogden.

She gradually stepped out of the carriage as though immersing in bathwater that was too hot. The Duke of Kent's estate had done that growing trick again. It had surely doubled in size since yesterday. Perhaps Mr. Kelsey had done some incredible spell to make it loom. To intimidate her. To punish her for accepting the dinner invitation.

But it wasn't very well *her* fault, now was it?

She should have said no. She should have sent a telegram directly to the duke himself and told him exactly what she thought of him, his society, and his mistreatment of his servants. Then again, her work with his bloody aspector wasn't finished, and such a communication would make any future meetings, however accidental, incredibly awkward. Elsie did not enjoy feeling awkward.

"Is it the right place, miss?" her cab driver asked behind her, likely wondering at her hesitation. It was difficult to mistake any other place in Kent for Seven Oaks, surely. But Elsie couldn't find her voice, so she nodded dumbly. The driver lingered a moment longer before whistling out the side of his mouth and whipping his horses' reins. Then he was gone, and she stood alone at Seven Oaks, unescorted. But she was nearly old enough to be a spinster, wasn't she? Just a few more years to go. And what uptight totty one-lung would think her worthy of gossip, anyway?

She wound her fingers together, the lace of her gloves chafing. She was in her maroon dress, the one she wore to church on the days she cared, and Emmeline had pinned her hair meticulously in the back and curled the shorter pieces in the front. Her hat sat like a resting bird atop it all, complete with feathers. She wore no jewelry—what she owned was not real in chain or stone, and she was certain the duke and his family would notice and judge her for it. The collar of the dress was high, besides.

It looked like the mansion was baring its teeth at her.

"Miss Camden?"

Elsie started, seeing for the first time a footman approaching her. A well-groomed footman, to be sure, but too young to be the butler. She offered a timid smile, and Elsie wondered how well the man was treated. Had the Cowls indeed been mistaken, or were the duke and duchess merely excellent at keeping up appearances? "I came out to see if you'd arrived, miss. Mr. Kelsey was worried you'd gotten lost."

I'm sure he was, she thought. Would the spellmaker punish her for her inability to show up to work today? What if he used the dinner to publicly announce her secret? Or perhaps he would insist they skip the dinner so Elsie could prowl the tenants' land in her nicest vestments?

She considered running all the way back to Brookley. The sun was setting; maybe she'd make it by morning. Now *that* would be a good bit of gossip: Elsie Camden stumbling into town a ready mess, her finest dress ripped at the hems. She could practically hear the story in the Wright sisters' voices.

She plastered on a smile. "I did get a bit turned around, thank you."

The footman nodded and gestured toward the monstrous house. Elsie's legs felt so stiff she almost wondered if she'd gotten stuck in one of Mr. Kelsey's spells again. But she managed to follow the man clear to the entrance, where a second footman held open the door.

It struck her again that the servants certainly looked healthy enough. That was good. To think Elsie might have become a maid herself had she stayed in the workhouse. Not at an establishment like this, of course. Somewhere more cramped, danker. Aristocrats didn't hire from workhouses.

The footman wound Elsie through a few halls, past more servants, and up a set of stairs to a spacious drawing room. The gilded paintings seemed to dance in the candlelight, the furniture was fine and brightly colored, and the biggest bouquet she'd ever seen sat in a porcelain vase on a low table.

She tried to act as though the casual display of wealth didn't affect her.

She didn't know the four women in the room, all dressed in finery save one, whose dress seemed about on par with her own. The oldest, a willowy woman who wore her years well, acknowledged her first. Her neck glittered with sapphires.

Elsie felt sorely out of place. Her eyes jumped between chairs and sofas, trying to find somewhere she could sit quietly and unobtrusively until the food was served—

"You must be Elsie Camden!" The willowy woman approached her, arms outstretched, a brilliant smile lighting her face. "Dear, forgive the nature of our introduction. Men can be so nonplussed." She took Elsie's hands like they were long-lost friends.

Elsie's jaw dropped. This was a noblewoman, was it not? But she was so . . . *nice*.

The woman took advantage of Elsie's bafflement and subtly looked her over. Elsie flushed, sure the woman was measuring up her attire, but to her surprise, she said, "And you're on the taller side. That's good."

Elsie's jaw snapped back into place. *Why is taller good?* But the answer came to her before she could speak, nearly choking her. The stranger was referring to her height relative to that of Mr. Kelsey.

The woman swept right over her voiceless stutter. "My name is Abigail Scott. The duke is my husband."

Elsie was holding hands with a duchess.

"This"—the duchess released her and gestured to two women, both younger than Elsie, the first about sixteen—"is my daughter Ida and my daughter Josie." Josie looked barely Ida's junior. "And this is Master Lily Merton, whom I also invited to dine with us tonight."

Master Merton, who looked to be a little older than Ogden, scuttled up to her. She was titled in the way of spellmaking, but she didn't look like the standard well-to-do lady. She was short and plump, with a round face that looked like it perpetually smiled. Her hair was curled and a little old fashioned, her dress violet, modest, and simple, which made Elsie feel less out of place. "My dear, it is excellent to meet you. I hope you don't mind the intrusion. The duchess's family is a dear one, and Miss Ida is showing so much promise in aspecting!"

Elsie blinked and turned toward the older daughter. "You're an apprentice?"

But Ida shook her head. "Not yet. Perhaps. But I do show promise."

Master Merton nodded vigorously. "I just have to convince her to join the spiritual alignment!"

Ida smiled shyly. Though Elsie didn't know the girl, she hoped she'd take the opportunity to study aspecting. There were so few women in the field, especially in Europe. Only the privileged who showed natural talent could try their hand at it, along with a sprinkling of the sponsored poor, who were often discovered only when spellmaking professors held recruiting events and didn't charge a family their firstborn child to participate. That left many potential aspectors turned away. Back to the cabbage fields.

Had Elsie been anything but a spellbreaker, she'd never have amounted to anything. The Cowls certainly would never have found use for her.

"I'm sure you will succeed," she tried, and Master Merton's eyes gleamed with pleasure. "I think it a very good profession for a young lady."

"Quite possibly," the duchess echoed. She perked at footsteps in the hall. "Here we are. My dear Miss Camden, Mr. Kelsey will escort you. And Master Merton, I would be honored to have you on my left."

"What a pleasure, my lady," Master Merton enthused, clapping her hands. Her good cheer was such that Elsie couldn't help but smile, too. "Oh, we have so much to talk about!"

The door on the near side of the room opened, revealing Mr. Kelsey. He held it for the duke, who noticed Elsie and grinned before shifting his attention to Master Merton and offering her a thorough welcome.

Mr. Kelsey approached Elsie as soon as he walked in. He looked a little irritated, but the lines in his tanned forehead smoothed themselves as he approached her. Goodness, it was easy to forget how large he was when not comparing him to normal-sized people. His eyes dropped to her skirt and back up, lingering, and Elsie couldn't tell whether he approved or disapproved.

Not that it mattered. Indeed, it most certainly did not. Elsie had merely straightened her posture because her corset was pinching.

A duke, a duchess, their daughters, and a master aspector. Mr. Kelsey was the only thing bridging the gaping class barrier between Elsie and the rest, and even that bridge felt insurmountable.

Elsie spoke first, quietly. "I could not get away this morning. It all went to pot, giving me barely any chance to breathe. I will try my best tomorrow."

Mr. Kelsey considered a moment before offering an arm. "Fair enough."

Elsie eyed him, hesitant to lift her hand. "Fair enough? Just like that? No jabs or threats?"

"If you meant to go back on your word, you would not have come."

She frowned and took his arm as the duke led the duchess toward the dining room, Master Merton beside them. As she watched them, she felt the bulk of Mr. Kelsey's muscular arm against hers. Who would win if he were to arm wrestle Ogden?

Heat crept up her neck, but she ignored it, loosening her grip to keep her focus where she needed it. "I merely wished to try the elegant food that is sure to grace the duke's—"

Spells.

Two of them. The first she'd noticed before—a forestlike scent that almost but not quite blended with his usual fragrance of newly cut wood and oranges. It was on Mr. Kelsey's person, right there on his torso. But another spell lay beneath it, calm and muted, barely noticeable. She couldn't identify it; the first enchantment was too pungent. But there were certainly two.

The second spell was so powerful that she couldn't detect it with her usual senses—she simply felt its existence, not unlike the sensation one got when being watched. The only reason she'd noticed it now was because she stood so close to him.

Why? And why were there *two*?

"—table," she finished, barely recalling what they'd been discussing. God help her, she *needed* to know what those spells were, but short of seducing Mr. Kelsey out of his clothing, she didn't think she'd be able to pin it down.

Now she *really* needed to distract herself, for her errant thoughts were making her blaze like the bloody hearth. Elsie tucked the notion of secret spells into the back of her mind and thought very hard about snow.

Mr. Kelsey led her toward the door, and the sisters followed after them. Were this a real dinner party, there would have been two gentlemen to escort them. But it wasn't, and the duke had already proved himself unusual by inviting her to dine with them in the first place.

On the taller side. She nearly snorted. And yet the banter had eased her nerves.

The dining room, of course, was as grand as the drawing room, though a little less busy in its décor. The table was not terribly large, and Elsie wondered if it had leaves to extend it, or if this was the smaller of two dining rooms. The duke sat on one end and the duchess on the other. Master Merton sat in the esteemed seat to the duchess's left, and Bacchus sat to her right, with Elsie beside him. Across from Elsie sat Ida, and beside her, Josie.

Footmen brought out the first course. Elsie didn't know what it was, but it smelled wonderful.

Cabbage, she reminded herself. *Everyone else is eating cabbage.*

"Bacchus tells me you're from Brookley," chirped the duke. "I've passed through the place. It has a certain charm to it."

Elsie nodded, unsure how she felt about her personal information being shared. But of course Mr. Kelsey would have needed to relinquish *something.* "It does, Your Grace. I am very fortunate to be there." She mentally kicked herself. If she admitted to her history in the workhouse, she'd surely be ousted from the table.

The duchess added, "He's very tight-lipped about you."

It took Elsie a second to realize she meant Bacchus, about her. She swallowed, suppressing relief. "Well, that is, we're really just acquaintances."

The duchess gave the duke a look that Elsie did not like. A knowing look.

Mr. Kelsey said, "Miss Camden has impeccable taste in ballrooms," and lifted his spoon to his mouth. Elsie watched to see if he'd dribble anything into his beard, but he proved quite adept at eating with facial hair. How irritating.

"Is that so?" asked the duchess.

"Master Merton," Elsie began, her appetite starting to slip away from her, "when did you first notice potential in Miss Ida?"

"Oh, I wasn't even the first to notice! That was Master Thompson." Because aspecting did not have a feminine title for women, Elsie was unsure at first if Master Thompson was male or female. "He went to university with the duke's brother," the aspector continued, "as did Mr. Kelsey's father, if I remember correctly?"

Mr. Kelsey nodded, more interested in his soup than the conversation. Elsie envied him his silence. As the newcomer to the table, she wouldn't be allowed much of it.

"He just had a hunch, apparently. Like drawn to like, I suppose," Master Merton prattled on. "I was there when he tested her. A dozen drops in her hand lit up like the sun!"

Miss Ida blushed.

"How interesting," Elsie said. "I admit I know little of magic myself"—*do not look at Mr. Kelsey*—"but my employer is an aspector. Not nearly at your level, of course."

"Is he?" the duchess asked.

Stop talking about your personal life!

Elsie nodded. "And Miss Josie"—*what's something refined young women do?*—"do you . . . sing?"

After a long conversation about music, the second course arrived, and Elsie found she had a bit more appetite. Ida mentioned the opus thefts, which instantly engaged Elsie's attention, but the conversation was quashed by the duchess. "Let's not speak of terrible things we have no control over," she said firmly. Elsie wondered if the prospect of her eldest becoming an aspector made the duchess uneasy, what with the news in the papers of late.

The duke instead chatted about dog breeds, and Master Merton conversed enthusiastically. Elsie was content to merely listen until the third course arrived, and she once again became a topic of interest.

"You mentioned working for an aspector?" the duke asked.

Elsie clamped her hands together under the table. "I . . . yes. A novice, really. He's an artist—"

"He does very well for himself," Mr. Kelsey interjected, his voice smooth and confident. "As does Miss Camden."

She paused at the compliment. But what did Mr. Kelsey know? Either way, it was a delicate attempt to bolster her standing, and for that she was grateful.

"But of course." The duchess nodded. "Remind me how you two met?"

Mr. Kelsey said, "I would have had to tell you the first time to remind you, Your Grace."

The duchess swatted her hand in the air. "I've told you about formality, Bacchus."

Josie said, "But we're dining," referring to the formal occasion.

The duchess gave her youngest daughter a pointed look, and Josie dropped her attention to her meal.

"Just in the market." Elsie tried to recall what she'd told Emmeline. "I was . . . having some trouble with a door. Mr. Kelsey graciously aided me."

His lips quirked at the near truth.

"Oh yes." Master Merton nodded enthusiastically. "The days are getting hotter and more humid. The wood swells right up! But you know a spell for that, don't you, Mr. Kelsey?"

Mr. Kelsey set down his fork. "I do, but I'll not be enchanting another's door. More often than not, a firm push will do well enough."

"So pragmatic," the duchess chimed. She dotted her lips with a napkin. "All that talk of music. Josie, you'll play for us after dinner, yes?"

"Of course!" she replied.

"I—" Elsie began, but her mind proved stubborn in fathoming an excuse. She could stay up a little later tonight to finish her work for Ogden, couldn't she? No doubt he'd have a list for her after another long day at the squire's. He had seemed so harried earlier. Not like himself.

"Miss Camden is not local, and it grows late," Mr. Kelsey said. Elsie wasn't sure if she should bless him or be offended that he wanted her gone so quickly. "It'd be best if she departed." Then, catching himself, he added, "but I would enjoy your music, Miss Josie."

Josie grinned.

"Oh dear, yes. I'm sure your escort is waiting," said the duchess.

Elsie forbade her cheeks to blush. They nearly listened. "Yes, she'll be here any moment." And she'd be charged a premium if the driver had to wait. With all the cabs she'd been hiring, Elsie would be going to the poorhouse soon.

The rest of the meal went smoothly, with Master Merton talking of the excitement of aspecting and the Spiritual Atheneum in London. When the last plates were taken away, Mr. Kelsey forsook his port to escort Elsie to her imagined chauffeur.

The cab wasn't there.

"I did ask him to return at eleven." Elsie stood in the gap in the stone wall, wringing her hands. Her voice might have been a touch defensive.

Mr. Kelsey regarded her in a way that made her warm. "You handled yourself well."

She straightened. "I'm no scullery maid." *Not anymore.* "I know etiquette well enough." Thanks to Ogden and her novel readers. She softened quickly. "Thank you, for protecting my privacy."

"It's not difficult; the duke and duchess know their etiquette as well. I have other plans for tomorrow, but we'll go to the tenants' land on Thursday. I have a suspicion of some curses."

"Curses?" Spiritual spells.

"I could very well be wrong." He rubbed his half beard. "I'll get you a carriage."

"Like I said before, it would be best if I do not arrive home in a duke's carriage."

"You must have very determined eavesdroppers at home if it concerns you." He stifled a yawn. Either he was used to turning in early, or Elsie's conversation was dull.

Obviously it was the former.

They returned to the house, where Elsie waited in the vestibule while Mr. Kelsey obtained the carriage. Elsie wondered how many the duke owned.

When it came around, Mr. Kelsey escorted Elsie to the door, even offering a hand to help her in. His hands were large but not unwieldly. Warm.

She pulled hers free the moment she had her balance.

"Until Thursday." He nodded and shut the carriage door.

The horses jerked forward, and Elsie gripped the seat to remain upright. Something crinkled under her hand. A piece of paper had been left on the cushion.

She picked it up, just making out the bird-foot seal in the moonlight. The Cowls.

CHAPTER 9

Bacchus had heard of the increased homicides among aspectors in Europe, England in particular, but the security swarming Christie's Auction House would make Buckingham Palace envious.

A uniformed officer pushed through part of the gathering crowd, waving away pedestrians with frantic arms. Another officer near the door asked for the names of arriving bidders before allowing them entrance.

Rainer, who had braved the crowd while Bacchus waited for the queue to move, reappeared at his side. "Spoke to a footman. There was an attempted theft last night."

Hence the security—the rumors had some heft to them, then. Apparently, the criminal or criminals at work were just as chuffed to steal the opus of an already deceased aspector as they were to kill a living magical worker. Bacchus peered up toward the auction house's rectangular windows. "Here?"

Rainer nodded. "They didn't catch the person, so they're being careful."

Interesting. A policeman blew a whistle nearby; it was deafening.

"Move along!" shouted the frustrated officer from before. His eyes landed on Rainer and Bacchus. "Don't you speak English? *Move along.*"

Bacchus's eyebrows drew together. "I believe I'm in the correct line."

The officer looked genuinely confused. Bacchus tried not to let irritation mark his features—this was just the way of things. He would never be fully accepted into high English society, not with the way he looked.

The sooner he left England, the better. With any luck, he'd get what he needed at this auction. Earn his mastership and book his passage home, the coveted ambulation spell written on his soul.

"This line is for the auction house," the officer stated dumbly.

"I'm aware," Bacchus replied.

The officer paused for a moment, then distracted himself with an older couple who had stopped to gawk at the fanfare. "Move along!"

The crowd shifted, and Bacchus finally reached the front of the line. Rainer spoke for him. "Bacchus Kelsey."

The large man with the ledger eyed them for a moment before scrolling through the paperwork. He drew a line across the page with a pencil. Tipped his head toward his companion.

The second, shorter man said, "Turn out your pockets, please."

Bacchus gritted his teeth—he didn't recall those before him being asked to do this—but obliged. He didn't carry a lot on him, and Rainer had his coin. An exorbitant amount of money saved for years for this very purpose. Money he would have gladly given the Assembly of the London Physical Atheneum were they not pompous hornswogglers.

His belongings were rifled through, and Bacchus kept his eyes on each gloved hand, ensuring nothing slipped into the wrong pocket. The officer then instructed Bacchus to lift his arms to be searched.

It was incredibly tempting to put the man in his place. To freeze him with a spell, or turn him green. To reprimand him for not respecting his betters, however much Bacchus hated the very notion. Once he had a title, such things would be easier to evade, but he'd been hesitant to take the master test. Until he did, there was always the chance the assembly members might change their mind and allow him to use the ambulation spell for his advancement rights. A slender chance, to be sure, but a chance, nonetheless. One he hoped he would not need to rely on. Master Bennett's opus was to be one of the first items up for bid.

So Bacchus submitted silently, and security did its job quickly. His things were returned to him, along with a blue paddle marked **18**, denoting him as an aspector. Only those with blue paddles were allowed to bid on magical items. Withholding a sigh, Bacchus proceeded inside.

He took a seat in the middle of the auction room, a large gray-walled space decorated with a few portraits and a tasteful amount of décor, while Rainer waited in the back with the other servants. Bacchus wanted to blend in, but he needed to be sure the auctioneer noticed him. Turning the paddle in his hands, he watched the podium until the auctioneer, his mustache long and graying, stepped up to it.

The first item was a painting of a teapot that went for a surprising amount of money. The second was Master Bennett's journals, five in total, well worn and engraved. One would think the personal musings of a father would be kept in the family, but if there was any chance Master Bennett had shared a spell or two in those pages, they would be worth a great deal. Unsurprisingly, the bound books went for double the cost of the painting.

Bacchus stiffened when the next item came out. Before it was even announced, he knew this was the opus he sought. A thick tome, bound in polished, red-hued leather with half a dozen burgundy ribbons streaming from its spine. The pages, clamped shut, had rough edges that sparkled when the book was placed on its easel. This was the opus of a true master, and a wealthy one at that.

"The opus of the late Lord Master Cassius Bennett, physical aspector, deceased 1894. Opening bid will start at five hundred eighty pounds."

A price that could make a man weep. But this was a master opus.

Bacchus's hand tightened around his paddle as he forced himself to wait. A man in gray near the front lifted his. Five hundred eighty pounds. Six hundred. Six hundred twenty-five. "Six fifty? Do I hear six fifty?"

Bacchus's paddle surged into the air.

His bid was noted with the tip of the auctioneer's pen. "Six seventy-five? A truly magnificent opus. No? Six seventy."

The man in gray raised his paddle.

Bacchus raised his.

A woman in the back raised hers.

Sweat pricked Bacchus's hairline and spine. The bidding continued apace, but he practiced forbearance, waiting for a lull.

"One thousand and twenty?"

He raised his paddle.

So did the man in gray.

His palms began to sweat. With a start of five eighty, he'd felt confident the bidding would stay under his cap. Neither the painting nor the journals had taken long to find a buyer. This competition had begun to drag, however, the number climbing ever higher.

The woman, after whispering to her companion, raised her paddle for one thousand seven hundred and fifty pounds.

Bacchus raised his. "Two thousand three hundred." His low voice carried across the room.

A small gasp sounded from the row behind him.

Almost immediately, the man in gray raised his paddle, and Bacchus's heart dropped to his ankles. "Two thousand five hundred."

Bacchus could not meet the price, let alone beat it. Not without taking foolish measures, succumbing to debt, and hurting those who depended on him.

"Going once," called the auctioneer.

It tempted him. Surely he could make it work. Just a small push, a little discomfort, and the tome would be his. *Might* be his. He hadn't a clue how much the man in gray was worth.

His arm twitched as he squeezed his paddle. He *needed* that spell. If he didn't get that opus, he didn't know where to turn next.

"Going twice." The threat echoed between the walls.

He wanted to claim he was so desperate for the spell because he needed it for his tenants, his property, his holdings. It was true, in a sense—it would help him serve them—but they didn't need him. Ultimately, the spell was for him.

Bacchus's fingers slackened in defeat.

"Sold to eleven!"

But he was not defeated yet.

Several grumbling people stood and made their way to the door as the next item was brought out for bidding. Not wishing to draw attention to himself, Bacchus remained seated for the rest of the auction, which drew out far too long with far too many petty things. The whole time, he kept his eye on the man in gray. He looked to be in his forties, well groomed. He was balding and had a straight spine. He also remained for the duration of the auction, bidding on two other items, winning one of them.

When the bidders were finally dismissed, Bacchus pushed through the crowd to the edge of the room, keeping an eye on the man in gray. Not a difficult task, given his height.

Rainer found him. Before he could offer any condolences, Bacchus said, "Tell me you know that man's name."

"Felton Shaw," Rainer replied without hesitation. "Owns several gentlemen's clubs."

"Aspector?"

"Yes, but rumor says he's topped off."

Topped off? Meaning he had already reached his magical limitations. Some people, no matter how much they paid and how much they studied, simply couldn't become powerful aspectors because their bodies lacked the ability to hold enough spells. Topping off was usually kept private. Shaw was either barely a master or he'd paid handsomely to get that blue paddle.

Did he even have the paperwork to own a copy of an opus?

Right now, the man's reasons didn't matter.

Mr. Shaw took his time finding his way out, choosing a side door instead of fighting through the crush at the back. Bacchus stuck his manners in his pocket and pushed his way through the crowd, taking long strides once he was free. He met Mr. Shaw at the turn of the hallway.

He bowed. "Mr. Shaw, congratulations on your wins. I hope to strike up a matter of business with you."

The older, smaller man lifted a monocle to his eye and studied Bacchus for an instant. "I'm listening." He sounded unsure.

"The opus you won," Bacchus began.

"The copy, you mean. Yes, you did a good job of driving up the price."

That's how auctions work. "I would pay a fair sum just to read one of the spells within it. I'm ready and willing to provide you with the proper certificates."

Mr. Shaw's eyebrows climbed into the brim of his hat. "Is that so? I don't know every spell it contains, mind you, only what was listed in the description."

A description that had not been released until after Bacchus entered the auction house. "I seek the master ambulation spell."

The Englishman's countenance fell slack. "That's illegal."

"I assure you it is not; I am a registered aspector and have the necessary clearance."

"I will not sell any of the master spells." Mr. Shaw took a step forward, but Bacchus stopped him with raised hands. His pulse hammered in his wrists.

"Allow me only to memorize it. It is for my own progress. I will pay handsomely."

He was offering the man a silver tea platter with cups full of gold. He'd give it all just to know what made that spell work. He *needed* it.

"Two thousand—"

"No." Mr. Shaw cut the overly generous offer into pieces. "I have plans for the master spells, plans that are more lucrative even than your coffers. I must decline."

He stepped around Bacchus.

Bacchus spun. "You are a man of business. Surely you must see reason—"

Mr. Shaw paused only long enough to spit, "Ask me again, and I'll alert security."

Bacchus froze and watched the petulant, rich Englishman stalk away. The urge to pick him up and throw him into a wall—no magic required—burned in his arms. His pulse sang in his ears.

First the assembly, and now this. He couldn't wrap his mind around all the stuff and nonsense. Had England changed so much in the few years since his last visit? Was there some sort of political thread he wasn't cutting? Why was this *so bloody hard?*

To frustrate matters further, he was already growing tired. He moved his hand to his diaphragm, to the spell etched into the skin there. It wouldn't hold forever. Bacchus had only so much time. Time that spilled through his fingers like sand.

Ripping his hand away, he balled it into a fist. He would not give up. If he had to travel all of Europe, scour the Americas . . . he'd find a way somehow.

He barreled out of the auction house with Rainer on his heels, ignoring the whispers that followed them.

CHAPTER 10

If all three of Elsie's employers ever demanded her attention at once, she would be in quite a pinch. As it was, Mr. Kelsey was preoccupied, the stonemasonry shop was in shape, and Ogden was busy, giving Elsie a rare chance to redeem herself to the Cowls.

The letter that had been tucked into her things after her dinner at the duke's residence had not mentioned the door spell at all, to her surprise. Instead, she'd been given another task. She was to disenchant a carriage that had been hired to transport local poachers to court. It was a time-sensitive matter, and so Elsie moved quickly, even when it meant cutting through traffic or overpaying a cab driver to run his horses wild. Her personal funds were depleting quickly, but the Cowls hadn't sent coin for travel in their last missive. Perhaps this was to be her punishment.

Not that it mattered. If no one intervened, men, *boys*, would be hanged for hunting animals on land owned by rich men. They just wanted to feed their families, and yet the neck of a human was priced the same as that of a pheasant. If Elsie could help them escape, she would do her part. Whatever it cost. She yawned, so many short nights catching up to her, but sleep was hardly important.

She went to London and found the public carriage house in question; the man she presumed ran it sat just outside, a newspaper in his hands and a cigar in his mouth, his hat pulled low to keep out the sun. Elsie walked past him, casual, before glancing over her shoulder and slipping inside the carriage house.

She nearly bumped into the tack on the wall and quickly side-stepped it, hiding herself among the vehicles stored within the space. The first spells she sensed were those on the wheels of a hansom cab. However, she doubted the Cowls would have sent her to intervene if the vehicle in question were a self-propelling carriage. Disabled by a spellbreaker, it wouldn't be able to leave the carriage house much less be used for transporting anyone. So she moved on, searching for a vehicle with strengthening spells, bars, anything to denote the kind of vessel that might deliver "criminals" to their doom.

The farther into the carriage house she stepped, the darker it became, and everything began to look the same. *What a bother.*

Elsie persisted in her search, knowing the driver and authorities could come at any moment. Finally, she found it—a carriage bolstered by glowing runes of protection and fortification, which she pulled apart like hot ribbon candy. They pulsed light once before fading, like the last drag on a cigarette.

Voices at the front of the carriage house sent gooseflesh over her arms; Elsie hid behind a cab and held her breath. To her relief, they didn't come any nearer. A vehicle was pulled out and driven away, and the man in charge resumed his reading of the day's paper.

Holding her skirt close to prevent sullying it, Elsie carefully tiptoed her way toward freedom. Just as she stepped into the light, however, the caretaker looked up, his eyes beady and questioning.

Elsie put her hands on her hips. "I don't suppose you rent omnibuses?"

He looked at her like she was mad. "Omnibuses? What does this look like, a rail station?"

Acting offended, Elsie turned on her heel and stalked away, going around the back of the carriage house to access the road home. Having spoken of omnibuses, she was reminded she could save a penny or two by taking one, and so she headed toward the market, eyes searching for one.

She'd just reached the sprawl of shoppers when a familiar voice reached her ears and stopped her in her tracks. She turned slowly, searching the crowd until she saw his face.

Alfred.

Alarm rushed up her limbs like a swarm of termites. She hadn't seen him in nearly two years. He didn't look any different, except for his hair. The ginger locks were a bit longer, styled differently. He was only one shop down from her, walking to a carriage with two heavy bags on his arm. A smile split his freckled face. It sent a knifepoint into the center of Elsie's chest.

"You don't have to carry those." The handsome stranger who would later introduce himself as Alfred hurried across the street, outstretching his hand, offering to take the sack laden with canvas.

Elsie flushed at his approach and stuck her nose up. "Good sir, I am perfectly capable of carrying my own things, else I would not have purchased them."

But she had let him carry her bags. And walk her to a carriage. And ask her name and where she lived, starting something he would kill just as easily months later.

Elsie blinked, coming back to the present just in time to spy Alfred's companion, which only twisted the metaphorical blade piercing her breast.

The widow. The one they'd met when Alfred had taken Elsie out to dinner for her birthday. But . . . not a widow anymore. Not by the way they touched each other, shared a carriage, and—yes, that was a ring on her finger, wasn't it?

Heat spread from her ribs, clawing down her legs and arms before turning to ice. So the woman hadn't been a passing infatuation. Hadn't left him for the weasel he was. He'd married her.

Married *her*.

Alfred turned just then, meeting Elsie's eyes for a split second. She panicked. There was no use hiding. What would she say? What would—

But he merely stepped into the carriage and shut the door.

Her lips parted. He'd . . . He'd *seen* her. And he hadn't cared. He hadn't given her so much as a nod. A tip of the hat.

A breeze swept her hair as the carriage passed. Elsie thought she heard an "Excuse me" behind her, but she couldn't bring herself to move, so the old woman huffed and stepped around her.

The past bubbled up like hot tar. Oh, how it hurt to be left. She had been abandoned by her mother and father, her siblings, and never—not one single day—had she forgotten it. *All* of them had left her, a child unable to care for herself, with strangers who'd been foolish to show a sliver of kindness. None of them had ever attempted to find her.

They'd seen something in her, something Elsie still had not discovered, that was unacceptable. And they'd fled from it. Alfred had done the same. He and Elsie had courted for months. Talked about marriage. Family. A future.

And then he'd left as abruptly as her parents had. Somehow, he'd seen that bit of her that was detestable, and he ran from it. Ran right into the arms of another woman, who now lived the life Elsie had once dared to imagine for herself.

The conclusion was inevitable.

She was unlovable.

Tears blurred her vision, but she blinked them away. The sound of trotting horses broke her reverie. *Blast it!* Her vision cleared just in time to see the omnibus leaving, the enormous carriage's horses pulling into the thoroughfare. It was full to the brim, people crowded within and on top, but the two tiny platforms on the back were free.

Somehow Elsie summoned enough sense to run after it and catch the pole on the omnibus's back end, planting her feet on the right platform. Gripping the pole until her knuckles blanched, she rode with her face in the wind, letting it dry her out until her eyes burned.

She felt stiff as a wooden board by the time she reached Brookley, grateful that the stonemasonry shop sat near the edge of town and not in the center of it. The last thing she wanted was attention. Her head was hollow, her hands sore.

She saw the squire's cabriolet on the street by the front door. No. The last thing she needed was *that man* inside her home.

She stalked past the carriage, only to stop when she heard the spell on his horse's flank—a chirping spiritual spell that would allow an aspector to speak to the animal to better train it. The same spell the post office used on its post dogs. Elsie unwound it with a flick of her finger and trudged inside through the side door. Let him think the spell was haphazardly placed and came off on its own. It wasn't an uncommon issue.

"Elsie! Where have you been?" Emmeline said as Elsie started up the stairs. "The dressmakers put up a new display, and I thought it would be fun to stop by and—what's wrong?"

Elsie couldn't summon the will to pretend everything was all right. Not yet. Shaking her head, she said, "It's nothing. I just . . . need to think for a moment." She slipped into her bedroom, grateful Emmeline didn't try to follow after. She closed the door, tore off her hat, and fumbled with her chatelaine bag. Coins and a fan had spilled onto the floor by the time she got her hands on her handkerchief.

She caught the tears just before they rolled down her face.

Sitting on the edge of her bed, Elsie chided herself for crying. She'd already recovered from this. It wasn't the loss of Alfred that bothered her, precisely. She was better off without him, though the night he left her still stung. *It's not right, Elsie,* he'd said. *You and I. It's been fun, but I've found someone actually suited to me.* And he'd taken his umbrella with him to leave her soaking in the downpour just down the street from his house, miles away from her own. She'd been sick with fever for two weeks after that, sick with heartbreak even longer. But Elsie was a strong woman. The Cowls knew it. Ogden knew it. Even Mr. Kelsey knew it.

Yet the soundest logic in the world could not heal her old wounds. It could not silence the voice that insisted she was unlovable. Unlovable. Unlovable.

She sobbed into the handkerchief until there wasn't a dry spot on it. Until the room began to grow dark. When there wasn't a stripe of energy left in her, she flopped onto her pillow and stared at the wall, her eyes dry and aching, her throat tight.

She didn't say anything when a knock sounded on the door. Nor did she protest when it cracked open, revealing Ogden in the doorway.

"Oh, Elsie," he said, warm and sad. "What happened?"

She merely shook her head. She couldn't speak even if God demanded it of her. A frog would be better understood.

Ogden stepped into her room, leaving the door ajar, and shoved her knees over so he could sit on the edge of the bed. Just like he had when she'd first arrived there. He had acted the part of the father she couldn't remember, reading her bedtime stories and telling her old fables. It was his fault she had an addiction to novel readers.

She'd wondered, back then, if he was as lonely as she was.

She hid her face in her stained handkerchief.

"Someone say something to you?" he guessed feebly. Elsie was not prone to hysterics, especially not in front of other people. She refused to be the seed of someone else's gossip. "The Wright sisters?" he tried again.

She shook her head.

"Might as well tell me, or I'll stay here all night, and the neighbors will talk."

A sore chuckle popped up her throat. Anyone who really knew Ogden knew any scandal between them was nigh impossible.

He touched her elbow. "Not the squire?"

"No." Her voice was raw and childish. She hated it.

Ogden waited.

After a few almost smooth breaths, she said, "I saw Alfred."

She needn't explain further. She'd been employed here, just as she was now, during their courtship. Emmeline, new and excitable, had suggested ideas for the wedding dinner and Elsie's dress almost daily. Ogden had stressed over finding her replacement. They, too, had been shocked when it ended faster than night turns to day. She'd dedicated herself more fiercely to the Cowls than ever after that. This was just a painful reminder of where her loyalty belonged.

"Oh, Elsie."

She shrugged. "Just for a minute. Doesn't matter. H-He didn't think twice of it."

He rubbed her arm briskly like she'd bruised it. "I'll have Emmeline bring dinner to your room."

I'm fine, she wanted to say, but her throat burned with the lie.

"With some warm milk," he added.

God help her, she really was eleven again.

His hand stilled. "You're a bright young woman, Elsie. You have no idea the things awaiting you in this life."

And oddly . . . she felt better. They were simple words, but they carried a strange power. A firm assurance she didn't quite understand. She thought she felt . . . but no, that was a hair tickling her face. She brushed the thing away. It would take hours to pull the pins out of the knots she'd made of it.

Ogden patted her elbow and stood from the bed. She heard him linger at the door for several seconds before closing it.

Elsie fell asleep before Emmeline could bring her a tray.

CHAPTER 11

"I suppose you're going to compensate me after my employment is terminated?" Elsie asked, picking her way around a mud puddle formed by the morning's rain. She traversed a wide dirt road that stretched from Seven Oaks toward the bulk of the duke's tenants, and while the overhead sky was currently dry, the lurking, morose clouds promised more rain to come.

Mr. Bacchus Kelsey, half a step ahead of her, scoffed at the idea. He wasn't in a jovial mood, not that jovial was his usual demeanor. But he was a little stiffer than usual, a little colder, too. Elsie didn't think it had anything to do with the weather.

She stepped over a stone, glad she'd had the forethought to don sturdy boots for today's blackmailed labors. She wore a simple linen dress, one she wouldn't care *too* much about dirtying. The hem was already collecting whispers of mud. Elsie would wash those out herself rather than explain to Emmeline how she'd come by them. Another late night ahead of her, then. At least she'd caught up on sleep.

Even so, she knew she couldn't carry on her triple life for much longer. If she spent much more time away from Brookley, she'd get herself in trouble. Goodness, it felt like she was a character in one of her novel readers, and if she'd learned anything from those sensational stories, everything would culminate into a ghastly event meant to entertain someone else—perhaps, in this case, God—at her expense.

She should try her hand at authorship someday. She might be good at it.

You may have more time than you think. What if it's the steward who is keeping Mr. Ogden busy, not the squire? What if Mr. Parker's giving you the time you need? Wishful thinking, perhaps, but she hoped it was true.

When they crested a small hill and the first homes began to dot the greenery ahead of them, Mr. Kelsey said, "The crops haven't been doing well. They thrive in the tenants' individual gardens, but the farms are waterlogged and close to rot."

"It did rain today."

He cast her a withering look.

Elsie sighed. "Well, I can certainly take a look."

He didn't reply, so she simply followed him into the tiny village, averting her eyes, wishing not to be recognized. *Out for a stroll,* she'd say if asked. *Consultant. Curious about the duke's grounds. Eager for Mr. Kelsey's company, is all.*

Not today. The man was practically a storm all in himself. Maybe he'd also run into a past lover. What kind of woman, precisely, would interest a man like Mr. Kelsey?

"Perhaps the queen will decide it's too dreary and hire the Physical Atheneum to clear up the sky, hmm?" Elsie offered. It wasn't fully a jest—it had happened before. With the ability to control temperature and water vapor, powerful physical aspectors *could* create storms, even dismiss them. For a city as large as London, it would take . . . many working together. Elsie wasn't sure of the exact number. But Kent would feel some of the effects.

If Mr. Kelsey replied, she didn't hear it. They stepped between two homes, Mr. Kelsey nodding to a woman comforting an infant on her shoulder. To the right, Elsie spied a physical spell, small and faintly blue, shivering as though cold, at the center of the stone wall. It vanished just as quickly.

When they were out of earshot, she said, "I don't suppose you want me to take the fortifying spells off the homes as well?"

He glanced at her, his green eyes such a contrast to his deeply tanned features.

She shrugged. "Make them more dependent. Easier to cow. The like."

"I don't know why you have it in your mind that the duke means to make enemies of his own tenants." He sounded tired. "Those spells are new, besides."

She paused for a moment. Only a moment, for Mr. Kelsey's long strides easily put distance between them, and she'd rather not run after him in front of so many onlookers. Mr. Kelsey had placed the spells, then. Recently. To strengthen the houses. That could be helpful only to the people who lived here.

Perhaps it had been done in an effort to save the duke money, but it was kind regardless. Not that she'd mention it.

Elsie saw the field in question up ahead—rows and rows of young plants, perhaps corn. She'd never been a farmer, but they did indeed look waterlogged and sickly, almost more brown than green, and spots dotted the leaves like freckles. She paused at the edge of it and crouched down, touching the soil. It wasn't any damper than the rest of the county.

"Anything?" Mr. Kelsey asked.

She stood. Glanced over her shoulder, feeling the prickling of distant stares.

"They'll lose interest soon enough," he assured her.

She took two handfuls of her skirt and hoisted it to the top of her boots. "May I?"

Mr. Kelsey gestured ahead.

She walked down the row, trying to avoid hurting the sad crops at her feet. A few had given up hope and lay uselessly on the dirt, stems too weak to stand.

Please let there be a spell, she thought, chewing on the edge of her tongue. *I can't fix it if there isn't.* And then these people might be denied even their cabbage.

She walked the entire row without so much as a glimpse, sound, or smell of a spell. Mr. Kelsey stood a third of the way into the field, watching her. Skipping a few rows, Elsie stepped carefully back, searching. Smelling, listening. Keeping her senses open.

Again, nothing. Perhaps the tenants would have to move the field. It wasn't too late to plant anew . . . but preparing another piece of land this size would be a difficult task.

She passed a few more rows and traversed the farmland once again. She was a quarter of the way through when she thought she heard something—a sound like a cricket's cry, punching the air before vanishing altogether. She stepped back. Nothing. Crouched—

There.

She gently pushed apart two plants. This time she heard it more clearly, the chirp subtle yet distinct, too wrong to be a hiding insect. A spiritual spell, then. After removing her gloves and shoving them into her collar, she gave up hope for manicured nails and dug into the dirt, the chirping becoming stronger until she found it nearly a foot down. Tiny but strong, its song buzzed in her ears, the sound clear enough now that she saw its knots in her mind's eye.

Mr. Kelsey approached from the west. "Did you find something?"

"Can you hear it?"

He shook his head.

She touched it. "There. It's a spiritual spell, but one I don't recognize. Does the duke or any of the people here employ magic in the fields? To help the plants grow?"

"Often, yes. Did you not find them?"

Elsie shook her head, wondering if a spellbreaker had also been present recently or if, perhaps, the aspector hired to initially boost the crops had never made it to his appointment. "This might very well be the curse you suspected, Mr. Kelsey." She wondered if the Cowls knew about it, but she doubted it. It was very well hidden.

Mr. Kelsey cursed. Or so she thought. It was under his breath and hard to decipher, but it had the sharpness of a curse.

Without waiting for his command, Elsie poked at the spell, searching for its threads. It took her a full minute to find the first one. Her concentration must have been obvious, for Mr. Kelsey didn't interrupt her until she was finished. She stood up and brushed off her skirts, then blinked as blood rushed back to her head.

Mr. Kelsey took her elbow.

"I'm quite all right," she said, but she didn't pull away until she was sure she wouldn't fall and ruin the dress completely. He had a firm but gentle grip, unlike when he'd manhandled her a week ago. She didn't *dislike* it. "I wonder if there are more."

"We'll look," he said. Elsie liked that he included himself in the work, though his aspector blindness made him quite useless.

She studied his face. "You know who did it?"

"I have a very strong suspicion."

She did love a bit of gossip. "Do tell."

He set his jaw, relaxed it. Rubbed his forehead. "The Duke of East Sussex. His wife is a master spiritual aspector and a jealous cow of a woman."

"My, my." Elsie pulled her gloves from her collar. "Such a sharp tongue you have."

"You would call her worse, I'm sure. She wears spells like a heavy perfume and deals them out as freely as the law will allow. The rest she does where the law can't see."

She frowned. "What business is it of hers if this farm fails or succeeds?"

Mr. Kelsey shook his head. "She's a jealous woman. Envies Duchess Abigail a great deal. Perhaps she's cross about Master Merton's interest in Miss Ida; rumor is she's topped off on her magical potential and it's made her bitter."

Topped off. Elsie thought of Ogden's struggle to learn a new physical spell. He was only a novice-level aspector, and he had already emptied his magical cup. She understood discussing one's magical potential was a taboo topic in polite society.

"As far as I know," Mr. Kelsey continued, "she's been forgotten by the Spiritual Atheneum. I honestly can't think of anyone else with motivation."

"She must be a rather self-motivated woman, to come out here and get in the dirt herself."

"She has done as much before. In other ways." He rubbed his half beard. Unfashionable as it was, Elsie thought it suited him rather well. What did those whiskers feel like? "I'm sure I have something in my repertoire to return the favor."

Why on earth are you thinking about his facial hair? She focused on the conversation at hand. "I didn't think you the petty type."

He scowled. "If these people only understand dirty politics, then I'll speak their language."

"While you mimic it quite well"—she stepped over some plants to get better footing—"I fear any sort of similar revenge will only hurt the duchess's tenants, and I'm sure they stay far from the political game."

He glanced at her, the scowl dissipating. She raised an eyebrow.

"You're right, of course." He sighed.

Hands on hips, Elsie scanned the field. She was nearly in the center of it. *If* there were more spells, she imagined they'd be at either of the far ends. She checked the sky. If she left in the next half hour, she could get home without the need to explain her absence. And yet . . . she found herself disliking this spiritual aspector who had turned her jealousy into a weapon wielded against the innocent. She didn't need a directive from the Cowls to see justice done.

"I presume the Duke of East Sussex is in London with the rest of Parliament, since his estate is not a comfortable ride away?"

He folded his arms. "I believe so."

"Then his duchess would be there as well."

His eyes narrowed. "Your point?"

"I assume your reference to her wearing spells would mean those of vanity? Physical and temporal, perhaps? Those are rather simple spells. Quite easy to unravel. I need only run into her, and she might not even notice." She smiled. "It might be enough of a message." Elsie *was* feeling a little reckless.

And she would very much like to stay busy today, if only to keep her thoughts where she wanted them and not allow them leave to stray to Alfred. Or her parents.

Unlovable.

She rubbed her hands together, cleaning them as best she could, before pulling on her gloves. "I'll even do it free of charge." She'd have to find an excuse for her absence if Ogden noticed. She really needed to be more careful. While she doubted Ogden would turn her out, she wanted him to be glad to have her.

Mr. Kelsey's lips quirked. "We sound like children, don't we?"

"Have you never noticed that children have a much happier disposition than adults? Perhaps you might know where the naughty Duchess of East Sussex is staying."

He considered that a moment. "Let's check the rest of the field. And then you *will* ride in a duke's carriage, Miss Camden."

"And you will ride on horseback outside of it." She offered her fakest smile. "For the sake of propriety."

He accepted the offer with a nod, though oddly enough, Elsie found herself wishing he'd fought her on it.

∽

Elsie stood in a short, sunny alleyway, feeling like she was eight years old again. Perhaps they were being foolish, immature, even reckless, but she could not deny she was excited. Her work with the Cowls was always so precise and clandestine. So impersonal.

She could get caught. In fact, if the situation seemed too dangerous for her to act, she would not. Petty revenge certainly wasn't worth the noose, however much the woman deserved it. But if the spells were simple enough, she could work swiftly, invisibly. She'd done it before.

Honestly, it was a soft punishment for a woman trying to starve an entire village.

"There." Bacchus peered onto the main street beside her. The word was especially rich, and Elsie realized he'd said it in his Bajan accent. She tried not to smile as he gestured subtly toward the road. They stood close, half-masked by a small shop for used book and leather repair. A tall but plump woman exited the ribbon shop Bacchus had indicated, dressed in scarlet almost too bright to be tasteful. Was that *velvet*? Goodness, the jacket alone would cost a fortune. She had black hair curled and pinned under a matching hat. Her features were quite lovely, her eyes large and nose small, lips red without paint. She looked too young for a woman in her fifties, which was the age Bacchus had guessed her to be.

Elsie set her quarry: Duchess Matilda Morris, disgraced spiritual aspector, crop ruiner, face liar. The Cowls certainly wouldn't like her.

Duchess Morris walked by a much smaller, plumper woman with gray-streaked curls bushing out from a hat. They seemed to be speaking about something astonishing.

Nobility gossip. How delightful. Though if the duchess had a companion, Elsie's plan might not work.

Elsie stepped into the street, checking the way for horses before hurrying along. She thought she heard Bacchus snap something about being careful. But there was no need to give chase; the two women took the stairs right into the next shop—a millinery.

Slowing her step, Elsie followed, catching the door right before it closed. She feigned intense interest in the window display just inside the entrance.

"I still think it might be bad driving. But I'm beginning to worry. It's not a long trip." Duchess Morris glanced over a few hats with her lip curled in disgust.

"Alma is an aspector, she'll be fine." The woman with the ruddy cheeks picked up a spool of ribbon and laid it across the back of her hand, noting the color against her skin. There was something in her voice familiar to Elsie. She dared a closer glance.

It was Master Lily Merton, from the dinner at Seven Oaks. Elsie turned away quickly, not wishing to be recognized. Or did she? Could she get closer to Duchess Morris if she struck up a conversation with Master Merton first? Would Master Merton know enough about spellbreaking to notice what Elsie was doing?

Doubt crept up her spine. But if it would put Bacchus Kelsey in better spirits, he might let her go sooner. No more lying and slinking around without pay. No more being under his thumb. Elsie did not enjoy being a debtor.

And it might be nice to see him a little more chipper, besides.

"And what will she do if some highway robber accosts her? Bless him? I'm the one who convinced her to take a holiday. What an awful start." Duchess Morris wrung her hands together. "She should have arrived by now. Her sister's telegram was practically manic. Ugh, this place is no better than the last."

Elsie watched from the corner of her eye. *Does the squire know this Alma, too?* she wondered, half-serious.

The owner of the shop stood right there, his brow wrinkling at the woman's insult. Duchess Morris waved a dismissive hand and started back for the door. "I'll send Marie for it. This is a waste of time."

Master Merton returned the ribbon and nodded her thanks at the disgruntled milliner, but another trinket caught her eye. She wandered off, leaving Duchess Morris waiting by the door. Master Merton and the shop owner were distracted. No witnesses.

Elsie steadied herself with a deep breath. She just had to get the timing right. She waited until Duchess Morris grew impatient and headed for the exit, then Elsie turned suddenly—

"Oh!" she exclaimed, barreling right into Duchess Morris. They fell over together, crashing into a table of wares that barely kept them from toppling to the floor. A smattering of tiny temporal runes smelled so strongly they made Elsie gag, and a physical rune she wasn't familiar with glimmered at her, already fraying at the edges. *Perfect.* It was cheaply made and would come apart on its own soon, anyway, so no one could point a finger at Elsie for its disappearance. In a feigned effort to get up, Elsie swiped her hand across the woman's face, catching the physical rune with her thumb. It came apart so easily even another spellbreaker might not have noticed.

"Get off me, you clumsy hag!" Duchess Morris growled in frustration. She pushed Elsie away just as Elsie pulled the threads of a second rune apart. Only two—she hadn't time for more, and there had to be at least a half dozen on the duchess's face alone.

"Oh my!" The millinery owner grabbed Elsie and pulled her upright.

"Miss Camden?" Master Merton asked, wide-eyed.

Seeing Elsie was uninjured, the shop owner quickly sought to aid the woman of higher worth. "My lady, are you all right?"

Master Merton's face pinched. Hushed, she said, "You'd best make yourself scarce," and then pushed her attention to the duchess. "Oh, Matilda! What a bother!" She took Duchess Morris's arm and helped right her. "What an unlucky thing."

The sternness in Master Merton's tone startled Elsie. Finding herself, she bowed her head. "My apologies! I wasn't thinking."

"Obviously." Duchess Morris righted herself and adjusted her skirt. Her brows pulled together, yet they left no creases or wrinkles on her forehead—a spell must have concealed that. But her nose, her *true* nose, jutted from her face like the edge of a cleaver, pointed and sure of itself. Fine lines appeared on the corner of her mouth below it—but only one corner. The other was as smooth as a babe's bottom.

Elsie bit the inside of her cheek and offered a curtsy. The milliner stared.

Master Merton, not yet seeming to notice the change in Duchess Morris's face, turned to Elsie and jerked her head toward the door. She was right, of course. Better that someone of Elsie's social class not stick around for the punishment of a duchess.

But Duchess Morris shifted, blocking Elsie's way to the door, and grabbed Master Merton's wrist. "Really, Lily." Elsie readied a defense, but the exasperated duchess ignored her, instead dragging Master Merton to the exit. Elsie lingered behind to put distance between them, picking up the items she'd knocked off the table and offering another apology to the milliner. Once she deemed it safe, she, too, stepped back out onto the street.

Bacchus strode up to her, watching the backs of the two fleeing women. "You are a natural, Miss Camden." That earlier gloom had dissipated from his manner. The excursion had been successful in two ways, then.

"But of course." She adjusted her hatpin. "If you'll kindly see me home, Mr. Kelsey, I have a growing list of chores that needs my attention."

He almost smiled.

CHAPTER 12

At home, with her hat and chatelaine bag put away and an apron tied around her waist, Elsie finished arranging the tea service in the kitchen before carrying it upstairs. Shifting it to one arm, she knocked lightly and waited for Ogden to invite her into the sitting room.

He lounged on his settee, arm across the drooping back, looking tired but otherwise well. Across from him sat Abel Nash, wearing the same clothes he'd worn the last time Elsie had seen him. He glanced at her briefly and grinned before turning back to Ogden.

Elsie gingerly set the tray on the end table nearest Ogden. Began filling his cup.

Then she saw it, and froze.

There, under an unopened letter on the edge of the settee, was the next novel reader. The continuation of *The Curse of the Ruby*.

She squealed and clanked the teapot against the teacup, spilling a few drops.

Both men glanced at her.

She cleared her throat. "The usual?"

Ogden raised an eyebrow. "When did you start asking?"

Elsie hurriedly dropped a half spoonful of sugar into the cup, followed by far too much cream. Ogden was plenty fit, however, so it didn't seem to be doing him any harm. She set the prepared cup aside and grabbed the empty one, eyes darting to the novel reader. She could make out most of the words on its cover: *Unveil the truth . . . in a time where darkness . . . and he must make his choice.*

Oh my.

"Elsie."

She quickly filled the second cup. "My apologies. The tea is ready. Unless you stopped liking it plain, Mr. Nash?"

He shook his head, his too-long blond hair dusting his eyelashes. "Never could dislike anything you made, Miss Camden. My thanks." It was a wonder he made Emmeline uncomfortable, charming as he was.

She served Ogden first, then Nash.

"Oh, take it, Elsie." Ogden tried to sound exasperated but did a poor job of it. "The letter is yours, too."

"Is it? I mean, oh! The post. Why, thank you, Mr. Ogden." She snatched the novel reader and the letter atop it with both hands. Beneath it she spied a folded newspaper, the word *poacher* catching her attention.

Continued from page 2 . . . insists that the escaped poachers will be caught and brought to justice. "It isn't merely about a pheasant," Bamber said. "It's about common decency and respect."

Elsie's lips parted. Escaped poachers! It must have been from the carriage! She'd been successful, and now the boys would go free—

"Elsie?" Ogden asked.

Lifting her head, she asked, "Will that be all?"

Ogden waved her off with a limp hand, and Elsie gladly left the men to their business.

The window of her room was closed, making the room noticeably stuffy, but she didn't bother opening it. She had a tendency to vocalize her reactions to stories, and passersby on the street had no need to hear that.

Elsie leapt onto the bed on her stomach, her corset biting her hip as she adjusted to a more comfortable position. *Let us see if the baron figures out—*

Oh, letter.

She paused, taking note of the rough paper, sealed with a dot of uncolored candle wax pressed flat with a thumb. The magazine slipped from her fingers as she snatched up the paper. Turned it over. Read her name, written in flowing handwriting. She knew that handwriting—it belonged to the postmaster who served Juniper Down. Where she'd last seen her family.

This letter was from Agatha Hall.

Jerking upright, Elsie snapped the wax and opened the short letter. Her hope instantly cracked—it would be another missive telling her no Camdens had passed through, and no one had heard word of them. But the familiar mantra wasn't in these words.

> *Elsie,*
> *I know you're hopeful. I know you're dedicated. But the Camdens aren't coming back. It's time to give up, lass. Nothing will change, and you're costing us postage we can't afford. I was happy to help you then. Now it's time to leave things be and move on with your life.*
> *Sincerely,*
> *Henry Hall*

Agatha's husband.

Elsie stared at the letter, not quite comprehending its meaning. She read it again, slowly. *Nothing will change.* Those words stood out starkly against the cheap paper. *Nothing will change. Nothing will change.*

The Camdens aren't coming back.

They wanted her to stop writing. Stop asking. Stop wasting their shillings. She crumpled the letter in her hand. Strode to the unlit fireplace and tossed it in. So what? Had she really expected anything else after all these years? She had friends, here in the stonemasonry shop, and she had the Cowls. Their work mattered. The part she played made a difference.

It was enough, wasn't it?

Elsie found herself staring out the window for an inordinate amount of time. She struggled to come back to herself, but her thoughts were . . . not there. She was a blank canvas. But that was all right. Better than the dripping paint she'd been the night before.

She needed to busy herself, that was all. It wasn't as if she lacked for things to do! She had to catch up on her missed work.

So she strode downstairs to the studio, leaving the novel reader forgotten on her bed.

~

It was only an hour's ride to Seven Oaks in Kent, but that morning it felt like Elsie rode clear to Liverpool. She'd left at the crack of dawn, right after Ogden had departed for the squire's home. He'd sounded hopeful about finishing the project soon, which meant Elsie had to sort out just how to balance this mess.

She had made the trip early because she needed a trinket to present to Emmeline tomorrow, for her eighteenth birthday. This was the only time she had to find one. Fortunately, Emmeline was easy to please. Unfortunately, much of Elsie's funds were being squandered on cab fare.

The driver let her off at the market street, and she thanked him silently with a wave, having already paid his fee. She rubbed her lower back as she walked. The town was awake but only just; not yet crowded, no voices hawking wares. But there were people out and about, setting up and settling in. A few men nodded to her as she passed, and she returned the gesture twice before pinning her hat a little lower. With her luck, the Cowls would send her on another mission to Kent, and someone on the street would recognize her.

She found a little Romany cart down a side street. From them, she purchased a pin studded with polished quartz. Emmeline could wear it to church. Normally Elsie would be pleased with such a find, but she couldn't bring herself to feel any pride today. Stowing the pin in her bag, she started toward Seven Oaks.

"Miss Camden?"

She turned at the sound of the familiar voice just as Mr. Bacchus Kelsey came strolling up beside her. His darker coloring and blue frock coat made him blend perfectly with the street lit with fresh dawn, like an artist had painted him there. An artist with a very good hand. His eyes looked spectacularly green, like endless rolling hills just before twilight set in.

Pinching herself to remain present, she nodded to him. "Good day, Mr. Kelsey." *He is only kind because you're helping him. Because he's forcing you to help him. Bah!*

"You're early." He fell in step beside her. He held two old-looking books in his hands, but Elsie didn't try to read the titles. Not today. With Emmeline taken care of, her mind turned elsewhere, sitting on some forgotten easel, waiting for the artist to remember her.

"I don't believe we set a time," she countered, watching the cobblestones pass underfoot.

He thought a moment. "I don't believe we did."

She nodded. It wasn't a long walk to the duke's estate, though she wouldn't have minded a long walk. They were good for the body and the mind. A walk after a rainstorm, especially, but it hadn't rained yesterday or last night.

"Are you well?"

She glanced up at him, and the cylinder of her thoughts spun a moment before firing. "I believe we've only been chatting for a few seconds, Mr. Kelsey. I doubt you've had enough time to gauge my health. But yes, I am well."

"Hmm." It was a sound of disbelief.

The market street bent near the end, almost like a river, and they took the turn together. On another day Elsie might worry someone would eye them and wonder after her, a young woman strolling with a man, but no one paid her any mind, other than the occasional nod. They didn't even notice Mr. Kelsey, but perhaps they were used to him by now.

Once they cleared the market street and reached the road that stretched to the estate, Mr. Kelsey asked, "Are you in trouble with your employer?"

Which one? she almost asked, but instead said, "No."

"He's treating you well?"

She blinked a couple of times, feeling the need to wake up. "Mr. Ogden treats me very well. Like a daughter." *Daughter.*

The word sat like a lead ball in her chest.

"I believe you are lying to me."

She glared at him. "Mr. Ogden—"

He raised his free hand. "About your state of mind, not your employer."

Elsie raised her chin. "You never asked about my state of mind, Mr. Kelsey. One generally perceives the question of wellness in relation to the body."

"Now you are being more yourself."

She folded her arms. "Am I?"

"Yes. You're being difficult." He said it with a sliver of humor.

Her arms dropped back to her sides as quickly as she had lifted them. "I'm sorry. I don't mean to be."

"And now you're apologizing, which truly alarms me."

She sighed. She could see the top of the duke's estate through the trees.

The lead ball in her chest was maddening.

"Since you already think me a criminal," she tried, focusing again on the road, "I don't suppose it does any harm to tell you." She'd like to tell someone about Mr. Hall's letter, about the death knell of her foolish hopes, and she'd already worried Emmeline and Ogden enough over her drama with Alfred.

Mr. Kelsey was silent. Listening.

She straightened her back, as though that would add dignity to her situation. She had already begun to regret her offer of information, but it would do her good to let it out. And what was Bacchus Kelsey to her? He already knew her biggest secret.

"I came to work with Mr. Ogden"—she left out her time with the squire—"from a workhouse."

Mr. Kelsey hesitated. "That . . . is not uncommon. Unless changes have been made to the system concerning the impoverished."

Elsie shrugged. "I was in a workhouse because I lost my family. Or they lost me. On purpose, I suppose." She rolled her lips together. She never spoke about this to anyone, not in detail. Ogden knew some of the particulars, but she'd told him only because she had to prove she had as much experience as many of his older candidates. It was strange speaking about it now, like reciting poetry in German. "I mean, we stayed with a family in a small town west of here one night, and only I remained in the morning. And so I write to that family every now and then, to see if they've received any word of my parents or siblings. And yesterday they wrote me back telling me to stop wasting their postage."

When Mr. Kelsey didn't respond, she took her eyes off the cobblestones and looked up at him. His gaze was unfocused, like he was thinking.

"I suppose that's why I'm such a vagabond," she tried, but the humor fell flat. "And I would appreciate you keeping it to yourself. I have a good standing in Brookley, you know."

Mr. Kelsey shook his head. "No, I . . . I mean to express my sympathies. I am . . . not sure how to do it."

"I appreciate the attempt."

"If it is any consolation, I myself am a bastard." When she gaped at the confession, he dismissed it with a wave. "My father did not treat me any differently for it, but he never married my mother. She was of a common background and hailed from the Algarve; my grandparents didn't approve. But your story is not one I've heard before. And I've heard many."

She regarded him for a moment, but his words were genuine. "Is Barbados so exciting?"

"I suppose that depends on your definition of excitement." It was not a jest. "But I do offer them. My sympathies, that is. I'm sorry the family is not more understanding."

She pinched the seam of her left glove. "They had little enough coin, and it's been fifteen years! I can hardly blame them." She thought she did a good job of making her voice sound light.

They reached the duke's stone wall, the one that still made Elsie's wrists itch when she looked at it.

Mr. Kelsey stopped abruptly.

"Miss Camden," he began, very serious and suddenly rather tall. "I have decided your debt is repaid. Twice over, considering. You have no more need to drag yourself here to ensure my silence. Your secret is forgotten."

Elsie stared at him for a second. Just like that? "Well, if pity is all it takes, I should have told you my life story sooner!"

He held up a hand. "It is not pity."

She paused, regarding him. Something stupid and hopeful fluttered in her chest.

"I'd already decided as much before I saw you this morning," he said. "There is little more I need your services for, besides."

She flinched at the words before biting the inside of her cheek and forcing her expression to relax. *Doesn't need me.* She tried not to dwell on it. She barely knew the man, and yet her chest had grown heavier at the declaration. Frustration—thank the Lord, she could work with frustration—steamed under her skin. Not frustration at Mr. Kelsey, but at herself for feeling *hurt*, of all things, by his dismissal! She should be glad. She *was* glad. No more sneaking away to Kent, no more late nights finishing her work, no more shillings spent on cabs. In fact, she'd been mistaken. It wasn't disappointment that feathered beneath her ribs, just surprise. Surprise and relief. Most definitely.

"All right, then." She paused to give him a chance to recant. Not that she wanted him to. Blessed freedom! "I don't suppose you'll reimburse my expenses to journey here this morning."

She expected him to refuse, but to her surprise, he reached into his wallet and handed her a few shillings. Plenty to see her back to Brookley.

Elsie felt awkward accepting the money, but it would be more embarrassing to suddenly change her mind, so she put it in her reticule. She found herself at a loss for words at their unexpected parting. She couldn't thank him—he had blackmailed her, for goodness' sake! But he'd also been true to his word. But she wouldn't thank him for that. That was expected of a gentleman.

"I suppose I'll head home." She pinched her chatelaine in her hands. "Good day, Mr. Kelsey."

He nodded. She started down the road, brushing the tangle of her feelings aside. But a new thought rose to mind, and she paused. Turned around.

"If I could ask you a personal question."

The statement took him aback. He looked less stern when caught by surprise. The softening of his features made him more handsome. Not that she thought him handsome. Hardly.

Before he could respond, she rushed out, "Since we're being so honest with each other."

His eyes narrowed. "Very well."

For a moment she considered tact—surely it was too personal to ask such a question—but the mystery had been weighing on her, and there wasn't a roundabout way of doing this. If she wanted to know, she would have to be straightforward. "What spells do you wear?" she blurted.

That really took him by surprise. His face opened as though she'd just told him the origin of the universe.

She spread her hands in a sort of apology. "I do have a knack for sensing them."

He moved stiffly, awkwardly, before deciding to busy his free hand by stroking his beard. "Of course you do."

She waited. If he didn't tell her, the suspense would drive her mad.

Turning, Mr. Kelsey leaned against the stone wall. "I suppose there's no harm in telling you. I trust you to keep my secrets, if only because I already know yours."

"Yes. Please, remind me again."

He studied her face. Elsie put a hand on the back of her neck—a rather ineffective attempt to cool an oncoming blush. After a moment, he pushed off the wall, tugged down his waistcoat, and stepped a little closer.

"When I was a youth, I began to exhibit the symptoms of polio."

Whatever Elsie had expected, it was not that. Her lips parted, but she dared not speak.

Mr. Kelsey glanced away. "My father brought me here, as there are no master temporal aspectors on the island. The spell you sensed is one that slows the spread of the disease." He looked uncomfortable, but his voice remained even. "It will not hold forever, of course. Spells cannot stop time, only impede its effects. In truth, the reason I've come here is not merely to test for my mastership, but to obtain a spell that will help me once the disease spreads."

"I see." Her gaze dropped to his torso. As a youth . . . How long had the spell been there? Ten years? Fifteen? Aspecting could do a lot for one's health, especially if one had the money to afford it. But it couldn't cure something as severe as polio. Just as it couldn't stop aging. Only slow it.

"My condolences."

"I will not subjugate you to unwanted sympathies if you will return the favor."

She nodded. "Of course." Paused. "And what of the other?"

"Pardon?"

"The other spell."

His brow knit together. "I don't know what you mean."

Her hands went to her hips. "Really, Bacchus. And here I thought we were being friends."

He took another step toward her, almost close enough for discomfort. Close enough for her to smell the temporal spell beneath his clothes. "What do you mean?" he asked again.

She gawked at him. "But I know I felt it . . ."

Confusion glimmered in his eyes.

She rolled her lips together. Swallowed. Lifted a gloved hand. "May I?"

It took him a moment to understand, but he nodded.

And so Elsie, after checking the street for onlookers, reached forward and splayed her hand against his chest, just over his diaphragm.

Well, that's . . . firm, she thought, ignoring the warmth creeping up her neck. There was the temporal spell, its scent like a sunlit forest floor. But there was a layer under it. A tightly knitted spell that made her think of the runes sown in the fields. Nestled away, out of sight. Just as before, she couldn't see, hear, smell, or feel it, but she *sensed* it in a way she couldn't describe. Whatever it was, it was powerful, to call to her in such a way. To conceal its alignment.

She took her hand away. "You can't feel that?"

He shook his head and sighed. Had he been holding his breath?

"There are two spells on your person, Bacchus Kelsey." She met his gaze. "One layered under the other. I cannot decipher what the first is without removing the temporal spell, but I am sure as a gun that it is there."

Mr. Kelsey lifted a hand and placed it where Elsie's had just been. "You must be mistaken."

"I am not."

But he shook his head. "There is no other spell on me. It would have interfered with the temporal spell." He sounded like he doubted his own words.

"The aspector who slowed the polio wouldn't have sensed it. Have you never worked with a spellbreaker before?" She lowered her voice. "A legal one, I mean?"

"No." He sounded almost defensive. Or simply confused. "No, I haven't."

She rubbed her hands together. "I didn't mean to upset you."

"I'm not—" But he turned away, not finishing the statement. He rubbed his eyes. "You are untrained."

She folded her arms. "You determined that by my wildly unsuccessful work, did you?"

He clutched his books. "I'll . . . look into it. Thank you, Miss Camden."

The words might as well have been a whip, the way they snapped through the air. Elsie stepped back as though she could avoid their sharpness. *He really didn't know.* The temporal spell was of such a sensitive nature . . . perhaps she shouldn't have told him of the second, not in his moment of vulnerability. But it was too late to do anything about it now.

Unsure what else to do, Elsie nodded, and Bacchus Kelsey turned for the estate, disappearing behind its wall.

CHAPTER 13

He did not believe Elsie Camden had lied to him.

But he also did not want to trust her.

Bacchus stood in his bedroom, looking out the window at the grounds below. He did not spend a lot of time in this space; he used it merely for sleeping—something he needed too much of lately, thanks to the stunted polio. There were always things in need of doing, tasks in need of completing. Standing still was bad enough. Soon he would be forced to *sit* still.

But here he was, pensive, staring out the window like an invalid, lost in his own thoughts.

He still remembered the day his father had brought him to Master Pierrelo. He'd been almost seventeen, already taller than his father. They had just returned from his mother's funeral in Portugal. His father had made sure she was comfortable all her years, but he'd never truly involved her in Bacchus's life, outside a single visit and a handful of letters. Whether or not she wanted to be part of Bacchus's life, he wasn't sure; but as a bastard, he would have lived a more affluent life with his father than his mother. Regardless, Bacchus had been sick from the loss of his mother, the travel over the sea, and the onset of his disease.

He remembered everything the temporal aspector had said. Remembered the spell warming his skin. *This is not a cure,* Master Pierrelo had cautioned. *Only more time.*

Bacchus had taken that warning to heart. He'd researched, studied, and worked until he had a plan in place. A plan that revolved around a spell he had not yet obtained. A spell that might help him move his legs once paralysis set in. If not, it would be an extension of his hands, allowing him to work without ever needing to stand.

If pity would have swayed the physical assembly, Bacchus might have shared his story with them. But men determined to be uncaring were never persuaded otherwise.

He touched his chest. He could still feel the prints of Miss Camden's fingers there. He hadn't thought her touch would affect him, yet the pressure of her hand lingered like she'd cast her own spell. In that brief moment, he had seen more of her than she usually revealed—sadness limning her eyes, frustration creasing her brow. But the certainty with which she'd declared the existence of another spell, one he had *no recollection of,* had dissipated any tender feelings.

He didn't know how large the rune was, but Miss Camden insisted on its presence. How long had she known? Had she learned of it that first night, when he'd caught her discharging his spell? During the reenchanting of the wall? Or perhaps at Isaiah's dinner, when he'd escorted her into the dining room. Perhaps he'd let his guard down, allowing the lighting and her sharp blue eyes to put him at ease—

Had she told him about the spell to torture him, let him stew in worry as revenge for making her work? Did she mean to continue her employment? But he didn't blooming *pay* her, damn it.

And truthfully, she didn't seem like that kind of woman. Though she masked it well, Bacchus suspected she genuinely cared about people, despite her . . . illegal tendencies.

No, he did not believe she'd lied. He only wished she had.

He took to the narrow writing desk in the corner. Readied a pen. Wrote briskly, scratching the paper, ignoring the few places where the ink bled. Shaking the message dry, he folded it over and scrawled *Master Jacques Pierrelo* on the back. Although she had told him the master wouldn't have sensed the first spell, the man might know something.

Someone had to know something.

Letter in hand, Bacchus charged for the door. He pulled it open, finding a startled footman on the other side.

The servant bowed. "My apologies, Mr. Kelsey, but you're needed in the drawing room."

He huffed. "What for?"

The man twisted in discomfort. "Perhaps you'd best see for yourself."

Eyeing the servant and hating the way every single Englishman danced around his intent, Bacchus nodded, pocketed the note, and strode toward the drawing room. The manor was huge, but the room wasn't far. He reached it and opened the door. The duke paced before the pianoforte, obviously disgruntled about something. The duchess had her back to him. A constable stood erect near the other entrance.

"What is this?" Bacchus asked, shutting the door behind him.

Isaiah said, "He only means to question you, Bacchus."

Bacchus turned toward the constable. "What has happened?" *They found out about Elsie.* His stomach tightened. He'd made a promise to her, and he intended to keep it . . . that, and the thought of the woman behind bars filled him with dread.

"Please sit down, Mr. Kelsey." The constable, a short, rounded man in full uniform, gestured to one of the chairs. Bacchus selected one that allowed him to see all three people in the room. He took his time, trying to think of excuses for both himself and Miss Camden, ones that wouldn't immediately convict her.

The constable pulled out a pad of paper and a pencil. "What is your relationship to Felton Shaw?"

"Felton Shaw?" He repeated the foreign name, trying to hide the relief lightening his shoulders. "I don't . . . Wait." Wasn't that the name of the man Bacchus had lost the opus to at the auction three days ago? "A gentleman in his forties, brown hair cut short? Wealthy?"

The constable nodded.

"I am barely acquainted with him." What was this about? "He attended an auction at Christie's Auction House this past Wednesday. Wore a gray suit. We bid on the same opus. He won."

"And that was the end of your acquaintance?"

"No. I spoke to him after the auction about purchasing a spell from the opus. He seemed interested until I named a master spell. Then he dismissed me somewhat forcibly and left."

"You did not follow him?"

Bacchus narrowed his eyes. "No. And my servant did not, either."

The constable nodded, eyes on his paper. "Your servant's name?"

He didn't like the way the man asked his questions, as if he were insinuating guilt. *Cooperate, Bacchus. The duke will protect Rainer.* "Rainer Moor. What is this about? Has Mr. Shaw filed a complaint against me?"

"Mr. Shaw is in hospital in serious condition." The constable finally looked up. "He was stabbed last night, after his home was broken into. Robbed."

Bacchus stiffened.

"Among the items taken was the Bennett opus. The only other witness is suffering from a head injury he will likely not recuperate from."

The duchess slumped, covering her face with her hands.

"That is . . . terrible," Bacchus managed.

The constable agreed with a dip of his head. "You were seen having a confrontation with him at the auction house."

"I would not call it a confrontation."

"Where were you last night, Mr. Kelsey? Between the hours of one and three a.m.?"

"Sleeping." He let the obviousness of the statement leak into his tone.

"Where?"

"In my bedroom. Until midnight, I was sharing some Madeira with the duke in his study." Though truthfully he didn't care for the drink—he preferred rum. "Before that, I dined with the Scott family and listened to Miss Josie practice the pianoforte."

The duke interjected, "Just as I told you."

The constable nodded. "You have excellent character witnesses, Mr. Kelsey." He made a small gesture toward the duke and duchess. "If I have more questions, I will return. I recommend not leaving the country anytime soon."

Bacchus relaxed, but only slightly. "I do not plan to." Not until he had the spell he needed.

He wondered, briefly, if he'd be the one hospitalized had he won the auction.

"And your servant?"

"Rainer sleeps with the other servants in the household. There will be many witnesses to his presence here."

The constable glanced at the duke. "Your Grace, if you would take me downstairs, so I might inquire?"

"Yes, of course." The Duke of Kent crossed the room quickly, gesturing to the door behind the constable. "Right this way." Then, in the hallway, likely to the butler, "No need, I'll escort him myself."

A long breath passed through Bacchus's lips. He leaned back in the chair. "I take it the stolen goods have not been recovered."

The duchess shook her head, distressed. "No. Oh, my dear, I hate it when my husband stays up late with his drink, but I am so glad he did it last night."

Bacchus nodded. Isaiah Scott had made the offer upon noticing Bacchus's distracted state. He'd been mulling over Elsie Camden—and her declaration of a second spell—ever since her dismissal.

"First Alma Digby goes missing, and now this." The duchess dotted her eyes with the knuckle of her index finger. "Not to mention Baron Halsey and Viscount Byron! Oh, their poor wives . . . I think I'll walk the gardens. Would you care to join me?"

Bacchus stood. "I might see how Rainer is faring, if that's all right."

"Yes, of course." She waved him away.

Nodding his respects, Bacchus left the room, heading for the servants' hall.

Less than half an hour later, the constable departed, having crossed Rainer's name off his list.

∽

Elsie could not seem to finish her latest novel reader. Sometimes the words blurred together. Sometimes her imagination floated to other things. Sometimes she pictured the baron as an Algarve man, and that threw off the imagery she'd worked up in her head for the tale.

Even here, sitting in a small chapel with the story tucked into a hymnal, she could not read. And so she listened to an unfamiliar preacher speak on pride, and occasionally turned to admire the stained-glass windows. She should be happy, now that things were back to normal. The last week had been nothing *but* normal. No sneaking off to Kent, no surreptitious notes from the Cowls. She might not hear from them for months. Even Ogden had finished up his work with the squire and was home more. Elsie liked having him home. Liked the subtle feeling of family that snuggled up against the walls of the stonemasonry shop.

And yet she was unsettled.

Ogden had taken them to Dulwich today. The church was small, but there was a spiritual aspector present regardless, one so young he had to be an intermediate magician, at best. He couldn't even grow a beard yet, Elsie was sure. Then again, the baron in *The Curse of the Ruby* certainly didn't have one.

At least she needn't worry about unwanted blessing spells.

She shut her hymnal and set it on her knees. Ogden was tracing crooked stars on his leg. Emmeline looked ready to fall asleep, the quartz-tipped pin stuck through her collar.

Elsie pinched her, causing her to choke on a little gasp, then handed her the hymnal. Usually, Elsie gushed about the story to Emmeline at night, once their hair was unpinned and their dresses put away, but she simply couldn't concentrate this week. Poor Emmeline had been pining to know what happened next. She couldn't read terribly well, but she could read well enough. When she looked down at the sneaky novel reader, she smiled and turned back to its first page.

She'd gotten to page 7 by the time the sermon ended and the congregation filed out. There were a good deal of gentlemen and ladies present, wearing their ultrafine clothing, waving themselves with cloth fans, though it wasn't even June yet. Ogden had found an old comrade or some such to chat with, and Emmeline remained perched on her seat, engrossed in the magazine, so Elsie pushed past all the well-to-dos, out into the early-afternoon sunlight.

Stretching her arms overhead, she started down the street, wanting to stretch her legs before being sausaged back into the cab. She heard chatter around her about a recent ball, a hunting party, and a vote for something. Oddly enough, Elsie didn't want to hear the gossip today. And so she strolled to the edge of the street, where it opened onto a small park. She circled the park, admiring the trees, before heading back. Most likely, neither Ogden nor Emmeline had noticed her absence yet.

A plump woman on the other side of the road tripped on a raised cobblestone, spilling the stack of books, papers, and ledgers in her arms. Quickly crossing, Elsie hurried over to help.

"Oh, thank you, dear," the woman said as Elsie handed her a parchment scrawled with diagrams.

Elsie paused. "Master Merton?"

Master Lily Merton glanced up. "Oh! What are the chances, us running into each other again! Only this time I'm the one tripping."

Elsie handed her a ledger. "You should have a manservant with you to carry these things."

"Oh, no, I can't stand the sound of people while I work, even bustling servants. Emma, would you hand me that?" She pointed to a fallen pencil.

"Elsie," Elsie gently corrected, snatching up the pencil.

"Oh goodness, I knew that." She stood, and Elsie helped her, ensuring nothing else tumbled off the stack. "Well, it's still nice to run into a familiar face!"

"Are you not from Dulwich?" Elsie asked.

The older woman shook her head. "No, not at all." She frowned. "Oh, my dear Miss . . . it was Camden, right?"

Elsie nodded.

Master Merton let out a breath that made her cheeks sag. "The atheneum just let go *three* of its acolytes. We've such a mess on our hands." Leaning forward, she added, "And that is putting it mildly."

"The atheneum terminated their contracts?" Elsie asked, unable to quell her curiosity.

"They're with the bobbies now," she said, using the nickname for the police force. Again lowering her voice, she added, "Suspected of having stolen or lost opuses. A few of them have been missing for some time. Now the rest of us, the elderly included, are having to step up and fill their spaces. I've been to two churches already today, and I have a paper I need to finish." She jerked her chin toward her abundant research. "I feel it in my hips already and it isn't even luncheon. Pah!"

"I'm terribly sorry." Elsie glanced at the ledgers. "The atheneum is missing opuses?" It was her understanding the spellbooks were kept locked away behind secret doors, so even the sneakiest thieves couldn't find them.

Master Merton shook her head, her short curls dancing around her ears. "Don't repeat that, please."

"But there's been a lot of activity with opuses lately." Elsie matched the aspector's volume. "I've heard of . . . murders."

Master Merton nodded, grim. "Oh yes. It's not related, of course. A couple of our foolhardy acolytes decided to cause some trouble or tripped their way into it." She clicked her tongue. "I don't like reading or hearing the news, my dear. It's too dreadful. How can a person be cheerful when bogged down with all of that?"

Elsie's stomach tightened. "Of course. Where are you headed? Let me help you."

"Oh no, I'm just down this way, really. I imagine you need to get back to your family."

A pang hit her chest. "I do."

The smile returned. Cheerfulness did suit Master Merton better than worry. "Thank you, dear. Pass my regards to the duke's family for me."

I don't think I'll be seeing them again. But she nodded.

When she returned to the church, Ogden and Emmeline were waiting outside for her, Ogden checking his silver pocket watch.

"Sorry," Elsie said upon reaching them, "I went for a stroll and had to gather a library's worth of material for an acquaintance who'd dropped it."

Ogden nodded. "Fair enough. I'm eager for luncheon. Shall we?"

He offered his arms to Emmeline and Elsie. Pinching a smile, Elsie took his left and let her employer lead them toward a cab for hire. *Family,* Master Merton had called them. They were, in a sense. But truth be told, were Emmeline to procure another position, or get married, she'd have no real reason to keep in touch—Emmeline had her own family. Three sisters and both parents. Even Ogden had relations. No children, and his parents were deceased, but he had a smattering of nieces and nephews he saw at Christmastime. Sometimes with Elsie in tow, sometimes without. Because while Ogden really was like a father to her, he wasn't her father. He and *his* family had no true obligation to her.

The ride home was uneventful, especially since Emmeline had now thoroughly engrossed herself in the novel reader and did not come up for air until they arrived in Brookley. Only once they were inside did Emmeline hand the story back and grab her apron.

Elsie watched her, bemused. "What are you smiling about?"

The maid giggled. "There's kissing."

Elsie blinked and opened the magazine, trying to guess what page Emmeline had left off on. Kissing? How scandalous!

Her ears heated, which was, of course, foolish. She'd been kissed before, though that had been some time ago.

Horse hooves sounded outside, but Elsie didn't pay them much mind. She tucked the novel reader away and grabbed a second apron. "Let me help you. I'm famished." *And need to occupy myself.*

"Just cold cuts and potatoes, I think." Emmeline had a peeler in her hand. "Could you set water on the stove?"

Elsie grabbed a pot and filled it at the pump sink, set it on the stove, and stoked the fire. "I might eat them raw at this point."

Emmeline snickered. "Won't take too long, not if I cut them extra small."

A knock sounded on the front door.

"Emmeline!" Ogden yelled from upstairs. He always went straight upstairs after church. He hated his formal attire.

"I'll get it." Taking off her apron and wiping her hands on it, Elsie hurried to the studio. It was Sunday, so the front door was locked, but on occasion a visitor still popped by. Ogden might have invited someone for tea. Elsie stashed the apron under the counter before coming around to unbolt the door.

Bacchus Kelsey stood on the other side.

CHAPTER 14

Elsie gawked at him a long moment. Then she shoved him from the doorway, followed him outside, and closed the door behind her.

"What are you doing here?" she asked in a hard whisper. Her heart was beating too fast for it to be explained by the effort of pushing the door, and her blasted ears were heating again. She swept back a few curls in an attempt to hide the color.

"I need your help." His voice sounded wary. He was well groomed, but there was a tiredness about his eyes and a tightness to his features, as though he hadn't relaxed in days. He was close enough for her to smell wood, citrus, and mushroom.

She could faintly sense the spell beneath his clothes.

Releasing the door handle, she asked, "What's wrong?"

"Nothing that was not wrong before." He grasped his hands behind his back. "But I need to know what the second spell is. It's driving me mad."

She nodded, slowly. It would drive her mad as well. "I might have to take off the temporal one first. They're right on top of each other."

"I know." He glanced toward the heavy carriage outside the house. *That* wouldn't draw attention at all. "Which is why I need you to meet with the aspector who placed it, so he can replace it after we've sorted this out. I dare not let too much time pass without it."

Elsie opened her mouth. Closed it. Her stomach wound in knots. Jerking her head toward the back of the house, she tromped around the corner to wait for him. The moment Mr. Kelsey came into view, she said, "I can see two very large issues with that. First, the Temporal Atheneum is in *Newcastle upon Tyne*. That's, what, eight, nine days away? I can't just leave for a fortnight. Second, as previously discussed, I don't have a ready chaperone." And she wouldn't get one. How much harder would it be to hide her spellbreaking abilities with an old matron following her every move?

"I can pay you."

That perked her interest. "Well, that's certainly a better offer than blackmail."

He looked satisfactorily mortified. "Elsie—"

"Also, what am I to do, hide out in the brush with you to take off the spell? Then sit on my backside while you run in and get the spell replaced?"

He let out a long breath. "Master Pierrelo will not ask to see your registration. No one will. It's in bad taste."

Rolling her lips together, Elsie considered. "That does not move Newcastle upon Tyne closer to London."

"No, but he's visiting family in Ipswich." He said each word carefully, his green eyes locked on hers. Goodness, he had remarkable eyelashes.

"Ipswich," Elsie repeated, focusing. "That's still a three-day journey."

"We can do it in two."

"I may not be gently bred, but I don't think it's a wise idea to be trapped in a carriage with a bachelor for two—no—*four*, days."

He rolled his eyes. "You make it sound like a chore."

Folding her arms, she countered, "Not that your dry disposition isn't pleasing, Almost-Master Kelsey, but I do have a reputation."

"We'll take separate carriages."

Elsie paused. That might work if he could arrange it, but—

"And how do I explain such a long absence to Mr. Ogden? No one in this house knows about me."

"Tell him you're visiting fam—" He stopped himself, but not before the suggestion stabbed her already sore heart. Today was destined to be terrible, she could feel it. "Do you have any distant relatives, friends, something to use as cover?"

"I used all my *cover* on Kent."

Mr. Kelsey rubbed his beard, considering. "I will make something work."

She dropped her arms. "And how will you do that?"

"Trust me."

Two simple words, but they made Elsie pause. *Trust me.* Could she? Bacchus Kelsey had been a thorn in her side, but he *had* kept his word to her before. She owed him nothing now. He was pleading for help.

She wanted to give it.

She studied his face. The new lines of stress there. The nice set of his nose—

Oh, stop it.

"Very well." The relief was notable on his features. "If you can make it happen, then I will go. But you'll have to be very convincing. Now leave, before I have to explain why there's a *duke's carriage* outside the masonry shop."

"Thank you, Elsie. Thank you."

She waved a dismissive hand, and as directed, Mr. Kelsey departed. Elsie stayed behind the house until she heard the horses pull forward. Then she peeked around the corner and watched the carriage disappear down the road.

Four days with Bacchus—two there, two back. She quite liked the way her Christian name sounded on his lips, though she'd rather hear it in his native dialect. She tried to imagine how it would sound. *Elsie. El-sie.*

"Oh, hush," she whispered to herself. Though there was no denying the pain in her chest had dissipated. Now it was time to wait and see what sort of plan an advanced physical aspector could hatch to steal her away.

She certainly hoped he was successful.

∽

Ogden had a habit of making his shelves look like mayhem.

He placed things haphazardly when he put them away, sometimes on the shelf easiest to reach, sometimes on the highest one. She would have understood the habit better had he simply put things away in the most convenient spot, but the highest shelves were quite high. One had to *try* to stow something there. It made no sense. Elsie occasionally tried to talk to Ogden about his organizational habits, and he always nodded as if he were listening, but her encouragement made no difference. He still put his paint away in three different places, chisels here and there, and sometimes his lunch pail would even find a place near the floor. It was no wonder he struggled to remember where his tools were.

Retrieving a ladder, Elsie began her reorganization project by tackling the topmost shelves, pulling things down to sort them. It wouldn't hurt to dust the entire wall; lint bits stuck under her fingernails.

It was as she stretched on her toes to grab a book from the shelf that the culprit walked in. "Elsie, I've just gotten the most interesting letter."

She snatched the book and set it on a lower shelf, one she could reach from the ground. "And what is that?"

"There's a new women's school in Ipswich—"

Elsie tottered and grabbed the ladder to steady herself.

"—for accounting and secretarial training. I'm surprised they even know who I am, but they're offering a week-long course for my employees for a rather inexpensive sum."

Elsie cleared her throat of incredulity. "Really?" *Clever, Bacchus.* Dusting off her hands, she climbed down the ladder and crossed the room. Ogden handed her the letter.

"Accounting. I already know my figures." She looked over the smooth penmanship. Had he written this himself? How many confidantes did he have? "Oh, but it's advanced . . . hmmm. That is inexpensive. I could pay for it myself."

Ogden stuck his hands on his hips the same way he did when a nice-looking man came around the studio. Always looking out for her, he was. "Are you interested?"

Elsie considered how best to play this. She hated lying to Ogden, but it was for a good purpose. Not like she was going off on a tryst.

"A week long?" She feigned consideration. If nothing else, the Cowls' demands had taught her to be convincing. "But it would be useful, to help more with the books."

"You're already quite helpful with the books." He took the letter back, examining it.

He was doubting, so Elsie added, "The squire's work is done. If there were ever a time to go . . . perhaps I could see what it's about, and if it's good, we could send Emmeline for the next course."

"You'd have to leave tomorrow to make this class." He spoke half under his breath.

Elsie hesitated a moment before saying, "I . . . suppose I don't need to go. I'll stay. I have shelves to organize."

She saw the sliver of guilt form between Ogden's eyebrows. Frowning, he glanced at the shelves. "I'll pay for half."

Elsie smiled. "It's settled, then." She kissed Ogden on the cheek. "It will be an adventure."

And she'd make sure Bacchus paid her back.

⌒

Elsie waited outside Brookley on a gray day for her ride. The sun had not quite come up, though even if it had, the gray-smeared sky would have hidden any of its cheeriness. It sprinkled ever so slightly, but not quite enough for an umbrella.

Not a pleasant portent, as such things went.

A large carriage drawn by four horses pulled up on the muddy road; Elsie stepped back to prevent mud from splashing her purple dress. It was one of her nicer dresses. Not that she had any particular reason for wearing it. The mud didn't splash on anyone else, either, for Elsie had insisted on waiting on her own, using the weather as her excuse. Ogden had accepted it well enough, but she had the feeling Emmeline was eagerly peeking through the drapery upstairs.

At the same time she noted there was no second carriage, Bacchus Kelsey kicked open the carriage door, his hair hanging loose. "I couldn't convince the duke to give me two."

Her stomach erupted into moths that attacked her throat, seeking a way out. She supposed it wasn't *entirely* improper—times were changing—but . . . well, what would she have to say about it, anyway? *I'm sorry, I insist you ride on the roof for the sake of my reputation, which of course no one actually cares about.*

Besides, it would be nice not to sit here alone the entire time. Mr. Kelsey could be pleasant when he wanted to be.

One of the servants—John, wasn't it?—ran up to grab her valise. Picking up her skirts, she said, "I'll be sure to keep the curtains drawn to prevent wagging tongues."

She hid a smile when he stepped into the rain to help her to her seat.

⌒

They'd ridden for about ten minutes before Elsie's thoughts needed voicing.

"Is there a lot of crime in Barbados?" she asked.

Bacchus, whose sun-kissed hair hung in tight waves over his shoulders, looked at her curiously. "Not much. Why?"

"Perhaps I'm getting better at eavesdropping or reading the news, but it seems a good deal is happening *here*." She knit and unknit her fingers over her lap. "I ran into Master Merton again on Sunday."

"Is she well?"

"Well enough. She was a bit frazzled. Quite a few opuses had been stolen or misplaced by some acolytes at the Spiritual Atheneum. They were dismissed, of course, and she was covering for one of them, I believe."

Bacchus—Mr. Kelsey, that was—frowned. "Interesting."

"Is it?"

He folded his arms over his broad chest. "There was a constable at the duke's last week, asking questions about a Mr. Shaw, who recently won a copy of an opus at an auction. He, too, was robbed. Though he still has his life, unlike others."

"That's unfortunate," she said. "Was he a friend of the family?"

"No. But I was seen talking to him, so I was a suspect."

"You've been absolved?"

"Apparently so."

She nodded slowly. Tugged on the curtain, hoping for more light. She got little. Rain pattered against the carriage roof.

"Will your man be all right out in this?"

"He insists he will be. He doesn't like tight spaces."

She smiled at that. "You went to this auction? For an opus, or something else?"

A soft growl came up Bacchus's throat. "For the same opus that was stolen from him. It contained a master spell I wish to learn."

"You've tested already?" Something in her abdomen squeezed. Master aspectors were eligible for titles. Upper class. Just like the rest of the toffs.

But he shook his head. "Not yet. I wish to advance with that spell in particular. Because I know you'll ask, it's an ambulation spell."

"Ambulation?"

"It would allow me to move the objects around me without touching them."

She blinked. "That's . . . fascinating." To think how much easier it would be to organize the shelves! She wouldn't even need a ladder. But no amount of aspiring would ever grant Elsie such a spell—spellbreakers were unable to learn aspection.

"I'm sorry you lost," she offered.

He shrugged. "It is something I'll revisit after we meet with Master Pierrelo."

She licked her lips. Glanced to the opposite window. "Are you sure he won't ask after my certification?"

"Does anyone ask after Mr. Ogden's?"

"Well, no . . ."

"You'll be fine. I'll ensure it."

"Thank you." She looked at him, the way he filled a good half of the carriage. "Why is your hair down?"

His eyebrow quirked. "Why are you concerned with my hair?"

She bristled, embarrassed, forcing her eyes away from the long, dark, sun-kissed waves. "Well, you certainly aren't. It's hardly fashionable."

He snorted. "It's annoying to wear back for long trips. I can't rest my head against the wall."

Elsie rested her head back to test the statement. Before her hair could get in the way, however, the back brim of her hat hit it. Yes, that *would* be aggravating for a trip of this length, wouldn't it? Elsie hadn't taken a multiday ride in a carriage since the workhouse had burned down.

She pulled the pin from her hat and removed it, setting it on the bench beside her. She rested back. It wasn't too bad, but a hairpin jabbed her scalp. "I see what you mean."

"Hmm." Bacchus glanced out the window. They were passing by a squat little village with sad houses. Elsie wondered whose stewardship it was to maintain. "Thank you," he added, "again, for agreeing to this."

"The women's school offer was quite clever. But I'll need to have some sort of new math skill to show off when I return, if it's to be believed. You also owe me five shillings."

His lip rose into a half smile. "I'll see what I can teach you, and you'll be reimbursed. I'm also more than willing to cover your services, this time around."

She smirked at that. "Also, you're welcome." She stretched out her legs as much as the cramped space would allow. "I admit I'm curious to know about the spell myself. You've really no idea what it could be?"

"None." He sighed. "It's kept me awake at night, trying to sort it out. If it's beneath the temporal spell, then it happened in my youth, before . . ." He touched his chest.

"You have seemed tired."

"I usually am. It's a symptom." His eyes took on a brooding look as he dropped his hand.

"I'm sorry."

"Don't be."

"I can be sorry if I want to be, Mr. Kelsey. It's a nice change to have the upper hand, besides."

His lip quirked again. "I suppose that's what this is. I'm in your debt now."

A tremor of guilt wound between her breasts. "I didn't mean it that way. I . . . want to help you. Truly. I won't even charge you for it."

He glanced at her, his eyes almost the same color as the hedges outside. "You are a confusing woman, Miss Camden."

She mulled that over. "I think if you leave off the part about tres-passing, I'm rather easy to understand."

He chuckled. "I'd have to agree."

Content, Elsie rifled through her bag for her novel reader. There was just enough light to make out the words.

She finally managed to finish it.

CHAPTER 15

Aspecting was different from other professions in most European countries. It was the only means for a poor person to change his fortune completely.

That is, few members of the lower class could afford the tutelage, let alone the drops each spell cost. But if a man showed enough promise, and showed it to the right people, he could get a sponsor. And if he excelled to mastership, he could make a good deal of money doing magic, and even earn himself a title.

He, Elsie thought, because women of the lower class were never given such opportunities. Only elite ladies were considered for aspecting, as with the Duke of Kent's daughter.

She considered this as they entered a modest house just outside a sugar-beet farm in Ipswich. Master Jacques Pierrelo was a master aspector at the Temporal Atheneum. That meant he was wealthy. But this was not the home of a wealthy man. There weren't even warding spells around the place to protect it—and given the recent rise in crime against spellmakers, that was unwise.

The estate belonged to Master Pierrelo's brother, who was a wainwright and not a spellmaker. It was Bacchus's—Mr. Kelsey's—understanding that the brother had inherited it from their deceased father. Which meant this was likely the home Master Pierrelo had grown up in. It wasn't a run-down house, or a small house, really. Not like the cottages dotting the Duke of Kent's land. It was just a little smaller than the stonemasonry shop and all its adjoining rooms, and while its architecture was old, the furniture was nice. Elsie couldn't help but think the master aspector had been responsible for that.

That made her like him a little more.

Their guide, a cheerful woman in her fifties, introduced herself as Mrs. Pierrelo, but Elsie suspected she was the aspector's sister-in-law rather than his wife.

"Oh yes." She ushered Elsie and Mr. Kelsey deeper into the living area. "He mentioned you might come." She looked at Mr. Kelsey when she said it, but her eyes flitted to Elsie, silently assessing the reason for her presence. The question in them faded into a jolly sort of warmth.

She'd likely concluded they were married. Well, Elsie wasn't going to bother correcting her. Better let the falsehood lie than explain the truth, especially since they had no chaperone.

"He's just outside," said Mrs. Pierrelo. "Make yourselves comfortable in the parlor, and I'll let him know you're here."

If the family had children, they had grown up and moved out already. The parlor Mrs. Pierrelo led them into looked to be a small bedroom converted into a sitting space. Elsie's own bedroom was a mite larger, but this space was comfortable. It had been used recently, for red embers burned in the little hearth, driving back the chill of the rain. Mrs. Pierrelo dropped two quarter logs on it before hurrying on her way.

"Cozy." Elsie selected a wooden rocking chair to sit in. Had Mrs. Pierrelo used this very chair to rock her babes to sleep?

Bacchus eyed her.

"What?" she asked.

"I'm trying to determine if you're jesting or not."

Elsie stuck up her nose. "I *do* think it's cozy. Comfortable. Quaint, in the best of ways. I'm not the one living in a duke's mansion, Mr. Kelsey."

He nodded, bemused. After spending two days and a night in a carriage together—they'd stayed at a small inn, in separate rooms, the night before—Elsie was starting to understand his subtle tones and nuances. For instance, three days ago, she might not have translated his fairly stoic countenance as bemused.

She had not told him, but from Colchester to the Highwoods, he had slipped into his Bajan accent.

Mr. Kelsey's bemusement wore off quickly, however. He paced the room, rubbing his hands together as though cold. Nerves.

"It will be quick." She noted a loose thread on the cuff of her left sleeve. "I'll see what it is, take it off if necessary, and the spell will be back on swift as a blink."

She expected him to retort that he was aware, or that he was not a child, but his only response was a barely perceptible nod. His lack of a reaction only made her more nervous for him.

Elsie's heart jumped when footsteps sounded on the stairs. She rose from her chair, clamping her hands in front of her. Dropping them. Clutching them behind her.

She dropped them again when a well-dressed man roughly the age of Mrs. Pierrelo entered the room. His hair was a faded brown and thinning, his eyes dark and large. He must have been handsome as a youth.

Bacchus met him instantly, extending a hand in greeting. "Master Pierrelo, thank you for meeting with me."

"Of course. The plans were already laid; it's of little inconvenience to me." He spoke with the slightest trace of a French accent, which made Elsie even more curious about his life story. Glancing at Elsie, he added, "I see you've married since I last saw you."

Elsie glanced away, but Mr. Kelsey was not perturbed. "No, you are mistaken. This is the spellbreaker I've hired to assist us."

Elsie pasted on a smile and offered her best shallow curtsy. "It's a pleasure to meet you, Master Pierrelo. Don't mind the dress; I'm afraid I'm the only one the institution could spare at such short notice."

The older man paused for just a moment before nodding. "Of course, Miss—"

"Camden," she said, trying not to let her voice sound tight. There was less of a chance either she or Mr. Kelsey would slip up if she used her own name, and besides, this man wasn't going to investigate her. He had no reason to.

"A second spell, you believe?" He turned to Mr. Kelsey.

"Yes. A spellbreaker visiting the Duke of Kent noticed it. But we cannot determine what it is until your spell is removed." He hesitated. "You're sure it is not one of yours?"

Master Pierrelo shook his head. "As I said in the letter, I only placed one spell." Then, meeting Mr. Kelsey's eyes, he added, "Your father didn't pay me for any more, lad. Though I suppose you've outgrown that term, hmm?"

He smiled at his own joke. Mr. Kelsey was a full head taller than the master aspector and a good deal wider as well.

"All right, then." Master Pierrelo cracked two of his knuckles. "This shouldn't take long, I presume. Would you prefer to sit or stand?"

"Standing is fine, thank you." He moved away from the fire. Looked at Elsie. There was something new in his gaze, although she couldn't quite decipher what it meant.

"Right," she mumbled, moving in front of him. He nodded his permission, and Elsie touched his chest. His heart was racing; he was nervous. And—

"Oh dear." Her cheeks warmed. She hadn't quite thought this through, had she?

"What's wrong?" asked Master Pierrelo.

163

Lowering her hand, Elsie cleared her throat. "Well, I didn't think of it before, Mr. Kelsey"—she tugged on that loose thread on her sleeve—"but I'm afraid . . . I'll need you to remove your shirt."

Her ears warmed. She stepped back to give him space. "That is, I presume the spell is on the skin."

"Of course," said Master Pierrelo.

Once again, Bacchus moved easily with the change in tide. If he felt awkward, he didn't show it. He slipped off his coat and draped it on the nearest chair. Then unbuttoned his waistcoat. Laid it atop the chair as well.

Elsie wanted to look away, but she couldn't bring herself to. *Because I'm a professional,* she reminded herself.

Or at least, she was pretending to be.

He pulled off his ascot, then tugged off his linen shirt by grabbing the back of its collar.

Oh my.

Elsie put both hands on the back of her neck to cool her flush. If she let her cheeks redden, she would look an absolute fool before both of them!

The only man Elsie had ever seen shirtless since the workhouse was Ogden. And while he was stout and in good health . . . it wasn't the same.

Bacchus Kelsey was not bad looking in the slightest.

She glanced at the floor, giving herself a few seconds of composure. When she thought she had it, she straightened her back and forced nonchalance into every fiber of her person.

"My apologies," Bacchus whispered.

Her gaze flitted to his face and away again. She waved a dismissive hand. "All part of the job, Mr. Kelsey." Taking half a step forward, she attempted to sense the spell. Bacchus's masculine scent, the one edged with citrus, was strong, but so was the earthiness of the temporal spell. It was a master-level spell, certainly. And though she couldn't see it with her eyes, she knew it was a large rune that began halfway down his chest and ended an inch above his navel. The start of a trail of dark hair sat just above the waist of his trousers—

Good God, woman, focus! She placed her hand on the rune. Bacchus jerked just slightly—her hands must have been cold. She focused on the chill in her fingers so she wouldn't think of the warmth of his flesh or its firmness, because if she thought about those things, the blush would only worsen. But of course Elsie's thoughts strayed as they were wont to do, her mind moving from the temperature of her fingers to the mesmerizing contrast of their skin tones—hers fair and almost peachy, his a rich bronze. The spell buzzed beneath her touch, as though it knew its demise was nigh. Beneath it lay another. Something she could sense like a person watching her, but couldn't yet see, hear, smell, or feel.

"Expertly made, Master Pierrelo." She focused her attention on the work at hand. "I feel almost sorry to remove it."

The compliment did its job; the master smiled.

"Ready?" she whispered.

Bacchus nodded, his gaze never leaving her.

She ran her fingertips down the length of the rune, testing the metaphorical knot and searching for the start of the pattern that would unwind it. Bacchus's skin pebbled under her touch.

Don't think about that. Focus.

It took her a moment longer. *There.* Bottom left. Then bottom, center, top left, top right. It took her a few heartbeats to find each thread, and she paused between the sixth and seventh—this *was* a master spell, after all, and the Cowls had never hired her to vanquish something so complex. The spell resisted her, complacent in its roost on Bacchus's skin. It was as though it grumbled, *No, I'm helping him. See?* But Elsie picked at it, bringing up her other hand to finish the job.

To the eyes of the two aspectors, it probably looked like she was playing make-believe. But the unwinding had done its work—the rune's scent soured before it pulsed a faint shimmer she could just barely see as it gave up its life.

A second, darker symbol appeared beneath it, a faded blue tinted green from the pigments of Bacchus's skin. No shimmer, as though someone had laid it in reverse, and the glow was beneath the skin, not above it.

"Oh." She took a half step backward, looking at it. It was unlike any other rune she'd ever seen. It sat almost like a child's drawing that had failed to wash clean. It was a third of the size of the temporal spell. Elsie didn't need to touch it to see it was a master-level spell. And the fact that she could see it meant it was physical.

"What is it?" Bacchus asked, his voice strangled. She thought she could *hear* his heartbeat now.

"I don't know," she confessed. "I've never seen its like before. And it doesn't . . . There's no light to it."

"Light?" asked Master Pierrelo.

Elsie nodded. "Physical runes have a sort of shimmer to them. This one looks like it was smeared on with wet chalk. I . . . Do you have something I can write with?"

"Physical?" Bacchus asked, touching the rune Elsie knew he couldn't see.

The master aspector ducked away from her peripheral vision, but she didn't follow him with her eyes. She didn't want to look away from the rune. It didn't pose any danger to her, but it was strange. She didn't like it.

"What's wrong?" Bacchus asked.

She shook her head, trying to get her thoughts around it. Before Master Pierrelo returned, she whispered, "It's like someone didn't want you to find it."

His muscles tensed.

"Here." Master Pierrelo handed her a piece of stationery and a charcoal nub. Backing up to the chair that had half of Bacchus's wardrobe slung over it, she leaned on the armrest and sketched the rune to the best of her ability.

"Do you recognize it?" She held up the drawing so both men could see.

Both brows furrowed. "No," Bacchus said.

Master Pierrelo shook his head. "One doesn't need a knowledge of runes to use magic; they're just an invisible force to mark that it happened. They're the language of magic itself, I suppose."

"Information about them is freely shared?" Elsie asked. "I could research this?"

Master Pierrelo nodded. "I believe so, yes. At one of the atheneums."

Atheneums that Elsie didn't have access to. Biting her lip, Elsie set the drawing down and approached Bacchus once more. She didn't bother asking for permission this time; she planted both hands atop that dark rune.

Firm, indeed.

She hesitated.

"What's wrong?" Bacchus's voice leaked genuine concern.

"This is one hell of a knot," she said. Master Pierrelo clucked his tongue in disapproval at her language. "Perhaps we should return to London and learn what it is before I try to remove it."

Try. Although she was quite sure she could. Elsie had never met a spell she couldn't untie. Some just took more effort than others.

"No." Bacchus's voice was sharp. "No, I want it gone. It was hidden and placed without my knowledge. I cannot see how it would be beneficial."

Master Pierrelo shrugged. "Perhaps it was instituted by your parents for good reason when you were a child."

But Bacchus shook his head. "I want it gone."

Elsie looked up at him. This close, with her hands still pressed against his skin—it felt intimate. And yet it didn't bother her. No, just the opposite.

But seeing the trepidation in Bacchus's countenance, she pulled free of the reverie and set to work, prodding the rune, searching for its end. It was well hidden, blast it. She carefully moved her fingers toward its center, searching. She probably looked like a new lover who didn't know what she was doing, but she *had* to find the end. She tried again, slower this time.

There.

The threads were as fine as strands of hair, and the last one had been tucked artfully under the others. Like the aspector who had placed it *did* have a knowledge of runes and had crafted the spell in order to deliberately conceal its beginning and end. This confirmed her suspicion: whoever had set this spell had not intended for it to be found.

Pausing, she met Bacchus's eyes once more. He studied her intently. "Are you sure?" she asked.

"Yes." His pulse was like a hummingbird under her hands. "Please."

She tugged at the thread. It took her just as long to find the second, and then third, but the more she unwound, the easier it was to locate the next loop. As she got to the end of the knot, the rune finally sparkled.

Then it vanished.

Bacchus gasped and stumbled backward.

"What?" she asked, whipping her hands back like she'd angered a snake. Her eyes moistened. *Oh God, I've killed him, I've done something terrible, I'll never forgive myself!* "What, what's wrong? Did I hurt you?"

Master Pierrelo rushed forward to steady him. Bacchus's Adam's apple bobbed as he swallowed. Stray strands of hair fell from the tie at the nape of his neck.

He inhaled deeply, nostrils flaring.

"Bacchus?" Elsie squeaked. Her hands trembled.

He held up a hand in reassurance. "I'm not hurt, Elsie. It's fine." He straightened and, somehow, was taller than he'd been before. His back stood straighter, his shoulders squarer.

Her eyes darted between Bacchus and Master Pierrelo. "Then what?"

"It was like . . . like something punched me." Bacchus touched his diaphragm, right where the second spell had been. "But . . . in a good way."

"Are you well?" Master Pierrelo asked, going as far as to touch Bacchus's forehead.

"I am." He shook free of the temporal aspector's hand. "I'm . . . *very* well." He lifted his hands, flexed them. They looked darker, their tan color richer. And . . . yes, it was the same for his face as well. As though he'd just spent the entire day in the July sun. His eyes were remarkably bright as well; so clear, so green.

Elsie's brain was a jumble of vines. "What do you mean?"

"I mean." He lifted his arms, lowered them. "I feel like I've *finally* rested. Like my body has been working at half capacity until this moment. I'm not . . . I'm not *tired* anymore."

Elsie's lips parted. Bacchus had often looked fatigued, although he had explained it to be a side effect of his disease.

"Mr. Kelsey," Master Pierrelo began slowly, "I am no doctor, but . . . I do not think you have polio."

Bacchus snapped to attention like the man had thrown water in his face. "What?"

Master Pierrelo rubbed his chin. "Do you *feel* sick?"

He paused. "No. I . . . don't think I've ever felt this hale in my entire life." He ran his hands down his chest, up his arms, as though his body were completely new to him. His eyes were round and wondering, more amazed than a child's on Christmas Day. Elsie's skin prickled like feathers danced beneath it. *She* had done that.

"Hmm." Master Pierrelo thought for several seconds. "Whoever put this first spell on you did it before you ever received my administrations . . . I suggest you take the young lady's drawing and see if you can determine what it was."

Desperately needing something to do, Elsie grabbed her drawing and handed it to him.

Bacchus's fingers trembled ever so slightly as he took the page and studied the charcoal rune. He let out a long breath, perhaps trying to orient himself into this new way of being. "Then we're off to London."

He said we.

Elsie clasped her hands together. Certainly Bacchus could get her into the Physical Atheneum. She could get her hands on those runes as well. Help Bacchus, and perhaps help herself to a few spellbreaking books at the same time. Everything she knew, she had taught herself.

"I think that wise. If you *want* me to redo the spell . . . ," Master Pierrelo offered.

But Bacchus shook his head. "No. No, not yet. I need to know what this is. As soon as possible."

He folded the paper and stuck it in his trouser pocket, then grabbed his shirt and tugged it over his head. Elsie handed him the remainder of his garments, eyes averted. Something about watching him dress felt just as scandalous as watching him undress.

If this wasn't a novel reader come to life, she didn't know what was.

Clothed, Bacchus said, "Let me pay you for your time."

Master Pierrelo stayed him with a raised hand. "You've not yet taken up a quarter hour of it. I'm sorry you've traveled so far only to not need my services. Go. And let me know what you discover, if only to satiate my curiosity." He eyed Bacchus. "This is a mystery more than ten years in the making."

So it had been ten years since Master Pierrelo had laid *his* spell. How long had the other one been in place?

Bacchus shook Master Pierrelo's hand again, and Elsie did the same, despite it being a masculine gesture. Why shouldn't she? She was a professional spellbreaker, as far as he knew, and it was not nearly as scandalous as putting her hands all over the bare chest of a virile bachelor, now was it? And because it wasn't every day she met a master magician, she thought she might also attempt to get some information.

"Master Pierrelo," she said, "what do you think about the opus crimes in London?"

The spellmaker frowned and released her hand. "They aren't only in London. I don't know much; the less I'm involved, the safer I am."

He seemed resolved not to say more, so Elsie nodded and wished him well. Perhaps the fear of being struck down was one of the reasons Master Pierrelo had traveled back home for a time. Still, it would have been nice if he'd said, *I rather suspect a certain squire. Would you like to hear about it?*

She nearly had to run to catch up with Bacchus. His stride was longer than usual. So eager was he to leave for London he nearly forgot to thank Mrs. Pierrelo for her hospitality, and he completely forgot to acknowledge her husband, Mr. Pierrelo, who sat shining his shoes in the corner. Elsie waved her apologies in his wake and followed him back to the road.

"Elsie." He turned around suddenly, the carriage only a few paces away. Rainer and John weren't there; they'd likely taken off to tour the town.

Elsie barely noticed their absence. She was too entranced by the fact that Bacchus had used her given name, now for the third time.

He grabbed her upper arms, and his lips parted in a true smile, his teeth white as pearls. "You've saved me, Elsie."

She grinned, heart turning over backward. "I wouldn't say that so soon; you don't know what that thing was."

"But I *feel* the difference." For a terrifying moment she thought he would lift her in the air, but his hands tightened only a fraction before releasing her, and she felt strangely sad for the separation. Bacchus raised his arms, then grabbed his hair, staring up at the drizzling sky like he looked into heaven itself. "I feel . . . amazing. Whatever it was . . . you've cured me."

Her chest warmed at the compliment. Although she did a great deal of good under the guidance of the Cowls, her role was never acknowledged. She'd never been *thanked* before. "You're very welcome, Bacchus."

Her tone wasn't exactly jubilant, so he paused in his celebration to look at her. "What's wrong?"

She tugged on that stubborn loose thread on her sleeve. "Do you know *who* did it? *Who* could have put such an awful spell on you?"

He sobered almost instantly, and Elsie regretted being the cause of it. His green eyes shifted back and forth, as though reading his memories like lines in a book. "No. No, I don't." He frowned.

"Well, we know what the rune looks like."

He nodded. "The London Physical Atheneum should have what we're looking for."

"You said we." She stuck her finger out as though accusing him. "That means I'm coming. A gentleman doesn't recant his word, Mr. Kelsey."

His lip quirked. It wasn't as warming as his true smile, but Elsie would take what she could get. "Of course. I certainly won't strand you here. Miss Camden, I may very well owe you my *life*."

"Oh, I doubt that." But she flushed despite her words. "I'm rather tired of that carriage, but I would like to leave as soon as possible."

"Yes." He turned. "As soon as we find John and Rainer."

"We'll have plenty to do while we wait," she said and, when he turned back, added, "You have a great deal of accounting to teach me, Mr. Kelsey, if our story is to be believed when I return home."

He smiled at her, halfway between a lip quirk and his full, beaming smile. "You're correct. How good are you with ratios?"

The thread on her sleeve bothered her now, so she strode to the valise on the back of the carriage to retrieve her sewing kit. "I don't use them often, so I suppose we can start there, and I'll sound very educated to Mr. Ogden."

Unclipping her valise, Elsie cracked it open—the last thing she needed was Bacchus peeking over and seeing her underthings or the like. She rifled about for her miniature sewing kit and, specifically, the pair of scissors inside it. Her finger touched a sharp corner, and she grabbed it, but it was too narrow to be the kit, and her novel reader was at the top of her belongings. Curious, she grabbed the thing and pulled it free.

All the blood that had ambled into her face during the last half hour sank back down. She knew this gray parchment. Didn't even have to check the seal before opening the letter.

Did they follow me here?

She hadn't seen the letter at the inn last night, but she hadn't exactly rooted through her valise when getting dressed this morning.

> *There is a weapons shed in Colchester with enchanted arms. The constable there is unkind to those who can't pay his bribes. He would do well with less power.*

There was an address and a five-pound bill—*five pounds!*—in the letter as well. Elsie's pulse picked up. She'd already passed through Colchester. Had her mysterious contact intended for her to do it then?

They'd pass through again, on the way home. But what excuse could she give Bacchus for having to make a stop, and without his company? Five pounds . . . this was to cover all her expenses privately.

Her heart sank. She *wanted* to know about Bacchus's rune. Wanted to unravel the mystery beside him. Wanted to share his carriage. It was a strange feeling . . . In the past she had never been anything but excited to carry out the Cowls' orders. But right now . . .

"What is that?" Bacchus asked, peering over her shoulder.

She shoved the letter beneath the waistline of her skirt. "Oh, Mr. Kelsey, I'm afraid I won't be able to go after all." Disappointment dripped down her limbs like the misty rain surrounding them.

Mr. Kelsey came around the carriage. "What do you mean? What was that letter?"

She puffed out her chest and put her hands on her hips. "It's private correspondence."

"But you only broke the seal now?" He looked over her head—following his gaze, Elsie spied Rainer at the end of the road.

Ignoring the comment, she said, "I need to go to . . . Hadleigh. I forgot to mention it. It came up after your visit on Sunday." She tugged her valise free of the carriage.

"Hadleigh?" His brows drew together. "Where is that?"

"West. Out of the way." She turned toward him, the handle of her valise clutched in both her hands. "I'll take a separate cab."

His look was incredulous. "How far west? I'm sure it wouldn't be too much of a bother—"

"You need to get to London," she insisted, quieter. Looking at him with tense eyes. *Just do it,* she pleaded. "You need to find out what that spell is. And I have to do this alone."

He frowned. "I don't think that's wise."

"I don't believe you have a say in the matter."

Those words added a hard line down the center of his forehead. "What I mean is, it's not safe to travel alone."

"Then I'll take an omnibus instead. Or the train."

"I don't und—"

"Bacchus." Her voice was hard but hushed, and she stepped in closer to be sure he heard her. "Please. I need to do this, and I cannot explain. I will get home safely. I'll even send a telegram. I'm asking you not to fight me on this."

He hesitated, looking her up and down. "This has something to do with the doorknob, doesn't it?"

The doorknob with the heat spell. The one she'd been unraveling when he caught her.

She said nothing.

He stepped back, pinching the bridge of his nose as though a headache had erupted there. "Elsie—"

"You said you'd pay me for my services, no? This is the payment, letting me go on my own without complaint and with the utmost understanding." She forced a smile. "Here comes Rainer. No need to keep waiting. It's a mystery ten years in the making, remember?"

She turned from him and stepped around the carriage, heading in the same direction from which Rainer came. She paused, looking back over her shoulder, and pasted on a smile. "Take care of yourself, please. And let me know what you find."

Quickening her step, Elsie took the first turn she could without getting hopelessly lost, just to break away from his line of sight.

Bacchus Kelsey, blessedly, did not follow her.

CHAPTER 16

For a time it seemed the cab could not go fast enough. Elsie was sure she'd see the Duke of Kent's carriage outside her window, or worse, following her. But Bacchus honored her request and did not pursue her. Which strangely made her wish he had.

No matter. She'd cashed in the banknote and now rode privately, her valise on the bench across from her. Cabs didn't always go long distances, so she did have to change two more times before finding a boardinghouse to stay in for the night, and she left early the next morning to make it to Colchester.

Once there, she had the driver leave her off at a local hotel, suspecting it might be noticed if the carriage left her off at the address on the note. Best not to take chances.

After leaving her bag in the room, she took a casual walk past the shed. It was guarded not by spells, of course—that would have been too easy—but by people. The true nature of the money in the envelope dawned on her. She'd need to stay in Colchester until she learned the guards' schedule. Perhaps they'd be particularly God-fearing guards and the Sabbath would send them home, but she couldn't rely on that.

That first day, Friday, she strolled past the shed three times. The second time, four hours after the first, there was a new man at the entrance, and he was replaced by two men come evening. She didn't recognize the guard on watch the next morning, but did recognize the one that afternoon. She never caught them changing shifts.

The Cowls wouldn't assign you a task you're unable to complete. Not without sending help.

The local church started at nine in the morning. Thirty minutes past that, a siren sounded a ways off. Its whine struck fear into her heart, and she stayed where she was for a solid ten minutes. When no one came after her, she crept back to the shed, surprised to see it unwatched. Surely it wasn't a coincidence. A Cowl must have set off the alarm or caused a distraction of some sort, knowing she'd be there.

She itched to follow the sound of the alarm, to find a Cowl or, perhaps, someone else who worked for them, but time was of the essence.

She moved quickly.

The room was hot and dim, but she saw enough to make her cringe. All sorts of weapons and tools hung on the walls. How many of these were used against the poor, especially those *driven* to crime by starving bellies and desperation? The thought made her shudder. She nearly sprinted along the walls, running her hands across handles, avoiding blades. She found the enchanted weapons quickly; they were in the back, sharing a wall.

She didn't recognize the spells on them except for a temporal rune for preventing rust. She undid everything, untying knot after knot until her wrists itched. Then, her bodice sticking to her chest with perspiration, she fled. She thought she heard a man yell after her as she went, but she ran until her corset became suffocating and sweat dripped from her hairline, and by the time she looped back to her hotel, she had no pursuers.

She departed for Brookley the same day.

This week had been one of the most stressful times in Bacchus's life.

All those hours he'd spent stewing over the second spell, unsure what it could mean, had worn on him. He'd hated Ipswich, too. All of the sugar farms had made him think of home in the worst way possible. He hated sugar plantations. Hated what they represented—the fall and mistreatment of his friends' and neighbors' ancestors, a legacy that still clung to them even sixty years after emancipation. He hated sweets for the same reason—the sweetest thing he could stomach was pawpaw.

And then the spell prolonging his life had been removed, and the mysterious second spell had been broken, and . . . he felt marvelous. Healthy, strong, invigorated. Like he was thirteen again. The transition was so confusing, so blissful. His outlook had brightened almost instantly. He could get his mastership easily now; the ambulation spell didn't matter.

He could do anything he wanted.

And yet his glee had been short-lived, not only due to the knowledge that someone had purposefully sabotaged him with that spell, but because of the emptiness of the carriage. He felt the lack of a woman who, he had to admit, was rather . . . amiable.

Amiable. Even he felt the wrongness of the word. Yes, she was amiable, but it was something else that drew him to her. He could still feel the cool touch of her fingers over his chest and stomach. It had dissipated his anxiety and stoked something even more maddening. Something he hadn't wished to dwell on before, given their circumstances.

Now she was gone, and he couldn't be more confused.

He no longer suspected Elsie of thievery, but she guarded her secrets so closely. She'd seemed so honest with him, so frank, on their trip to Ipswich, and just as quickly she'd shut down. Fled without reason. Abandoned a mission she'd seemed intent on seeing through.

What had been in that letter? A threat? Blackmail? Or was he letting his imagination get away from him? He'd wanted to ask her to explain herself. But her eyes had looked so worried, her mouth resolute, and she'd just broken the bonds he had unknowingly worn since adolescence. And so he'd let her go, leaving himself to simmer in unanswered questions.

Rather than head straight to London, he returned first to Kent, wanting to update the duke and see if Elsie's promised telegram had arrived. He arrived on Sunday to find there was no telegram, and the duke had fallen into poor health while he was away. It was not the first time it had happened, but it concerned Bacchus, nonetheless. The duke's entire family was at the end of their line, worrying over him. And so Bacchus had spent most of his Sunday pacing the long corridors of the estate, tormenting himself. He must have been a sight, for even Rainer and John kept their distance.

Early Monday morning, he returned to London, to the Physical Atheneum.

He'd written ahead to request an appointment regarding his advancement. But when he arrived, the first place he went was the library. The maze of books became an utter labyrinth once he began walking through the shelves. They hadn't seemed so imposing in passing.

He spotted an elderly steward in one of the larger rooms and approached the man.

"You, are you employed here?" He sounded impatient. He tried to reel himself in, but the questions were boiling over. He could solve at least one of them now: What rune had marked his skin?

As for Elsie's—Miss Camden's—well-being, he was forced to wait.

The steward looked over his spectacles. He appeared to be frowning, but perhaps that was simply the way the loose skin of his face hung. "Never seen a Spaniard in these parts."

Bacchus doubted he'd ever seen a Spaniard period, as Bacchus wasn't one. He stuffed his impatience into his stomach and chose not to correct the man. "Do you know of any volumes depicting runes?"

He blinked, the spectacles making his eyes large and birdlike. "Runes? Those are spellbreaker books. Down in the basement. Why?"

"Thank you." He stepped away. Paused. "Would you kindly point me in the direction of the stairs?"

The man did, with a crooked finger, and Bacchus crossed the floor with long strides. Bookshelves like sentinels stood in his way, but eventually he found a stairwell basked in shadow, thanks to a burned-out lamp. He took it carefully, the temperature lowering by the step. The smell of mildew snuck into his nose as he reached the bottom.

The area was poorly lit, so Bacchus took one of the lamps off the wall and brought it with him. Two others shared the space: a woman nearly as old as the steward, and a boy who could not have yet been twelve. The woman squinted at Bacchus; the boy, his hair mussed, pored over a book. Her apprentice, he suspected. Perhaps he was a spellbreaker in the making. Hopefully he did not have the tome Bacchus sought.

The man had not said *where* in the basement the books would be, and so Bacchus forced himself to slow down, to read spines and labels, which were severely lacking in information. He pulled out the folded paper in his pocket to again study Elsie's drawing. The symbol looked almost Asian, but the curls on the edges lent it more of a French aesthetic. Not that it mattered. Magic was universal.

Tucking the paper away—thinking about Hadleigh, where Elsie claimed to have gone—he investigated one row of books, then another only a quarter full. On to the next shelf. At this rate, he'd have to ask the old woman—

Encyclopedia of Runes until 1804, a book spat at him. The spine was the same width as his hand, and when he pulled it free, he grunted at its weight. The thing might as well have been made of iron. He expected dust, but got little. Either the tome was used often or the stewards of the library took their jobs very seriously.

He searched for a table, but the only other one was back by the woman and her apprentice, and he'd rather have privacy. So he returned to the quarter-full shelf and set down both the lamp and the book, opening the latter.

It had three to four spells per page, labeled in alphabetical order. Fortunately, the thing was also segmented into four sections: novice, intermediate, advanced, and master spells. He flipped to the last quarter and slowly turned the pages, moving the lamp closer.

So that's what the ambulation spell looks like, he thought, tracing his fingers over the complex coils of the spell he'd tried so hard to obtain. A spell he no longer needed, thanks to Elsie. His stomach tightened. He ignored it.

The ambulation rune would do nothing to teach him the Latin spell that would actually enable him to use it. The name had a plus sign by it. An advanced master spell, then.

He turned the page. Upon closer inspection, the ink was actually colored to match the alignment of the spells. The physical spells were blue, rational spells red, spiritual spells yellow, and temporal spells green. The yellow ink had faded, making the spiritual runes hard to read in the poor lighting, but Bacchus had a mind for only the physical runes.

He dismissed spell after spell, turned page after page. Thought he heard the woman and boy move from their table to the stairs. He neared the end, turned the page.

Saw the rune immediately.

His breath caught, and he slammed a hand onto the page as though the rune might leap away. The blue ink was faded nearly to black, and the name had two pluses by it. A *very* strong spell.

The letters seemed foreign for a moment. Bacchus held the lamp even closer. The word revealed itself. *Siphon.*

He formed the syllables with his lips. *Siphon.* A siphoning spell? And on the following page, the rune was inversed. Squinting at the faded text beneath the images, he read on the first, *Dare,* and on the second, *Accipere.* Latin. *To give* and *to receive.*

A physical aspector had somehow placed a high-ranking master spell on his person and . . . siphoned his strength away from him? Given him symptoms two doctors had diagnosed as the early onset of polio? Had the aspector kept the stolen strength for himself? Bottled it up? Let it drain out with the sea?

Why?

He gripped the edges of the book until his fingernails left marks in the covers. His only consolation was knowing that whoever had benefitted from sapping his strength could no longer tap it. But where had it happened? Barbados? England? He'd been to New York and France as well, but he had absolutely no memory of the event . . . or of the person who'd done it. Had a rational aspector been present as well, to wipe his mind clean?

Now he was getting into the absurd.

Siphon. He knew when, roughly, it had happened. Before his parents had brought the first doctor in. But . . .

Closing his eyes, he racked his memory. He'd come to England often as a boy. Gotten seasick once on the journey back. Had that been the start of the siphoning, or had it not occurred until he was home in Barbados? But Barbados was not renowned for its aspectors. Bacchus has been one of few, though American spellmakers were known to holiday there during the winter months . . .

He slammed the book shut. He couldn't make sense of it . . . and he had to accept that he might never know. He could investigate in Barbados first, ask his aging nursemaid, but she had never accompanied him and his father on their trips. She'd fretted over him. Wept over the diagnosis! Had she known anything, surely she would have said so. And to think his father would never know the truth . . .

He pulled away from the shelf, dragging the light with him. *Let it go,* he heard his father say in his memory. *It will do you no good, allowing it to fester.*

He'd said it to him often, first when he was the only foreign-looking boy on the English streets, and later when his temper rose over inconsequential things.

He couldn't let it go, not yet. But he would tuck it away until he could investigate further.

In the meantime, he had a mastership to obtain.

CHAPTER 17

When Elsie returned to Brookley, the first place she went was the post office to send a vague and inexpensive telegram to Kent: *All is well.* She casually asked Martha Morgan first if any new crimes regarding opuses had appeared in the papers and, second, if the squire had been in town. Martha claimed she hadn't seen any news on the aspector crimes, but the squire had been in just yesterday.

No murders while the squire was at home. The information stoked Elsie's growing suspicion. If only she were a registered spellbreaker . . . she'd have access to the atheneums and be able to weave through the highest circles of aspectors and pick their brains, glimpsing secrets journalists didn't, or perhaps couldn't, put in the paper.

But she wasn't registered and never would be. What could she, Elsie Camden, do? It wasn't like Ogden would ever be targeted. She'd have to wait for the answers to come to her just like everyone else. A novel reader without a clear-cut publication date.

Valise in hand, she hurried home. She didn't even make it to the front door before Emmeline scared her halfway to Liverpool.

"Elsie!" the younger woman shrieked, nearly tripping over the basket of laundry she was midway through hanging. She rushed for Elsie and hugged her. "How was it? Was it exciting? It's been so boring here without you. And your next novel reader came! But Mr. Ogden said I couldn't read it without your permission. I've been going wild wondering what will happen next. Is this the last issue?"

Elsie laughed, which lightened her in a way she hadn't realized she needed. "Perhaps we could read it together, while I put my feet up. If Ogden isn't desperate for help, that is."

"Oh"—she took Elsie's valise—"you must be exhausted. I didn't even think of it. We'll look at it tomorrow."

Elsie took the luggage back. "I'm well enough to carry my own things. Where's Ogden?"

"In the studio, last I saw."

Elsie squeezed Emmeline's shoulder before trekking into the house, setting her valise at the bottom of the stairs. She pulled her gloves off as she walked. Sure enough, Ogden was in the studio, his tarps over the floor, a canvas half-painted blue sitting before him.

"Work or pleasure?" Elsie asked.

He startled, fortunately pulling his brush back before he could tarnish his work. "Oh, Elsie! So good to see you back. How was it?"

She'd already rehearsed her words in the cab, so they flowed from her lips as easily as if they were true. "It was rather dreadful, honestly. Everyone invited was in a position similar to mine, including a few secretaries. But they treated us like a bunch of ninnies, like we barely knew how to read, let alone put our shoes on the right foot. I didn't learn much of anything." She sighed. "I'm glad to be home." That much, at least, was sincere.

"Oh dear." Ogden rested his brush on his palette. "I shall have to write them with my disappointment."

Elsie nodded. "I'll get you the address." Which was code for *I'll wait until you forget you asked*. Stifling a yawn with a knuckle, she asked, "What can I get for you, Ogden? I suppose you've lunched already."

He reached to the floor to grab a bottle of white paint. "Go rest, Elsie. I'll have plenty for you to catch up on in the morning."

"You're sure?"

"Am I ever not?"

She smiled. "In that case, a little mouse told me my next novel reader arrived."

He chuckled. "That little mouse was supposed to leave it on your bed for you."

"I've not yet been upstairs, so I'll check." She paused halfway to the door. "Mr. Ogden, you read the paper."

The bottle of paint spit onto his palette. "Yes . . ."

"Then you know there has been an alarming number of thefts and . . . murders . . . as of late."

He paused. Set down the paint and his palette. "Yes, I've noticed. Sometimes I wonder if it's better to be informed or ignorant. Or, rather, informed and depressed, or ignorant and happy."

Elsie nodded. "If only one could be informed and happy."

Standing from his stool, Ogden said, "Ah, but that is not the way of the world. Journalists do not pay their rent reporting on how well things are going, unless it is in regards to the queen."

She twisted her fingers together. "I merely wish we could do something about it."

"Careful, Elsie. You'll sound like a Tory."

She offered a weak smile. "Why do you say that?"

"Most of the crime that has been reported on lately has targeted the upper class."

"True," she said carefully, "but it's not really worth nicking from those who don't have money. Or magic."

Ogden nodded. Sat, and picked up his brush and palette. He began randomly dabbing white paint onto the canvas: first near the top, then to the side, then down to the right. It made no sense, even if he were attempting clouds, but there was a strange sort of pattern to it. Elsie could almost guess where Ogden would touch his brush next. "That is true. There does seem to be a theme running through it. Or perhaps the newspapers are focusing solely on lords and aspectors because it makes for a more interesting story."

She chewed on her thumbnail. "Perhaps."

"If it helps"—he dabbed the center of the canvas—"the squire is unworried about it. It came up, my last day there."

Elsie clicked her tongue. "The squire doesn't care about anything but himself. If anyone were to go after opuses, it would be him. He loves power. And what's more powerful than magic you can cast for free?"

"Be careful, Elsie." He lowered his brush. "You never know when one might be listening."

She stiffened. Glanced at the door, then the window. They were alone. "You mean to scare me."

Though his mouth turned up at one end, Ogden shook his head. "I don't. But you needn't fear. You've no opus to steal, and mine isn't worth more than a page."

The words, half in jest, struck Elsie to her core. Ogden was right, of course—righter than he realized. Spellbreakers didn't have opuses. They could only dismantle spells, not learn them.

He considered a moment. "If things ever do get bad, we'll steal away, you, Emmeline, and I. Ride up to the Thames, maybe even the St. Katharine Docks, and take a discreet boat out to the channel. How's your French?"

Elsie snorted. "Very poor, indeed. Let us hope it does not come to us relying on my French." Leaving Ogden to his work, she passed through the kitchen to grab some bread and butter to eat, then hauled her valise up to her room. All her clothes needed laundering and ironing; she'd get to that tonight, before she went to bed. The novel reader was indeed on her coverlet, but Elsie went through her valise before looking at it, ensuring there were no more notes stowed away.

How did they get into the bag in the first place?

Part of her wished she hadn't seen it. How much more could she have learned about Bacchus Kelsey had she slipped into the London Physical Atheneum with him? Not only the mystery of the spell, but the mystery of the man.

Not that you have any right to know. Really, Elsie.

Forcing her thoughts back to rational things, she moved toward the window and stared down at the street below. It was empty but for a couple of men who stood off the main road. Neither of them glanced up at her, or showed any interest whatsoever in the stonemasonry shop.

"Will you ever tell me your secrets, Cowls?" she whispered to the glass. "Will you deem me worthy and bring me into the fold?"

She wondered if they'd consider her more valuable if she started ignoring their missives. She didn't fear they'd reciprocate in any foul manner; they'd only ever been kind to her. Mr. Parker was certainly kind. No, her worst fear was that they'd stop asking altogether.

Heaviness weighed down her eyes, and she rubbed it away. She *could* use a rest. Lifting her gaze from the street, she peered over Brookley, into the green distance. *Did you find your rune, Bacchus? Will you tell me, or have I tried your patience, too?*

It was fruitless to worry over it. But that didn't stop her.

Drawing one of her curtains, Elsie retired to bed, focusing on her novel reader to keep her thoughts at bay.

She fell asleep halfway down page 3.

Elsie was sweeping the porch when a post dog jogged up to her, its pink tongue hanging out as it panted.

"Why, hello." She set the broom against the wall and moved to the bag attached to the dog's neck. She pulled out two letters, one addressed to her and one addressed to Ogden. She studied the handwriting on the first, but it didn't match that of the postmaster in Juniper Down. Her heart sank just a little—Mr. Hall had meant every word, hadn't he? She wasn't ever going to hear from them again.

But who else would have written to her?

Her breath caught as hope flared in her chest. She pet the dog on the head. "No treat on me today, Ruff. Off you go."

The dog turned around and trotted back toward the post office.

Forgetting the broom, Elsie ran inside. She set Ogden's letter on the kitchen table and took the stairs two at a time, diving into the privacy of her room.

She ripped the letter open and read the bottom of it first:

> *Sincerely,*
> *Bacchus Kelsey*
>
> *Thank you for the telegram. I just received it.*

Her heart fluttered. He'd found the rune. Or at least, he'd gotten home safely.

Just read it, she chided herself.

> *Miss Camden,*
> *I hope this letter finds you in the privacy for which it is intended. I was successful in finding the rune in question. You were correct—it's of the physical nature. It is the mark of a siphoning spell, one that I was not aware existed. It appears to be complex and rare.*
> *I believe it is the cause of my symptoms. I continue to feel well. I owe that to you.*

Her skin warmed. Despite herself, she smiled.

I have been in contact with Master Ruth Hill of the London Physical Atheneum. She has offered me the choice between a gem spell and a substance spell to complete my mastership. Once I choose, the rest of my repertoire will need to be earned on my own.

I thank you again for your help during this trial. I pray you are well.

Sincerely,

Bacchus Kelsey

Thank you for the telegram. I just received it.

He didn't mention her abrupt departure. Kind of him.

So why was she crying?

Lowering the letter, Elsie dabbed at her eyes with her sleeves. She hadn't yawned, and there was no dust in the air. Had she picked up a head cold while traveling? But she didn't feel stuffy. Or achy. That is, not achy in the manner of a head cold. No, this ache was centered in her chest.

She reread the letter. Sniffed. It was a goodbye, in a sense. She no longer had a debt to repay. He no longer needed her services. And he was testing to be a master aspector. Once that happened, he'd be titled, putting his rank far above her own. Which hardly mattered, anyway. He'd likely return to Barbados once he had what he'd come for. There'd be an entire ocean between them.

It's better this way, she told herself, dabbing another tear. She managed to keep the crying light, the way heroines always cried so prettily in novel readers. But it left a hard lump in her throat, one that dug in with claws. But it *was* better this way. Whenever Bacchus thought of spellbreaking, or perhaps of polio, he would think of her. And he would think of her kindly, of the way she'd helped him, or perhaps her humor. She would forever live in his memory as a likeable acquaintance.

It was better that he leave, because that meant he would never get close enough to her to discover that utterly unlikeable *something* that drove everyone else away.

The Camdens aren't coming back.

She thought of Juniper Down and the workhouse. Of Alfred, hand in hand with another woman. It was miraculous that Ogden had yet to kick her out.

She folded the letter and slipped it between the books on her shelf. A stray tear dropped off her jaw and onto her hand, but she wiped it off with her skirt. Yes, it was better this way.

The lump dug in, hard.

Really, Elsie, she thought, since she could not speak. *What were you expecting, romance? From a man who thinks you're a criminal? Who could be a baron next month, for all you know?*

She thought of the depth of his laugh. The way his skin felt beneath her fingers.

No. Stories like that were meant for novel readers, not real life.

It really *was* better this way. The loss of her family, her siblings, Alfred . . . It still hurt, and it had been years. How much worse would the sting be to have a man like Bacchus in her life, only to be discarded by him, too?

She drew in a sharp breath, which eased the lump. Drove it down deeper, where it was a little easier to ignore. She had too much to do today to sit up here wallowing in self-pity.

"Elsie?" Emmeline called up the stairs.

She rubbed her arm across her eyes. Cleared her throat. "I'll be right there!" The volume helped keep her voice even. She needn't give Emmeline a reason to reject her as well, though the maid seemed to like everyone, Nash aside. Hurrying to her small table, she dumped out what little water was left in her pitcher into her washing bowl and dotted it on her eyes and cheeks, cooling them. Then she stood erect and forced herself to take a big gulp of air. Repinned part of her hair.

If Emmeline noticed anything amiss, she didn't mention it.

Elsie woke to a thumping chest. The tendrils of the strangest dream curled beneath her skull. She'd been trapped in a room full of kitchen supplies, all the exits blocked by stacks upon stacks of bowls. In her desperation to escape, she'd knocked over the largest stack—

Something clamored down the hallway.

Not a dream.

Leaping from bed, Elsie called, "Are you all right?" not knowing if it was Emmeline or Ogden. Practiced hands struck a match and lit a candle. "Emmeline, is that—"

"Help!" Ogden bellowed.

Something heavy hit the floor.

Gasping, Elsie ran for the door, nearly putting out the candle in her haste. "Who's there?" she cried, nearly screamed. Ogden's door was ajar at the end of the hallway. Something else fell over. A scuffle, broken glass—

Elsie swung into the room just as a shadow passed through the window. Her candle struggled to hold its light. Her heart leapt into her throat.

A moan sounded from the wall.

"Ogden!" she cried, rushing to his side. One of his eyes was starting to swell shut. She lifted the candle, searching for blood, but found none other than in the split on his brow.

"What's happening?" Emmeline appeared in the doorway, her eyes huge.

Setting the candle down so forcefully she nearly sent it out of its holder, Elsie shouted, "Go wake the neighbors, and send Mr. Morgan for the constable! Hurry! He's getting away!"

Emmeline froze for a full second before grabbing the skirt of her nightdress and barreling down the stairs.

CHAPTER 18

"The men are searching now." Constable Wilson examined the window. The perpetrator had escaped that way, despite it being two stories above ground. He'd shattered a pane in his desperation to open it. "Seems you got off lucky."

"I beg your pardon?" Elsie snapped, wrapping her shawl more tightly around herself. They had all taken up posts in Ogden's bedroom, lit with candles and lamps. Ogden sat on the trunk at the foot of his bed, pressing a cold slice of meat to his eye, while the constable paced back and forth across the room, occasionally taking notes. Elsie lingered near the window, wanting to see everything the constable noticed or wrote. Emmeline fidgeted by the doorway.

"You've found nothing stolen yet—"

"We've only checked his cabinet!" Elsie interjected. His drops had not been touched.

"—and a black eye is better than what it could have been." Constable Wilson looked pointedly at her.

Elsie pinched her lips together. He *did* have a point. It could have been much worse. Thank God it was not.

The constable squinted out the window. "Good, the lights are on."

"Lights are coming on all over the town," Elsie said.

He pointed his pen across the way. "I was referring to the post office. Mr. Morgan is sending a telegram to the High Court of Justice."

Elsie's stomach sank. "The High Court? Whatever for?"

"Mr. Ogden is an aspector." He said it matter-of-factly, as though Elsie hadn't known. "Her Majesty has sent out missives that the court is to be alerted of all life attempts and robberies involving aspectors."

Life attempts. Had Elsie and Emmeline not woken, had Ogden not stirred and managed to fight back, would he be dead now? Would they be talking to a coroner instead of a constable? Would the London Physical Atheneum, to which Ogden was registered, be descending upon them like termites to take away his meager opus?

Shivers ran down her spine. "Do you truly believe there's a connection to the other crimes?"

"I mean to follow orders, Miss Camden."

Elsie shook her head. "You know him, Wilson. He wouldn't be a target." She glanced at Ogden, but he didn't look offended.

The constable nodded. "Indeed. You are only novice level, correct, Mr. Ogden?"

He nodded. "Not for lack of trying."

"What will happen?" Elsie asked, voice tight.

"I imagine they'll send a team immediately, both to hunt the perpetrator and to interrogate you."

From the doorway, Emmeline squeaked, "Truthseekers?"

Elsie clawed at her shawl as cold dread wound through her bones. *Truthseeker* was a fancy title for the spiritual aspectors who worked for the High Court of Justice, the highest court in England, which dealt with magic-related crimes the atheneums couldn't handle on their own. The title had its origins in the fact that spiritual aspectors had tricks up their sleeves that lent greatly to investigation, the greatest being their ability to pull truth from even the most stubborn man's throat.

Or woman's.

One truth spell, and a spiritual aspector could pull every one of Elsie's secrets into the light.

"We're the victims," she protested, already knowing it would do no good.

"You have nothing to worry about. But I will need you to return to your rooms until they arrive."

Elsie's fingers went cold. "Do you really think this is necessary?"

At least the man had enough feeling to give her a sympathetic look. "It's protocol."

Setting her jaw, Elsie pushed past him to Ogden and placed a hand on his shoulder. "You're all right?"

"Just this." He shifted to indicate his eye, then winced.

Turning, Elsie said, "You'll call the doctor, too?"

Constable Wilson answered, "As soon as I have a man to spare." He indicated the door.

Elsie dragged her feet on her way back to her bedroom.

ॐ

Lightning danced beneath Elsie's skin. *They won't ask about your abilities,* she told herself as she paced the length of her room. *Why would they? We're the victims.*

She heard a cacophony of shod horse hooves and wheels. Peeked out her window, but she couldn't see the arriving carriage, only hear the exhaustion of the animals pulling it. Sweat slicked her palms. There were so many questions they could ask. So many, and Elsie wouldn't be able to resist answering, unless she broke the spell before speaking. Would a truthseeker notice?

"Calm down," she whispered. She drew in deep breaths, squared her shoulders. She had no reason to be fearful. If they noticed she was discomfited, they'd ask more questions. More questions meant more truths.

And she didn't think she'd be able to barter free labor to keep a truthseeker quiet.

A pang stung her heart.

Footsteps came up the stairs. Elsie ran to her bedroom door and pressed her ear to it, listening. A few pleasantries were exchanged—she recognized the constable's voice but not any words—and then a door shut. They were starting with Ogden.

More footsteps neared her door. Elsie leapt back from it, and a moment later, a knock sounded.

She opened it and looked at the constable.

"Make yourself comfortable, Miss Camden." He again looked sympathetic. "It will be just a few moments now."

Elsie stuck up her nose. "I don't suppose I have time to get dressed."

Fortunately, the man didn't point out that she could have done so while waiting for the court carriage to arrive. "I'm afraid not."

"Very well. And thank you for your help."

He nodded. She closed the door. Opened it again, a few inches. Moved her chair over to the window and sat, looking down at the light-stippled shadows below. Half the town appeared to be awake. She thought she could make out the Wright sisters.

Were she a less refined woman, she would have shouted, *Go home!* out her window. But she didn't.

She was too scared to unlock it.

She was still sitting there, wringing her hands, when the truthseeker knocked on her door ten minutes later. The man was about Ogden's age, perhaps a little older, though fatigue might have aged his features. He was balding in a very unfortunate manner, losing the crest of his hair while the sides still clung on. He didn't have an unkind face, but she suspected his nose had been broken before. She prayed it was from an accident and not violence.

She glanced at his hands. What kind of criminals did he enchant? Did he have . . . *other* methods of seeking truth?

She swallowed.

"No need to be nervous, Miss Pratt. It's merely procedure." He shut the door behind him. It struck Elsie as somewhat funny that she was alone in the room with a man and it wasn't considered improper, but the absurdity of the situation didn't cheer her up.

"I'm Miss Camden." She hated how timid she sounded.

"My apologies." He stepped close to her, and despite her best efforts, Elsie tensed. What would he ask her? *What are your secrets? What are you hiding? Is there any reason you should be incarcerated?* "And my condolences. We'll get this taken care of quickly."

She nodded stiffly. Without further ado, the truthseeker placed his palm against her forehead. Did he feel how clammy it was? What if the spell didn't take because of what she was? What if she was found out—

She felt the spell as it formed, like grains of sand dusting her skin. It rang like her ears sometimes did as it knotted together, heavy on her skin.

It dug into her soul.

She cringed.

"What is your name?" the truthseeker asked, pulling a pencil and pad of paper from a carryall.

"Elsie Camden."

"Your age?"

"One and twenty." She tried to think something else, like twenty-three, but found her thoughts blanked when she did.

She did *not* like this. *Hurry up so you can take it off!*

"Tell me the events that happened tonight."

"I went to bed at ten—" Her tongue twisted, cutting off her words. "Perhaps later? Eleven?"

That spilled out just fine. Apparently the truthseeker could catch lies she wasn't even purposefully making. How was she supposed to remember precisely when she'd gone to bed?

The aspector simply nodded.

"And I slept until I heard a clamor. I thought it was part of a dream." She hadn't meant to say that last part. She'd felt . . . *compelled* to. "I lit a candle and chased after the sound, and I found Ogden on the floor. A shadow vanished through the window. I told Emmeline to get Mr. Morgan, our neighbor, for help."

The man nodded, focused on his notes, not on her. "And what did the culprit look like?"

"A shadow," she repeated. "I saw nothing more. Not even where he went."

"Or how he got down?"

She shook her head. The man didn't seem to notice, so she said, "I suppose he jumped. He shattered a windowpane."

"For what means does Cuthbert Ogden use his aspection?"

The questioning had taken a jarring turn, and it took her a moment to answer. "For his art. He knows very little. He changes the color of things. Softens stones. He can change the opacity of an object. That's all I've seen him do."

"He knows no other spells?"

"He struggles to learn them. Just a few weeks ago, he floundered with an intermediate spell."

The man hummed to himself and scribbled on his pad. "Thank you, Miss Camden. I think that will be all."

Relief fountained up like it had been pumped by the queen herself.

He moved into the hallway. Gestured with a hand. A young man— he was barely eighteen, if that—strode into her room with mussed hair and an unhappy countenance. A lad grumpy from being woken in the middle of the night. Without any semblance of manners, he grabbed Elsie's head and wiggled his fingers across it.

The spell vanished.

Elsie took in a deep breath. Stared at the man as he stalked back out of the room. *A spellbreaker.* She'd never met another one before, not that she was aware. Questions bloomed up her neck and gathered on her tongue. So much she wanted to ask him! Were their methods the same? When had he realized what he was? What sort of training had he received? What work did he do? How much was he paid?

But the young man turned the corner, out of sight. Of course, Elsie couldn't have risked asking the questions even if he had stayed.

She waited for a long moment, listening to the voices coming from Emmeline's room. Seeing no harm in it, she rose and tiptoed to Ogden's room. He had a salve smeared on his eye, a small bandage across his brow. The doctor must have come.

He offered her a weak smile. She sat with him until the constable returned and the truthseeker and his entourage descended the stairs to return to London.

"A few more questions for you, Mr. Ogden," Constable Wilson said.

Ogden sighed. "I don't know what more you can get out of me, but go on."

Elsie patted his shoulder and left, seeking to console Emmeline—and to find out if the truthseeker had asked them both the same questions. But when Elsie arrived at Emmeline's room, she found it empty, a single candle burning on her bedside table.

"Emmeline?" Elsie asked, crossing to the window. Shielding her eyes, she peered outside.

The maid was on the road, talking to the Wright sisters.

Elsie cursed and turned from the window, determined to silence rumor before it could take root.

Master Ruth Hill had given Bacchus two options for his mastership, both of which were master versions of spells he already knew. The first was a hardening spell, something one could use to make wood strong or metal brittle. But the master version was known as the "gem spell" because it could be used to harden rock into precious stones. It was heavily regulated by the government and required registration to learn.

The second was a state-changing spell, the most basic form of which a novice could learn with water. It did essentially the same thing a stove did: change water to gas. Or the opposite—change water to ice. The more powerful the spell, the more easily a person could change the state of any given matter. The more stubborn the matter, the more intense the spell. This master-level spell would not only allow him to bend more materials to his will—it would also allow him to skip a step with many. Turning water vapor directly to ice, for example.

Bacchus chose the latter spell.

He sat in Master Hill's private parlor, which, while small, was elaborately decorated almost to the point of untidiness. The wallpaper was roses and red stripes of varying sizes, accented by hibiscus; the carpet was cream; the furniture covered with baubles and books, Russian eggs, and Brazilian ceramics. Either Master Hill was very well traveled or she kept well-traveled merchants very rich.

He was capable of writing the Latin for the spell himself—he was capable of *so much* now that the life wasn't being siphoned out of him—but he did not protest when Master Hill took the brush to his arm, a vial of blue ink held delicately between her aging fingers. Bacchus had rolled up his sleeves for the purpose, and Master Hill's brushstrokes were professional and small. Not once did she make a mistake, and she paused just briefly to tuck a stray piece of graying blonde hair behind her ear. Bacchus read each word as she traced it down his arm, memorizing the incantation. After he absorbed the spell, he would no longer need the words to perform the magic, but he might want to teach it to another aspector or perhaps keep a record of how the spell was achieved. It was generous of her to let him watch; it was not unheard of for spellmakers to be blindfolded when receiving a new master spell in order to keep it valuable.

When Master Hill finished and most of the ink had dried, she handed him so many drops he could barely hold them all. Drops he'd paid for himself, but that didn't matter. He'd been prepared to spend much, much more on the ambulation spell he no longer needed. They glowed vibrantly, brighter than candles. Bacchus still remembered being nine and having his father, who was not a spellmaker, place a single drop in his hand out of sheer curiosity. It had lit the room, and within the year, he'd been registered with the London Physical Atheneum.

Master Hill then held out an old book to him so he could read the spell aloud, but he didn't need it. He had already committed the words to memory.

"*Versandus naturam. Mutandus viam. Natura versat. Via mutat. Ultimum finemque. Per et intus. Supra et sine. Ultimum. Finem. Audi potentiam meam. Flecte voluntatem meam.*

"*Muti.*"

The drops in his hands glittered and vanished, leaving him with an empty fist. Simultaneously, the ink absorbed into his skin like it had never been there at all. A surge of warmth coursed through him as the spell wrote itself into his internal opus, forever a part of him. Even in death.

"Thank you." Bacchus lowered his arm and let out a stiff breath.

"You've earned it, *Master* Kelsey." Master Hill had a knowing grin on her face. "I am glad you returned to us."

Master Kelsey. That had a pleasant ring to it. Bacchus stood, feeling a little taller. Feeling . . . indestructible. He rubbed his hands where the drops had been. No trace of them remained. Even after all these years, he still thought it odd how the universe simply claimed its payment in exchange for sorcery.

"Here."

He glanced up. Master Hill held out a candle. It was nearly used up, enough for a quarter hour's worth of light, perhaps. White wax and a burnt wick.

He accepted it. "Is the morning light not to your liking?"

Ignoring his question, she strode to the nearest window and opened it, then bid him to follow. "You show great restraint. Most of my pupils jump to use their new magic the second the ink is absorbed."

He smirked. Glanced at the candle. Tightened his grip on it.

"If you would hold your hand outside," Master Hill continued with an amused tilt to her mouth. "Ice to steam is one thing, but most solid matter becomes rather . . . animated when forced into a gaseous form. And we must always account for temperature."

Bacchus nodded. Physics was one of the required courses aspectors of the physical discipline had to study. Leaning out the window, Bacchus outstretched his arm. He noted that Master Hill took several steps back.

Thought moved so much faster than speech. A person could think a hundred things in the time it took for him to utter a single word. With time, Bacchus would be able to think this spell even faster than he already did.

The candle *exploded* in his hands, sending a flash of searing heat through his hand and up his arm. Enough for him to yelp and drop the inch of wick still clasped in his fingers. He'd admittedly pictured the candle simply puffing away. Saying the magic was "animated" was a vast understatement.

He also understood why Master Hill had insisted he try out the ability on something so small. The candle's scent lingered in the air as its molecules drifted away. Rose petals and lavender.

It smelled a little bit like Elsie.

Master Hill switched places with him and pulled the panes closed. "How does it feel?"

He flexed his hand. The burns weren't severe, but would smart for the next hour or so. Could he perform the feat with gloves on, or would that serve only to vaporize his gloves? "Amazing. Thank you."

"There is a ceremony, of course." She stepped away from the window and the sounds of the city beyond it. "But you don't seem one for pomp and circumstance."

"I am not."

She cupped his larger hands in her pale, small ones. "I admonish you, then, not to stop here. Continue achieving. Advancing. Fulfilling your potential, because I see a great deal of it in you. There are many in the world who will try to stifle it, because of jealousy or because they think it is not the way of things, but they are wrong. You and I are more similar than you might think, Bacchus Kelsey. And while it may not be your goal to join the Assembly of the London Physical Atheneum, you should always *have* a goal. Do you understand me?"

She had such a maternal look to her face, such insistence in her pale eyes. Bacchus wondered after her background. In England, as with most countries, only women of fine breeding had the opportunity to become aspectors. Women who already had a step up in life. He found himself very much wishing to know her story.

"I do. And I believe you have much more to teach me, magic aside."

She smiled, patted his hands, then released him. "I do, if you'll hear it. I'll ring for tea."

She moved to a bellpull on the wall. Bacchus crossed the parlor, looking over the simple but refined decorations on the mantel. A large mirror hung above it, allowing him only to see himself from the chest up. He'd wound his hair back tightly, and from the front, it almost looked like he wore it short, like Englishmen did.

Turning from the mirror, he strode toward the more comfortable furniture. Master Hill had set him up in a hard chair in the corner of the room for the spell. He found an upholstered chair beside a table that had three days' worth of newspapers gathered in a stack, the newest at the top. A familiar word caught his eye, and Bacchus leaned forward to read the headline.

The Bandit Strikes Again! Workshop in Brookley Latest Target.

༄

"*This* is why you don't talk to the Wright sisters!" Elsie spat, throwing the day's paper on the dining table. "Sixpence says they're the ones who went squealing to the press."

"Elsie." Ogden's voice was firm but tired. He leaned over his lunch of kidney pie, supporting his head with one fist.

Emmeline, a little taken aback, said, "Well, isn't it exciting? To be in the paper? Our names are not mentioned, besides. You shouldn't be so upset."

Thank the Lord our names aren't in it, Elsie thought as she dropped hard into a chair and jabbed a fork into her own slice of pie. Elsie was supposed to be invisible. Unextraordinary. Useful to the Cowls. She wouldn't stay invisible for long if people started taking an interest in her place of work.

"They embellished the lot of it," she griped, shoving the pie into her mouth. The pastry was warm and flaky, and it dissipated some of her frustration. "They say just enough to stir the imagination, so people think it's some grand tale. And neither the constable nor the truthseeker confirmed the attack was related to the opus-stealer's crime spree!"

The reporters had made Ogden out to be some fascinating specimen on par with Viscount Byron and the baron. With their luck, people would start claiming his prices were too high, since he apparently had so much money to sit back on.

She glanced at Ogden, feeling a sudden stab of unease. What if she was wrong? What if it was more than she thought, and the would-be thief came back to finish what he'd started? The thought of losing Ogden was too much for Elsie. She would crumble to nothing were he ever taken from her. He was the closest thing to family she had.

Pulling away from the destructive thoughts, she added, "I'll talk to the glazier and get the pane replaced as soon as possible. And the locks changed."

"Thank you." Ogden sipped a cup of tea. "I think that would be for the best."

Elsie managed to be amiable for the duration of luncheon. In truth, Emmeline was hard to stay angry at—she was like the little sister Elsie never had. Or rather, the little sister Elsie could not quite remember. Her siblings were vague shadows on her memory; most of what she knew of them came from Agatha Hall, whose memory wasn't terribly sharp, either. One would think a girl of six would remember her family and what they were called, but for some reason Elsie just . . . couldn't. Something about that time, somewhere between waking up in the Halls' home and sitting in a row of other children at the workhouse, was broken. Dark and dense and heavy in her mind. She did think she had a brother named John, or perhaps Jonathon. Of course, John Camden was such a common name she had never been able to find any leads. Sometimes Elsie wondered if her family was a fancy she'd invented out of loneliness and the Halls had merely played along until they tired of it.

Finished, Elsie helped Emmeline clear the table until a customer came. She spoke with him—yes, Ogden did do busts, and yes, he was the one from the paper—and organized a few things, placed Ogden's work orders where he could see them, and set off for the glazier. It was a standard-sized pane the intruder had broken, so she didn't need to deliver measurements. The glazier would come tomorrow morning to fix the window. And the blacksmith, who also knew locksmithing, would come by that evening to evaluate their security.

"Oh, Miss Camden!" crooned a canary-like voice as Elsie started back home. She knew the voice well; she'd eavesdropped on it many times when she didn't have a novel reader to occupy her. Now, however, it made her cringe.

Alexandra Wright. And her sister, Rose, right behind her.

Elsie's body tensed like her bones had turned to vises. She couldn't recall a single time she'd heard either woman actually say her name, let alone speak to her. Elsie preferred to remain invisible, just as the Cowls did. And right now, she wished to be a cat that could turn tail and clamber up a drainpipe.

Unfortunately, magic did not work that way.

The sisters approached with suspiciously wide smiles and beady eyes. "We're so dreadfully sorry for the break-in! How horrid! And so fortunate that no one was hurt."

Elsie glanced down the road, toward the stonemasonry shop. "Not badly, at least," she said.

"Emmeline was not specific at all, poor thing." The two exchanged a look that was supposed to appear concerned, but their acting wasn't up to snuff. "Surely the perpetrator didn't go through your room as well? How frightening!"

Something hot boiled at the base of Elsie's throat. "Yes, very. Too frightening to speak of. If you'll excuse me."

She pushed past the duo.

"Oh, but Miss Camden! We're simply trying to console you as any loving neighbor should—"

Elsie kept walking, lengthening her strides until she practically ran. Perhaps it was rude, but she didn't mind being rude to rude people. *They'll forget me and move on to someone else by next week.*

She'd have to warn Emmeline to stay away from them.

Arriving home out of breath, Elsie barely had time to hang up her hat before Emmeline, sleeves rolled to her elbows, popped out of the kitchen and said, "Elsie, I'm to send you to the sitting room as soon as you're home. We have a guest. He arrived not ten minutes ago!"

"Oh?" She touched the sides of her hair, smoothing down loose strands. "A customer?"

Emmeline shook her head, eyes wide. "He is quite the sight! Straight from the Americas, I'm sure!"

Elsie froze while her stomach slapped against the floor.

When she moved again, it was to bound up the stairs.

Her limbs buzzed with energy as she approached the door to the sitting room, which was slightly ajar. She quickly shook out her skirt and smoothed back her hair. The door hinges squeaked when she entered. Both men in the room looked over, though Bacchus had to turn around in his chair to do so.

A surge of excitement swept through her middle. Bacchus. Here. In her house. He looked so radically out of place Elsie wondered if she'd hit her head fleeing from the Wright sisters and this was the wishful creation of her unconscious mind. She was terrified and gleeful at the same time, similar to how she felt when reading the climax of a good book. Except this was much more visceral. This was *real*.

What are you doing here? she almost blurted, but the double time of her heartbeat created a blessed disconnect between her thoughts and her mouth.

"Elsie, your good friend Master Kelsey dropped by to see if we were all right," Ogden explained. "That paper has certainly circulated the news quickly."

Master. Had it happened already? Cold disappointment tempered the storm in her stomach. But—

He'd come to see if she was all right? Didn't that mean he cared about her welfare? It wasn't yet evening—how quickly had he ridden over after hearing the news?

Desperate for a moment to think, she stumbled, "Would you, uh, like some tea?"

207

"Emmeline's taking care of it. Come, sit." Ogden gestured to a chair. He didn't appear angry, only puzzled. "Master Kelsey says you met in the market?"

Elsie's gaze flitted like a fledgling sparrow from Bacchus to Ogden, to Bacchus, to the mantel, to Bacchus, and back to the chair he occupied. By the time she reached her own seat, she'd investigated everything in the room, and *Master* Kelsey a dozen times over. "Yes, when I went to get those paints." *Truth.* Her mind spun through everything that was safe to share. She sat. Tried to read Bacchus's expression, but he was so bloody good at hiding his thoughts all she got was stoic curiosity, if such a thing existed. "You've tested, then?"

"It was not so much a test as a formality of my acceptance, but yes." His English accent was crisp, flawless. His green gaze swept over her quickly. Elsie checked her posture.

In reply she said, "We are generally unharmed, though as you can see, Mr. Ogden took the brunt of the attack." Ogden's eye was a nice mix of yellow, red, and violet, and it would only be darker tomorrow. Remembering herself, she added to Ogden, "The blacksmith will be here tonight, the glazier tomorrow."

"Thank you," he said.

Turning to Bacchus—it was unreal to have him sitting there, in their sitting room, looking so normal, so *present*—she asked, "How is the duke? Mr. Ogden, I don't know if Mr.—Master—Kelsey told you, but he's staying with the Duke of Kent. Apparently he was good friends with Bacchus's late father." She was talking too fast.

Master Kelsey. Master *Kelsey.* She certainly wouldn't get used to that. And the more she dwelled on it, the smaller their sitting room seemed, the plainer her dress became, the simpler her life, her interests, and her employment. One word, one title, had done all that.

She hated it.

"He did mention it, yes."

Emmeline stepped in then, carrying the tea service. She set it down, but Bacchus politely declined, and Elsie waved her cup away, stomach too tight to accept so much as a sip. Ogden, however, took his, sugar and cream and all.

"The duke is unwell," Bacchus finally answered as Emmeline departed, looking over her shoulder every fourth step. "I often forget how old he is, how mortal."

"Oh no." Elsie leaned forward. "Not terribly ill, is he?"

Bacchus shook his head. "A temporal aspector came by, but the duke is seventy already, so he could only do so much. The outlook is rather dim."

"I'm sorry to hear it." Ogden set aside his tea. "I imagine you are close to him."

"Will you stay?" Elsie asked. Then, realizing how pleading the words sounded, she added, "I-In Kent, I mean. For the duke's convalescence."

He nodded. "Of course. But I did not come to share my grievances, only to ensure you were dealing well with your own."

Ogden replied, "Journalists will embellish any story to make it sell. It was a by-the-books failed robbery, I'd say."

"I agree with you, about the journalists." Bacchus folded his hands together. His sleeves seemed more fitted, as did the shoulders of his frock coat. Goodness, was it possible for the man to get even *larger* now that the siphoning spell wasn't sucking his strength away? "But you are an aspector, and if your attack is related to the other crimes, it could be a serious matter."

Ogden chuckled. "Then the culprit is indeed getting desperate."

Bacchus seemed to consider this.

"And you?" Elsie tried, still struggling to discern his state of mind. "You're well? Outside of the duke's health?"

He nodded. "Very well." There was an intonation in the words that warmed her, like he was thanking her yet again for his newfound vivacity. "As for the duke, time will tell."

Of course, Bacchus was going to leave eventually, no matter how long he stayed. From what he'd told her on the way to Ipswich, he had no interest in furthering himself with the London Physical Atheneum. His real life was in Barbados, where he didn't have to fake an accent or complain about frigid weather. She knew that—had reminded herself of it often—and yet she was glad he'd come to see her. Perhaps he would stop by again before sailing the River Thames. Perhaps.

The small talk ran low, and Elsie heard the front door open downstairs. Ogden must have heard it as well, for he stood, tugged down his shirt, and offered a hand to their guest. "I thank you for looking out for us, Master Kelsey. It's unnecessarily kind of you."

He nodded. "I hope your eye heals quickly."

They ventured downstairs, Elsie wringing her hands together, and had just turned toward the studio when Emmeline, flustered, came barreling down the hall. "M-Mr. Ogden, Nash is here for you."

"Tell him now is not a good time."

The blond-haired man appeared in the hallway behind her, dressed casually in a linen shirt with no cravat or waistcoat. "Sir, if I might—"

"Not *now*, Nash." Ogden didn't shout it, but he might as well have. The venom in his voice gave Elsie pause, and even Bacchus looked askance at him.

The deliveryman looked offended—even enraged—for half a second, but he didn't say anything as he turned and strode away, exiting through the studio door. Elsie thought he'd slam it, but he didn't.

Emmeline sighed in relief.

"My apologies." Ogden rubbed his forehead, then again adjusted his shirt. "I suppose last night has caused more stress than I care to let on. Nothing some work won't fix."

He nodded politely to Elsie and Bacchus before following Nash's footsteps into the studio.

"I . . . Why don't we exit through the back door, hmm?" Elsie offered, exchanging a look with Emmeline she hoped said, *Make sure Ogden is all right.*

She led the way, and Bacchus followed silently behind her, though he might as well have been a wolf breathing down her neck, the way he loomed. At the back door, glancing over her shoulder to ensure Emmeline hadn't strayed, she whispered, "You've no luck figuring out who did it?" She was very close to him—close enough to detect a spell, if he still had one. The faintest scent of cut wood and oranges danced around her, no longer seasoned by that earthy note of the temporal rune, and she again thought about the feel of his chest beneath her hand. She cleared her throat and willed her skin not to flush.

It took Bacchus a moment to answer—she hadn't been very specific, so she didn't blame him. "No. I will look into it, but I fear it will be a fruitless endeavor. It happened long ago, and I cannot even connect which continent it happened on." He sighed and slipped his hands into his coat pockets.

"How very strange."

"Are you honestly well, Elsie?" His eyes seemed too knowing for some reason, like they could burrow beneath her skin. She dashed her traitorous thoughts away, fearing he'd pluck them right from her head. "You are unharmed? You have no concerns?"

She thought of Ogden's flaring temper, so unusual for him. "I'm certainly concerned," she admitted. "But what is there to be done? The man, thief, whatever he may be, is gone, and none of us got a good look at him. The constable can't search for a person with no description. And the truthseeker didn't seem interested."

"They alerted the High Court?"

The front door opened and closed, meaning Nash was on his way again. "Ogden is an aspector. It's procedure, apparently, with everything happening." She offered a weak smile. She still couldn't believe the attack was related to the ones previously in the papers—Ogden was a feeble spellmaker. Yet the incident had still left a mark on her nerves. "No need to worry. I've avoided shackles once again."

"Good." He averted his eyes in thought. "I wonder if it is only one person. There's such a breadth to the crimes, and no real evidence to speak of. If we start connecting every crime in the aspector world, we'll never solve anything. The academy, for example."

That gave her pause. "What academy?"

"The aspection academy that filters into the atheneums." When she didn't react, he continued, "A wing of it burned down, killing a professor and two apprentices." He frowned. "Their opuses weren't recovered, but that's to be expected in a fire. And yet even that is being attributed to this bandit."

She tried to ignore the gooseflesh rising on her back and arms. "That's . . . terrible."

Rubbing his beard, Bacchus hummed his agreement.

Elsie wondered if the squire had been to the academy on one of his trips to London. He'd need a reason to visit, having not a magical hair on his body. Perhaps Bacchus was right, and it wasn't one great murdering criminal, but several wayward souls trying to cause a storm. Or perhaps the uprisings of the seventeenth century were upon them once more, the magicless and downtrodden attacking aristocrats, stealing their opuses so they could have some semblance of power for themselves. "Ogden may be right about journalists," she offered. "And about him being a target for his opus. He barely knows more spells than my shoe, really."

His lip quirked at that. If only he would smile at her, fully, one more time. But she couldn't bring herself to ask, nor to be witty enough to merit it.

"Give my best to the duke, Bacchus." She touched his sleeve, then instantly regretted it when her cheeks warmed. "Take care of yourself, and . . . let me know if I can help."

It was a foolish offer. If their acquaintance deepened, he might discover what Ogden and Emmeline still had not. He might catch sight of her wrongness.

He nodded. "You as well. I . . . might place a few wards on my way out."

"I would like that, thank you."

They stood there awkwardly for a moment before Elsie opened the door. "I don't mean to insult you by sending you out the back—"

"I'd rather not interrupt Mr. Ogden's business." He offered her a nod, the hair gathered at the nape of his neck bouncing slightly, and departed. Just like that. Elsie forced herself not to watch him go. She needn't stand in the doorway like some lovesick pup.

I'm not lovesick, she snapped at herself, closing the door a little too hard. Bacchus was merely an adventure. A fancy. Proof that she read too much fiction.

Perhaps she should switch to scientific journals for a while. She couldn't think of a better medicine for her twisted insides at the moment besides warm milk.

The studio door opened and closed. Best she help the next customer.

But when Elsie stepped into the studio, it was empty, save for Ogden hacking at a lump of clay in the corner.

"Did Emmeline leave?" she asked.

"I believe she's in the dining room." Ogden's focus stayed on the clay.

Elsie glanced to the door. "Didn't someone just come in?"

Looking up, he shrugged. "I didn't hear anything."

Odd. Perhaps her mind had merely sought out an excuse to change the pattern of her thoughts.

"Elsie"—Ogden turned his stylus in his hand—"is that man courting you?"

Her cheeks burned. "Goodness, no. I barely know him."

He nodded halfheartedly. "It would be good for you, after . . ." He didn't dare say *Alfred*, not when that wound was so newly opened. "Though I'd hate to see you heartbroken again, my dear. And heartbreak is inevitable across the class divide."

He might as well have taken that carving tool and stabbed it through her breast.

"I'm well aware." She forced the words to be light. "But like I said, I barely know him. And he's off to Barbados soon, besides."

"Is that where he's from? I didn't know if it was rude to ask."

Elsie rolled her eyes.

Ogden paused. "Hand me that order, would you?" He gestured weakly toward the counter. Fortunately, Elsie knew what he meant. She strode over to retrieve the latest work order—

A gray envelope poked out from beneath it.

Her breath caught. *How?*

Perhaps she hadn't imagined the opening and closing of the door, after all. Had they *just* delivered this? But how could it have escaped Ogden's attention?

Grabbing the envelope, Elsie bolted around the counter and out the front door, ignoring Ogden's alarmed cry that followed her. She ran out onto the street, turning, looking everywhere there was to look.

She'd been too slow. No strangers lingered around the house, no one in hiding. Not that she could see.

Pinching her lips together, she stole away to the shade at the back of the house and brought the crescent-moon-and-bird-foot seal to her face. Broke it. Read the name of her next target.

The London Physical Atheneum.

CHAPTER 19

Elsie did not like doing her job at night. It made her feel like a criminal. Which she wasn't. At least, not at the heart of the matter. What God-fearing person, for example, would call Robin Hood a criminal?

It really was a matter of perspective.

She shivered, though it wasn't terribly cold in London. Wasn't even raining. With excuses of being lost and feverish, or perhaps looking for her cat, in her back pocket, Elsie approached the massive Physical Atheneum.

It had guards, yes, but not many of them walked the grounds. Like many wealthy places, the atheneum relied on magic to guard its doors. Magic did not require an hourly wage, nor did it fall asleep on the job. That, and the atheneum was never empty. There was always someone out and about, studying or prepping or snoozing at his desk. Still, the Cowls had given her instructions for how to proceed, and she followed them with exactness. She would very much not like a repeat of the doorknob incident in Kent. If she was caught here, she doubted her captor would be as lenient as *Master* Bacchus Kelsey.

She needed to be swift, regardless, for she did not want to risk connecting him to this in any way, even if it was for the good of the people. The atheneum certainly wouldn't see it that way. In truth, Bacchus might not, either.

Tonight's task involved a great deal of walking, but Elsie came at the atheneum from behind—the northwest side. She found the lounging garden mentioned in her letter, a long path covered in pale stone, studded with benches and potted bushes trimmed to look like spheres. She approached carefully, favoring the long shadows cast by the half moon, searching for the first spell.

She spotted it right before she stepped in it—a night-activated spell that caused the ground to surge up around anything that put pressure on it. She undid it easily, having unraveled the very same enchantment at the duke's estate. She found the next one less than two feet away. Crouching, her skirt bunched between her knees, Elsie crept along that way, ignoring how the runes made her itch.

She was not surprised at the Cowls' reasoning for sending her here. Magic was a tool that could help all of society. Or hurt it, as was the case with the curse in the duke's fields. But magic helped plants grow, tamed animals, eased transportation. It kept bodies working, children healthy. And so anyone who hoarded it for pride and profit hurt those who lacked access to it. Even Bacchus had been denied a spell he'd needed, and he was *one of them*.

Elsie wondered how many useful spells were hidden in the library of the great fortress before her, withering away, unused and forgotten, helping no one. Once her work was finished, others more daring than she would sneak in, copy the spells, and distribute them. Perhaps if spellmakers were not so bloody gluttonous, they wouldn't be robbed or murdered in their beds. This way, there would be more for all . . . if the lower classes could obtain the necessary drops to absorb magic as well. But sharing the wealth of the spellmakers would be another task for another day.

The "suction" spells—Elsie hadn't a better name for them—ended when the stone did. She proceeded even slower than before, pausing once when she thought she heard something nearby . . . but silence settled, minus her rapid-fire heartbeat. There was another spell here, somewhere, although she saw nothing on the ground—

There. For a moment she thought it was a spiritual spell, for she *heard* it, faintly, like a mosquito close to the ear. But as she neared two identical statues standing across the path from each other, she spied glimmering *physical* runes on each of them.

The barely audible sound made sense. She'd undone an enchantment like this once before, a few years ago. The two sister spells formed an invisible barrier that if broken, let out a horrible noise. It was an alarm, likely activated by darkness as the suction spells were.

If she set off this alarm, she didn't think she'd be able to run far enough to hide before someone found her. Reaching one hand out carefully, ensuring her fingers never passed the inside of the rune, she loosened one end. Then the opposite end. A small loop in the center, then the bottom, until the spell let out a weak croak and vanished. She needn't worry about the sister rune—without anything to connect to, it would be harmless.

Still, Elsie held her breath when she passed between the statues, sighing in relief when nothing happened. Her chest felt too warm beneath her corset, but when she searched for other alarm spells, she found none. Nerves, then.

Approaching the building, Elsie glanced up at the nearest window, which started about a foot above her head. If the Cowls were correct, there was one spell left—one that forbade passage through all ground-floor windows from the outside. Once she eliminated that, the Cowls could sneak into the library, copy the spells they needed, and flee. If she lingered long enough, would she see one of them?

And what explanation will you give Ogden if you're not in your bed come morning?

Given the assault he'd suffered, he was liable to contact the authorities at once. Which would require her to answer questions best left unasked. No, she needed to be quick.

Retreating into the garden, Elsie tipped over a pot, dumping out its soil and flowers. She froze over the mass, hearing footsteps nearby. She listened closely to them until they faded and her calves burned from her prolonged squat. Heaving the pot up, she carried it back to the window and stood on it.

The spell came alive beneath her fingers, beckoning her. Elsie worked with both hands, having to jump up twice to reach the top of the rune. She felt exposed, and sweat slicked the curve of her spine. When the spell broke apart, it took every ounce of discipline she had not to bolt away. She needed to replace the pot in case the Cowls' man did not come until tomorrow night. She couldn't give anyone a reason to be suspicious, else she'd have to do this all over again. And if her work was discovered, there *would* be patrolling guards.

Feeling oddly stronger than she had moments before, she carried the pot back and shoved dirt into it, heedless of what it did to her dress. The unrooted flowers were a mess, but she stuck them into their beds, anyway. No one would notice unless they looked closely. She swept loose soil into manicured grass and crept, with painstaking slowness, out the exact way she had come.

As far as she knew, no one followed her.

Elsie stepped out of the way as Squire Hughes exited the post office. Not out of deference, but because she was sure the man would simply mow her over if she did not. He neither held the door for her nor made eye contact. He simply charged past, nose held high, and headed toward his horse, which Elsie noted was newly respelled.

Biting the back of her tongue, Elsie slipped inside the post office. One of the post dogs whined in the back, and Martha Morgan shuffled around a few letters in the cubbies against the wall behind the desk.

"Good afternoon, Martha," Elsie said.

Martha peeked over her shoulder. "Oh, Miss Camden! One moment, if you would." She finished organizing the small stack of envelopes in her hand before giving Elsie her full attention. "How can I help you?"

"I need to send a telegram to Brixton, addressed to Mr. Allen Baker." She unfolded the note in her hands where she'd written Ogden's instructions. "The piece will be ready tomorrow." Elsie fished out the appropriate coin and laid it on the desk.

Martha scrawled the message down. "I'll send it straightaway."

"Thank you." Elsie folded the paper and turned for the door.

"Miss Camden." The voice came from Mr. Green, the postmaster, as he strode in from the house connected to the post office. "Good timing. I've just received a telegram for you."

Martha smiled and lifted her eyebrows, as if to comment on the timing, before heading to the back room.

"For Mr. Ogden?" Elsie clarified.

"For you." He handed her the envelope.

Elsie did not like opening her private post in public, but curiosity got the better of her. Hoping it might be from Bacchus, she opened the brief message.

Her heart skipped. Not Bacchus. Juniper Down.

Elsie. We were wrong. Someone is looking for you. Come as soon as you can.

The message was only that, and yet it was everything.

She must have blanched, for Mr. Green asked, "Is everything all right?"

Elsie nodded dumbly. "It's . . . perfect. Thank you."

And then she ran from the post office as though on the wings of a storm.

⁃

"Ogden!" Elsie screamed the moment she rushed into the house. "Mr. Ogden!" She turned around the corner and nearly ran into Emmeline. It was a short distance from the post office to the studio, but Elsie wheezed like she'd run miles. "Where is he?"

"S-Studio." Emmeline gawked. "What's happened?"

But Elsie couldn't bear to delay. She hurried to the studio, Emmeline on her heels. Ogden was standing, his painter's smock half-untied.

Fear blanched his face. "What's wrong?"

Elsie practically leapt at him, grabbing his upper arms in her hands. "I got a message from Juniper Down! Someone is looking for me! Ogden, it must be my *family*!"

He gaped at her and let out a long breath. "You're sure?"

Emmeline squealed.

Elsie smiled. "Who else would go to that out-of-the-way place and ask for me by name? Please, I'll do anything, but let me go. I must leave immediately. I'll take the train, make it as far as Reading—"

He worked his mouth. "You just heard of this?"

Fishing out the telegram, Elsie handed it to him. He read it, and as he considered, Elsie passed it to Emmeline.

"This is incredible." Emmeline grinned. "Oh, Elsie, you've waited so long!"

"I'll pay for temporary help," she said to Ogden. "Whatever you need—"

Ogden, somewhat baffled, shook his head. A small smile played on his lips. "That won't be necessary. If you leave now, you can be on a train before nightfall."

Elsie laughed and kissed Ogden on the cheek. "Oh, thank you, thank you. Goodness, I need to pack."

Emmeline chirped, "I'll get your laundry off the line," and ran from the studio.

Elsie darted to the stairs, taking them two at a time up to her room. Pulling her valise from beneath her bed, she laid it open on the mattress and rummaged through her wardrobe. She liked to take care with how she packed for a trip—especially a trip of an undetermined amount of time—but all she could think of was getting to Juniper Down.

They'd wait for her. Surely they'd wait for her! *We've waited this long, what is another day?* And she could do it in a day if she slept on the train and in the cab. Only a day between herself and her family! Who was it? Her mother? A brother? She dared not hope it would be all of them.

Emmeline came up shortly with Elsie's laundry, which was mainly underthings. Thanking her, Elsie folded what she thought she'd need and crammed it into the valise. Just as the valise was getting full, Emmeline returned with a cloth-wrapped parcel.

"So you don't get peckish." She set it in Elsie's hands.

"Oh, Emmeline, thank you." She straightened. "I'll need my savings passbook." Money for the train ticket, the travel . . . and she had no idea who had come for her. What if they were destitute and needed help? "Ogden!"

"He just stepped out! To the post office, I think, to inquire about replacing you for the week."

"Of course." She barely registered the remark. God help her, she had so many questions and no time to think them.

"I'll get you some more cheese." Emmeline hurried back down the stairs, her footsteps eager. Elsie followed after her as far as Ogden's bedroom, which she entered unabashedly. She used to clean it, after all.

"Passbook, passbook," she whispered, looking over his sparse furniture. He kept all their savings passbooks in here, often added to them himself, out of generosity. Elsie hadn't needed to use hers for quite a while. *Where is it?*

She moved to his desk and opened the top right drawer, searching through the pens and papers within. Several had large scribbles on them, connecting random dots. Something about the drawings seemed almost familiar, but she couldn't think of why. They lacked Ogden's usual artistic eye.

The drawer beneath it held various bottles of blue aspector ink, and the third was filled nearly to the brim with old ledgers. In the left drawers, she found receipts—had he given those to her to document yet?—framing tools, and old letters.

Bother. She retrieved his key from beneath his bedside table and went to the cupboard where he kept his drops, opening the door and sorting through the contents of the locked cabinet. No passbook. Where on earth could it be? She needed to get to London before the last train left, or she'd waste an entire day—

Locking up the cupboard, she returned to the desk and checked its drawers once more. She rifled through receipts, lifted ledgers. Pulled open the drawer of inks and pushed them forward and back. Nothing.

She closed the drawer hard and heard a *chink!* Fearing she'd broken a bottle, she opened it again, ready to find a blue mess staining the wood. But the bottles were fine.

She shut the drawer again, the *chink!* sounding again, but a little softer this time. She paused. It didn't sound like glass hitting glass . . . so what was it? Not her passbook, certainly, but curiosity had her opening the drawer again. Nothing but ink bottles, one nearly empty, three full, one half-full. She shifted the drawer back and forth, hearing the high-pitched *chink!* even though the bottles were not hitting one another.

She shifted each vial, one at a time, until she found one in the back that was empty. It *looked* half-full, but upon closer inspection, the glass had been tinted blue halfway up the bottle. She shook it, hearing something rattle beneath the glass. What on earth?

Uncorking the thing, she turned it over, and a long, metal-tipped stamp fell into her palm. What purpose would Ogden have for hiding a seal—

She stopped breathing when she saw the image at its end. A bird foot over a crescent moon.

The symbol of the Cowls.

Her jaw dropped. Then, as though the thing were a live ember, she shoved it back into the bottle, corked it, and replaced it in the drawer. She slammed the drawer shut and retreated two steps.

The Cowls . . . Ogden was *one of them*?

But it made so much sense. How their letters had always found their way into her most personal spaces, without a trace. Like their deliverer knew precisely where she'd find them. Besides which, he'd always been so generous with her time, as if he knew she was putting it to good use.

Had Ogden always been one of them, or had he converted to their cause after hiring her? Had he discovered something she had not, and been inducted into their fold?

He undoubtedly knew one thing . . . He knew she was a spellbreaker.

Gooseflesh prickled her arms and legs. All the questions she'd wrestled with since the night of the workhouse fire flooded back. Why had he kept it a secret? For Emmeline?

It struck her that Mr. Parker probably wasn't involved at all. Ogden had said, *The squire has his hands in all sorts of nefarious affairs.* Was that what his steward had been hiding? Not his penmanship, but a letter trying to sort out one of Squire Hughes's misdeeds?

But of course it was Ogden! He was an artist. It wouldn't be hard for him to disguise his handwriting . . .

She needed to think on all of this, to decide the best path forward, and yet it felt as if she'd opened a new book with too many pages. She had to get to Juniper Down *now*.

But the Cowls . . .

"Elsie?"

She jumped at Emmeline's voice. Smoothed the sides of her hair. "Emmeline. Do you . . . know where Ogden keeps our savings passbooks?"

She considered for a moment. "Did you check under the bed?"

"I . . . no."

Jittery, she crouched by the bed and pulled out a wooden box of documents. Sure enough, all three of their passbooks were stored near the top. Elsie grabbed hers and held it to her chest. She didn't know how much money she'd need, so she would withdraw all of it. There were still bandits about—

Juniper Down. The Cowls. Her *family*. Ogden.

Her head was going to explode.

Hurrying to her bedroom, Elsie stuck the passbook into her chatelaine bag and closed her valise, noting a second cloth package of food tucked within it.

"Thank you, Emmeline." She hauled the valise into the hallway. She dragged it down the stairs and set it on the table, then worried her hands as she waited for Ogden to return. He came through the door less than a quarter hour later.

"I'll take you to London," he said the moment he stepped into the dining room. He took her valise in hand. "Send us word as soon as you can."

Elsie nodded, unsure of what else to say.

She hoped he didn't notice her awe.

CHAPTER 20

She could have asked him about it on the way to London. There were so many ways Elsie could have started the conversation. *Mr. Ogden, do you know what I am?*

Or, *I found an interesting knickknack in one of your drawers.*

Or even, *Why didn't you tell me you were one of the Cowls?*

Granted, *Cowls* was a nickname Elsie had invented. It wasn't what the group actually called itself.

In the end, she didn't say a word, knowing the ride to London would never be long enough for all of her questions. And if Ogden *was* angry that she'd inadvertently snooped and discovered his true identity . . . What if he did something that forbade her from going to Juniper Down?

She *had* to go. This was more important than . . . anything.

Elsie purchased a hotel room for the night in Reading, the closest train stop to Juniper Down, although she might as well not have bothered. She paced her small room for hours, then failed to sleep on both the chair and the bed. It wasn't until near dawn she managed to drift off, only to wake to a rain-choked sunrise with a tiny bit of drool on her pillow.

It was just as well.

She dressed quickly, making herself nearly as presentable as she'd been for the duke's dinner, though she couldn't truss up her hair the same way Emmeline did. She would see her family *today*. The very thought made her heart flutter.

She wondered if Bacchus would still be in England when she returned. Would he want to know about this wonderful turn of events?

Someone had *found* her. Come back for her. This changed everything.

Smiling at herself in the small mirror on the wall, Elsie pinned her purple hat carefully to her hair. Then she packed up her valise and lugged it downstairs, where a concierge kindly hired her a carriage. The driver took her southwest, toward Juniper Down, a tiny village barely worth a dot on a map. She hadn't been there since she was six. Never visited, only written. She wondered if it still looked how she remembered it . . . though she mostly just remembered the interior of the Halls' house.

She wrung her fingers together until her lace gloves threatened blisters. Then she practiced what she would say. If it was her mother or her father—or perhaps *both*!—she'd of course ask why they had left. Why they'd waited so long to come back for her. But that couldn't be the first thing out of her mouth. She wanted to start on the right foot. She wanted to make them happy they had at last come for her. The questions would follow.

If it was a sibling . . . *Where have you been all this time? Do you remember me? Did they leave you, too?*

Her throat constricted on that last one.

Surprisingly, Juniper Down came too soon, even with the driver having to stop to ask a farmer for directions. It was a tiny place, with only one carriage-sized road running alongside it, and it was in poor care, judging by the way Elsie jostled about. The horses stopped, Elsie's heart leapt into her throat, and the driver opened her door.

"Sure this is it?" he asked, lending a hand to help her down.

Coming around the carriage, Elsie scanned the place. There was farmland off in the distance. The houses weren't too dissimilar from those of the duke's tenants, though they varied a little more in size and looked to be in worse repair. Each had a small garden. Narrow dirt paths crisscrossed around. An old man in a chair by a beehive near the road squinted at her.

Sensing her hesitation, the driver shouted, "Ho! This is Juniper Down, is it not?"

The man bellowed back, "'Tis! What's it to ya?"

Drawing in a large breath, Elsie turned back to the driver. "I'll find it, thank you."

The man nodded and pulled down her valise from the back of the carriage. "Good luck to you."

Elsie nodded and stayed on the road until the carriage turned about and pulled away. Then, trying not to chew on her lip, she approached the old man.

"I'm sorry, but do you know where the Halls live?" she asked.

"Henry's lot?" he repeated, eyeing her. All his clothes, including his hat, boasted at least one hole, and here she was in one of her best dresses. Perhaps she had made a mistake, primping before coming here. But the man lifted an empty pipe and pointed it south. "Down the road, they is."

He didn't offer to escort her, which was just as well. "Thank you," she said, and followed his direction.

The noises of young children—one of them a crying baby—reached her ears. A woman knelt in her garden, pulling weeds. Another drew water from a well, watching her pass. She wore a black hat and black ribbon around her wrists. Was she in mourning? Folk here likely couldn't afford a special wardrobe for it.

Elsie nodded to her and continued on, soon spying a little girl also in black, and a black-dyed dress hanging on a clothesline. How terrible. What had happened here?

The path forked up ahead, but fortunately a woman perhaps in her late thirties stepped out of her house just then. "Oh!" she exclaimed, looking Elsie up and down. "Are you in from Foxstone?"

Elsie shook her head. "I'm from Brookley, actually. Near London."

The woman whistled. "What are you doing in these parts?" She shook her head. "Don't mean to be rude, just curious. Are you lost?"

Elsie's shoulders began to ache, and she forced her posture to relax. "Only a little. I'm looking for Agatha Hall."

"Agatha?" The woman stepped onto the path and gestured for Elsie to follow. "She's just around this way." They passed an older woman washing clothes. "Here to see Agatha," the first said, as though the other had asked. They continued along, but Elsie heard the second woman pass the information along to someone else before leaving earshot.

"Right here." Her guide gestured to a house that looked like all the others. "Need me to come along?"

"Uh, no, thank you." She nodded her gratitude and, holding her breath, approached the house.

She knocked thrice, feeling eyes on her back.

Footsteps sounded within, followed by a sharp word, likely to a child. The door opened. Elsie barely recognized her—she was working off the memory of a six-year-old child, after all, and the woman had aged since then. Perhaps it was the dress, or the obvious fact that Elsie didn't belong, but Agatha knew her immediately.

"Elsie Camden!" The words were uttered on a gasp. "Oh goodness, you came. And so fast! Come in, come in." She put a hand on Elsie's elbow and ushered her inside.

The home was cozy. Small. An old dining table took up half the room, and the bottom floor *had* only one room. A narrow set of stairs led up to what Elsie presumed would be one or two bedrooms. A boy of perhaps ten sat by the window, polishing a pair of shoes. There was a fire in the hearth, warming a great iron pot, and the air was overly hot, but it smelled like bread and earth. That smell was more familiar to her than anything else she saw.

Elsie set down her valise, her manners fleeing her. "Where is he? She?"

"He," Agatha corrected. "And he didn't stay. I mean, he's here, but he ain't *here*." She turned and ventured toward a wooden shelf. Pulled an envelope from it and handed it over. The edge was smeared with some sort of grease. "Sorry," she added, gesturing to it, "one of the littles got to it."

An envelope? Elsie turned it over. No seal. "What's this?"

Agatha shrugged. "He wouldn't say much about it. Only to give that to you."

Clutching the envelope in her trembling hands, Elsie asked, "How old is he?"

Agatha shrugged. "Maybe a bit older than meself. Grew out a beard; swear he was clean shaven when you all came around the first time, but it's been so long, and it was only the one night."

Father, she thought, and a chill flowed down her arms. "But he's still here? In Juniper Down?" She broke the wax on the envelope. It was made of fine parchment. The letter within was delicate, the paper small.

"Said 'nearby.' Must've been staying round Birmingham, the way he talked."

Birmingham? That was a ways north of here. Had he been there this whole time?

Elsie held the brief message, written with a fine hand, up to her face.

By the plum where the road turns for Foxstone. Come alone.

That was it.

Elsie turned the paper over, but there was nothing else upon it. Did he want their meeting to be private? Did he intend to wait by the tree day by day until she arrived? It made little sense to her, but Elsie was used to short, direct messages like this.

"Where is the road for Foxstone?"

"That where he is?" Agatha asked, but she pointed toward a corner of the house. "Goes east that way, curves through a bit of a forest. You got to turn right after that, or it'll send you to Pingewood."

Elsie turned for the door. Paused. "Thank you so much, Agatha. Might I keep my things here?"

"Of course. Bring him back, if you like, and I'll see you both fed." She smiled. "I'm right happy for you, Elsie. Glad it turned out."

Nodding, Elsie stepped back into the sunlight. A few people, including children, were lurking around the house, likely curious about what had brought a stranger to the Halls'. Ignoring them, she ventured east, searching for a path wide enough to be called a road. After finding it, she glanced over her shoulder once, but no one followed her. Most likely they were pestering Agatha with their questions. Some of them might even remember the little girl who'd been abandoned by her family fifteen years ago . . . but Elsie would worry about that later.

The way was farther than she expected; the woods weren't close, but she was in a hurry, and she kept up a brisk enough pace that her ribs hurt by the time she reached them. Forcing herself to slow, Elsie scanned the sparse trees, keeping to the center of the road. *Father,* she thought, disbelieving. She tried to remember the lines she'd rehearsed in the carriage, only to find them forgotten.

Why come back now?

Why did you wait so long?

What is your name?

The woods broke, and Elsie couldn't help herself—she hurried again, ignoring the stitch re-forming beneath her corset. After another minute of walking, she saw the fork up ahead, as well as a crude, faded sign that pointed toward Foxstone. Sure enough, there was a massive plum tree a short ways to the west. Upon seeing it, Elsie left the road behind and trekked through the long wild grass, crinkling the letter as she picked up her skirts.

She was nearly there when a man stepped out from behind the tree. She slowed, her tongue twisting, her entire body a pulse. He was tall, just like she was, with a prominent nose and dark eyes, unlike hers. His tan spoke of days out in the sun, and his hair was long and straight, streaked with gray that made it look the color of sand. It might have been Elsie's color, years ago.

She stopped a few paces away from him, surprised at the hardness in his face. Lost for words, she tried, "Hello."

Her father lunged at her, his calloused hand grabbing her neck. Elsie stumbled backward until she hit the plum tree's trunk.

It was only then she saw the pistol leveled with her forehead.

Speech fled.

"You won, I'm here. Tell me what you want."

Elsie gaped. He spoke with an *American* accent.

This was not her father.

Confusion, fear, and disappointment swirled within her. She grabbed the man's arm, but he easily overpowered her, and she could not lift his hand from her neck. She croaked, "Who are you?"

He scowled. "Don't play games with me, Elsie Camden."

He knew her name. He *had* come looking for her, then. But why?

When she didn't answer, he said, "I read your articles. You thought we'd do this on your terms? I looked up your workhouse records. I know what you want, but I'll kill you before I utter the words." He dug the pistol into her forehead.

"Stop!" she screamed, writhing, though it cut off her dwindling supply of air. "Help!" The call was little more than a rasp. Clawing at the man's grip, she said, "What articles? I've no idea what you're talking about!"

He sneered. Stared at her for a moment. Released her, but kept his gun level. Elsie bent over, gasping for air.

"You're too young." He lowered his gun slightly. "Who sent you?"

Straightening, she looked at him, incredulous. "Who *sent* me? You did, you blunderbuss! I got a telegram saying you were looking for me!" Her words tight, she said, "I-I thought you were my father." He must have faked his dialect with Agatha. Either that, or she'd simply gotten it wrong.

Confusion lined his forehead. Elsie shivered with the effort of keeping her thoughts organized and her heart in one piece.

"What articles?" She pushed the question through her sore and tight throat, eyeing the gun. She didn't think it was enchanted, not that it mattered.

"The newspapers. Magazines. All over Europe and the States." He glared at her, and his gun twitched. "You're a pawn."

"I'm no one's pawn. Put that bloody thing away!" She gestured toward the gun. The man lowered it a fraction more, so he'd only blow off her knee instead of her head. "I'm no writer. You've the wrong person."

"No." He shook his head, but he stepped back. He glanced around, as though expecting someone to jump out of the grass and tackle him. "No, it's you. You must be an apprentice." He raised the gun again.

Elsie lifted both hands. The letter fell to the ground. "I work for a stonemason!"

"You're an aspector. And I'm telling you now that you won't have it." His arm tensed.

"*Stop!*" she shouted again, half hoping someone would hear, but the road remained empty. "I-I'm not! I'm a spellbreaker, I swear it." Dangerous, to offer her secret to a man holding her at gunpoint, but it was the only thing she could offer to prove he'd mistaken her for someone else. "I'm only looking for my family. They left me in Juniper Down when I was a girl. That's why I have a workhouse record. I swear it!"

He lowered the gun again, which fountained cool relief up Elsie's stomach. "Prove it."

She opened her hands. She needed a spell first.

He stepped forward; she retreated. He raised the pistol. Elsie held still.

He touched her forehead, and Elsie felt a spell seep into her skin, the same one the truthseeker had used. A spiritual aspector, then. The spell crept over her skin like a worm, and she tried her best not to cringe.

"I've never published a newspaper or magazine article in my life." She was glad for the spell if only because it verified her words. "I haven't the faintest idea who you are." Then, reaching up, she felt for the threads of the rune and pulled it apart, relieved when its magic dissipated.

The man holstered his gun. "An *unknowing* pawn." He shook his head. "Watch yourself. If our paths cross again, I won't be so forgiving."

He headed for the road.

"Wait!" Elsie charged after him. "Tell me what you—"

His gun reappeared in his hand. "I *will* shoot you if you follow me."

Stopped in her tracks, Elsie held up her hands in surrender. She kept them there until the mysterious foreigner turned for the woods. He vanished, and moments later, the galloping of horse hooves swept into the distance.

∞

Elsie stood by the plum tree for a long time, staring at the bit of road where the man had vanished. She stood until her spine and knees ached. Then she dropped to her knees like a dress freed of its mannequin. Her head filled with the complaints of crickets, and a spot on her cheek started to burn where sunlight scissored through the leaves. Confusion simmered like tea in the back of her mind, but its pungency was nothing compared to the hard truth rooting her.

Mr. Hall had been right. They were never coming back.

Her tongue felt swollen in her mouth, her ribs bruised, her stomach empty. All of her, empty.

Had it been so foolish to hope? To think *someone* from her faded memories had remembered her, thought of her, determined that she wasn't so unlovable after all, and come looking for her? She'd been ready to give them everything—forgiveness, understanding, kinship, and every penny she'd saved since she was eleven years old.

But they hadn't come. *He* had.

Blinking her eyes to clear her vision, her thoughts sluggishly turned toward the American. What did he mean, a pawn? A pawn of *what*? Newspaper articles, under her name? And they had to be traceable to England, and to this area, if he'd known where to look up her workhouse records. Where to find the Halls. And it was *her* name, not a pseudonym. What exactly did the articles say? And why her?

Why *all of it*?

She finally moved—rubbing her eyes to alleviate a headache pounding beneath her skull. Would the Cowls know? Ogden? More kindling to add to her fire of questions. So many questions.

It was her corset that finally got her moving. It wasn't comfortable, out in this heat and in that position. Her skirt was thoroughly wrinkled, too. So Elsie stood, her legs shaky, and dragged herself back to Juniper Down. The echo of her footsteps sounded hollow to her ears. Her mouth was dry. Her back hurt.

The little town seemed to have forgotten her as she approached. She spied another family in all black and gray, among them an older woman, a mother perhaps, with a drawn face. Elsie felt for her and her loss. She felt it keenly.

She spied two others dressed for mourning before reaching Agatha's house. She was sweeping off her porch.

"There you are!" she exclaimed when Elsie's shadow drew near. She spied around her. "He's not coming with you?"

Her lungs constricted, but she managed a quiet "No. Later."

Agatha nodded. "Will you be staying the night? We can make you a space by the fire, unless you want to share a bed with the children."

Stay the night. Would she? Elsie wanted nothing more than to be back in Brookley, in her own bed, the shutters drawn and the door locked. "I'm not sure." Then, eager to shift the conversation from herself, she asked, "Why are so many mourning?"

A frown pulled at the woman's lips, and she set the broom against the door frame. "Most terrible thing. Happened almost a week ago now, but they're expecting the ashes anytime now."

Elsie touched her chest. "Oh dear."

Agatha nodded, a tear coming to her eye. She dabbed it with a rough knuckle. "Poor lad. He was only fifteen, and had such a future ahead of him. Got a sponsorship for aspection, he did."

Elsie's stomach sank, and she almost wished she hadn't asked. She didn't know how much more bad news she could take. "A sponsorship?"

"The Crumleys' boy. Been studying for three years already. They pinned their hopes on him, and now it's rubbish." She shook her head. "Terrible way to go, too. Died in the fire at the academy. Weren't too big a flame to start, we've heard, but the local firemen couldn't put it out. Their water staffs had been disenchanted."

Elsie rolled her lips together, then stiffened. Her breath caught in her throat, and it took half a second for her to push it out. "Water staffs?" she asked. Pre-enchanted tools that called up water from the ground and even the air. Hands cold, she added, "Y-You said this happened a week ago?"

"A week tomorrow." Elsie's expression must have been dire, for Agatha laid a comforting hand on her shoulder. "Terrible, isn't it? Him and another boy, as well as one of their professors. To top it off, there ain't even an opus to send home. Fire ate it up, too. Professor John Clive—that was his sponsor—sent his regrets himself, before he . . ." Agatha's words caught, and she turned her head to clear her throat.

"Sorry, lass, that one is still fresh." Withdrawing her hand, Agatha took in a shuddering breath. "Still can't believe it. None of us can."

Elsie tried to swallow and found she couldn't. "Agatha. Where . . . Where is the academy?"

She tilted her head, confused by the question. "Up in Colchester. Why?"

Elsie might as well have bled out on Agatha's doorstep. It couldn't be a coincidence. The same time, the same place, the same magic . . .

She had disenchanted those water staffs.

Which most certainly meant the Cowls had started the fire.

CHAPTER 21

Elsie stumbled back from the porch.

"Miss Camden?" Agatha followed her. "Are you all right?"

She couldn't breathe. It couldn't be true. It simply couldn't be. Ogden was one of them, after all, and he didn't have a foul bone in his body! And she . . . all those deaths . . . *she* . . .

"Just . . . too much today," she muttered, sure she sounded intoxicated. "I need a moment."

"There's beds just upstairs—"

But Elsie shook her head and fled from the house. Fled so fast she was tripping over her skirts. She stumbled all the way to the well by the road, then gripped its sides and leaned over the dark pit, cool air from between the stones whispering against the sweat on her face.

It's a misunderstanding.

"Oh dear, you look sick. Don't turn up your stomach in there, though." An older woman approached, hair pinned messily under a threadbare cap. "Take a sit here. You're Agatha's visitor, ain't you?"

Elsie numbly allowed the woman to guide her to a nearby stump. To draw up some water for her to drink. Elsie swallowed the stale liquid until her belly hurt and she had to stop or suffocate. She spilled some on her dress, but couldn't bring herself to care.

"There." The woman set the bucket aside. She, too, had black on her, though her dress was a simple brown. She offered a soiled handkerchief, but Elsie waved it away. "Did you get some bad news, dear?"

Elsie cradled her aching head in her hands. "You could say that." She could still feel the end of the pistol against her forehead. The touch of the *weapons* beneath her hands in Colchester. The Cowls had offered such a compelling explanation in their letter.

But who else would have disenchanted the water staffs?

She felt a hand on her shoulder. It tightened in reassurance, then lifted. "It's all bad news around these parts. Might help to get it off your chest."

Elsie could have laughed at the notion were her body not so heavy. "I doubt that."

She picked at the black scarf tied around her left sleeve. "One of our own lost a boy."

"I heard. I'm . . . sorry." She had to croak out the last word.

"Just yesterday we got a telegram saying his sponsor had passed, too." The woman's voice squeezed tight, and she coughed. "So terrible."

Lifting her head, Elsie asked, "Professor Clive?"

She nodded. "Agatha must've told you."

Elsie sighed.

"It's all a mess, what's happening in London. All those stolen opuses. It's terrible."

Sitting up straight, Elsie said, "His opus was taken?"

"The report claimed as much. He didn't just go missing; there was vomit on the library floor, full of poison. Someone broke right into that atheneum and did him in." She wiped her wrinkled eyes with the handkerchief. "One less good man in this world." Managing to smile, she added, "At least your ails can't be as bad as that, hmm?"

But Elsie's body felt cold in the afternoon heat. "Which atheneum?"

"The London one."

Elsie stood, nearly knocking her head on the edge of the well's roof. "There are two in London." She knew she sounded forceful, but she had to know. "Physical and spiritual."

Don't say physical. Don't say—

"Well, he was a physical aspector, so I suppose the first." She eyed Elsie like she was half-mad.

Maybe she was. She was ready to scream, or weep, or . . . she didn't know. Her thoughts were retreating from her, almost to the point where she forgot to breathe.

Too much of a coincidence. *She* had been in Colchester. *She* had disenchanted security at the Physical Atheneum just before leaving for Juniper Down.

"I need to talk to your constable," she croaked. Gossip was well and good, but she needed solid information, not hearsay.

The woman stood. "What's wrong? I . . . We don't have one just for us. You have to go to Foxstone."

Elsie swallowed, blinking rapidly until her unshed tears sank down into a hard ball in her throat. "I will pay a florin to whoever will drive me."

༄

"I don't know, miss," the young constable said when she, with the help of a man from Juniper Down, stopped him outside a small millinery. The shop had already closed for the day. Without the patience to introduce herself properly, Elsie had immediately barraged him with questions about the recent sequence of murders and opus thefts.

Adjusting his hat, he continued, "We're just small folk, even here in Foxstone. If you want to know more, you'll need to head to a city. Reading, perhaps?"

And so Elsie did.

⁂

Elsie was tired yet restless as she rode a mail coach to Reading. Her urgency had not been enough to convince someone to take her so late on the Sabbath. At least the constable had been generous in letting her take a room in his home, but she'd returned to the streets before dawn, eager to travel at the first opportunity. It took every bit of control she possessed to keep from weeping in the privacy of the cab.

She clung to the notion of a misunderstanding. It couldn't be her. It could *not* be Ogden.

She went first to the police station on Friar Street, but the constable was not in, and the only other officer available was young and uneasy with her request, so Elsie got directions to the constable's home from the post office. She went on foot and, after finding it, knocked incessantly on the door. A nearly grown child answered, looking perturbed, as Elsie had apparently interrupted their luncheon. Their table was set, food barely touched. A woman leaned forward to get a better view of her, but the man rose and came to the door, dismissing his son.

He was tall and broad shouldered, with a severely receding hairline. He wore a blue peelers coat, so Elsie had no doubt she'd found the right house. The lines on his forehead suggested he was annoyed by the disturbance, yet his eyes were quizzical.

"Mr. Theophile Bowles?" Elsie asked, heart hammering.

"I am."

She took a deep breath. "I know I am interrupting, but I badly need to speak with you concerning the recent crimes regarding aspectors and their opuses."

He drew back. "The journal is hiring women now?"

Normally Elsie would have bristled at the comment, but she didn't have the strength to be indignant. She might as well encourage the assumption. "I assure you, the story is crucial. My own employer was nearly a victim. I'm ready to pay you for your time." Her life savings might as well go to some use.

Mr. Bowles paused, then glanced back at his family. Rubbed his eyes. "Come in, Miss . . . ?"

"Camden. Thank you." She stepped inside, tripping over her own relief that he was inviting her in. She knew the records were public if they were in the papers, but she wouldn't know where to go next to access them if he turned her away.

To his wife, Mr. Bowles said, "Just a moment," and gestured toward a back room, barely large enough to be a bedroom. It had within it a desk, a bookshelf, and a small harp in the corner. Mr. Bowles sat behind the desk. Elsie remained standing.

He pulled out a thick book from a desk drawer and flipped through it, silent enough to make Elsie feel awkward, before pausing near the center of the pages. "Which are you concerned about? Only one occurrence happened in my jurisdiction."

"But you're made aware of others, yes?"

He paused, nodded.

"From the beginning, if you would."

He raised an eyebrow at her, but he did as she asked, listing off an unfamiliar name and location, and the crime: murder. The next crime, a robbery, had happened in a town Elsie had never heard of. Another name, location, minute details. He turned the page. "Baron Halsey attacked and murdered in his bedroom, opus stolen, May 4. Viscount Byron attacked and murdered at the London home of Walter Turner, opus stolen, May 10. Theodore Barrington—"

"Wait." Elsie stepped forward, knees stiff. "Did you say Turner?"

Mr. Bowles rescanned the passage as though he'd already forgotten it. "Walter Turner, yes."

"London home?" The words came out on a whisper. "The viscount was . . . murdered there?" She recalled what Mr. Parker had told her, and the article in the paper. A witness claimed he'd been struck by lightning. And—

"I believe the viscount's sister is married to him. He was visiting." He looked up as though waiting for permission to continue.

Elsie stepped to the side so she could lean on the bookshelf. It took every ounce of courage she could muster to keep her face smooth. Hadn't she disenchanted a hidden door on the back wall of a Mr. Turner's home? So someone could sneak inside, find his room, and use a lightning spell . . .

The constable read three more names before another caught her attention, and she again requested he repeat it. He did, with dwindling patience. "Alma Digby, missing person, believed to be potentially connected."

"You cannot share the details?"

He sighed.

"Just for this one, and I'll leave you to your meal," she promised, hearing the desperation in her voice. "E-Even if it's only what I'd find in the papers, should I take the time to research."

Mr. Bowles leaned onto his fist, and Elsie thought he was trying to remember. "She was—is—a spiritual aspector traveling for a holiday. Went missing en route. I believe there was evidence of a highway robbery. Miss Digby had ordered a magic-armored carriage, which we found, but the spell protecting it had been removed."

Elsie couldn't breathe.

Mr. Bowles stood. "Are you quite all right?"

She managed a nod.

"Let me get you something to drink—"

"No." The word was too forceful. Her lungs felt like blacksmith bellows. "No, I'll see myself out. Thank you."

She stormed back through the house, not even bothering to thank Mr. Bowles's family for their time. The hot afternoon air slapped her as she stepped outside. She kept walking, unsure of her destination, needing to expend the energy building inside her.

She had snuck into a carriage house and broken spells on its vehicles.

She had created an easy path into Mr. Turner's home.

She had broken the water staffs that could put out the fire at the academy.

She had cleared a path into the London Physical Atheneum, where Professor Clive was murdered.

Pausing, Elsie gasped for air, her ribs aching. A cab passed by her.

How many more was she connected to? And each one assigned to her by the Cowls.

By *Ogden*.

"Oh God," she whispered, holding her middle. "It's him." *He* was behind it all. *He* had sent her those letters. *He* had never once complained about her time away, because she'd been doing *his* bidding.

The American had been right. She *was* a pawn.

And the attack on the stonemasonry shop . . . It *didn't* match the other crimes. It had happened shortly after Elsie expressed her worry about the stolen opuses. Had it been a cover? Had Ogden attacked *himself,* or hired someone to do so? Then what, paid off the truthseeker? Used an opus spell to thwart his interrogation?

She hunched over, sure her stomach would upturn the remains of her breakfast—she hadn't eaten since. Wasn't sure she'd ever want to eat again. She was a tool in the greatest crime spree of the century. She'd blindly followed all of it, thinking she was doing good, thinking—

How long had he been using her? She . . . She'd *loved* Ogden. He was the father she couldn't remember. Always kind, always ready to listen. He'd never made her feel small or useless. And yet, just like all the others, he didn't truly care about her. He was simply a dot in a network Elsie didn't understand, a puppet master pulling her strings to do awful, *heinous* things in the name of good—

"Miss, are you all right?" asked a voice, but Elsie waved the person away with a sharp jerk of her hand. Footsteps faded behind her.

Her body shook as she held it all in. The information, the questions, the screams, the tears. Straightening, Elsie hobbled to a lamppost and leaned against it, trying to digest the truth, poisonous as it was, and decide what to do about it. She had to say something to the authorities. Come up with a story that wouldn't indict her. She had to stop him somehow—

Oh God in heaven. Emmeline.

She was still there. Sharing a roof with a murderer. And despite her world turning inside out, Elsie knew one thing for certain: Emmeline was an innocent in all of this.

Elsie had to get back to Brookley. She had to get back *now*.

CHAPTER 22

The train gave her time to reflect, and she hated every minute of it.

Am I a murderer?

Thank the stars I didn't ask Ogden about the seal.

Is Nash part of this? Is that why Emmeline is so uncomfortable around him?

Does Emmeline know anything? No, of course she doesn't . . .

How many more crimes am I connected to? No, I don't want to know.

I want to know.

I don't want to know.

How will I convince Emmeline to come away with me without Ogden overhearing?

Should I send a telegram ahead, pretending to be a buyer, and set an appointment with him?

Where will I go when this is all over?

She wrung her hands together until they were sore and dry. When the train stopped in London that evening, Elsie grabbed her valise and dragged herself to the platform. She'd barely slept, and the only food she'd eaten since breakfast was a bite or two of what was left of Emmeline's packed morsels. Her stomach was a tight knot, and not one she knew how to dis-spell.

"Goodness, is she traveling alone?" Elsie turned slightly to see who'd spoken, and saw two women watching her. Women in fine dresses with their hair meticulously curled. A mother and daughter, if she guessed right.

Elsie averted her eyes and picked up her pace, but she still caught "This thing will bring in anyone, won't it?"

But Elsie didn't have time to care about gossips. Valise in hand, she kicked her skirts as she hurried from the station. Lugging her things about was becoming bothersome, but what else could she do? At least she wouldn't have to linger at the masonry shop to pack a bag.

She thought of all the things she'd have to leave behind, for she'd need to get Emmeline out of there as quickly as possible. Dresses, books . . . Her heart hurt, not for the things, but for the home she would have to leave behind. The stonemasonry shop was her life, and despite it all, it was a very good life. Deep down, she still couldn't accept that Ogden, *her* Ogden, could have . . . but there was no other answer for it. And if by some grace of God there was, it would have to come out after she and Emmeline were safely away.

Where? To Juniper Down, perhaps. The Halls had kicked her out before, when she was merely another mouth to feed, but she was a capable woman now, and she could work crops and clean a fireplace. Emmeline as well. Or they could go far away, to Liverpool or the like, and get a job in service. They wouldn't have a reference from Ogden, but times were changing. Maybe they wouldn't need one.

There was also Bacchus. Unless the duke had passed while she was away, he might still be in Kent. Perhaps, if things got ugly, she could steal away to Barbados—

Stop thinking like a fictional character. She switched her valise to her other hand. She had her savings, and Emmeline would have something, and Elsie had already mentally listed anything she might be able to sell. They'd get by, one way or another—

A flash of yellow caught her eye, and Elsie paused right there in the street, earning a curse from a factory worker as he ran into her.

Nash.

The way was crowded despite the evening hour, but Elsie was sure it was him. His usual smile was nowhere to be seen, his face tight and serious. Perhaps he was innocent of any wrongdoing, but the way Emmeline had always felt so cowed in his presence bit at Elsie. And so, when he turned the corner, Elsie found herself picking up her skirts and hurrying after him, taking one turn and then another when she saw the bright flash of his hair disappearing down a side road. She pardoned herself countless times as she took off after him, accidentally swinging her valise into passersby or nudging them with her shoulders. The throng thinned, and soon she was following Nash much more covertly, though she felt she stuck out like a whale in a bathtub with her luggage.

Finally, the man turned into some downtrodden flats in desperate need of repair. Third door, two-story. Elsie dipped around the side, stowing her valise out of sight. Should she confront him head-on? Act like she was in town on some sort of business, and Ogden had told her where to meet him? Should she be stealthy and sneak up behind him? Perhaps ask the neighbor if she might come in and press her ear to the wall? That wouldn't be strange at all—

She deliberated for several minutes before Nash made the decision for her. He re-emerged with a bag over his shoulder, his strides more purposeful now. He took off down the road quickly.

Elsie, coming around the building, eyed his door.

Then she snuck around back. She used her hatpin to unlock his window, and lifted it.

This was utterly the least elegant thing she'd ever done.

When Elsie dropped into the narrow, filthy kitchen beyond, her skirts toppled over her head, and if Nash had any roommates, they'd certainly gotten a good view of her knickers. Fortunately, the flat appeared to be empty once she righted herself. Empty and dark. And dank.

Something about the atmosphere raised gooseflesh on Elsie's arms. She proceeded quietly, though the floorboards creaked like an old woman's jaw. This was most certainly the dwelling of an unrefined bachelor. The furniture was sparse, belongings few, and yet the place looked untidy. Mold grew in one of the corners. A half-eaten plate of *something* sat on a nearby chair. It had to be at least two days old.

Elsie eyed the thin stairs leading to the second floor. After ensuring the front door was locked, she carefully ascended them.

There was only a single bedroom up top. A narrow bed, a window that had never been washed, a side table that looked to be used as a desk, a narrow wardrobe without doors, and a chest. Elsie shifted to the wardrobe, looking inside. Nothing except clothes. There was a single drawer, but it was empty. Just her luck—she really *was* a criminal now. Best Bacchus never hear of it . . . not that it mattered. She couldn't add him to the tangle of her thoughts, not now, or she'd douse the entire flat in a new rain of tears.

Focus. She crept to the chest, and a familiar shimmer danced on its lid.

"Hello," she whispered, crouching before it. No lock, but a spell that fused the lid to the base. A lock Nash likely undid with an enchanted key. A lock that was unpickable.

Except to her.

Grasping the ends of the simple rune, she pulled them apart, and the spell puffed into the air like face powder. She lifted the lid.

Her stomach sank.

It was full of firearms. Enchanted weapons. Lockpicks, cudgels, a few things she couldn't identify. Touching one of the blunt rods, Elsie spied a physical spell. Parts of the rune were familiar to her, but she wasn't quite sure . . .

She swallowed. If she had to guess, it was a lightning rod. Not one used to diffuse a storm, but to bottle it. Viscount Byron's demise instantly came to mind.

Was *this* Nash's true job? He was not a delivery boy, but an . . . an . . .

Assassin.

Elsie practically leapt from the chest, and the lid smacked loudly down. Pulse racing, legs desperate to flee, Elsie turned for the stairs—

—but in her peripheral vision, she spied a familiar parchment on the side table. It was thick, gray. *Cowls.*

Her fear flared into anger. How *dare* he be a part of it, too. How many people did she dance for?

Three strides were all it took to cross the room. She recognized the writing on the letter. It matched every other letter she'd ever gotten from the "Cowls." Now that she knew, it *did* look like Ogden's—if he were trying to disguise his hand. The flourish on the T . . . something about it was painfully familiar.

> *Again at Seven Oaks. Disregard the heirloom opus and go*
> *for the Master. He's too much of a distraction.*

A chill rushed through Elsie's body.

Seven Oaks was the Duke of Kent's estate. And the only master there was . . .

The Cowls' next target was Bacchus Kelsey. The duke must have owned another's opus. That had been the first target. But now . . .

"Oh God," she muttered, dropping the letter. "Oh God, oh God."

Nash had been in a hurry. Night was falling. Perhaps he was heading to Kent even now, as Elsie rifled through his things.

Not Bacchus. *Not Bacchus.*

She flew down the stairs and unbolted the door, too anxious to care if she was seen. But she made it only a few steps before turning back.

She'd forgotten her valise and didn't want to leave anything connecting her to Nash. Snatching it, she hurried to a busy street and nearly got herself run over trying to flag down a carriage that had no intention of stopping. But she stepped right in front of the next cab, forcing the driver to stop or run her over.

"Are you mad?" The man had long gray sideburns poking from beneath his hat, and his two black horses stamped nervously.

"Where are you going?" Elsie *did* sound mad, but she didn't care. She even grabbed the reins so the driver could not leave her.

The man sputtered. "What's it to you? I've passengers heading for the train."

"They're close enough! Let them out here and take me to Seven Oaks. I'll pay you three times your asking price."

He paused, considering.

"Now, man!" Elsie cried.

The driver jumped from his seat, and though his passengers had likely heard the entire exchange, opened their door and said, "Way's too crowded, but the station's just ahead! Out you go!" He grabbed their luggage and practically chucked it onto the cobblestone. The passengers—two women and a man—gawked, and one of the women complained in an accent Elsie couldn't place. But to her relief, they got out, and she got in.

"As fast as you can go," she pleaded, pulling her gloves off her sweating hands. "Please. It is a matter of life and death."

"Duel?" the driver guessed, but he didn't wait for an answer. Returning to his seat, he whipped his horses forward.

Elsie could only pray she wouldn't be too late.

∞

"Well, it was quite a scare, nevertheless." Master Lily Merton raised her spoon to her lips. She sucked the white soup down, dabbed her mouth with a napkin, and added, "I would have so hated to see our dear Miss Ida join our ranks out of *necessity*. A career of any sort is much more enjoyable when chosen through passion."

It was unsurprising that the Duke of Kent's health was the primary subject of conversation for the first course of dinner—the first meal the duke had been able to take with the entire family in a while. Bacchus couldn't have been more relieved to see him well. The temporal aspector's spell had taken well enough, and the duke had gradually regained his strength. Master Merton of the London Spiritual Atheneum was an unsurprising addition to their dinner. She had nearly cemented herself into Ida Scott's future. Indeed, in the past week, Miss Ida had practically assaulted Bacchus with question after question regarding aspecting, until he'd given her a gentle reminder that physical aspectors studied different subject matter than spiritual, and so her experiences would greatly differ from his.

"I wouldn't say necessity," chimed the duchess. "Do not mistake me, I love my husband"—she passed a tender look to Isaiah, who had finally gotten his color back—"but we would not fall into shambles upon his passing. I may not have a son, but our nephew is kindhearted and well meaning, and there are sufficient funds set aside beyond that."

The duke raised his glass. "Though I have decided I would like to see Ida utilize her talents."

Bacchus couldn't tell who beamed more: Miss Ida or Master Merton.

"Bacchus," the duchess said, perhaps to steer talk away from her husband's near demise. It had troubled her greatly, and even now, with the duke's recovery, she worried he'd relapse. They all did. "Are you sure you won't stay with us a while longer? I'm sure Ida, at the very least, could learn from you."

"Master Merton would likely do a better job of teaching her." Bacchus stirred his soup. He'd had an appetite, but it seemed to have been scared off by the duchess's inquiry. And of his future trip in general.

He craved home, with its familiar faces, privacy, and balmy weather. And yet something about the plans made him feel uneasy.

The uneasiness made him think of Elsie.

"Our alignments are very different." He swallowed back the thoughts. "And I've lands to manage back home."

Which was true, though he had full confidence in his manager. And the voyage was no quick journey, as it took three weeks to cross the Atlantic to Barbados.

"When do you leave, Master Kelsey?" asked Master Merton.

"Within the week." He finally lifted his spoon to his mouth.

"It must be very beautiful." Miss Josie, the younger sister, rushed in, likely eager for a chance to join the conversation. "The island, I mean. Always sunny."

"And often rainy," he pointed out, "but it's a different rain than here. It's warmer and has more purpose."

Miss Ida chuckled. "Do you mean to say English rain has no purpose?"

Bacchus shrugged. "Is there a purpose to watering stone?"

"I'd love to feel warm rain," Miss Josie said dreamily. "Even in the summer, the rain isn't warm."

"I think," interjected the duke, "that it is. Perhaps one day a year. Next month we might be lucky."

The duchess smiled behind her napkin.

"I think," Master Merton began, but a *thud* from elsewhere in the house—Bacchus thought it might have been the front entry—vibrated up the exterior hall. Everyone paused in their dining and turned toward the door. There were sounds of an argument, though Bacchus could make out only one speaker, and it was a woman.

A few of the words carried through the silence that filled the dining room: "—don't understand! . . . see him . . . might die!"

Bacchus stood. *Elsie?*

The duchess followed suit. "I think someone is bullying Baxter," she said, naming the butler.

The moment Bacchus took a step toward the door, he heard a soft curse behind him. He turned, but the foul word had not come from any of the dinner guests. He peered toward the heavy curtains drawn across the windows.

Heavy footsteps sounded in the hallway. The opposite door burst open, and sure enough, Elsie toppled through, her hat askew. Her wild blue eyes found him. "Bacchus! You have to—"

Lightning shot out from the drapes.

Bacchus dived, and the electric bolt blasted through the backrest of his chair. He hit the carpet, tasting static in the air. Both daughters screamed. Master Merton cried, "What's the meaning of this?"

"Get the duke!" Bacchus shouted, grabbing the chair in front of him and throwing it back toward the windows. The air prickled again, and lightning raced across the room, flashing bright in his vision.

"Fire!" Miss Josie shouted.

Cursing, Bacchus turned toward the second ruined chair, which had fallen on the fine carpet, a small blaze springing up from it. He crawled toward the fire, intent on putting it out, and at the same time Elsie screamed, "I know who you are, Abel Nash!"

That voice cursed again, this time louder, and a man dressed in all black, his face hidden save for his eyes, leapt out from the curtains. The duchess pulled the duke toward safety, and Master Merton ushered the girls toward the rear exit. Baxter rushed into the room.

But the man—Abel Nash—had eyes only for Bacchus.

Wielding a lightning staff, the thin man charged and flung its head forward.

Calling upon a spell, Bacchus threw up his hands and demanded the air to *move*.

The lightning flew just over his head as a gust of wind slammed into Abel Nash's body, shoving him back toward the curtains. It wasn't enough to knock him against the wall, and the assailant proved surprisingly nimble, flipping over upon landing, returning to his feet in an instant.

It was then that Bacchus realized this man was an assassin—*the* assassin—armed and ready to take out a master aspector. To steal yet another opus.

Bacchus was his next target, and somehow Elsie had known it. Had her shouts called this criminal from his hiding place early?

There was no time to think of it.

Bacchus darted toward the fire and calmed it with another spell, then grabbed a broken chair leg. He armed it with a spell for speed and hurled it at his attacker. The wooden missile whistled through the air like a bullet. The assassin disintegrated it with a burst of lightning and ran forward, closing the space between himself and Bacchus.

The duchess screamed.

Bacchus sprinted to meet the man, causing him to hesitate; Bacchus was by far the larger opponent. Before they collided, Bacchus dived to the ground and pressed his hand to the carpet, willing the floor to *open*.

It did, but not quickly enough to send Abel Nash into the basement. Nash leapt out of the way and pointed his lightning rod.

It sparked as Elsie collided with him, knocking them both to the ground. The lightning grazed Bacchus's leg, searing his skin and igniting the fabric of his trousers. He clenched his teeth and snuffed the embers with his hand.

Turning, he saw two servants in the doorway, Master Merton gaping, and Miss Ida still at her side, tugging on her sleeve. "Go!" he bellowed. "Now!"

Master Merton's gaze flickered from him to Elsie to the assassin. Perhaps she hesitated because she wished to help, but spiritual aspecting would do no good in this situation, unless she had a curse ready and could get close enough to Abel Nash to touch him.

She grabbed Miss Ida's forearm and jerked her toward the door.

Bacchus looked back just in time to see Elsie take an elbow to her face as the assassin flung her away.

The burning in his leg blazed to fill his entire body.

Flying to his feet, Bacchus grabbed another chair and, bespelling it with speed, flung it at the man. It went wide, but the assassin ducked, nevertheless. The chair bullet crashed into the wall, ruining a portrait as it smashed into hundreds of splinters.

From a kneeling position, Abel Nash aimed his lightning staff and sent a fiery bolt for Bacchus's head.

Bacchus jumped to dodge, only to realize he was on a path to collide with the dining room table.

His hands touched it first, and the entire center leaf shifted from solid to liquid as his master spell overtook it—shifting it directly to gas would have been the equivalent of setting off a bomb. The lightning bolt soared overhead and *cracked* as it struck the opposite wall. Bacchus dropped into a puddle of strange woody liquid that was already beginning to resolidify. Pain surged from his head into his shoulders, not from the landing, but from the sudden and extreme use of the spell.

The air prickled. The lightning rod had been activated again, and he didn't have enough time to escape.

He turned just as the blinding light shot at him—and the familiar silhouette of a woman stepped in front of it.

"No!" he shouted, but the lightning hit—

—and then vanished.

Blinking spots from his eyes, Bacchus pushed himself upright. Elsie's shoulders heaved with her breaths. Both of her arms stretched in front of her as though frozen there. She stared with wide eyes. So did the assassin.

It took another heartbeat for Bacchus to understand what had happened. She'd dis-spelled the lightning. *As it struck her.*

He'd never heard of such a thing.

The awe fled Abel Nash first. He flung the staff forward again, a huge serpent of lightning flying for them. Bacchus wasn't quick enough to tackle Elsie before it hit. She moved her palms up slightly, and the light surged into them—the brightness was nearly blinding, but Bacchus could have sworn he saw a glimmer of blue where light hit skin. A broken rune.

The lightning choked out, leaving them both unscathed.

Bacchus acted immediately. Grabbing a shard of porcelain from a broken dinner plate at his feet, he bespelled it with speed and chucked it. The porcelain zoomed through the air like a bullet before piercing through one side of the assassin's chest and bursting out the other, spattering blood as it went. It collided with a curtain and hit the floor, breaking into three pieces.

Abel Nash's knees quivered. The lightning staff fell from his hand and hit the floor. He followed after, dead.

CHAPTER 23

Elsie stared at the bleeding, slumped body of Abel Nash on the floor and did the very thing she'd always promised herself she'd never do.

She fainted.

It was brief, a quick blackening of her vision. The sensation of falling. A snippet of memory, lost. But when her senses returned, she found herself bent back in a very uncomfortable position, held aloft by a single strong arm that smelled remarkably of oranges.

"Elsie. Elsie!" Bacchus's voice was low and close. A second arm joined the first in supporting her, warm and sure. "Someone call the police!"

"Already done!" The butler she'd been arguing with mere minutes ago ran back into the room, surveying the damage with wide eyes.

Straightening and steadying herself with the crook of Bacchus's elbow, Elsie took stock of the room, intentionally keeping her eyes away from the . . . corpse. Ahead, the floor gaped like an open mouth. Chairs, dishes, and cutlery were a mess. Part of the table was missing, and there was a brackish puddle on the rug beneath it. Charred gouges scarred the walls, ceiling, and carpet.

She could still feel the heat in her hands from the lightning strikes. She'd dis-spelled enchanted staffs before, but never what they emitted. The runes on the lightning had a similar feel—so fast, so hot—but she hadn't even seen the threads, the knots. She'd just . . . done it.

She didn't understand it at all. But she was still alive. And so was Bacchus.

Bacchus.

She threw her arms around him and buried her face into his collar. She felt his quick pulse beneath her nose. Tears wet her eyelashes. "I didn't know if I'd get here in time." His shirt muffled her words.

Just as embarrassment began to surface, those strong arms encircled her. "We made it, Elsie," he whispered, words flavored with his Bajan accent. "We're all right, thanks to you."

In that moment, Elsie had never felt safer.

Bacchus pulled back, but kept one arm around Elsie as he guided her into the poorly lit hall. She reached for the wall, her legs feeling weak, and lowered herself to the floor. Bacchus crouched across from her.

"Are you well?" He took her face in his hands. "Should I call the doctor?"

She grasped his hands, squeezing his fingers. "Bacchus, it's Ogden." Her voice caught. Voicing the words made it so much more real, and it felt as though that morbid piece of porcelain had cut through her, not Nash. "He's the one behind it. The opuses. It's him."

His green eyes narrowed. "What?"

She glanced down the hall, and Bacchus followed suit. She wasn't sure who else in the household, if anyone, had witnessed her grand spellbreaking, or if they'd even recognize it as such. But Elsie would rather not add incarceration to her extensive list of worries.

She swallowed. Then, to her chagrin, tears sprang to her eyes.

"Bother," she muttered, wiping them on her sleeve.

Bacchus tucked some of the mess of her hair behind her ears. "You're safe, Elsie. Nash is dead."

But she shook her head and released him, breaking away from his warmth, his concern. "You don't even know." She hated the squelch to her voice. She wiped her eyes again, then a third time. The bloody things wouldn't stop leaking. "I did it, too, Bacchus." And there it was, an ugly piece of her, displayed for him to see. She'd so hoped to stay in his good graces before he left. But to stop Ogden, she had to confess the truth. "The doorknob. All of it."

"You're not making any sense," he murmured, and he wiped away a tear with the pad of his thumb.

She laughed. "Could you please not be tender while I tell you what a terrible person I am?"

He hesitated, then sat back on his heels.

Checking the hallway for eavesdroppers once more, she went on. "The ones I wouldn't tell you about. The Cowls. The ones who . . . who hire me for spellbreaking. I didn't know it, but Ogden is one of them. And they are behind the theft of the opuses."

His brows drew together.

She wiped her God-forsaken eyes again. "Every time they needed me to do something, they sent me a letter—it was always through letters—and told me about all the good I was doing. How I was helping someone in need. How I was stopping a wrong going unpunished. How I was balancing out the world. Freeing innocent boys, helping farmers, keeping families in their homes . . ." She laughed again, but it ripped up her throat in a most unpleasant manner. "And I did as they asked, blindly. For a *decade*, I did it all so blindly. But in the last year, it's been so frequent. More and more. And then I found their seal in Ogden's room. And when I went to Juniper Down, I realized every spell I've broken for them is connected to one of the thefts, one of the murders. *I* was the key that unlocked all those doors. *I* helped kill all those . . . people . . ."

259

She covered her face with both hands, the guilt unbearable. If only the floor would open up *here* and swallow her whole. Dying in a basement didn't sound completely terrible at the moment.

She thought she heard new voices in the house. Had the police arrived?

She felt him shift. "Elsie——"

Ripping her hands away, she said, "You must tell them. *Now.* The police. I swear to you as the sun rises in the morning, *Ogden is the criminal behind all of this.* Please!"

Her voice rose with every word, until even the servants down the hallway were looking at her like she was a specter risen from the grave. But Bacchus, bless him, was taking her seriously—he left, and she hoped it was to carry out her request.

She stared down the servants. "Are you deaf? Cuthbert Ogden of Brookley is a killer! Tell the police!"

They scattered.

Closing her eyes, Elsie leaned her head back against the wall. Her wrists itched something fierce, and the annoying sensation flowed up her arms as though carried in her veins. She tried to scratch, but her sleeves were so damn tight.

She sat there for a while, listening to the back-and-forth of servants, the occasional wail. The duchess came by once, asking after her. Elsie managed a half-hearted assurance, and the woman let her be. The itching started to recede.

Would the police require a testimony? Would they use another truthseeker? She'd have to confess her spellbreaking to make her story work, wouldn't she? Or was there some other way around it? She needed to think, but she'd been thinking so much lately. Her brain was exhausted.

Grabbing some wainscoting, Elsie heaved herself to her feet. She needed to go. She needed to protect Emmeline. Heaven help her, she would be so frightened if she was in that house when the police arrived—

Several policemen chattered among themselves in the dining room, pointing at the body and the damage, taking notes. Someone had informed them of the situation on the way over, perhaps. Could she slip out without being seen? It would be hard to find a cab back home, since she hadn't told the previous one to wait for her. She hadn't told the driver anything, merely left his coin on the seat and bolted for the house—

"Elsie."

She jumped, hand flying to her breast. "Bacchus, you blend with the shadows." She'd had enough frights for one day.

He offered her that subtle near smile. "Let's pull you away from all this."

Elsie eyed the policemen in the dining room. Two blocked the sight of Nash's body.

"I'm not turning you in," he assured her, and took her hand, guiding her down the hallway. The noise of the investigation slowly quieted behind her. A relief.

He stopped by a massive staircase to the first floor. Turned toward her and took both her shoulders in his hands. "You never answered me. Are you hurt?"

"No. Not really." Her gaze fell to the floor.

He let out a long breath, forceful enough to stir her mussed hair—she couldn't recall where her hat had gone. "That's twice now."

"I wouldn't have broken in if that butler weren't such a daft—"

"I mean twice that you've saved my life."

She lifted her gaze almost unwillingly. His hands on her shoulders were too warm, and a flush crept up her neck. She cleared her throat. "Well, if you want to focus on that part of it."

He chuckled, which almost helped her relax.

"Bacchus," she pressed, "you did hear me, didn't you? I'm *part of this*." Her voice dropped to a whisper.

He lowered his hands, but only so they held her upper arms instead of her shoulders. "Did you at any point know or suspect that you were part of it?"

She paled. "Of course not!"

"Then you're fine."

"But the police—"

"I told them Abel Nash confessed Ogden's name before his demise. I told the others that I'd invited you to dinner and you must have seen Nash sneaking in. The police shouldn't question you outside of a recounting of the events that occurred tonight. As long as they match my retelling, you'll be fine."

Elsie gaped, a numbness she hadn't noticed lifting from her limbs. "But a truthseeker—"

"The duke has sway. They won't use one on you."

She rolled her lips together. "You're interrupting me a great deal tonight."

He smirked at her.

Remembering herself, Elsie pulled away from his touch and folded her arms against the chill that rushed in to replace his warmth. "Thank you. Truly." She glanced toward the dining room again. "They came quickly."

"The duke owns a telegraph. And the High Court employs spiritual aspectors who can project themselves to further the message."

"That's fortunate." Her pulse quickened. "Oh, poor Emmeline. She'll be so confused. I need to get to her."

"You didn't come from Brookley?"

She shook her head. "Reading. Before that, Juniper Down."

"Why were you away?"

Her shoulders sank. "Well, funny story. I was led to believe my father had come looking for me, but it turned out to be some highwayman who'd mistaken me for someone else."

Bacchus ran a hand down his face. "Elsie, I—"

But a police officer swept down the hallway at that time, his hard-soled shoes echoing in the corridor. Bacchus stiffened. "Has word come in?" The man must have been walking from the direction of the telegraph.

The young officer hesitated a moment, perhaps unsure what he was allowed to share, but he gave in easily enough. "Cuthbert Ogden has fled his home, but a neighbor claims to have seen him headed north."

Elsie's chest tightened. The last vestiges of hope dissipated, making her feel like a dried corn husk. She added Ogden's name to the list carved into her heart. He was yet another person who'd left her behind. Another father who'd abandoned her. Maybe he'd always planned to, once Elsie's usefulness ran dry.

Elsie rubbed her wrist. "Why would he head toward London? If *I* were a fugitive"—she very much did *not* like how that sounded—"I wouldn't go into the crowds. I'd run away from them."

"He has the cover of darkness," Bacchus offered. "He can get lost in the throng."

Elsie bit down on the knuckle of her index finger hard enough to leave prints. Pulling it free, she asked, "Would you ask after the maid? Emmeline Pratt? Make sure she's all right?"

"We do have priorities, miss. Any staff will be seen to." He tilted his hat toward her and continued on his way toward the front entrance, perhaps to report to someone outside. Elsie watched him go, her stomach cramped.

After several seconds, Bacchus asked, "Are you hungry? You're welcome to stay here tonight, until we sort this out."

"I doubt I'd be able to sleep." Though she'd gotten precious little of it lately. It suddenly struck her that the policeman had said a neighbor had seen Ogden leave home. He'd taken off before the police had arrived. Why? "How would Ogden even know to flee?" she asked. "I sent no word ahead, and I know Abel Nash didn't, either." She paced at the end of the stairs. "They shouldn't have too much trouble catching him. He doesn't own any horses. You can't get a cab at night in Brookley unless you order it ahead of time. But there's no possible way he'd have known to do that—"

If things ever do get bad, we'll steal away, you, Emmeline, and I. Ride up to the Thames, maybe even the St. Katharine Docks, and take a discreet boat out to the channel. How's your French?

She froze.

"Elsie? What's—"

"He's going to the docks. Of course." She spun toward him. "Bacchus, I think I know where Ogden is going." It was strange that he should have told her, and in such detail, yet there'd been a certain look on his face as he said it. He'd been in earnest. He'd considered an eventual escape and planned it in advance. "We have to stop him! With all these opuses . . . he's powerful, and if he flees . . ."

Bacchus's face darkened. He considered only a moment. "We have to tell the police."

This time, Elsie agreed with him. She loved Ogden, but . . . "Yes, tell them. If they leave now . . ." But would a carriage be fast enough to catch up? How much of a head start did Ogden have?

Bacchus rubbed his jaw. "How well can you ride?"

Elsie paused. "I . . . I know how to stay on the saddle, at least."

"Good enough. The police will take the main roads; we'll ride the back routes." He offered her his hand.

She took it.

 ⟳

There were many docks that lined the River Thames, but if Elsie knew how Ogden thought—and despite the secrets he'd kept, she thought she did—he'd aim for a smaller, more discreet boat.

She could be completely wrong. And if she was, the outcome would be the same as if she'd taken Bacchus up on his offer of food and rest. But if she was *right*, that would change things. Yet she couldn't think of what she'd possibly say to him when, *if*, she saw him again. Her chest hurt at the mere thought.

The ride was hard. Elsie had traveled on horseback before, but she'd never taken lessons. The Duke of Kent's thoroughbreds were lean and amazingly fast, which Elsie might have marveled at were she riding for pleasure at a slow, serene pace.

As it was, she clutched the reins with white knuckles, her skirt flapping immodestly behind her, because there was no way in hell she was riding this thing sidesaddle. Fortunately, holding on for dear life was the only thing really required of her; the animal was well trained and followed Bacchus's mount unquestioningly, its nose nearly touching the first's whipping tail.

The beasts were tired by the time they neared the pier. Bacchus slowed, and Elsie quickly adjusted herself for as much modesty as she could manage, though it was hardly one's first concern when chasing a traitorous murderer. Her heart panged again at the thought. Ogden . . . She never would have guessed it to be him.

Even now, she struggled to believe it.

A gaping loneliness yawned inside her, but she couldn't dwell on that now.

They trotted by a hospital, and the large warehouses of the pier came into sight, each six stories high and built of sturdy yellow brick. She noted two dockworkers by a gaslight up ahead.

"I don't see him." She was breathless and sore, despite the horse being the one who'd done all the running.

"It's a big place," Bacchus whispered, pulling back on his reins and turning his animal about, scanning the area.

Though the ground seemed a little too far away, Elsie dismounted, floundering but managing to stay on her feet. Her thighs instantly burned in protest, but she ignored the discomfort, removing her shoes and starting for one of the docks. Bacchus called after her, but she ignored him. She may not have been an experienced horsewoman, but she *did* know how to slink about unnoticed.

The docks were long and cool underfoot. She strode beneath the eaves of the warehouses, passing dark windows and locked doors. She dared to jog, her legs protesting. Holding her shoes in both hands to keep them from knocking together, she peered about the next corner. There was only one boat tied up here, a small one with its sails up. The area was fairly well lit, but shadows clustered around the blocky warehouses. She heard the subtle movement of water and her own pulse in her ears.

Turning the corner, Elsie jogged again, trying to hear beyond herself, wishing she had sharper eyes to see through the shadows. There was another dockworker across the way; he didn't seem to notice her. Footsteps followed, but she didn't bother to check them—the stride, the heaviness, that was Bacchus, with a slight limp likely due to the lightning that had grazed his leg. The knowledge that he was close gave her courage.

She reached a wooden bridge connecting two of the docks and started across it. Perhaps it was an angel tilting her head or merely a stroke of luck, for she spied movement in the shadows on the dock opposite her, across the water. She'd spent so many years with Cuthbert Ogden, days and nights, rain and sunshine, that despite the darkness and the distance, she recognized him.

"There!" she hissed, and pointed. The shadow vanished into one of the warehouses. Panicked, she spied around for a boat or raft that could carry her over—by the time she paddled her way there, he'd be long gone!

The bridge shifted as Bacchus stepped onto it. He dropped to his knees and reached down into the water. Elsie caught the edge of a shimmer.

A bridge of ice crackled across the river to the very place she had pointed.

"Oh, you wonderful, brilliant man," she whispered, hurriedly replacing her shoes. Bacchus dropped onto the makeshift bridge first, found his footing, then helped her. The ice was rougher than it was slick, but Elsie dared not sprint. Still, she moved as fast as she could, keeping her arms out to maintain balance.

They reached the other dock, Elsie managing to heft herself up before Bacchus could offer her a hand. Her pulse thundered through her limbs. She took off immediately in the direction Ogden's shadow had gone, and Bacchus followed without complaint. Bless him. Sentimentality aside, after seeing what he did in the duke's dining room, Elsie was grateful to have him with her.

She wondered as she wrenched open an unlocked door—perhaps a lock-picked one—if she should call out to Ogden. She'd spent nine years in his household. She didn't understand him, now that she knew the truth, but this was the same man who'd consoled her when she was sad, who'd put money away into her savings account, who'd teased her at dinnertime. Would the sound of her voice be enough to make him pause, or would he flee all the faster?

The only lights in the warehouse came from the glow of gaslights through the windows. The air smelled slightly of mold, and as Elsie dashed down a long hallway, her footsteps almost in rhythm with Bacchus's, she noted stacks of linen, or perhaps cotton, bundled and ready to ship.

They paused at an intersection. The faintest sound of footsteps echoed in another hall.

"This way," Bacchus murmured, taking her hand and pulling her to the left. Despite the limp, he was fast and surprisingly nimble as he ran; Elsie sprinted on her toes to keep up. They were getting close now. They were the pursuers, while Ogden was trying to find a path to flee or somewhere to hide. That would slow him down. It would—

She sensed it only a moment before they reached it. "Bacchus, stop!" She yanked back on his hand, but his momentum was too great. Their fingers pulled apart, sending Elsie sprawling onto her backside. Meanwhile, Bacchus nearly flew out of his boots when his shoes, of their own volition, slowed down significantly.

"What on earth?" He waved his arms to keep balance.

Elsie's chest heaved with heavy breaths. That spell could have broken his leg.

"Let me find it." She hurried forward on her hands and knees, sniffing for the earthy spell. Not here, but . . . up and to the left?

She found the temporal spell on a support beam against the wall. She'd never seen one set like a trap before—

As she unraveled the spells, her stomach sank. "Opuses. Bacchus, he's using opus spells." Yet more damning evidence against him.

Bacchus stumbled forward when the magic released him. "Perhaps you should go first."

She nodded, fearful to run, but too anxious for caution. They didn't get far before she felt a crackle in the air, just like with Nash's lightning staff. Turning the corner, she saw a bead of lightning shoot out from the right edge of the ceiling.

"Go under it." She hugged the wall. Avoidance would be quicker than asking for a boost so she could reach the rune. The lightning zipped through the air again, causing her hair to stand on end, but it didn't hit her.

Bacchus followed without question.

She heard a door slam ahead and took off running, only to smash into the wall to her left.

"Damn it, Ogden!" she blurted as the wind sputtering up from the floor pinned her in place. Air swirled around her like she was in the eye of a cyclone. Bacchus used the exact same spell to push the wind in a different direction, allowing Elsie to push past the trap. He followed.

"I don't suppose," she managed between breaths, "that you can do that in reverse? Suck him toward us?"

"No."

Elsie made out the outline of a door up ahead. She searched for runes but saw none—

"Stop!" she shouted, digging in her heels. Bacchus ran into her, nearly bumping her into a wooden crate against the wall. Elsie had just recognized the symbol glimmering atop it.

"A mobile spell. This would have crushed us." She crouched and pulled the rune apart, then pushed past the bin unscathed. She cursed. "We have to find another path. He's getting away!"

Her toe hit something metal on the ground—a crowbar. Elsie considered it for only a moment before snatching it up. She couldn't cast spells, but she could certainly swing this.

"It will be easier once we're outside." Bacchus moved past her and grabbed the door handle, opening it just as Elsie spied the slightest glimmer of a spell.

The ground shifted upward like a giant mouth, knocking Elsie into the crate. Cement, stone, and wood contorted and surged up and around Bacchus—a giant version of the spell he'd once laid for her at the duke's estate. The one that had seized her shoe.

But this one swallowed him clear up to his neck.

"Bacchus!" she cried, finding her feet and rushing toward him. He might as well have been trapped in a mountain! She ran her hands over its uneven bumps, searching for the rune.

Bacchus grunted, trying to move, but he was pinned completely, his limbs immobile within his close-fitting prison. "Bloody . . . ," he began, but didn't finish whatever foul thing sat on his tongue. "He's getting away!"

Elsie spied the slimmest glimmer in a crack. Her skeleton seemed to puddle inside her. "I found it, but it's on the other side of the rock. Your side." She tried to push her fingers through, cutting them as she did, but she couldn't chip the cement. Stepping back, she wedged the crowbar in. It chipped away at the cement a little more, but it wasn't hard enough to break the stone. Elsie put her weight on it, but it seemed the crowbar would break before the concrete mound did. Panicked breaths tore up and down her throat. "Maybe I-I can find something else. A hammer—"

"Elsie, leave me. Go."

She shook her head. "I'll get you out—"

"You'll lose him!" he barked. "Go!"

"Can't you melt it?" Desperation squeezed her voice out an octave higher than usual.

Bacchus shook his head, though he was barely able to do so. "This is stone. Do you know what the liquid version of stone is? And it's too large to shift to gas. I'll kill myself *and* you."

Her breaths became rapid. "Can you try to change just a little of it? If I can get through—"

"*Go*, Elsie, before it's too late!"

"*I don't leave people!*" she snapped, hands fisted against the bespelled mound. She panted, seeing red, feeling as cold as Bacchus's aspected ice.

Bacchus hesitated only a moment. "No, you don't."

Swallowing, she glanced up at him.

"Elsie." His voice was firm yet somehow melodious, his Bajan accent slipping through. In the moonlight streaming from the open door, his eyes glowed. "*You're* the one who can stop him. Who can get past his spells. He might listen to you. You need to go *now*, or you'll lose his trail, and this will all be for nothing. I believe in you."

"But—"

"I know you'll come back." His eyes were intent, bright as emeralds. "Elsie, please. *Go.*"

She held his gaze for a heartbeat, cradling her injured fingers against her breast. He was right. She needed to go. But she could only undo spells, not create them. She was armed, somewhat, and after what had happened with Nash . . . she might be able to get past Ogden's spells if she focused. But what if she couldn't? She'd die, and Bacchus would be trapped here until a worker found him . . .

Her own possible demise flashed across her mind. Was she ready to die to stop Ogden?

It was what Robin Hood would do.

She started for the door. Paused. Glanced back to Bacchus.

She rushed toward him and, stepping onto one of the crags of his cement cage, lifted her face to his and kissed him on the cheek. His half beard was rough and startling against her jaw. Her nerves sparked, but it was done.

"Thank you," she whispered, and without a second glance, she bolted out the door and across the dock.

Her employer might be able to slow her down, but in doing so, he left a clear path.

Follow the runes, find Ogden.

CHAPTER 24

There was something oddly familiar about the spells she chased, but Elsie couldn't quite put her finger on it.

She disarmed an enormous weed that shot up through cracks in the concrete, grown with a temporal spell. Removed, albeit with shaking hands, a rational spell on a warehouse wall that created the illusion of a giant spider. Leapt over a gap a physical spell had created in the boards of the bridge. Disenchanted another that had fused several boards together to create a wall.

There were no dockworkers or security seeking out the cause of the noise, which worried her. Was St. Katharine's so empty at night, or had Ogden already . . . *eliminated* them?

Before she followed the trail into the next warehouse, an owl swooped down at her at a strange angle from the direction of the river, and Elsie shrieked despite her need to be undetected. She wouldn't be able to remove the spiritual spell driving the animal to attack her, so she bolted for the door and slammed it shut behind her, crowbar squeezed in her clammy right hand. The bird's talons scraped against the door half a second later.

She raced through the warehouse, following runes scattered with a flare of insanity, some placed on the ceiling, others the floor or random places on the wall, even when the location was a poor choice for the spell. Through it all, that strange sense of familiarity nagged at her, but she didn't have time to think about what it meant. Or the fact that she'd kissed Bacchus Kelsey while he was in a compromised position. Good heavens, what had she been thinking? At least it had only been on the cheek.

At least she wouldn't have to face him again if one of Ogden's spells caught up with her. Or if she caught up with the man himself and their reunion went awry. *You have to risk it,* she reminded herself, searching, listening, feeling, and smelling for opus spells. If she caught up to him and came out the victor . . . it would be all right. It would allow her to right her wrongs, to an extent. God knew she had to try.

She pulled apart a density alteration spell hovering midair, slightly to the left, which made the air too thick to walk through. It was the eighteenth spell she'd encountered.

Her wrists and arms itched as though bitten by a hundred mosquitoes when she pushed open the door at the other end of the warehouse. The burn of gaslight stung her eyes. The moon reflected off the nearly still river water.

And illuminated Ogden as he crouched at the edge of the dock, untying a small fisherman's boat. A sheaf of mismatched papers—*opus spells*—stuck out from the collar of his paint-stained shirt.

"Ogden, stop," she pleaded, raising one hand as though in surrender while stashing the crowbar behind her back with the other. She strode toward him, focused. Casting an opus spell required verbal activation, so at least she'd have warning. "Let's talk about this."

Ogden pulled the sheaf from his shirt, and Elsie paused as though he'd brandished a gun. He'd need only to whisper, *Excitant,* and those spells would come flying for her. "No closer," he warned. His voice came out hoarse, and his hands shook as they held the papers. Why? Was he afraid? Ill?

"You're sick." Elsie dared to take another step forward. Ogden wasn't young, but he was in good health. Yet maybe this run had overtaxed his heart. "Ogden. Cuthbert. Please. Let me take you to a hospital."

He stood suddenly, eyeing her. She thought she felt something in the air, something like snow—

She didn't *want* to stop him, now did she? Ogden was just going fishing. She had so much work to do at home. What was she doing here? Emmeline must be worried—

"Stop!" she screamed, hands flying to her head. The crowbar fell to the dock behind her. She was the least experienced with rational spells, but she sensed the quiver of one in the air between them. It dug into her thoughts, planting new ones.

I'm such a mess! I need a bath. Time to go home—

She clawed at the space before her until she found it. She'd have no luck were the thing planted on her head, but Ogden had not yet touched her. She pulled off one thread, then another. It was complex. A master spell.

Emmeline must be so worried! I must return at once!

"*Ogden!*" she screamed, clawing off another knot.

Go home. Go home.

No, come with me.

The sudden shift in the demands threw Elsie off balance. Now Ogden held out his hand to her, like he'd suddenly changed his mind. Like he wanted a companion. With his other hand he worked on untying the boat, opus spells shoved into his trouser pocket.

But . . . he hadn't selected a single page. Hadn't said, *Excitant,* to activate the magic.

He hadn't *used* an opus page for this.

I need to take care of Ogden! I must get in the boat—

Which meant . . . he'd cast it himself.

Another thread off, another. Her own thoughts battered against the false ones. Elsie's knees wavered.

"Come with me." Sweat beaded across Ogden's forehead.

It all made sense.

How scandalous that I'm out at the docks alone, at night! The spell pushed her away even as her employer beckoned to her.

Alfred. She thought of Álfred, after seeing him with his new wife. Crying on her bed. Ogden had come in and . . . everything had felt okay. Like her sorrow had simply been whisked away.

The police will know I'm involved. I should leave while I still can!

But then, *You're interrupting Ogden's holiday! He'll sack you if you don't leave!*

Wisps of memory surfaced between the claws of the spell. Offenses forgotten. Pain lessened. Anger subsided. Had he done all of that? Used magic to calm her each and every time?

Time to—

She pulled the last thread free, and the foreign thoughts dissipated. She gasped, collapsing to the dock. She'd been holding her breath.

That had been a master spell.

Ogden wasn't a flimsy physical aspector. It had been a cover. He was a master rational aspector. Unregistered, just like she was.

Ogden's nails dug into a piling on the side of the dock. He seemed to be resisting *her*. Like she was a magnet pulling him close. His tremors had grown worse.

"Ogden!" She ran toward him. "Stop!"

"You . . . can't . . . have her . . . ," he groaned.

His head flung up, but this time . . . this time she felt the rational spell coming. As if time had slowed. The rune was a fairy, unseen, but the pulse of its wing beats was unmistakable—

Her fingers flew and picked it apart. The last knot came close enough to graze her forehead, whispering something she couldn't understand before it died.

Just like in the duke's dining room, she'd dispensed with the spell before it could unfurl.

Even Ogden looked surprised. Something she should use to her advantage—because if he got into that boat, Elsie wouldn't be able to get him out.

She dashed forward, lungs straining against her corset, and tackled him, her shoulder colliding with his chest. He was so much larger and thicker than herself, but she mustered enough power to knock him onto the dock and lift his foot from the boat. He tried to grapple her. She fought to pin him down, her ear pressed to the base of his open collar.

That's when she heard it. The slightest click, like a dying cicada. The sound was so faint she might not have noticed had it not contrasted against the silence of their struggle.

A spell. A *spiritual* spell. And its placement . . .

Just like Bacchus.

Ogden shoved her off. She would have fallen into the river had two pilings not stopped her. She'd rolled through the spilled stack of opus spells, and many of them fell into the water, ruined.

Ogden leapt to his feet. Started toward the boat. He shook like a man riding a bull. Like he was . . . resisting.

She grabbed his shoulders; he collapsed to one knee. "It's a pattern, Elsie," he wheezed, eyes distant. "It's always been there—"

His lips smacked closed. Flinging her off, he strode for the boat, his limbs still shaking.

Pattern?

Pattern.

By the grace of God, it all snapped into place. The familiarity in the runes she followed to get here. Their sporadic placement. She'd seen it before.

In his paintings.

In the tiles for the vicar.

In the way he doodled on his knee at church.

In the re-sorting of his shelves.

In the scribbles on the papers in his desk drawer.

They were all the same. They were a pattern. An eighteen-point pattern. An eighteen-point *knot*.

He'd been trying to tell her. He'd been trying to tell her for *years*.

He got one foot into the boat, then the other.

Picking herself up, Elsie bolted after him and jumped. He broke her fall. He grunted when they landed, a bench digging into his back. His head struck a thwart, hard enough that his eyes rolled back.

Grabbing the edges of his shirt, Elsie ripped them apart, popping buttons. The rune wasn't readily apparent; it was so expertly placed . . . but she dug her fingers into the skin over his heart and sensed its song. It was wildly powerful—the strongest she'd ever encountered—but she knew the key. She knew the pattern.

She ripped it apart so roughly her nails left red trails on his skin. She started in the upper left and ended near the center. The spell screamed as it puffed away. Ogden gasped like a man come back to life. He bucked, knocking her off, and sat up, his hair mussed and his eyes wild.

Then they filled with tears.

"Elsie," he whispered. "Finally. You've saved me."

He collapsed into her lap and wept.

CHAPTER 25

Ogden was still incoherent when the police arrived. Elsie had managed to get him out of the boat, but he lay on the dock like a scared child, trembling.

When Elsie saw the lights of the oncoming officers, she balled up the remaining spells and pushed them into the river, where they sank out of sight. All except one. She'd picked up enough Latin to understand its purpose. Its importance. This one she folded tightly and slipped into her bodice.

"We were wrong," she said after they swarmed her. "He was just a pawn. Abel Nash used him as a scapegoat."

The words made her think of the American in Juniper Down. He had been right. She had been used as a pawn, too.

But whose? And how had the American known? Who *was* he?

The police questioned her. She asked after Bacchus and, seeing their confused looks, told them where to find him and to please hurry. She ached to lead them there herself, but Ogden . . . She couldn't leave him, not like this. Relief that he was not entirely the villain she'd feared him to be warred with the anxiety about what all this might mean. She gave vague, tired answers to the policemen's questions. Then she demanded Ogden be taken to a hospital.

Before they left, Ogden whispered, "I'll take care of the truthseeker."

The words echoed in her ears. But of course—a master rational aspector could easily make a truthseeker believe he'd already performed his interrogation. He could make him believe anything. That must have been part of the plan when the burglar—Nash?—broke into their home. The attack must have been an attempt to allay suspicion, engineered by the spellmaker who had controlled Ogden.

Elsie stayed with Ogden at the hospital. Waited in the corner as the same truthseeker from before entered, got a blank look on his face, and left. He told the officers Ogden was innocent—that he'd run only because he was scared. Nash had worked alone. The events of the night were just as confusing to Miss Camden as they'd been to everyone else.

That much was true.

Elsie wasn't sure what to believe.

$\sim\!\mathcal{O}$

Fatigue dragged on Bacchus like wet clothes, but he trudged through the small hospital regardless, following the directions the attendant had given him. The melody of an old parlor song his nursemaid used to sing played in the back of his thoughts. The burn on his leg from his fight with Abel Nash was a dull ache, and he still picked bits of rock and sediment from his hair. The police had taken pickaxes to his prison while they waited for a spellbreaker to arrive. It would have been a quicker job had Bacchus told them where to dig to get to the rune. But then he'd have to explain how he knew, and that wasn't possible. Not if he wanted to keep Elsie safe.

Bacchus Kelsey very much wanted to keep her safe.

He found the room. The door was cracked an inch. Knowing Elsie's preference for privacy, he wondered if the doctor had recently been in and failed to close the door after him. Mr. Cuthbert Ogden lay on a narrow bed in the center of the small room, sleeping, looking as though he'd aged ten years. Elsie sat in a chair next to him, elbows on her knees. Her hair was unkempt from the horse ride and the fight. The police had given Bacchus an overview of what had happened, though he'd rather hear Elsie's account. He suspected there was much the police didn't know.

He realized he hadn't been as quiet as he'd thought when Elsie started and turned around. As he pushed open the door and stepped out of the shadows, she jumped to her feet, wavering a little—she must have been exhausted. She rushed to him, and Bacchus readied for an embrace, but she pulled up short at the last moment, looking unsure. Instead she clutched his forearms.

"I'm so glad you're all right," she whispered, glancing back to Mr. Ogden.

Turning his arm around so he could take Elsie's hand, Bacchus asked, "And you? Are you hurt?"

Shaking her head, Elsie stifled a yawn. "No. Nothing rest won't cure."

"Then you should rest. I'll watch him."

A tired half smile tugged at her lips. "No. I need to stay. I need to be here when he wakes up. The travel, the fight . . ." Pulling from him, she moved to shut the door, then crossed to the far side of the room, by the window, gesturing for Bacchus to follow. When they were significantly out of earshot of any passersby, she whispered, "He was just like you, Bacchus. Had a spell I couldn't see. Couldn't *hear*. I don't know for how long . . . I didn't think a spell could be placed so secretly. They must have made him use his magic to steer me away."

Confusion niggled at him. "His magic?"

She chewed her lip a moment. Glanced out the window. "He's a master *rational* aspector, Bacchus. Has been this entire time. Unregistered, like me."

The confession drove back some of his fatigue. "You're sure?"

She nodded. Touched her bodice, then dropped her hand. "I'm sure."

Bacchus looked to the unconscious man on the bed. He never would have guessed. Rational aspectors . . . they were closely monitored, more so than any other alignment, because of the types of spells they could enact. Were Elsie to be discovered, she might luck out with imprisonment. But Mr. Ogden would be executed immediately.

"You have my word that I'll not share it," he murmured.

"I know you won't." She smiled softly, and Bacchus's chest tightened. For her to trust him so readily, after the way their relationship had started . . . it was significant.

Reining in his thoughts, he asked, "Who placed it? What spell?"

"A spiritual spell. One that controlled him." She shifted closer, warmth buzzing between them. "It's the most masterful spell I've ever encountered. Even more so than the siphoning one. I never would have untied it in time had he not whacked his head and given me clues."

"Clues?"

She waved the question away. Another time, then. "I don't know who placed it. We won't know until the true culprit behind the opus crimes is caught. He was so confused, Bacchus."

She picked at the seam of her sleeve. Bacchus took her hand once more.

"Do not blame yourself for your involvement," he whispered. As soon as he spoke the words, she glanced away. He squeezed her hand. "You have a strong sense of justice, Elsie. You genuinely thought you were doing good. Had you suspected otherwise, you never would have helped . . . What did you call them?"

"The Cowls. I thought they were . . ." Her voice shrunk. She swallowed. "They used my sense of justice against me. If they hadn't made me feel like I was doing something important, I might have been too scared to break the law."

Raising his free hand, he put the knuckle of his first finger under Elsie's chin and lifted her face so she'd look at him. "Do not disparage yourself for having courage."

She looked away, then back. She was so close. If he wanted to, he could lean in and—

He pulled his hand away. "What can I do?"

She took a moment to think. Glanced at their linked hands. "I know you're exhausted, Bacchus, but—"

"Name it."

"Just stay, until he wakes." She squeezed his hand back. "Just . . . stay."

Ogden was released the next morning. Bacchus used his own funds to hire the carriage back to Brookley. Their parting had been so bleary, so sleep deprived, that Elsie could barely remember it. But it had gone . . . well. She would be content if not for the myriad questions still plaguing her. How would they explain this to Emmeline? She and Ogden would have to work on their story together.

After she got answers.

Elsie waited only long enough for the horses to pull forward before she said, "I need to know what that spell was."

Ogden, who looked haggard, rested his head in his hands. "A spiritual spell. I don't know how it works. You would think mind control would be rational, but this was more than that. It went deeper."

"*Who* was controlling you?" Elsie ignored a bump in the road that jarred the carriage.

His hands looked limp between his knees. "I don't remember. He didn't want to be known. But it's been . . . a decade, Elsie. I can't remember exactly . . . The aspector didn't *want* me to know. It's mud. But." He hesitated and looked at her.

Her heart cracked down the middle. "But it must have happened when I entered your life."

The American's words whispered inside her head, *You're a pawn.*

He nodded, looking sick. "Elsie, the spell was there, but he couldn't control every aspect of my life. He couldn't control my thoughts. I think of you as a daughter. I . . ." He swallowed, and Elsie pinched herself so she could focus on a physical pain rather than the anguish blooming inside her. "I *was* hiring. He must have noticed me after I took you on . . . then realized what I was."

"A rational aspector," Elsie said, then cleared the forming lump from her throat. "A *master* rational aspector."

He nodded. "I was very careful with my spells. I made you think the drops only glowed faintly. I miswrote the spells on my arm so I wouldn't absorb them."

"Your physical spells—"

"Those were real." He rubbed his hands together. "I learned those before ever meeting you, for my art. I made sure you saw only those. I did what I had to, what *he* wanted me to, to keep you from figuring it out."

She shook her head. Why control Ogden and not her? Then again, the Cowls had come into her life when she was a child . . . They'd been her savior, her religion. One didn't need a spell to sway the heart of a desperate little girl.

A chill bloomed between her shoulder blades and coursed down her limbs. *She* was the one who'd fled to the stonemasonry shop from Squire Hughes's household. *She* had led the Cowls right to Ogden. They had learned his secret, and made him a prisoner.

Had Elsie stayed put, he would never have been their victim.

Oh, if only the carriage would swallow her whole. She pressed her hand to her chest, as though she could force her heart to stay in one piece by the pressure of her palm. *A decade.* A decade of having his will usurped by another, all because Elsie hadn't wanted to scrub dishes for a pompous nobleman.

Put it away. She tried to bury the realization deep. She needed to get all the pieces in place before she let them fall apart. *Put it away, for now.* But God help her, the anger hurt.

"Why did you not register?" Her voice was a harsh whisper, despite there being no way their driver could overhear. She needed to push on, to save her despairing realizations for another time. "Why have you pretended to be what you are all this time?"

He shook his head and leaned back in his seat. Stared at the crack of window between the door and the curtain.

"Ogden, I deserve to know."

"You do." His fingers dug into his knees. "I'm a liberal thinker, Elsie. Always have been. I used to be on the parish council, even."

She nodded, recalling that bit of history. She focused on it, to keep herself from darker thoughts.

"Did you know all registered aspectors, spellbreakers included, must report to the queen whenever summoned? To work on whatever she needs? To go to war if she demands it? The idea that I could sway a political ratbag with the power of my mind, without him ever realizing it, was intoxicating. At one point, I believed I could sway all of them to create just laws, *my* laws, and never get caught. And then, the idea that I could *convince* someone to love me . . ." His voice choked, and his hand went to his neck as though he could fix it.

Elsie pressed her lips together, her own throat tight. The folded opus page beneath her bodice poked her collarbone.

A full minute passed again before he continued, "You might have noticed. I don't love the sort of people I'm supposed to. When I started on this venture, I was young and foolish. I didn't respect the will of others. But don't worry. Life has a way of teaching us wisdom, when we're ready for it. I didn't get into too much trouble."

Elsie leaned forward and touched the hand still on his knee. "I don't blame you." She understood the desire to feel wanted, needed.

Ogden sighed.

"I never detected it before," she said.

He lowered his other hand from his neck to his heart. "You rarely got close enough. Even *I* knew it was well hidden. And when he was watching . . . I could *make* you not see it. Do it quick enough that you wouldn't sense the spell."

Hadn't she suspected as much? With his ability, he could turn her mind away from its presence, pluck the memory right from her brain. How often had that happened? Had she connected her work for the Cowls to the opus crimes before, only to have that knowledge washed away? How many times had she heard the song of the spiritual spell on Ogden's person, only to forget its tune completely?

"Then how do I remember now?" She couldn't face the other questions yet. "How did I get it off you?"

Ogden shook his head. "He was worried. Stressed. Elsie, I was *fighting* him as hard as I could."

The shaking. The stalling.

"And he, in the end . . . he wanted you, too."

Elsie pressed her lips together. That explained the contradictions in the rational spell he'd put on her. It was Ogden telling her to go home and this spiritual aspector's influence telling her to come with him. The Cowls wanted Elsie now, just as they'd wanted her when they'd taken her from the workhouse. How utterly ironic, for them to finally pull her into their fold. After years of Elsie pining for their approval. A few days earlier, Elsie would have readily joined them. She would have done so blindly.

That must have been why Ogden had told her about the St. Katharine Docks in the first place. Because he knew that's where he'd go if his controller ever decided to pull him from Brookley.

"I haven't openly fought it in so long," Ogden went on. "I wanted to appease him. I tried to make my efforts subtle. Thus all the churches."

Elsie straightened. "*That's* why we hop from cleric to cleric?"

Managing a weak smile, he said, "I wanted to study the spiritual aspectors. I wanted them to *see me*. I don't know. I was fishing for anything. It took me years to figure out the rune without him noticing. And years to tell you."

"Without him noticing," she finished.

He nodded.

She hugged herself. "I'm so sorry. I didn't—"

"You *couldn't*," he interjected. Now he reached forward, pulling one of her hands free and holding it between his own. "But I knew you were the only one who could free me. If I had left on that boat, I would never be free. It took years for me to learn the rune without him noticing. I gave you every clue I could. He realized it, in the end. But I would rather die fighting him than live as his puppet."

Elsie's thoughts flew back to Juniper Down, to the strange man who'd held a gun to her head. He had been a spiritual aspector. "The person controlling you wasn't American, was he?"

"What?"

She described the man in detail. She thought again on his mention of *articles*, but she still hadn't figured out what he'd meant by that. So much had happened she hadn't yet found time to consider it.

Ogden released her. His forehead wrinkled. "I . . . I don't remember. I *know* I saw him that first time. But the spell forbade me to think on it, and after so long, I can't recall. I don't think so. But this American knows something. What was his name?"

"I don't know." Failure tasted sour in the back of her mouth, but she stiffened. "But you could draw him, Ogden. I could describe him to you, and you could draw him."

His eyes brightened. "Yes." He smiled. "*Yes*, Elsie. I will."

⁀⊘

"Well, it's quite the misunderstanding!" Emmeline crowed. Elsie had never seen the young maid so angry. "To have them chase you like that!"

Emmeline stirred the pot of jelly like she was beating a rug, but she'd accepted the tale easily enough. Elsie and Ogden had both since cleaned up. Elsie thought of the police, the docks, the spells. And she thought of Bacchus. Of his seat beside her in the small hospital room, his low voice, his hand engulfing hers. When was he leaving for Barbados? Elsie hadn't even asked. He could be setting sail even now, for all she knew.

She thought of his cheek beneath her lips, which made her face burn. *Foolish woman,* she thought, breathing around a rusted spike in her chest. God save her, it shouldn't hurt this much. Maybe Ogden could smooth this sensation away from her, too. And yet . . . she wasn't sure she wanted it gone. It was too soon to tell.

That night, after Emmeline had turned in and things felt more or less normal, Elsie dressed down to her nightgown and robe. Sitting on the edge of her bed, she unfolded the opus spell she'd taken from the dock.

She couldn't read it in full. Barely in part. But she didn't need to—she could cast this spell without any knowledge. Without any drops. She traced her fingers over words she recognized: *Memoria, perdita.* Memory, lost. The word *oblivio* made her think of oblivion. She'd have to get a Latin-to-English dictionary, but she was almost certain this spell was one of forgetting. The faded red ink told her it was a rational spell, which leaned to her theory. And judging by its length, it might even be a master spell. From whom, she'd never know. But seeing the way Ogden had wept and trembled on that dock . . . Maybe it would come in handy. She hoped not, but she couldn't convince herself to do away with it.

She folded it carefully and slid it beneath her mattress—a temporary hiding spot until she thought of something better. She braided her newly washed hair over her shoulder and crept to Ogden's bedroom. She didn't bother knocking; he was expecting her, sketch pad, pencils, and charcoal spread across the foot of his bed.

She shut the door and sat on his trunk. Without waiting to be asked, she began describing the American.

"It will take a few tries." He started with the shape of the head and the narrow jaw Elsie remembered. "I won't influence you one way or another. Just tell me what you can remember."

"He was about your age. Tanned. Traveled," she offered. "His eyes were close set. Long hair. His hairline started . . . here." She touched her crown. "And there was a peak."

It took Ogden longer to draw than it did for her to describe. She looked over his shoulder every now and then, offering suggestions.

After nearly an hour, Elsie asked, "Where did you keep the opuses, Ogden? We should find a way to return them."

His attention never left the sketch. "I didn't. He took me somewhere, before the docks. I don't quite remember it. Somewhere dark and wet. A sewer, or maybe a sepulchre. I grabbed spells almost at random to defend myself before moving on." He slowed. "The mind and the spirit are interesting things. Separate, yet interlocked. Perhaps, if I can get my hands on the right library, I could study their boundaries for myself." He resumed sketching.

Elsie nodded, considering. Replaying last night's events in her thoughts. How Ogden, or his puppet master, knew to flee still confused her, but she didn't want to distract Ogden with questions, especially ones he likely wouldn't be able to answer. So she watched him draw instead. The sketch was beginning to come alive. It didn't look quite right, yet Elsie couldn't explain how without the American standing in front of her. As Ogden filled in the brow, however, he paused.

"This isn't him." He set the pad of paper on his lap. "I know it's not him."

Elsie rolled her lips together and took the pad in hand. *You're a pawn,* he'd said. Which meant he wasn't.

"It was worth a try."

"The eyes . . . The eyes aren't right."

Elsie stood. "You remember?"

Squeezing his eyes shut, Ogden rubbed his head. "I can almost . . ."

Elsie set down the pad and paced the room, thinking. She pulled her robe close around her. It was almost summer, but the room felt cold. Was it worth it to light the fire?

The fire.

She paused. "Ogden."

He glanced up.

She met his tired eyes. "It was a woman who took me from the workhouse. A woman with a"—she closed her eyes, picturing it—"a receded chin."

He froze a moment. "A woman," he whispered. He held still as a grave, focus shifting. A moment passed. He stiffened suddenly and picked up his pad and charcoal. He sketched in a frenzy, drawing, shading, then shaking his head and ripping the page free, only to start anew. "A woman. I can see it. A woman . . . Yes . . . Almost . . ."

He started with the chin, adding lines around it. He jumped from that to outlining the hair around the face. No style, no hat, no pins. And a forehead. He began a thick eyebrow, then smeared the lines with the side of his hand and redrew them thin. He sketched the eyes, paused. Looked away and let his fingers draw from memory.

"Something like . . ." He added a heavy lid and a brow that looked almost Russian.

A chill ran through Elsie's body. "God save us."

Ogden turned toward her. "You recognize her?"

Mouth dry, Elsie nodded. The woman was older now, and the picture was incomplete, but she knew that face. And she understood why Ogden had known when to flee.

"She's the one he was looking for," she said, words barely more than a rasp. "The American. She's in London. Her name is Master Lily Merton."

ACKNOWLEDGMENTS

Oh hey, lots of people helped me with this book! They are the best. No book is a one-man show, and there are many thanks to be passed around.

First, God. He usually comes at the end of these, but I'm moving Him up to throw off the readers who actually peruse this section. Thanks, God.

Second, alpha and beta readers. These are people who slog through my rough drafts with no glory and no pay. Rebecca Blevins, Cerena Felt, Tricia Levenseller, Whitney Hanks, Rachel Maltby, and Leah O'Neill. I appreciate you guys *SO MUCH*. Even my agent doesn't see my rough drafts!

A special thank-you to Caitlyn McFarland for helping me work out plot points, characters, and more on the phone and in person. And for letting me yell at you and call you names and then still liking me afterward.

Many thanks to Professor Thomas Wayment at Brigham Young University, who was much more useful with my Latin translations than the internet was.

So, so, so many thanks to my husband, Jordan, who also reads my crappy rough drafts, takes care of our kids so I can write crappy rough drafts, brainstorms ideas for my crappy rough drafts, and is every bit as chivalrous as a Victorian man should be.

Thank you to my agent, for getting this book into the right hands; my shiny new editor, Adrienne Procaccini, for helping me with the vision for this duology; and Angela Polidoro, who got up to her elbows in word grease to help me fine-tune this story.

Always, my utmost appreciation to the 47North team—author relations, copyeditors, proofreaders, fact-checkers, marketers, and so on. Thank you for making my dream job that much more awesome.

ABOUT THE AUTHOR

Charlie N. Holmberg is the author of the Numina series and the *Wall Street Journal* bestselling Paper Magician series, which has been optioned by the Walt Disney Company. She is also the author of five stand-alone novels, including *Followed by Frost*, a 2016 RITA award finalist for Best Young Adult Romance, and *The Fifth Doll*, winner of the 2017 Whitney for Speculative Fiction. Born in Salt Lake City, Charlie was raised a Trekkie alongside three sisters who also have boy names. She is a proud BYU alumna, plays the ukulele, and owns too many pairs of glasses. She currently lives with her family in Utah. Visit her at www.charlienholmberg.com.